beautiful Lies

beautiful Lies

JESSICA WARMAN

WALKER & COMPANY
New York

First published in the United States of America in August 2012
by Walker Publishing Company, Inc., a division of Bloomsbury Publishing, Inc.
www.bloomsburyteens.com

For information about permission to reproduce selections from this book, write to
Permissions, Walker BFYR, 175 Fifth Avenue, New York, New York 10010

Library of Congress Cataloging-in-Publication Data
Warman, Jessica.
Beautiful lies / Jessica Warman.—1st ed.
        p.   cm.
Summary: Eighteen-year-old identical twins Alice and Rachel have always shared a very special bond,
so when one is abducted the other uses their connection to try to locate her.
ISBN 978-0-8027-2338-3 (hardcover)
[1. Sisters—Fiction. 2. Twins—Fiction. 3. Abduction—Fiction. 4. Mystery and detective stories.]
I. Title.
PZ7.W2374Btm 2012   [Fic]—dc23   2011052330

Book design by Nicole Gastonguay
Typeset by Westchester Book Composition
Printed in the U.S.A. by Quad/Graphics, Fairfield, Pennsylvania
2 4 6 8 10 9 7 5 3 1

Like all the others, this one is for my husband, Colin, and for all the promises we've made to each other—and kept—over the years. And for our daughters, Estella and Esme, who are simply the best. I love you all.

beautiful Lies

CHAPTER ONE

It's one of those cool, crisp fall nights that make you feel like the air is ripe with possibility, like anything could happen. From where we stand on the jogging trail, my sister and I can see the whole city stretching out around us. On the farthest end, all the way across town, there is a dusk-lit celebration taking place, a huge tent holding overlapping threads of bodies, the sounds of their voices carrying across the wind, all the way to us.

"Ah. Oktoberfest at the Yellow Moon," she says to me, squinting, standing on tiptoes in her scuffed ballet flats, like if she stares at the party long enough she might absorb some of the excitement, which feels almost electric as it seeps from the crowd.

She looks at me, her face shadowed by the almost-darkness. Her lips are outlined with crimson liner and filled in with a deep shade of cherry gloss. "Don't you wish we could go?"

I wind a strand of long red hair around my finger, thinking. Someone nearby on the path is smoking a cigarette. I can smell it even though I can't see him, but he's in the shadows somewhere, probably close enough to hear us. "We're only eighteen." I smile at her. "We can't drink yet, Alice."

She smiles back. "You know that wouldn't matter." We have fake IDs. And even if we didn't, Doug the bartender would give us drinks. My sister and I work at the Yellow Moon as servers a few nights a week.

"It wouldn't work. Everyone would recognize us," I say. "Half the town's probably there. If we got drunk, we could get in trouble." We've stopped walking for the moment, pausing to gaze at the lights across town. In the moonlight, my sister looks ready for anything: she is confident, calm, her dewy cheeks flushed with anticipation.

"Wait," I say to her, "your eyes."

She bats her lashes. "What's the matter with them?"

A family strolls past: a mother, father, and a daughter who can't be older than maybe four. The little girl has three purple helium balloons tied around her wrist, bobbing in the smooth night air as she walks, her pink-and-white sneakers dirty, almost blackened at their edges with dust from the trail.

The family pauses to look at the two of us. My sister and I are standing face-to-face, our identical noses only a few inches apart, our dilated pupils aligned. The space between us feels alive, almost humming with invisible energy.

The mother wears cutoffs and a red tank top, even though the air is cool enough for jackets. She looks tired but happy, holding her daughter's hand. "You don't see that every day," she says to us, squinting through the dusk to get a better look. "You're identical. Yes?"

I don't break away from my sister's gaze. The corners of her eyes crinkle in a soft smile. She is my favorite person in the world. Tonight, even our breath seems to be in sync. "Yes," I say, "we're identical."

The mother kneels beside her daughter. "See, sweetie? They're twins."

She's right. Even though we're dressed differently, and even though my sister is wearing heavy makeup—while my face is bare except for some light blush and powder— we are an unmistakable matched set.

The little girl gazes at us, openmouthed. We both smile at her.

She looks at her parents. "I want to go home." She seems almost ready to cry.

Her mom and dad give us an apologetic look. "Kids," the dad says. He flashes an embarrassed smile, and I feel a surge of unease when I see that his teeth are crooked and yellow. I'm not sure why exactly; there's just something about him that makes my stomach turn. As the family begins to stroll away, it almost seems like the earth is tilting beneath me, moving my surroundings a hair off-kilter. I can almost taste the cigarette smoke in the air, rancid and thick. It smells toxic; I have the overwhelming urge to get as far away from it as possible.

As she's walking away, just once the little girl looks over her shoulder. She seems afraid. But of what? Of us?

"I think we scared her," my sister whispers. She giggles. "We're freaks."

"We aren't freaks." It's getting darker by the second. "Let me fix your eyes."

She begins to look through her purse, digging around in the contents to find a tube of black liquid eyeliner. She hands it to me.

"Hold still," I tell her. "Alice. Look at the stars."

She puts her small hands on my shoulders to steady herself. I take a step closer to her—so close that I think I can hear her heart beating, close enough that I can see the faint pulse in her neck and feel the warmth of her breath on my face. With a steady hand, I reapply the liner with smooth strokes. Even when I reach the inside corners of her eyes, the inky applicator tip almost touching her tear ducts, my sister does not flinch.

"There," I say. "Finished."

I can see a touch of anxiety behind her smile. "How do I look?" she asks.

I still smell cigarette smoke. The family from a moment ago is far away, three bodies bobbing against the horizon, growing smaller with every step. Soon they'll turn a corner and disappear altogether. I don't like being alone out here, so close to whoever is standing in the shadows, maybe watching us. I know I'm getting upset over nothing, but I can't help it; the air reeks of disease. "You look like Alice," I tell her. "You look like yourself."

"We could go home," she offers. "We could stay in tonight."

I frown. "A minute ago you were ready to sneak into Oktoberfest, and now you want to go home? What fun would that be? We said we'd go out. You wanted to come. Our friends are waiting for us."

"*Your* friends," she corrects me. "They don't like me anymore. Remember?" She looks around, sniffling. I know she can smell the smoke too. "I'm nervous," she says.

"Don't be. Everything is fine. You'll be great."

She looks at the lights from Oktoberfest across town again. "Bet they're having more fun than we will at the fair. We could go. I have my ID."

I follow her gaze, imagining how it would feel to be silly and drunk, the thrill that comes from truly getting away with something. She's right; it *would* be more fun.

But we have plans. "We already talked about this. We're going to the carnival. I'll be with you the whole time, Alice," I say.

Her lips—full and shiny, identical to mine except for their deep stain of color—form a slow smile. "I know you will, Rachel."

More confident now, she starts walking again, heading

toward the fair. When I look at her, the last few beams of sunlight almost completely below the horizon now, all I see are shadows against her profile, her sharp features softened, almost seeming to dissolve.

She glances at me, smiles again. "All right, you've convinced me. Now come on, before I change my mind. We'll be late." She tugs me along, our fingers still laced together. The gesture feels as natural to me as breathing. She is mine. I belong to her. This is how it has always been, even before we were born.

໐໐

On our side of town, only a few hundred feet down the path we're walking on, there's a whole different kind of crowd gathered for the annual autumn festival at Hollick Park. I can smell it before I see it, the gross odor of cigarette smoke replaced by whiffs of cotton candy, funnel cakes, and hot dogs.

"I want a candy apple," my sister says, holding my hand more tightly as we walk down the hill, toward the field crowded with people and vendors' booths. At the far edge of the park, there's a tiny carnival set up, a cluster of rickety-looking rides crowding the horizon. In the center of them, a Ferris wheel spins slowly, its metal beams strung with twinkling white lights, the structure towering so far above the rest of the fair that, at its highest point, the wheel almost seems to graze the moon.

"Rachel." I hear someone calling us—calling me. "Rachel and Alice! Behind you!"

We both turn around. "Here we go," my sister murmurs.

"Shh." I give her a look. "It's okay."

The voice belongs to Kimberly Shields, who we've made plans to meet up with tonight. Everybody calls her Kimber. She waves at us, beaming, her bright green eyes flashing beneath the fair's lights. She's still in her cheerleading uniform, obviously having just come from a football game. She's with two of our other friends: Nicholas Hahn, whose dad owns the Yellow Moon, and his girlfriend, Holly Willis, who goes to our church and volunteers in the nursery every Sunday, and whose family leaves their Christmas tree up year round.

At almost eighteen years old, Kimber Shields is an honest-to-goodness sash-wearing cookie-selling Girl Scout. A few weeks ago, when she was at the mall, an elderly man had a heart attack in the bookstore, right there in the Crafts and Hobbies section. Kimber was a few feet away, paging through a book on knitting. Without any hesitation, she got down on the floor and gave the man CPR until the paramedics arrived. She saved his life.

The five of us stand in a semicircle beside one of those games where you try to toss a ping-pong ball into glass bowls filled with water. One out of every five or six bowls has a fish swimming around in it; if you sink one, you get to keep the fish.

"Charlie would love this," I murmur, looking at the fish. Charlie is our cousin.

My sister stares at the game. "It's two dollars for four tries," she says. Her heavy black eyeliner gives her face a hollow look, making her blue eyes seem bigger than they actually are, their lids filled in with dark gray shadow, the effect both dramatic and kind of unsettling in its allure. Her beauty is different from mine tonight: more arresting, more intimidating somehow. When she's all made up, out and about, she has a presence that commands attention, and she knows it. Tonight she wears a plain, fitted white tank top and a denim miniskirt that's so short I almost can't believe our aunt and uncle let her leave the house in it, even if she is wearing tights underneath. Despite the way she faltered a few minutes ago, she is nothing but confidence now. Men who pass by us stop to look at her, even if they're with their wives or girlfriends. They can't help themselves.

"So? It's only two dollars." Nicholas—nobody *ever* calls him Nick—looks into his open wallet, thumbing through a bunch of ones. "You ought to try it, Alice. Win yourself a fish or something."

Nicholas lives a few blocks away from us, in one of the biggest and nicest houses in our whole city. In addition to the Yellow Moon, his dad, Mr. Hahn, also owns Pratzi's, which is a hoity-toity restaurant uptown. Nicholas's dad drives around Greensburg all the time in a silver Mercedes with tinted windows, blaring classical music, a lit cigar between his lips. People say he has ties to the local mafia, but I've always doubted it; I can't imagine that our town even *has* a mafia connection. Anyway, I know that Mr. Hahn is a jerk. For one thing, he's an awful boss; he's always flirting with the waitresses, making sleazy comments about the way we look, his gaze raking over us like we belong to him. And supposedly his first wife—Nicholas's mom—left because he used to beat her up all the time. He never got arrested for it or anything, but that's what people say.

Despite his family drama, Nicholas is a nice enough guy, well liked by pretty much everyone, cute in a nerdy kind of way. I'm actually surprised he and Holly decided to come out with us tonight; lately they've been devoting most of their time to geocaching, which is kind of like an elaborate treasure hunt using GPS. I don't know much about it beyond that, but Holly has told me it's a ridiculous amount of fun.

"For two dollars," my sister tells Nicholas, "I could go to the pet store and buy myself a goldfish."

"But the fun's in trying to win," Holly says. I can see her breath suspended in midair as she exhales; that's how chilly it is.

"I bet they're scared," I say, staring at the fish as they circle endlessly in their tiny bowls.

Nobody says anything. We all look at the game, its edges crowded with little kids, their parents standing behind them looking bored.

Finally, Kimber giggles. "Rachel, you're so funny," she says. "Fish don't have feelings."

My sister is chewing pink gum. She blows a bubble, snaps it loudly against her lips, and says, "So what you're telling us is, if a fish needed CPR, you wouldn't help it."

Kimber seems confused. "Alice, fish don't—you aren't—" She frowns, looking from my sister to me in frustration. "I earned my Good Samaritan badge for that."

"I know." I try to smile warmly at her. Kimber responds by frowning again, bringing her fingers to her neck to grasp a tiny golden cross dangling from a thin chain.

Kimber is a good person—she deserves all the happiness she can get. Back in the first grade, before I ever knew her, her parents went through a messy divorce. One night while she and her mom were sleeping, her dad set their house on fire. He went to prison, and Kimber was in the hospital for months. I've seen her getting changed in gym class; she has horrible scars all over her back and shoulders. She never wears tank tops or goes swimming with the rest of us in the summer. She's never even been on a date, though plenty of guys have asked—she's too ashamed of the way she looks.

There is a noticeable unease among my friends, who are doing their best to be kind to my twin. Things used to be different among us, but in the last six months or so, she has broken away from our group, preferring to spend her time alone. She's gotten a real taste for alcohol lately—pot too. As a result, her reputation has disintegrated to the point where some of our friends aren't even supposed to be around her anymore. This fact pains me, because I know her better than anyone. I know she's not a bad person. She just wants some peace, the opportunity to quiet her mind, which always seems to be working against her. She wants to silence her thoughts, but she doesn't have any idea how to do it aside from drinking or smoking until she can't string together a sentence anymore.

Sometimes I understand exactly how she feels.

We are essentially the same, she and I. Her and me. My sister, myself. When she takes off her makeup and brushes out her hair—when we first wake up in the morning, or right before we go to bed in the evening—nobody in this world can tell us apart just from looking at us. Only we know who is who. Knowledge like that, shared with only one other person in the world, can feel exhilarating. It's like we own a secret that nobody else will ever hold the key to, for as long as we both live.

⁓

Right now, my sister squeezes my hand to get my attention. "I'm hungry," she says.

"Me, too," Holly says. "I shouldn't be. I just ate a few hours ago." She opens her oversize purse—a designer knockoff that looks big enough to hold the contents of an entire minibar— and pulls out a prescription pill bottle. Holly is a skinny, nervous girl with light blond hair and pale skin. More often than not, she spends weekends at church retreats with her youth group. It's not like she has a choice, though; her family is so strict and conservative that Holly wasn't even allowed to shave her legs or get her ears pierced until she turned fourteen, which is really funny, because she was the first girl I knew to go on birth control, back in the ninth grade. By then she'd been dating Nicholas for two years. To this day, her mom has no idea what her little girl is up to. In my experience, adults usually don't.

"What are those, Holly?" Kimber asks, her tone suspicious. "Are those drugs?"

"They're obviously drugs," I say. I don't let go of my sister's hand. She seems restless, sort of like she doesn't want to be out tonight. Her behavior is a little odd; it was her idea to come.

She tugs me toward the candy-apple stand a few yards away, a bright-red neon apple glowing in the window of the vending trailer. Our friends follow behind us.

"Would you relax, Kimber?" Holly opens the bottle, shakes two of the pills into her hand. "They're for Evan's asthma. They suppress your appetite, that's all."

Nicholas looks at his girlfriend, vaguely interested in the fact that she's abusing her little brother's prescription medication. "Doesn't he need them? You know—to breathe?"

"Oh, he'll be fine," she says, swallowing both pills without anything to drink. "He has tons of them. These are, like, extras." And she holds out the bottle, offering it to us. "Anybody want one? You won't be hungry for the rest of the night."

She pauses. "But there's a very small risk of dizziness, blurred vision, and seizure."

Behind us, in the park's band shell, several musicians are setting up their equipment. The guitarist plays a chord. He's hooked up to an amplifier. The noise slices through the crowd, momentarily creating an almost complete silence as everybody stops to listen. Just for a second.

"What are we doing?" I ask. "Does anybody want something to eat? Alice wants a candy apple."

My sister's gaze shifts past my face. I can tell she's staring at the rides. "Actually, I want to go on the Ferris wheel. *Then* I want a candy apple." She smiles at me like a little kid. "Can we, Rachel?"

I turn around. Faintly, I think I can hear the gears grinding on the rides. Among all the food smells, there's a whiff of grease in the air.

"I don't want to. It's so high, Alice. These things fall apart sometimes; I've seen it on the news."

"She's right," Nicholas says. "Some guy forgets to tighten a bolt in the wrong place, and people end up getting killed."

"Come on." Holly nudges him. "It's the Ferris wheel." To me, she says, "It's for *kids*, Rachel. You'll be fine."

I glance at it again. Heights don't usually bother me. Tonight, though, the thought of being up in the air makes me uneasy. I don't know why. "Then come with us."

"Okay. We will." Holly looks from Nicholas to Kimber. "Right?"

Kimber nods. "Sure."

Nicholas shrugs, indifferent. "Whatever. I don't care."

The five of us, led by my sister, hold on to one another's hands and make a chain as we weave through the crowd together. Even though it's chilly, the air is crisp and refreshing. Families and kids are out in droves. We pass a few more people we know from school. I see our biology teacher, Mr. Slater, standing alone beside a kettle-corn booth and smoking a cigarette; he doesn't seem at all concerned that parents and students will see what he's doing. He looks miserable too, but that's nothing new for him. I see an elderly woman being pushed along in a wheelchair. She's had her face painted tonight; her nose and cheeks are colored red and black, like a cat's. We pass young couples with their hands in one another's back pockets, and a slew of high-school football players in lettermen jackets who have clearly been boozing it up. Holly almost knocks over a man on stilts as he makes his way through the crowd, a good four feet taller than everyone else, dressed like Uncle Sam.

And we pass carnies. They're everywhere, at least one at each booth, all wearing dirty clothes, most of them smoking cigarettes, their eyes gleaming as they call out to whoever's passing by to come and play, try to win your girl a prize, or to go for a spin on one of the rides.

When we get to the Ferris wheel, the ride has just come to a stop. The operator is beginning to empty the seats, one swinging bench at a time. The line grows shorter as, two by two, people climb on.

"I'm so thirsty," Holly complains. She makes a face like she's tasted something bad. "Nicholas." She pouts. "I'm so thirsty, baby."

"You want something to drink?" he offers.

She nods. "Yes, please. Lemonade."

My stomach flutters as we get closer to the ride. I stare up at the highest seat, imagining how it will feel to be stopped at the very top, swinging back and forth, helpless, and a twinge of panic ripples through me. I can smell the hot oil that greases the gears, the odor deeply unsettling for some reason. I'm not sure why I'm so afraid—the feeling has come from out of nowhere. All I know is that I don't want to get on.

"You need me to buy you some lemonade right now?" Nicholas asks Holly.

"Yes. Hurry up and you'll be back before we reach the front of the line."

He ducks away, disappearing into the crowd. My friends and I take small steps, getting closer and closer. I feel dizzy with dread. *Get a grip*, I tell myself. *It's a freaking Ferris wheel.*

But I can't calm down. I press a hand to my stomach. The air feels much colder all of a sudden. I can hear bits of conversation coming from all around me, but I can't focus on any of them, not completely.

"Rachel." It's my sister. She's beaming, cheeks flushed from the cold. "Come on!"

We're at the head of the line. She tugs me toward the empty seat. I don't know how Kimber can even think about riding alone. I'm sweating in the chilly evening, unable to speak, arrested by anxiety. I don't know what's wrong with me.

We sit down beside each other, and she rests her head on my shoulder. For the moment, sitting so close that I can hear the rhythm of our breath in sync, I feel a little bit better.

The ride's operator approaches us, ready to lower the metal restraining bar across our laps. Nicholas appears behind him, holding an oversize Styrofoam cup.

"Yay!" Holly claps from her place in line. "Thank you!"

The operator turns around. "Nope," he says, shaking his head. "You can't cut in line, man."

"Dude, I just stepped out for a second." Nicholas's tone is light, friendly. "Come on. I'm with my girlfriend."

"Sorry, kid. Can't do it. You'll have to wait for the next one."

And before I have a chance to realize what's happening, my sister slides out of the seat we're sharing. "You can ride with Holly, Rachel." She begins to back away, waving with both hands. "I'll catch up with you after. I want a candy apple!"

She turns on her heel and rushes away from us. It is such a typical Alice move—restless, impulsive—but I feel like she's only acting this way because that's the kind of behavior everyone expects from her. Almost immediately I lose sight of her in the thick crowd.

Holly climbs into the seat next to me. Nicholas is still standing beside the head of the line. He shrugs at us before stepping away, giving the finger to the ride operator's back.

"I guess that worked out," Holly says, clutching her purse against her chest. Without any warning, she raises her voice and screams "I love you!" at Nicholas.

The operator leans over us. With one hand, he pulls the metal bar downward, securing it tightly against our laps. "Enjoy your ride." His voice is flat as his eyes stare into mine. His breath on my face is so sour, so sickening, that I have to look away before I gag.

Our seat rises into the air. Beneath us, previous riders climb out, replaced by Kimber.

I search the crowd for my sister, looking everywhere for a glimpse of her red hair, for a sign of the face I recognize so well.

The wheel turns slowly at first, then begins to speed up. Across the field, the band starts to play. I recognize the music. It's "Sleep Walk" by Santo & Johnny. It was my parents' wedding song.

"Holly." My voice barely breaks a whisper. The music is too loud, the ride too fast.

"Whoo!" Holly kicks her feet with glee. Even though it's fall, she's wearing open-toed high-heeled sandals, her toenails painted a creamy shade of pink. She raises her arms, making spirit fingers in the air, and I get a whiff of her perfume. The smell turns my stomach again. I could almost throw up.

"Alice." My voice is louder, but Holly still doesn't hear me. She stands up a little in her seat, the metal bar pressing against her thighs, to blow kisses at Nicholas.

From high above the crowd, I can spot Uncle Sam on his stilts. I can see strands of customers, their bodies woven into ropes of flesh as they line up for food. I can see the candy-apple stand, its neon light glowing red against the crowd. But I don't see my sister anywhere.

Long before our births, we shared the same space in our mother's body. We are what's known as "monochorionic monoamniotic twins," which means we are identical twins who grew in the same amniotic sac and shared one placenta. It's a pretty rare phenomenon; when it does happen, both twins don't always survive, let alone thrive as we have—especially back when we were born. The chance of our simple existence is a marvel of nature. No matter where I am, no matter where she is, I have always felt her presence from somewhere within myself.

Until this moment. It is as though the thread connecting us has snapped, like something deep inside me has been severed. She is simply gone.

Chapter Two

My friends won't listen. They don't understand.

"Call her phone," Holly says, sipping her lemonade, uninterested in my panic.

We have to shout just to hear each other. The band is playing a Tom Petty song now; notes of "American Girl" bounce off the crowd that has gathered around the stage. Kids are perched on their parents' shoulders, up way past their bedtimes, their faces flushed with exhausted glee. Lots of them wear neon glow-in-the-dark necklaces that are being sold for five bucks apiece at a nearby booth. The booth is also offering snow globes with tiny replicas of Greensburg contained inside them. For a moment, I want to grab one, to stare at it until I see my sister somewhere within the miniature world, maybe only walking home early or hanging out with a friend she ran into. Except, like I said, my sister doesn't really have many friends lately. Maybe she's by herself, on the outside of the field somewhere, happily eating her apple. Maybe she went to Oktoberfest.

"Alice doesn't have a phone," I tell them.

Kimber frowns. "Who doesn't have a *phone*?"

"My aunt and uncle took it away." We live with our aunt Sharon and uncle Jeff. Aunt Sharon was my mom's twin sister. Twins run in our family; we've had three sets in four generations. But my mom and Aunt Sharon didn't get along; my sister and I had never met our aunt or uncle until they showed up to claim us nine years ago, even though we'd lived less than thirty miles away from them our entire lives.

My mom and aunt were fraternal, not identical. This fact is an act of mercy on the part of the universe—I cannot imagine how it would feel to be living with a woman who looked exactly like my mother, knowing every moment that it wasn't truly her.

"What did she do?" Nicholas asks.

"What did who do?" I can barely think. I feel a light trembling in my chest, almost no worse than a tickle. I'm wheezing. I never wheeze.

"What did Alice do to have her phone taken away?"

"Oh. She . . . uh . . . she got drunk."

Nicholas frowns. "That's all? She got drunk, and they took away her phone?"

"Um . . . it was worse than that," I say. The ground feels soft and unsteady beneath my feet. "Alice drank a fifth of my uncle's coconut rum. Then around three in the morning, she decided to go swimming in our neighbors' pool."

Holly, Nicholas, and Kimber stare at me, expectant. "So? What's the big deal, then?" Holly asks.

"She thought they were on vacation. They weren't." I take a step backward. My breath quickens. I need air.

"Rachel. You have to calm down." Kimber puts a hand on my shoulder. When she smiles, she reveals a slight gap between her top front teeth. "Alice has been gone all of ten minutes. She went to get a candy apple, that's all."

I'm shivering. When I breathe, my chest rattles, the wheeze deep and uncomfortable. "I should look for her. Maybe she went home. I should go."

Holly stares at me. "Rachel, you can't leave. You just got here."

I don't have asthma, but it's getting more and more difficult to catch my breath. "Can I have one of those pills?"

Holly and Nicholas exchange a momentary glance. But Holly says, "Sure, Rach," and rifles through her purse to find the bottle.

"One doesn't do much," she tells me, shaking a few into my palm. "I always take three or four. You're taller than me. You should take four." She pauses. "Maybe five."

"You'll kill her, Holly." Kimber pushes the bottle away from my hand. "How many does your brother take?"

"My brother," Holly pronounces, "is seven years old. He's fifty pounds. He takes one."

There are four pills in my hand. Without giving it much thought, I pop them all into my mouth. I take a long drink from Holly's lemonade to wash them down.

"I'm going home," I tell them. "Alice isn't here."

The crowd applauds as the band finishes playing "American Girl" and launches into "Honey Bee." As I start to walk away, Kimber grabs me by the arm. She doesn't let go until I turn to face her.

"What?" My breathing is labored. I can still smell the grease from the rides. The odor is so strong that it feels like it's burning the insides of my nostrils.

"We'll keep looking for her," she says. She has kind eyes, a sincere face. "We'll call you as soon as we find her, then you can come back."

"Okay."

She gives me a hug. Beneath her thin cheerleading sweater, I can feel the outlines of deep scars on her back. I bet they still hurt sometimes.

⁂

I push my way through the crowd, looking around for my sister, trying to ignore the certainty that she isn't here. Where else would she go? Aside from the Yellow Moon—which is a long walk, all the way across town—the only possibility I can think of is that she ran into Robin somewhere, but Robin has been gone for almost two weeks. Besides, she would have told me if she'd seen him around. And she wouldn't have snuck off with him regardless. She must be here somewhere. I can't imagine that she would have left without telling me.

The crowd begins to thin around the arts-and-crafts booths. Eager-looking women stand behind tables full of things like handmade stone jewelry, personalized calligraphy, and needlepoint. At one booth, there's an old man sitting in a wooden folding chair, using a pocketknife to carve something very small. There's an almost empty basket of peaches beside him.

I don't know why, but I stop. I watch him work for a few seconds. Maybe I pause because it's still so difficult to breathe; I have to calm down before I go up the hill behind the park, toward the jogging path that will take me home.

"Would you like a peach?" We're far enough from the stage that I can hear his raspy voice pretty well.

"A peach?" I echo. My stomach lurches at the thought of food. "No, thank you."

When I look down at the table between us, I almost gasp. There, laid out in neat rows on a plain white cloth, are dozens of tiny monkeys clinging to bowed trees, their deep-set eyes so visibly rendered that they almost seem to have expressions. They're carved from individual peach pits, each one no bigger than a sparrow's egg.

"What's the matter?" the man asks. "Don't like peaches no more?"

I blink at him. "What did you say?"

"You were just here, weren't you? You liked them fine."

He saw her. She's wearing more makeup than me, sure, and different clothes, but he remembers her face. He thinks it was me.

"When was I here?" Without any warning, there is a sharp pain in my chest. My knees buckle a little bit. The sensation feels like fire. I have to hold on to the table just to stay upright. I don't know what's wrong with me. It can't be the pills; I only took them a few minutes ago. Besides, the feeling is more than just physical—my adrenaline is pumping, my stomach turning—it's like my panic is manifesting into pain, the sensations urging me to go somewhere, to do something, to find my sister. Except I don't know where to look.

"Hey. You doing okay?" He holds the pit he's been working on, squints at it. There's almost no light around us. I don't know how he can see what he's doing.

"You saw my sister." I breathe. "We're twins. Did she say something to you? Was she with anyone?"

He shakes his head. "Twins. Huh. No, she didn't say much. Wanted to buy a monkey."

I lean against the table hard, trying not to show the pain I'm in. "Did you sell her one?"

"Nope." He stands up and begins to walk toward me. He's short and wiry, with a full head of white hair. He leans closer, so that our heads are only a few inches apart.

"I'll tell you something," he says, like he's sharing a secret. "I ain't in this for the cash flow." And he holds out the monkey he's just finished carving. "I gave her one."

He turns my palm upright and places the monkey in my hand. "Now you got one too." When I close my fist around it, the pit feels warm and damp.

"You look sick," he tells me. "You ought to get away from the crowd, honey."

The pain in my chest has subsided slightly, enough for me to walk.

"I will." I nod at the fist that holds the monkey. "Thank you."

"My pleasure. Pretty girls deserve pretty things." He winks.

༶

The old man's booth is close to the hill behind the field, where the jogging path begins. I don't know where else to look, so I head toward the path, hoping I'll find my sister as she's walking home.

After about a quarter mile, I make a left onto the street and head up another hill, toward my house.

It's only a little past nine. All the lights are still on at home, illuminating the rooms behind the windows. Except for the third floor, where she and I sleep.

As I'm standing on the front porch, I can see my aunt and uncle sitting on the sofa, facing the television. They don't know I'm out here. For a minute, all I do is watch them. My aunt looks sort of like a shadow of my mother; her features are similar, but somehow they seem less deliberately shaped. Like my mom, she's tall and has a slightly bumpy nose. Not *big* bumpy, more like uniquely pretty. They have the same skin tone, pale and lightly freckled. But that's where the similarities end. My mom was a redhead, while my aunt is a blonde. My mom was spontaneous and fun and goofy, while my aunt is serious and thoughtful all the time. In the nine years that we've lived with her, I don't know that we've ever seen her giggle. She doesn't talk about her sister too much, and we've never discussed why they hadn't talked in over ten years before our parents died. But I've gotten plenty of information from my grandma, who is always happy to share our family's secrets.

See, my mom believed she was different from other people. She thought she had a gift, that she was able to sense things other people couldn't. My grandma believes that she has one too—like it's hereditary or something. But nobody would ever think that sort of thing about my aunt Sharon. My aunt is just . . . normal. There's nothing special about her. And she swears up and down that my mom and grandma are—or were—far less *gifted* and more mentally unstable.

My uncle Jeff is okay—he's not nearly as unpleasant as my aunt—but he's also not particularly interesting. When he's not at work, he goes running on the path almost every morning and spends pretty much all his free time reading things like the *Wall Street Journal* and *The Economist*. He's a consultant. I've been living with him for years, and I'm still not sure exactly what a consultant does.

He and my aunt are watching *The Muppets Take Manhattan*, which means that, even though I don't see my cousin Charlie in the room anywhere, he can't be far away. Charlie loves the Muppets. He's nineteen years old. When he was born, his umbilical cord got wrapped around his neck during delivery, cutting off his oxygen for a few minutes. So Charlie is different from other men his age. But it's good-different. As worried as I am about my sister, when I see my cousin walking into the living room, carefully holding a full glass of iced tea in one hand, his other arm curled around a bowl of popcorn, it occurs to me that he's going to love the peach-pit monkey. Maybe I'll give it to him.

The three of them stare at me when I step inside.

Almost immediately, my aunt's lips form a stiff line. She'd be pretty, maybe even beautiful, if she weren't pissed off so much of the time. Sometimes she gets mad at my uncle too, but she almost never gets upset with Charlie. She's always stayed home with him. He can't be left alone for too long. When she has time, my aunt volunteers as a docent for the Greensburg art museum a few afternoons a week. She's like a tour guide, but for paintings. She was an art history major in college, before she had Charlie. My mom had an interest in art, but she didn't just study art, she created it.

"Where's Alice?" my aunt demands. It's like the sound of the name alone—*Alice*—makes her blood boil.

The wheeze persists. Can they hear it? I squeeze the monkey in my hand, trying to stay calm. Charlie crunches on his popcorn, his eyes fixed on the television. We'd wanted to bring him with us tonight, but my aunt said no. She didn't have a good reason. She can be overprotective.

"She isn't here." It's not a question.

"No, she isn't." My aunt crosses her arms. "Why isn't she with you?"

I take a deep breath before I launch into my plea. "Aunt Sharon, Uncle Jeff, please listen. I was riding the Ferris wheel, and all of a sudden Alice was gone. I couldn't find her anywhere. I think something's wrong. She wouldn't have left without telling me."

My aunt nods slowly. "Jeff? Are you hearing this?"

His gaze is fixed on the television. "I sure am."

"Who were you with?" she asks.

"A few people. Kimber and Holly and Nicholas. They said they would call me if they saw her, but that was over half an hour ago." My voice begins to rise. "You know she wouldn't leave without telling me. You *know* that."

My aunt presses her hands to her face. Her engagement ring, which is big and round, sparkles beside her wedding band, beneath the light of the living room's brass chandelier. "Rachel, your uncle and I have had a very long evening. I can't do this right now. You don't have any clue where she might have gone?"

"No! She just disappeared. Aunt Sharon, *please.* She would have told me if she were going somewhere. Listen to me." I'm almost yelling at them. I have everyone's attention now, including Charlie's.

"I found a cat, Rachel," my cousin interrupts, as though the news will calm me.

"Your cousin found a cat," my aunt confirms, staring

upward at the light. "The cat is pregnant. She's in the kitchen."

My uncle appears to be thinking, looking at me now. His index finger is pressed to the tip of his nose. When we make eye contact, he shrugs. He's obviously not too upset by the idea that my sister is missing. "We named it Linda," he offers.

I look at the three of them. My wheeze has subsided, but now I can feel my heart beating quickly in my chest. Holly's pills are kicking in. I shouldn't have taken so many. "What?"

"The cat," my uncle clarifies. "We named the cat Linda." The information seems to cheer him. He adds, as though I care, "After Paul McCartney's first wife." Charlie loves the Beatles.

"Jeff, wait. She's worried about her sister. Rachel," my aunt says, scooting over on the wide sofa, making room for me. "Come here."

I shake my head. "No. You need to call the police."

"The police?" She stares at me. "She's been gone less than an hour. Sweetie, come on. What are the police going to do? Alice is eighteen." But my aunt can see how upset I am. "Jeff?" she asks. "What do you think? Should we go look for her?"

My uncle is eating a handful of Charlie's popcorn now, chewing while he speaks. "If Alice can figure out how to turn back the odometer on my sports car, then I'm sure she can take care of herself for an evening."

I'm almost crying. "Uncle Jeff, this isn't funny. Please listen. I know something happened."

Charlie blinks at me. "How do you know, Rachel?"

"I know because . . . because I just *do.* I can feel it. It's like one second she was there, and then she was gone. I mean *gone.* Please," I beg, "call the police. Tell them she's missing. Say we can't find her. They'll know what to do. They can put out a bulletin, or search the fair, or—"

"Rachel, your sister has a criminal record. Honey, the police won't look for her yet. You need to calm down." My aunt's gaze flickers back to the Muppets.

Ba-dum, ba-dum, ba-dum, my heart thumps. I'm sweating. "If you won't call the police, then I will."

"What?" She seems alarmed by the idea. "Rachel, please don't do that. Think about this for a minute. Alice disappears. It's what she *does.*" My aunt has little patience for behavior that is anything besides orderly and whatever she considers "normal." Her own mother—my grandma—is certifiably crazy, which made for a miserable childhood for my aunt and mother; my grandma had a hard time functioning from day to day, and she's had more than a few stints in institutions, even when her daughters were young. My mom got over it eventually, but Aunt Sharon never has.

"Alice didn't run away this time." I can't explain to them how I know, though. They wouldn't understand any of it. Even *I* don't understand it, not completely. All I know is that I can't feel her anymore. Our connection has been replaced by a messy sense of dread that fills my whole body, seeping into the space around me.

My aunt and uncle exchange a look, communicating with their eyes, the way people who have been married for a long time can do.

"Okay, Rach," my uncle finally says, "if Alice doesn't come home tonight, we'll call the police in the morning. In the meantime, why don't you get in touch with a few of your friends? See if any of them ran into her."

"Fine." My voice trembles. My fingertips are numb. "I'm going upstairs."

⚬⌂

In our room on the third floor, I sit cross-legged on my bed, staring at my phone for a long time, willing it to ring. Willing it to be her, calling to say she's all right.

Alone in the room, I look around, trying to take some comfort in the familiar surroundings. My sister's bed, against the back wall of the house, is unmade as usual. Heaps of our clothing litter the floor. An easel sits beside the front window, holding a work in progress. It's a charcoal drawing of Robin, started weeks ago, abandoned when the relationship got messy. The walls are covered with sketches. Some of them are random objects—books and buildings and household things, studies from long hours spent after school in the art room. Lots of them are of Charlie, who is an excellent model. A few others depict a smiling young girl with a small gap between her top front teeth. I don't know her name or who she is, but there must be at least a dozen sketches of her in our room alone. In the lower-right corner of every drawing, so small you could barely see them, are the initials A.E.F. A talent for art is one of the few things my sister and I don't have in common.

After almost twenty minutes of sitting in near silence, listening to the sound of blood rushing behind my ears, trying to calm myself without any success, I know I have to do *something*. I can't sit here all night, waiting.

What I really want to do is call Robin. If he's around, maybe there's a chance he saw my sister at the fair and tried to talk to her. It seems unlikely, and he wouldn't have gotten very far with her if they did run into each other. But I can't call him. Robin is the only person I know who has never owned a cell phone. At least, he always claimed he didn't have one. No cell, no house line, no way whatsoever for anybody to get in touch with him unless he reached out first.

I sit, staring at my phone, trying to will it to ring.

It does. The sound makes me jump. I look at the screen to see who's calling, but it only says UNKNOWN NUMBER. It could be him. It *must* be him. It rings four times before I answer.

"Hello?" I ask tentatively.

Silence on the other end.

"Hello?" I repeat. "Who is this?"

"Hi." It's him. There's no background noise. Even though he's only said one word, I can sense that he sounds tired, or maybe sad. Where is he? What is he doing tonight? Who is he with?

"Robin," I say. "Where are you?" He tends to come and go as he pleases, showing up out of nowhere sometimes.

"I'm here," he says. "I'm talking to you."

"You have to tell me something," I continue. "It's important. Promise you'll tell me the truth, okay?"

Another pause. "Sure."

"Were you at Hollick Park tonight? There's a fair. You must have seen it." He lives on the opposite side of town, but everybody knows about the autumn festival.

I can *hear* him smiling. I can picture exactly what he looks like in my mind. "Nope," he says, "I've been here all night."

"Where are you?"

"It's not important."

"Robin," I say, "it *is* important. Why did you call me, anyway?"

"I don't know," he says. "I just felt like it, okay?"

"You haven't been around lately. What have you been doing?"

He ignores the question. "I've gotta go. Sorry. Listen, though—you know where to find me if you need anything, right?"

I stare at his portrait, which is so lifelike that it almost seems like he's right here in the room with me.

There's a pause in our conversation that seems to stretch forever. I can hear his thick breath. He's smoking a cigarette.

I imagine the room he might be in, all alone in his cheap apartment on the east end of town.

I squeeze my eyes shut in frustration. He is always like this, so nebulous. So difficult to pin down. "Right," I say weakly. "Fine. Thanks a lot."

I don't wait long for him to respond. After a few seconds, I take the phone away from my ear, press end, and toss it onto the bed.

Minutes pass, and he doesn't call back. But I continue to stare at his half-finished portrait near the window, trying to imagine what he's doing at this moment. I lay in bed, on top of my sheets, listening to my heart beating in my chest. I can feel my eyes moving in their sockets. My sweat dampens my clothing, and I get so chilly that I can't stand it anymore, so I finally get up and change into a pair of pajamas. Around two in the morning, I cross the room and climb into my sister's bed. I lay there for what feels like forever, until I can't hold my eyes open any longer. Downstairs, I hear Linda the cat meowing in the kitchen, all by herself, afraid of the dark night.

CHAPTER THREE

We were four the first time. We had a baby pool in our backyard. I was in the pool, playing with a plastic teacup set. My sister went inside to use the bathroom. My mother let her go in all by herself. The bathroom was right inside the back door, next to the kitchen.

My mother had dark red hair that she used to wear in a messy ponytail. She'd sit in her lawn chair beside the pool, keeping an eye on us while she read a book, smoking her cigarettes. She smoked all the time. I didn't realize until I was much older that it wasn't socially acceptable to smoke, much less around your children. My mom never finished college; instead, she had us. She married my father when she was only twenty-one. But this was a long time ago—back when it wasn't so unusual for people to get married so young.

Back then, to me, my mom always seemed happy. She laughed a lot, and some days when we were finished playing in the baby pool, she'd take us inside and we'd make microwave brownies together. She always let us crack the eggs. I remember her smell—it wasn't perfume or soap or anything like that. It was just the way she smelled, like cigarettes and teaberry chewing gum.

My sister was in the house using the bathroom that day, and I was in the pool. I sat with my legs folded underneath me, bent at the knees. It was a hot day, the kind of heat where you can see the sunlight shimmering in the air. The grass kept turning brown and was starting to die underneath the baby pool because it didn't get any sun, so my parents would move the pool around the yard to help the grass grow back, and finally we had all these big brown circles in the yard, like a map of every place the pool had been that summer.

My mother wore big, round sunglasses with pink frames. She was reclined in her chair, reading her book. All of a sudden I couldn't breathe.

I *tried.* I put my hands to my throat and struggled for air, but it felt like I'd swallowed a rock. I didn't cough. I gagged. I panicked, splashing around in the water, trying to breathe.

"Baby?" My mother put her book down. I shook my head at her. I couldn't speak or cry or do anything but work for air that wasn't coming.

"Sweetie, say something!" My mother rushed to me, picked me up from the pool, and lay me down on the lawn. She shook me hard. She screamed my name over and over. She slapped me across the face.

But no matter how I tried, I could not manage to take a breath. My mother picked me up like I weighed next to nothing and threw me over her shoulder, hitting me on the back as she carried me inside.

There, in the kitchen, lay my sister. She was on the ceramic tile floor. She wasn't breathing. She was bluish, her wispy red hair across her face, her little mouth wide open. I remember it all so vividly. I remember looking down at her and thinking, "That's me down there." Because I felt exactly what she was feeling.

My mother knelt beside my sister. She shook her hard. She screamed her name over and over. She slapped her across the face. Still, my sister did not breathe. Her eyes were open, but she wasn't looking at us. It was like she wasn't there.

My mother lay me down on the floor, her gaze filled with horror as she tried to help both of us at the same time. She struggled to lift up my sister and pound on her back. "Steven!" she screamed, calling for my father. Then she put her arms around my sister's stomach, hands clasped together against her small tummy like a knot, and pushed.

My sister spit something out. She coughed and coughed. Then she threw up all over the floor.

My mother gazed at the mess. With her thumb and index finger, she reached into it and picked something up. She stared at it, then she looked at me.

I was breathing again. It all happened in an instant. I felt fine.

My mother, though, did not seem fine. Her face was white. I looked at what she was holding. It was a big wad of pink teaberry gum.

That was the first time.

I dream of my sister all night long. At least that's how it feels; I read somewhere that dreams only last a few seconds, even though it might seem like they go on for hours.

We are standing on the running path, walking side by side with our fingers laced together gently, our arms swinging as we stroll along.

In the dream, I feel worried. There is a strong, cool breeze that whips my hair into my line of vision, obscuring my surroundings. I grip my sister's hand more tightly. "We should go home," I tell her.

She stops. She reaches toward me and brushes the hair from my eyes. "You go ahead. I have to stay behind."

"Why?" I ask, still holding her hand. I feel certain that I can't let go, or she might slip away forever.

She doesn't answer me. She looks up at the sky, which is overcast, thick with dark, puffy cumulus clouds. "It might rain soon."

"I don't want to leave you here," I say.

She smiles at me. "You don't have a choice."

Then the oddest thing happens. It's like she starts to fade, her form growing translucent, her hand slipping away from mine even as I struggle to maintain my grasp. The wind picks up, and she begins to blur around the edges. It's like an invisible hand is taking an eraser to her figure.

I want to lunge after her, to save her, but I can't move. I am frozen in place. All I can do is watch as she grows fainter by the minute. I open my mouth to scream her name, but I can't make a sound.

Just before she disappears, she speaks to me one last time. Her voice is strong and firm, so different from her appearance. "Don't. Tell. Anyone. Not a soul."

I find my voice, shouting her name even as she vanishes into thin air. I feel incredibly cold all of a sudden, unable to move, shivering, waiting for her to reappear. I stare at the empty space for what feels like hours, but she doesn't return.

ோ

I wake up with my legs tangled in her sheets, sunlight leaking through the cracks in our window's wooden shutters. It's 9:13 in the morning. I feel something in my hand; looking down, I see that I'm still clutching the carved monkey. I've been holding on to it all night.

Beside me, resting on the fitted sheet, is my phone. Its tiny message light is off. No missed calls. No texts. Nothing.

But the panic is still here; almost immediately, I realize that I'm sweating. The sheets are all wet. My sister, I know, did not come home last night. She isn't downstairs watching cartoons with Charlie. She isn't making herself some cinnamon toast in the kitchen. She isn't anywhere.

I put my feet on the floor. I stare at the monkey again, holding it up to the sunlight, noticing its precise detail. For some reason, I don't want to put it down. Each individual finger is visible against the tree trunk. Its mouth is an almost-perfect tiny heart shape. I've never seen anything like it.

I get out of bed and hurry downstairs. My aunt and uncle promised they'd call the police this morning if my sister wasn't back. We need to be looking for her. We should have been looking last night.

The house is a big old Colonial with creaky hardwood floors and thick plaster walls. The staircase leading to the third floor is wide and curved, the steps carpeted with an expensive Oriental pattern, held in place with brass poles. On the landing just outside the door to our bedroom, there's a cozy window seat overlooking the street, except that the view is obscured by a huge stained-glass peacock. The bird's tail is fanned into numerous slivers of color, its bright green eyes always open, watching, sometimes catching the light so that it almost seems alive. There's a huge landing on the second floor, its staircase gently sloping, open into the foyer.

The coolest thing about this place, though, is that there's a genuine hidden staircase. In the smallest second-floor bedroom, which is a guest room, there's a rectangular seam in the blue-and-white-striped wallpaper. If you press on the edge, right where you'd expect to find a doorknob, it releases a hinge on the other side, and part of the wall swings out to reveal a dark, narrow staircase. It leads to the kitchen, where there's a latch that opens from the inside. And in the kitchen, to the left of the refrigerator, there is a similar flat panel with no visible doorknob—just a slim rectangular crack in the wall. It's barely noticeable.

Nobody else in this house ever uses the secret staircase; it's dark and inconvenient, the steps are steep and narrow, and its unheated air is chilly. But I like it. In the months after we first came here, I used to hide in the wall for long periods of time in the afternoons, sitting with my knees pulled against my chest, thinking of my mother and father. I imagined that I was in a secret, magical corridor—kind of like the wardrobe leading to Narnia—and that I'd step out of the darkness and into my old life at my old house, and my parents would be standing in the kitchen like they'd always been there, like they would never go away.

It didn't work, of course. There was no magic. But in the cool darkness of the hidden stairs, if I listened closely to hear the whispered vacuum of air circulating past my ears, sometimes I almost believed that it could.

℘

This morning, I open the latch and step into the kitchen, where my aunt and uncle, along with Charlie, are gathered in a semicircle around a big cardboard box on the floor. Inside, there's a fat calico cat lying on top of an old yellow blanket, her breathing rapid and shallow, eyes so wide and glassy that they look like wet marbles.

My aunt looks at me. "Alice?"

I shake my head.

"Oh. Rachel." Pause. "Your sister still isn't back, then?"

"No." My eyes are watering, and I'm continuing to sweat. "Please do something."

"She didn't call you?" my uncle asks, not looking up from the box. The cat gives a low-pitched meow, in pain, and rolls to her other side. Her fine belly fur is licked so thoroughly that it's soaking wet, her swollen nipples a deep, angry shade of red.

"No. You said we'd call the police today. You *promised*." I close the secret door and stand beside the box, between my aunt and Charlie. "What are you staring at? It's just a cat." The house feels like an oven; a bead of sweat rolls down my forehead and into my eye. "Aren't you worried, now that Alice didn't come home all night? You said you'd listen to me. Aunt Sharon, you promised. *Please*."

"Oh, honey . . ." My aunt sighs. "Maybe we should call around first. She could be with Robin."

"She's not. I talked to him last night."

"You talked to Robin?" My aunt gives me a sharp look. "Rachel, he's—"

"I know. But I was so scared." The cat sort of gurgles and howls all at once. It wriggles around on the blanket.

"You're still worried, aren't you? Even though she's run away before?" My aunt Sharon picks up a mug of steaming coffee from the floor beside her. Charlie made the mug in a ceramics class that he took at the community center last year.

It's dark green and lopsided, a few of his big fingerprints visible in the glazed clay. My aunt uses it every morning, washing it by hand after she's finished drinking coffee, carefully drying it with a dish towel before placing it on the ledge of the kitchen window. Every morning.

I close my eyes for a moment. The feeling of dread is almost suffocating. "Something bad is happening. You have to believe me; I know her better than anyone." I open my eyes to give them another pleading look. "I can tell. I know it sounds crazy, but I'm certain of it."

My aunt glances at the clock above the kitchen stove. I can see that she's starting to worry, too, but doesn't want to show it too much. "Maybe Robin was lying to you."

The idea annoys me. My aunt and uncle don't like Robin, but they've never even *met* him. They don't know him at all. "He wasn't lying."

"Oh . . . would you look at that," my uncle whispers.

"Ew!" Horrified, Charlie brings his hands to his face. He separates his fingers, peeking out from between them. "Dad! It's so gross."

My uncle rubs Charlie's back. "It's okay, buddy. She's having her kittens. You should watch. You might never see anything like this again."

But Charlie's right; it *is* gross. I stare as the first kitten emerges, contained in a clear, gelatinous sac, its tiny paws working to break through the membrane without much success.

Charlie and I look at each other. He puts an index finger in his mouth to make a gagging gesture. In spite of everything, I smile.

"All right, Rachel. If she doesn't get in touch within the hour, I'm going to call the police," my uncle says, unable to take his eyes off the cat. He adds, "Sharon, where's the camera? We should be taking pictures."

"Within the hour?" I almost shriek. "Are you kidding? Call them *now*. You promised me." I look at the cat again. "And why would you want pictures of that? It's the most disgusting thing I've ever seen."

My aunt sips her coffee. Her expression over the edge of her mug is serious. To my uncle, she says, "I think Rachel might be right. Maybe we should call the police now, Jeff. Alice didn't come home last night. We shouldn't wait around all morning."

My uncle barely looks at her. "If you think so."

"I *do* think so. We can't just assume she's okay. Even if she did run away, the police need to know she's gone."

My face is flushed, my forehead wet with sweat; why hasn't anybody else noticed how warm it is in here? A flutter of worry beats hard in my chest. "Will you call right now?"

My aunt stands up. "Yes," she says, glancing at the box. As she's heading toward the phone, she adds, "Rachel's right, Jeff. That's the most disgusting thing I've ever seen." She means the cat. To me, she says, "I know you're worried, but please don't panic. The police will track down Alice. And when she gets home, we'll deal with her." She sighs. "Somehow."

I lean against the wall in relief, sliding downward until my butt hits the floor, pulling my knees close to my chest.

My aunt drops her mug. It shatters against the floor, coffee and thick green shards of ceramic all over the place, some of the brown liquid seeping into the side of the cardboard box.

Charlie looks at the mug, at my aunt, and then at me. His bottom lip begins to tremble. He starts to cry.

"What the hell, Sharon?" My uncle jumps to his feet, his arms spread out, the cat howling wildly below him, four newborn kittens in the box now, and when I look at my aunt again she's staring at me, a look of pure horror on her face, her expression crumpled somewhere between frowning and crying and screaming. She covers her mouth with a hand, shakes her head, steps toward me, and reaches down with her free arm to pull me to my feet.

"What is that?" Charlie asks, crying.

"Jesus." My uncle stares at me. "Charlie, go get the phone, buddy."

"Dad, what's all over the wall? Dad?" I've never seen my cousin so scared. What does he mean, what's on the wall? I am too afraid to turn around and look.

"Charlie. The phone!"

His footsteps heavy, my cousin runs toward the family room.

"What? What's wrong?" I've never been looked at this way before.

"Rachel . . . oh, sweetie. You're hurt." My aunt reaches toward me with a shaking hand.

"Aunt Sharon," I say, backing away, "you're scaring me."

And then I sense it. Something feels wet and cool on the back of my head, near my neck. It doesn't hurt; it tingles.

Slowly, I turn around to look at the wall.

The paint is a color called silk heaven. The kitchen used to be wallpapered. It was this garish gold-and-purple flower pattern. When we were fourteen, my sister and I spent an entire weekend scraping the paper off. You can't imagine the mess. When we were finished, my aunt let us help with the painting. Silk heaven. The words roll off the tongue. Aunt Sharon always keeps the kitchen so clean, so white.

The wall behind me is marked with a thick smear of blood, a bright-red stripe running vertically toward the floor. It's so red, such a vibrant, pretty color, that it almost looks alive. It is caked with hundreds of strands of my hair, shimmering beneath the light, tiny particles of gray scalp visible at their roots. So much blood. So much hair.

I touch the back of my scalp, gently, and feel a gooey mess. It's still flowing. I pull my hand away. I am holding a fistful of hair and scalp.

My aunt and uncle ease me to the floor. My uncle pulls off his shirt, holds it to the back of my head, and wraps his arms around me.

In her bare feet, her toenails painted a pink so light that it's almost white, my aunt stumbles on a shard of the ceramic mug, slicing open the edge of her foot. A blossom of red appears at the wound, but she doesn't seem to notice.

From the cardboard box, there is a chorus of hungry, sweet mewing. The kittens' cries start out quiet but then quickly become louder, the sound growing shrill, almost intolerable. The room dissolves into inky patches of light and darkness. From somewhere far away, somewhere dark and damp and cruel, I hear my sister calling my name. The pain comes through her and into me. I feel it for both of us. Everything hurts.

Chapter Four

Don't." As soon as I realize they're about to call an ambulance, I stop them. "I'm okay." I stare at my bloody hand, hair and scalp stuck to my fingers. For a moment, it occurs to me that I am really, *really* not okay. But I can't go to the hospital. That will only waste my aunt and uncle's time, when they need to call the police and focus on finding my sister.

My sister. Where could she possibly have gone? As I gaze at the mess of flesh and blood in my fist, I can only think the worst: that the same thing has happened to her—somebody grabbed her last night or somehow lured her away from the fair. She looked so pretty and self-assured, all the men sneaking glances at her when they thought their wives and girlfriends weren't looking. Did somebody want her enough to simply *take* her? I shouldn't have let her run away from the Ferris wheel. I should have protected her.

Charlie stands in the doorway to the kitchen, trembling

as he hands the phone to my uncle. My cousin is still wearing his pajamas. He doesn't look at me; instead, he stares at the box of kittens. He's taking deep breaths, visibly trying to calm himself. He's easily upset, and for years his therapist has coached him to rely on breathing techniques for relaxation whenever he becomes agitated. I hate the fact that I've worried him so much. More than that, I hate knowing that things seem like they're only getting worse. For me. For my sister. For everyone.

My uncle kneels at my side, attempting to peer at my wound as he continues to press his shirt against my scalp. "What did you do?" he asks. "Did you cut yourself somehow?"

I can't tell them what I think is actually happening. They would never believe me. They would never understand. My sister and I have been connected this way our whole lives—this isn't the first time something like this has happened to me. There was the incident with the gum when we were much younger, but it's more than just that; it's a million other, more subtle oddities that have piled up over the years, to the point where they can't all be dismissed as coincidence.

"Rachel." My uncle stares at me, worried. "Answer me. Did you cut yourself?"

"I don't know. I don't think so." I wince, feeling pain at the site of the wound for the first time as my uncle presses his hand against the shirt. "Please call the police," I say. "We have to help her."

"Rachel," my aunt pronounces, "you have a head wound.

You might need stitches. Don't worry about Alice right now." She glances at my cousin in the doorway. "Charlie, honey, go to your room for a while. Okay?"

Charlie shakes his head back and forth with worry. "I want to help."

"Everything will be okay," my aunt tells him. "Please go to your room."

I close my eyes as a rush of dizziness overwhelms me. I hear Charlie's heavy footsteps fading as he walks away. As my wound throbs, I imagine my sister alone somewhere, helpless, probably hoping that I'll search for her, that maybe somehow I'll find her. But before I can do that, I have to get out of this house.

"Rachel? Rachel? Sharon, I think she's about to pass out. Jesus. Sharon, do something!"

My eyelids flutter. For a moment, my vision blurry, I see my aunt standing beside me, holding her phone, just staring at it. My gaze drifts toward the floor, and I notice a ribbon of blood running from the cut in her toe.

"I'm okay," I repeat. I try to steady myself, then I realize that my bottom half has gone numb; I try to wiggle my toes, to regain sensation in my feet so that I can get up and call the police myself, if that's what I have to do.

After a few shaky seconds, I'm able to stand. I step away from my uncle, replacing my hand over his in order to hold the shirt against the back of my own head. I blink rapidly, trying to bring the room into focus.

"We should still . . ." My aunt's voice trails off.

"Wait, Sharon." My uncle puts a hand on her arm. He moves toward me. "Let me see how badly you're bleeding."

I still feel fuzzy. Even though I can breathe, I feel suffocated by dread, like someone has pulled a plastic bag over my head and the air is slowly running out. And the back of my head is beginning to ache dully, the pain throbbing to the beat of my pulse.

Carefully, my uncle lifts the shirt away. With gentle hands, he pushes aside my hair to better examine the wound.

"Rachel, are you sure nothing happened? Did you fall in the shower?"

"I didn't take a shower. Not last night or this morning."

"Maybe you hit your head somehow. You must have done *something*. Because it looks like—come here, Sharon, see for yourself—it looks like the hair has been yanked out. You've almost got a bald spot."

I've learned a thing or two from Charlie's relaxation techniques. I try to calm myself by taking slow, deep breaths. But it's almost impossible; it's like my lungs will not fully expand, like their elasticity is gone.

"My goodness," my aunt murmurs. "Rachel, what the hell did you do to yourself?"

A chorus of tiny mews sounds from the box on the floor. Looking down, I see that all the kittens are free from their sacs and have crowded around their mother's belly, eyes still closed so soon after their births, bodies wet and weak, tiny voices crying out for milk as they search blindly in what is, to them, complete darkness.

My uncle pours me a glass of water. After a few more minutes of holding the towel against my head, the bleeding seems to stop.

"I don't think you need any stitches, but we should definitely wash it off," my aunt says. "It could get infected."

I nod. "I'll go get in the shower. But first, will you call the police?"

My uncle takes a long, deep breath. He looks around the kitchen, at the red streak on the wall, and seems to notice the blood seeping from my aunt's foot for the first time. "We should clean up the room before we do anything else. Sharon, your toe."

My aunt doesn't even glance down. "It's fine. But poor Charlie's mug . . ."

"He can make you another one," my uncle offers.

My aunt gives him a sad smile. "Sure he can."

The kitchen goes silent, except for the constant mewing of the kittens. Beyond the walls of the house, outside on the street, somebody is blaring an old Bon Jovi song that I haven't heard in years.

My uncle cocks his head a little bit. "What's that? Music?" He makes a face. "It's Sunday morning."

"It's TJ washing his car," I offer. "You should know. He does it every weekend."

Our neighbors across the street, the Gardills, have a twenty-two-year-old son, TJ, who still lives at home. He drives a blue convertible, which he washes by hand every Sunday. When the weather is warm enough—and sometimes even when it's not—TJ works shirtless, presumably to show off his buff bod. He was pretty scrawny up until a few years ago, when all of a sudden he started to bulk up, going from a dorky-looking boy to a remarkable specimen of a man, seemingly overnight. I can look at him now and recognize on some level that he's most definitely hot, but it's like I can't forget the twerp he once was. My sister and I used to refer to him privately as "Pee-Wee." Even though the nickname doesn't fit anymore, we still use it all the time.

The three of us stand there listening as the song ends, followed by a DJ announcing that we're listening to station KZEP: All classic rock, all the time.

I attempt to smile at my uncle. "Since when is Bon Jovi classic rock?"

He smiles back, but the effort is weak. He doesn't answer.

"Rachel," my aunt says. "Go clean up, sweetie. When you're out of the shower, let me have another look at your head. We need to disinfect it. Okay?" And she kneels down, begins to gather pieces of the broken mug into her open palm. As she works, moving slowly around the kitchen, she leaves bloody half footprints all over the floor.

I don't move yet. "Who's going to call the police?"

"I will." My uncle holds up the phone in his hand. "I'll do it right now."

My inclination is to wait, to see for myself that he's called, but I believe him. Besides, I have other things to do right now.

So I head toward the stairs, walking slowly, bracing myself with every step in case I suddenly become dizzy again.

Once I'm on the landing of the second floor, I stop. I wait for a moment, listening to the sound of my uncle's voice as he speaks with the 911 dispatcher.

"I think that I, uh, need to report a missing person." He pauses. "My niece. Her name is Alice Foster. I'm her guardian . . . that's right."

Carefully, quietly, I open the door to my aunt and uncle's bedroom and step inside.

My uncle's wallet rests in plain sight on the night-stand. I don't have to look to know that, if I open his top nightstand drawer, I'll find the keys to his sports car. It's a Porsche. He only drives it four months a year, from May to August. The rest of the time, he stores it under a canvas cloth in the garage behind our house.

If I'm hoping to get very far, I'm going to need transportation. I walk to the nightstand on my tiptoes, even though the room is carpeted. I open the top drawer. I stare at the keys for a second. Then I take them.

When I step into the hallway again, Charlie is standing on the landing, staring wide-eyed at me.

"Hey, Charlie." My hands dangle at my sides. He can definitely see the keys.

"Rachel? Why were you in my parents' room?"

Oh, Charlie. He is kind at all times, curious and genuine and gentle. I love him dearly.

But I love my sister more.

"Can you do me a favor?" I ask him.

He notices what I'm holding, and I can see the struggle on his face as he attempts to piece together what's going on.

"What?" he asks, doubtful.

"I need you to stay in your room. Just for ten minutes. Go inside, close the door, and stay there. After ten minutes, you can do whatever you want. Okay?"

"Why do you have those keys?" he blurts.

"Shh. Quiet." I take a step closer to him. "I can't explain everything right now, but it's really important that you listen to me and do what I say. You believe me, right? I wouldn't lie to you."

My cousin's eyes are glassy with worry. His hair is uncombed. Glancing past him through the open door to his bedroom, I see the framed drawing that he keeps above his desk. It's a pencil sketch of his face, his lips turned upward into a patient smile, eyes staring brightly ahead. In the right-hand corner—so small and far away that I can only make out a hint of them—are the initials A.E.F.

I don't know exactly why I start to cry—I just do. I can't stop myself. Maybe it's because the dread is still all around me, seeping through my clothes and into my body, so thick that it seems to drip from my pores. Maybe because I am deeply certain that my twin sister is suffering somewhere, and I don't know how to help her.

My lungs crackle as I breathe, still unable to fully fill

my lungs. Charlie's face becomes a blur through my teary vision.

"Rachel? I'm scared." He puts a clammy hand on my arm. "Don't leave. Okay?"

"I'm just going upstairs. Don't worry about me." I smile at him. "Promise you'll wait ten minutes before you come out."

He doesn't answer for a long time. Finally, he says, "Okay. I promise."

I give him a hug. "Thank you."

I have no time for a shower. I hurry up to my room, quickly change my clothes, and slip on a pair of flip-flops. I pull my hair into a ponytail, my whole head aching now, and try to ignore the discomfort, along with the fact that my hair is covered in blood. I don't care. I grab my purse and phone. I find my backpack beneath a pile of dirty clothes, and then I kneel down and reach under my bed until I find the last, most important thing that I'm looking for.

I sit cross-legged on the floor beside a large rectangular cardboard box and lift off the lid. As I gaze down at the contents, I let out a breath I didn't realize I'd been holding.

Inside is all that's left of the life my sister and I once shared with our parents. There are our report cards from kindergarten through third grade; art projects that our small hands constructed so carefully, eager to impress our mom and dad; old Christmas tree ornaments; two Baby's First Year scrapbooks. There is a thick row of loose photographs arranged in no particular order. A small manila envelope contains some of my mother's old jewelry, including her engagement ring.

I've looked through this stuff a hundred times—my sister and I both have. But I'm not interested in any of it right now. What I want is all the way at the bottom, wrapped in a thin cotton blanket—the same one the nurses used to swaddle me in at the hospital, right after I was born.

It's money. Lots of it. Ten thousand dollars, to be exact.

Here in my room. Hidden in a box beneath my bed. I guess it's my money, in the sense that it's in my possession at the moment. But from a legal standpoint? A moral one? That's where things start to get a tad sketchy.

I hesitate, staring at it, overwhelmed by how much is there even though I've looked at it many times over the past few weeks. The money isn't mine; I found it. Actually, I stole it. And I can't ignore the possibility that its owner probably wants it back. Maybe whoever it belongs to wants it badly enough to go after the person who took it. And maybe they made a mistake; what if they confronted the wrong sister last night? What if something terrible happened, and it's all my fault?

I remember the dream I had last night. My sister's voice: *Don't. Tell. Anyone.*

But I have to tell someone. Without giving it another thought, I grab the money and stuff it into the front of my bookbag. Then I leave.

⌘

Back on the landing, I peek downstairs. My aunt and uncle are in the living room at the front of the house. They're talking

in hushed voices. The television is on, tuned to a muted episode of *Meet the Press.* I can hear Billy Idol's "White Wedding"
blaring from TJ's car stereo on the street.

It could almost be any normal Sunday.

Except that on any normal Sunday, my sister and I would
be downstairs with our family. We'd all be eating breakfast—
except for my sister, who can't stand to put anything in her
stomach before lunch. Right now we might be watching the
kittens, marveling at how tiny they are, how we've never
seen anything so *new* in our whole lives.

Instead of joining my family in the living room, I slip
down the secret stairway and into the empty kitchen. I tiptoe unseen out the back door and hurry toward the garage.
By the time the police arrive, I'll be gone.

CHAPTER FIVE

I drive slowly through town, constantly glancing at the side-walks, trying to get a good look at each person I pass, hoping I might suddenly recognize my sister among them. I imagine pulling up beside her, demanding that she get in the car.

"What's the matter?" she might ask, grinning, like her disappearance is nothing more than a hilarious practical joke. "Did I scare you?"

I'm so desperate to find her that the fantasy is pleasant in an achy sort of way. I let it continue, the scene unfolding in my mind with almost no effort on my part; it seems like my sister is describing it herself, from somewhere very far away.

"Here," she says, pulling something from her pocket. "I have a present for you." She opens her hand to reveal another peach-pit monkey. "Have you ever seen anything like it?"

I laugh. I reach into my pocket and produce my own identical carving.

My sister's eyes twinkle. She rests her monkey in my palm. "Look," she says, "they're twins."

But none of it is real. The longer I drive, the more sure I am that my sister isn't walking around on these streets, waiting for me to stumble upon her. I make my way down a steep one-way hill that winds around the back of the hospital and brings me out next to the local Catholic school, whose parking lot offers a shortcut to Pennsylvania Avenue.

The Porsche is out of place among the other cars parked along the street, all of which appear old and beat up. Pieces of trash—mostly empty soda cans and cigarette butts—litter the cracked, uneven sidewalks. Pennsylvania Avenue used to be considered one of the worst streets in town. It spans four blocks cluttered with huge old homes, many of which are broken up into low-rent apartments. You can tell just by looking that it's not a bright and happy place. Almost all the small front lawns are overgrown with weeds and strewn with random junk. For years this street was a notorious source of local drug activity. I think there have even been a few shootings.

Lately, though, people have been making efforts to clean up the area. About six months ago, a group of investors purchased most of the houses, a few of which are already undergoing renovations. The idea is to restore them to single-family dwellings and sell them for a huge profit once the whole street has been transformed. Marcus Hahn—my boss and Nicholas's dad—is the leader of the investment group.

He personally owns six houses on this street, all of which are on the same block, directly behind the Catholic school. Three of them are still occupied by tenants whose leases don't expire until the end of the year. Two of them are in the early stages of repair. And one of them is empty, the tenants gone since June, even though its cleanup isn't scheduled to begin for another few weeks.

I know all of this because, for a couple of months now, Mr. Hahn has been letting Nicholas use the empty house to entertain friends after school and on weekends. He's what you might call a permissive parent. Nicholas hasn't had a curfew since eighth grade, and he told us that on Christmas last year, his dad gave him a box of condoms in his stocking.

Nicholas has a key to 340 Pennsylvania Avenue, and as far as I know, his dad has never bothered to check up on what happens here. He doesn't care if we trash the place, Nicholas explained, because they're just going to gut it in a few weeks anyway.

As soon as he got a key to the house, Nicholas promptly made copies to distribute among his friends—my sister and I got one to share, and I have it with me today. After I've knocked a few times, once I'm confident the place is empty for the moment, I dig my key from the front pocket of my bookbag and let myself inside.

"Hello?" I call, stepping into the foyer. "Is anybody here?"

The place is enormous; it's one of the few homes on the street that never got split up into apartments. Still, it's a wreck inside. The hardwood floors are scratched and stained, probably beyond repair. The wallpaper in the dining and living rooms is peeling away in sheets. Little piles of rodent droppings line the baseboards. The electricity is still on, but almost none of the lights are functioning because the wiring is so bad. Even though the water works, there's only one usable toilet in the house, down in the basement. The spaces behind the walls and ceilings are infested with squirrels; if you listen carefully, you can hear them running around inside, their little claws scratching against the wood.

The house is always packed with kids on weekend nights, but otherwise it's usually empty. Over the summer, my sister would slip away sometimes, for a few hours here and there. She told me she liked being alone in this house. She said she'd lock all the doors and go up to the attic, where a huge window offers a panoramic view of the city.

"But what do you *do*?" I'd asked her more than once. I've been in the attic myself a few times; it's filthy. Aside from the unfinished wooden floor, there's nowhere to sit. The big window is painted shut, preventing any fresh air from getting in, so the room always smells musty and suffocating. Anytime sunlight shines through the dirty glass, you can see all the dust particles floating in the air.

My sister didn't want to tell me how she spent her time alone here. All she would ever do is give me a little smile and say, "Everybody deserves to have a secret, don't they?"

But she isn't here today. I check almost the entire house

twice, calling out to her, looking in closets and behind doors, hoping that maybe she snuck over here last night and fell asleep, or got locked in somehow, or was just having too much fun by herself to bother coming home.

Even as I'm searching, I know I'm not going to find her here. The more I look, yelling her name—waiting for an answer and only hearing the *scratch, scratch, scratch* of the squirrels behind the walls—the more frantic and disappointed I become.

After maybe fifteen wasted minutes, I find myself standing at the foot of the basement stairs. It's the only place I haven't checked yet. The basement is unfinished; it has a dirt floor and low ceilings, from which plaster is falling off in chunks. Behind them are rusty pipes and old clusters of wires, their insulation chewed away by squirrels and whatever other creatures might be lurking behind the scenes.

A few Saturdays ago, after the first football game of the year, Nicholas had a party here that lasted until four a.m. Sunday morning. My sister and I both came, along with practically everyone else from school. Jill Allen, the secretary of our senior class, brought three jugs of homemade liquor that she'd stolen from her parents' root cellar. Apparently it was some kind of family recipe going all the way back to Prohibition. We tried mixing it with everything we could think of— soda, juice, even Gatorade—but no matter what we used, our drinks tasted like poison and made our insides burn. The only upside was that we all got drunk very quickly. By midnight we were a bunch of fools, stumbling all over one another, making so much noise that you could feel the walls vibrating. Eventually the chaos started to make me feel sick. Looking for a quiet spot to rest for a few minutes, I came down to the basement, which was the only unoccupied part of the house.

Pennsylvania Avenue runs along a steep hillside; all the homes are built so that their basements have doors and windows looking out the back, while their front rooms are basically underground. I'd only been down there a few seconds when I heard footsteps on the stairs, presumably someone looking to use the only functioning toilet in the house.

I'm not sure why I wanted to remain unseen so badly, but for some reason I hurried deeper into the basement, into a cool, windowless room toward the front of the house. It was dark, but once my eyes adjusted I could make out a crooked wooden door on the opposite wall.

When I lifted the latch, the door creaked open to reveal another set of steps, much steeper and more narrow than the main basement staircase. I felt the walls around me until my fingers touched a light switch. When I flipped it on, the space filled with dim light. Beyond the second set of stairs was what appeared to be *another* basement. A sub-basement.

Ordinarily, I would have been curious enough to go exploring. But I was drunk, and the space below me looked creepy enough that I didn't want to check it out alone. I stepped a few feet into the stairwell so I could pull the door shut behind me, intending to wait until whoever was using the bathroom had gone back upstairs.

I slipped and fell immediately. There was no banister to grab on to. I tumbled all the way down on my butt, the unfinished wooden stairs scraping the backs of my bare legs. I was tipsy enough that it didn't hurt much, but I knew I was probably bleeding.

Once I'd recovered from my spill, I found myself in an area so tiny that it didn't even qualify as a room. It was just a hollowed-out square of dirt, more of a crawl space than anything. But there was something nestled into one of the corners. Even in the dark, I recognized its shape. It was a duffel bag.

In hindsight, I don't know why I took it back upstairs with me. I didn't think there would be anything of value inside. I wasn't even that curious. But I didn't think it through at all—I was in a hurry—so I grabbed the bag and tucked it under my arm and limped out of the crawl space, the scrapes on the backs of my legs beginning to burn.

Whoever had come down to use the bathroom was gone. Alone again, I unzipped the bag and peered inside.

It was money.

I'd like to think that, if I hadn't been drinking, I would have put it back where I found it. But that's not what I did. Instead, I rolled the duffel bag into a ball and stuffed it up the front of my shirt. I kept my arms crossed against my chest as I went back to the party. I didn't speak to anyone as

I walked out the door, straight to my aunt's car parked on the street, and stowed the duffel bag under the front seat. Then I returned to the house and got myself a fresh drink. It didn't occur to me until a few days later that whoever had hidden the money might come looking for it eventually. But did it really matter? Nobody had seen me take it. Nobody had even known I was in the basement.

Later on that week, as I sat on my bedroom floor and counted the bills for the fourth or fifth time, astounded each time by how much was there, I reassured myself that everything would be fine. I smiled. "Finders, keepers," I whispered.

❧

Right now, alone in the basement again, all I want to do is put the money back where I found it. The duffel bag is long gone, but I figure that won't matter to whoever stashed it in the first place. If whoever took my sister comes looking for the cash again, they'll find it all right where they left it, safe and sound, every bill accounted for. They'll let her come home. Everything will be okay. It has to be.

I can feel the adrenaline pumping through my veins as I make my way toward the little wooden door, unzipping my bookbag and reaching inside while I walk. All I have to do is run down the stairs, replace the money, and leave.

But as I reach for the latch, I freeze. My stomach turns.

The walls seem to rise up around me, swallowing me, all the light and air and hope slipping from the room like water falling through the holes in a sieve.

Somebody has attached a shiny metal combination lock to the latch. The door is locked.

I grab the handle anyway and lean my shoulder into the door, trying to force it open. It doesn't budge. I try again, then again, but the lock isn't going anywhere.

With sudden clarity, I realize that whoever padlocked the door is at least one step ahead of me, maybe more. I've made a terrible mistake.

The house seems to breathe as I take a few unsteady steps backward. The walls appear to tilt inward, like they might fold down upon me. There are noises everywhere: in the ceiling, the floors, outside and upstairs and beneath me. What the hell am I doing here? What if I'm not alone?

My fingers and toes are numb with panic. I'm afraid my knees will buckle as I start to run upstairs, frantic to get out of the house, but somehow I manage to make it all the way onto the street and into my car.

I lock all the doors and fumble with my key, forcing it into the ignition, pressing my foot so hard against the gas pedal that my tires squeal when I pull away from the curb. I'm almost to the highway when I realize that I left the front door to the house hanging open with my key in the lock.

⌒

I don't think about where I'm going as I speed away from Pennsylvania Avenue; it's like my hands steer the wheel automatically, my subconscious somehow directing me to a place where I might feel safe. Eventually I calm down enough to realize where I'm headed. I don't know where else to go, not right now. If anyone can help me at all, maybe it's Robin.

His home—it's actually half a duplex—is in a section of Greensburg known as Friendship. Nestled in between the railroad tracks and a patch of undeveloped land, the area is not the cheerful place that its name suggests. The streets are nearly deserted this early on a Sunday morning, and what little activity there is makes me even more uneasy than I was to begin with. The neighborhood is supposedly working on improving its image, but it's not quite there yet. At the bus stop next to a supermarket, a homeless man sleeps soundly, his body only partway covered by a child's filthy comforter embroidered with a scene from Winnie the Pooh. Farther down the street, just before I make a left onto Willow Circle, there's a block of commercial buildings, each entrance protected by metal gates meant to keep people from smashing the windows. The stores appear rundown and sketchy, offering services like paycheck advances, cash for gold, rental furniture, and used computers starting at $19.99.

As I come to a stop at the red light before my turn, a lone little girl makes her way down the street. She looks like she can't be older than nine or ten. She's pushing a shopping cart filled with small cardboard boxes. Their sides are stamped with the contradiction FRESH FROZEN FRIED FISH.

I don't know what prompts me to pull up beside her and open my window. Maybe it's because I know how it feels to be alone with nobody to help me, faced with a task no child should ever have to take on by herself.

"Hey. Do you need a ride, sweetie?" I smile at her.

She stops, looks up and down the empty street, then fixes me with a cool stare and raises a single eyebrow. "I don't need nothing," she says. "I'm good."

I force a deep breath, discomfort only halfway filling my lungs as the struggle to fully breathe remains persistent. I should leave her alone. I have more important things to do.

But then she stands up straight and wraps her arms around her skinny body as she shivers, rubbing herself for warmth. I can't leave her out here alone. I won't.

"Where do you need to go with those boxes? You shouldn't be walking around by yourself." And I smile again, trying to seem safe and friendly. "It's okay, really. I just want to help you."

She hesitates. Her gaze lingers on the Porsche, so out of place in this neighborhood. "I only gotta go a little bit farther," she says.

I shake my head. "That's okay. I'll take you."

She taps a foot against the pavement. All of a sudden, behind her, an ungated storefront called CHINA TASTE becomes illuminated. When the lights come on, the girl is immediately standing before a backdrop of decadent squalor. Inside the building, its windows big enough that I can see everything within the restaurant, ornate Chinese lamps hang from a stained drop ceiling. Small tables fill the room. An old Asian man shuffles around them. He carries an armful of vases, each one holding a brightly colored flower. He stops at each table to place a vase on the center. His actions are precarious and slow, and when I take a closer look, I see why he's struggling to do something so simple: he only has one hand. The bottom half of his left arm is completely gone, the empty sleeve flapping uselessly as he works.

The little girl turns her head to follow my gaze. Her lips curl into an amused grin. "That's Mr. Lee. He's called Freaky Lee. Know what he does? Has his wife massage his arm that ain't there. He says it aches all the time. Even though it's gone." She pauses, shades her eyes to peer at the sky, and doesn't say anything else.

It's like I've slipped into some other world, where nothing fully makes sense and the most random things seem significant. Why is this little girl telling me about a one-armed man right now? Her comment spooks me, as I think of my sister and our connection, which throbs with such clarity despite her absence. I'm wasting time. I should go.

Without another word to the girl, I put my window up and drive away, leaving her behind in the cold. After a few blocks, I make the left onto Willow Circle and go down the brick-paved street until I park in front of a small white house. I'm here. Finally.

His door is unlocked. I don't bother knocking.

Robin sits calmly on his orange sofa, smoking an unfiltered cigarette and watching television. He is hunched over with his elbows on his knees, wearing his usual jeans and white shirt. His hair is damp, like he's just taken a shower.

Robin stares at me in his doorway. He puts a hand to his mouth, gazing at me with shock and concern. "What the hell happened to you? Are you okay?" He stands up and hurries toward me.

"What?" I ask, confused, trying not to panic even as a creeping sense of dread spreads through me. *What now?* I think.

"Your face." He's so close to me that I can feel his breath warming the air between us. When he touches me, I flinch as his fingers brush my right cheek. I cannot stop myself from closing my eyes. I don't breathe. It is as though I can sense every groove in his fingertips, which are callused and tough from so many hours spent stretching canvas and gripping paintbrushes. There is usually paint in his hair and on his clothing, but not today. Despite his freshly scrubbed appearance, he smells like the turpentine he uses to clean his brushes.

"What's wrong with my face?" I ask, my eyes still closed.

He moves his hands to my shoulders and pivots my body to face a small round mirror hanging on the wall beside the door. "Look."

I don't know whether to scream or cry or both. I have two black eyes.

As I stare at my reflection, an ache begins to spread across my face. "What happened?" Robin asks again.

I hesitate. I know exactly what's going on. But if I'm

going to explain it to him right now, I have to start at the beginning.

"Would you answer me?" he persists. "Who did this to you?"

I don't answer. Turning around, I stare past him. Above the sofa, a large painting of a female nude, her form depicted in dark sepia tones, hangs from the wall. The girl's arms are outstretched, her legs folded into a V-shape and pointing to one side. The details are sketchy enough that, at a glance, a person might not even understand what they were looking at.

The painting took several hours. It was done in one sitting, on a dreary Thursday morning last spring, when I should have been in school. Instead, I was here. The girl in the painting is me.

"Robin," I begin, "nobody hurt me. Not really. That's why I'm here, though—I need to talk to you. Something bad is happening." I pause, my thoughts swirling, unsure exactly how to begin, so afraid that he might not believe me. My gaze flickers back and forth between the painting and Robin. Finally, I say, "My sister is gone."

He blinks a few times, unimpressed by my declaration. "Your sister?"

I nod. I am not wearing any makeup. My outfit—jean shorts and a pink polo shirt—is different from the style I typically wear. I know that most people would mistake me for my sister right now. Robin knows I'm an identical twin, but he's never even seen my sister. I wait for him to fully recognize me, to show some sign of understanding. I feel hopeful that, if anyone can see the truth, it might be him.

He looks like he hasn't been sleeping well. His hazel eyes are bloodshot. The skin around his lips is dry and chapped. "Well . . . do you know where she might have gone?"

I ignore the question. I know I have to tell him the truth right now, before we can go any further.

I don't know quite how to say it, but I do my best. "Nobody knows who I am," I whisper.

He's confused. "What do you mean?"

"I mean what I said. Nobody knows who I am. Not right now, anyway." I pause. "But you do. Right?"

He squints at me. "Of course I know who you are."

"Tell me. I want to hear you say it."

"Tell you what?"

"Tell me who I am. Tell me my name."

He cups my face gently in his hands. He tilts my head upward a little bit and steps closer.

"Your name is Alice," he says.

Despite everything that I'm feeling—all the fear and panic and pain—I cannot help but smile at him. "Yes. I'm Alice."

CHAPTER SIX

I've only known Robin for four months, but it feels like so much longer. Sometimes you meet someone and the connection is instant and undeniable. Aside from my sister, Robin is the only other person I feel close to. But we had a fight a couple of weeks ago. Until his phone call last night, I hadn't seen or spoken to him in thirteen days.

My aunt and uncle refer to him as my boyfriend, but they're using the term loosely. Our relationship was never really like that, even though I think we both wanted it to be. But it always seemed impossible. At age twenty-one, Robin is a little too old for me. Even though I'm eighteen and technically an adult, there's a quality to him that always made it clear to me that he was very much a *man*. It's sort of there in the way he carries himself, so self-possessed and poised despite his disheveled appearance. He has a quiet intelligence that can be disarming. I've seen him drink for hours without ever appearing tipsy or out of control.

It's not just his calm presence, though, that makes him so arresting. He is a mystery. I've never met any of his family, and he's never shown any interest in meeting mine. His face always has a five o' clock shadow, no matter what time it is. He wears the same uniform pretty much every day: a white T-shirt, baggy jeans, and a beat-up pair of Converse sneakers.

Like me, he is an artist. His paintings are all huge and intimidating, wild yet deliberate splashes of bright color applied with thick brushstrokes. Maybe I'm biased, but I think they're some of the most beautiful pieces I've ever seen.

His apartment seems so much cleaner today than I ever remember it being. The whole place smells like disinfectant. In the corner of the room, beside the kitchenette, a metal folding table serves as a breakfast nook. The table used to be constantly covered in pieces of mail, dog-eared books, dirty plates and bowls, and whatever else Robin didn't feel like putting away. Now the surface is wiped clean, without so much as a stray drinking glass. The kitchenette countertops— made of chipped white-and-gold Formica—are bare except for a lone open container of orange juice. There are fresh vacuum lines on the shaggy beige carpet. I didn't even know Robin *owned* a vacuum cleaner.

"So help me understand," he says. He presses the back of his hand to his forehead. Even though his hands are clean, there are rusty red-paint stains beneath his fingernails and along his cuticles. "You're saying that nobody else knows who you really are."

I nod. "Yes."

"And who are they mistaking you for?"

I stare at the carpet. "My sister. Rachel. We went to the fair together last night, and she disappeared. She still isn't home. And I came here because I needed to ask you face-to-face if you saw her yesterday. But you wouldn't have known it was her. She looked like me. I mean, she sort of *was* me." I falter. "Do you understand what I'm telling you?"

"I think so, yeah," he says. "You two . . . switched?"

"Yes."

He shakes his head, like what I'm saying can't possibly be true. "Alice, come on. Nobody would buy that."

I almost laugh out loud. "You've never even met Rachel. You've never seen the two of us together. We're identical."

"Okay, but still, there must be tiny differences. I'm sure your family—"

"My family doesn't know anything. We've been doing it for years, and we've been getting away with it. Robin, my aunt and uncle think that *I'm* Rachel. They think that Alice ran off last night, so they aren't worried. But they should be," I continue, my voice rising in panic, "because Rachel would never do anything like that. Something's wrong. I know it is."

He presses his lips together in thought. "I assume this has something to do with the bruises on your face?"

When he says the word—"bruises"—I flinch again. I can feel my eyes growing puffier by the minute. I have no idea how I'm going to hide this from my aunt and uncle;

makeup can only do so much. I hesitate. "I don't know if you'll believe me."

"Why not?"

"Because it will sound crazy. It's not, though. It's true."

"Alice—"

"Rachel and I have a connection," I blurt. "It's because we're twins. But it's not just that, Robin—we're different than other twins. I've told you before. We shared the same gestational space. That isn't how it normally works." I stop, watching him, trying to appraise his expression. He can be tough to read.

"You shared the same gestational space," he echoes.

I nod. "Yes."

"But isn't that true for all twins?"

"No." When I shake my head, the room goes a little fuzzy, and I begin to feel dizzy. I have to wiggle my toes in my shoes, reassuring myself of the floor beneath my feet in order to remain steady. "During their mother's pregnancy, normal twins will each have their own amniotic sac and their own placenta. Rachel and I shared them."

As he nods, I imagine him visualizing what I'm describing. "Okay," he says, "but that can't be so unusual, can it?"

"Yes," I say, "it's unusual. Not unheard of, but rare—only about one percent of all twin pregnancies. And when Rachel and I were born eighteen years ago, medical technology wasn't nearly as advanced as it is today. At least half of all monochorionic monoamniotic twins didn't make it."

Robin squints at me. There's a hint of satisfaction in his gaze. "But you two survived. And you're . . . perfect."

"No, Robin. We aren't perfect. We're freaks."

"Freaks?" He raises an eyebrow. "You're being a little dramatic, don't you think?"

I shake my head. "Think about it. First of all, we're genetically identical. That's not so rare, but *monochorionic monoamniotic* twins? That's far less likely. Add to that the fact that both of us survived when we were born almost twenty years ago, and it makes us very lucky, to say the least. But now think about this: even though monochorionic monoamniotic twins are genetically identical, they often look different from each other once they're born. Because of the complications from sharing one placenta and one amniotic sac, they sometimes develop at different rates in the womb— with one twin taking most of the nutrients from the other. Yet somehow, with almost no medical intervention, Rachel and I look exactly alike. What do you think the chances are, Robin?"

He studies me for a few seconds before responding. "And you think there's some sort of . . . what? A psychic connection between the two of you?"

"Yes," I tell him. "It's been that way our entire lives. I can sense her. I can tell when she's not okay. And sometimes it becomes . . . physical."

"Physical how? What do you mean?"

I gesture to my face. "I didn't do this to myself, Robin.

Nobody hurt me, either. This happened because somebody is hurting Rachel."

Robin looks around the room, almost like he's expecting a camera crew to jump out from behind a chair and tell him this is all a big joke. Except that it's not funny.

"Has this kind of thing ever happened to you before?"

I nod. "Lots of times. And there have been so many little things too, things that I sense before they happen to her."

"Like what?" He pauses, reaching toward me. "Come here." He takes my hand and tugs me onto the couch. I sit down beside him, let him wrap his arms around me, and rest my head against his chest. Our fight seems so ridiculous now that we're together again, his body warm and comforting, the pressure from his embrace somehow slowing my panic, absorbing my fear. I'm so grateful that he isn't laughing or dismissing me entirely. Instead, he's being kind; he's listening, trying to understand. He knows me, and he knows I wouldn't lie to him, especially not about something so serious.

"When we turned twelve, my aunt and uncle bought us new bikes for our birthdays. Rachel was so excited, way more than I was. It was a really pretty day, and my aunt and uncle told us we could go for a ride right away. The bikes were in our backyard, and before Rachel was even out the door, I *knew* she shouldn't go. I didn't know why, but I was certain something awful was about to happen. But there wasn't much time for me to do anything, and I was so scared that I couldn't think straight. I didn't know how else to stop her, so I grabbed one of my aunt's porcelain figurines from the mantel and I threw it against the wall. That got everyone's attention real quick. My aunt flipped out. There was glass everywhere, and I guess the figurine—it was shaped like a bird—was some kind of collector's item, so she started screaming at me, asking what the hell was the matter with me. But I didn't care, because Rachel didn't go outside and get on her bike."

When Robin speaks, I can hear his smile. "That's so . . . so *Alice* of you." He holds me closer.

"You're right," I say. "You really know me, don't you?"

He rests his head against mine. "I guess I do."

We sit in silence for a moment, and I can tell we're both thinking about our fight from a couple of weeks ago. I was the one who started it. We'd been seeing each other for three months, but there was so much he wouldn't tell me about himself. I still didn't even know his last name. We were at his apartment one afternoon, and I started looking through his mail while he was in another room, trying to figure it out, but everything was addressed to *Current Resident.*

When he confronted me, I got so angry—I was crying, begging him to tell me why he kept so many secrets. "How can you be my boyfriend if I don't even know who you *are*?" I'd demanded. I was throwing the mail all over the room, making a huge mess.

And then he said the most awful thing. At least, it seemed like the most awful thing at the time. "That's the problem,

Alice," he told me. "I can't be your boyfriend." He wouldn't say anything else, even though I begged him. I finally left; that was the last time I'd seen him until today.

"So what happened?" he finally asks. "After you broke the figurine and your aunt went nuts, did you tell Rachel not to get on her bike?"

I nod. "Yes. And by then I'd made such a scene that my uncle finally went out to look at the bike, I guess to make sure it was safe for her to ride. He was just patronizing me, I knew. But after a few minutes he came back inside, and he had this weird look on his face. Our bikes had come with these canvas pouches attached to their handlebars—you know what I mean, right? So we could have a place to keep stuff while we rode?"

Robin shrugs. "Sure."

"Well, I guess the bikes had been parked in our garage for a while, maybe a week or so. And Rachel's bike . . . there was a hornet's nest inside the pouch. They'd burrowed inside and built a nest while it was hidden. If she'd gone for a ride right then—if I hadn't done something to stop her—she could have been swarmed." I pause. "But I did stop her. And she was safe."

Robin exhales a deep breath. "Because you knew something would happen to her if she got on that bike."

"Yes. But there have been other things too, Robin." I rush on. "The summer before last, when we were sixteen, Rachel did a bunch of work in our yard. It was my aunt's birthday, and she wanted to do something nice for her. So she spent a whole afternoon pulling weeds beside our house, and when my aunt came home that evening, Rachel was excited to surprise her. But my aunt was worried; she told Rachel there'd been a ton of poison ivy growing among the weeds; my aunt had been meaning to have it sprayed for weeks. Rachel had been working in shorts and a tank top all day. She hadn't showered yet."

Robin shudders. "Well, that's unfortunate. She must have been a mess."

"She was, yeah. Even though she showered as soon as she found out, it was already too late. She woke up the next morning covered; she even had it between her toes. But here's the weird thing: I got it too. I got it all over me, just like Rachel." I stare at him. "I wasn't in the yard at all that day, Robin. I was at my grandma's."

He lowers his head. "That doesn't make sense."

"I know. But I'm not making it up."

"And you think she's in trouble now because of what's happening to you," he finishes for me. "You want to figure out how to save her."

"Yes."

"But Alice, do you have any clue at all where she might be? Do you even know where to start?" He sits up straighter, pulling away so he can look me in the eye. "Rachel is her own person. You might be her twin, but that doesn't make you responsible for her."

But it does, I think. He doesn't get it because he doesn't know everything—not yet. "Robin," I say, "I think it could be my fault that she's missing. Whoever took her . . . I think they meant to take me. Do you understand? I *am* responsible; it should be *me* who's missing, not Rachel. She didn't do anything wrong."

Robin pulls farther away, but I don't get the sense that he's trying to distance himself from me as much as he's simply trying to find space, to think about everything I'm telling him. Without a word, he gets up and walks toward the kitchenette. He opens the refrigerator and stands before it, staring inside.

The fridge is almost bare except for a lone stick of butter on the top shelf, a six-pack of light beer, and a wooden palate smeared with half a dozen shades of oil paint. Despite the glaring light from the fridge, the apartment otherwise dim, I can guess each color on sight: Burnt sienna. Cadmium orange. Cerulean blue. Chromium oxide green. Raw umber. Gold ochre. He grabs a beer, twists it open, and turns to me. "You want one?"

I shake my head. The bruises around my eyes feel damp and hot in the warm, moist air of the apartment. My whole body aches. Still, just being here with him makes me feel . . . different. Safer, maybe? Protected? But that's not it—not exactly.

I feel loved. Being with Robin makes me feel loved, despite everything else I've done, all the things that make it hard for me to stand myself right now.

Before he shuts the door, Robin reaches into the freezer and removes a plastic bag of frozen tater tots. "Here." He walks back across the room to me. I give a little yelp of pain as he presses the bag to my face. "Shh," he says, sitting down again. "It's okay, Alice. Everything will be okay. I promise."

I can feel the individual hairs on his arms brushing against my face. I want to lean into him and close my eyes shut more tightly, to fall asleep and wake up in a new day where none of this is happening. I want to believe him that everything will be okay. But I can't; I don't. Instead, I start to cry.

"Shh," he repeats. He pulls the bag of tater tots away, tilts my head upward, and stares down at me. I can tell he's trying to suppress a smile.

"What?" I ask, pulling back a little. "Why are you looking at me that way?"

His eyes crinkle at their corners, even as his grin wavers. "This is going to sound weird," he says, "but you look so pretty when you cry."

He's right; it is a weird thing to say. But I don't respond; I just lean into him again and let him hold me while I cry. Despite everything that has gone wrong in the past day, I have never felt so protected. I clutch his shirt in my fists, rubbing my thumb across the threads woven into soft fabric, unwilling to let go even when my phone begins to ring in my bookbag. I ignore it, squeezing my eyes shut more tightly instead, trying to pretend that it is only the two of us, that the rest of the world doesn't exist, that there is nothing beyond his front door.

After a few moments, Robin breaks the silence, his somber tone yanking me back to reality. "Alice," he says, "I don't know how I can help you. I've never met your sister, and I definitely didn't see her last night. I didn't go to the fair. I was here all night, alone."

"But you called me," I say. "You don't have a phone."

He pauses. "A friend stopped by."

"Which friend?" Before he has a chance to answer, something else occurs to me. "Robin, my aunt and uncle took my phone away last month. You knew that. I've had Rachel's phone since last night; you called *her* phone, not mine." Even as the thought materializes in my mind that he might have intended to call my sister, not me—that maybe something has been going on between them that I don't know about—I try to dismiss it. The possibility is too painful to confront.

"You gave me her number," he says quickly—maybe too quickly.

"I did?" I shake my head. "I don't remember that."

"Alice, come on." He gives me a reassuring smile. "Don't get crazy on me."

"Okay. I'm sorry. But who was here with you last night?"

"Alice, seriously," he says, ignoring my question, "I know you're worried about Rachel, but I don't think it's a good idea for you to look for her on your own. You need to go to the police." He stops for a minute, thinking. "Wait—you were about to tell me something a little while ago, before I interrupted you. What was it?"

I sit up, pulling away from him. I think of my dream from the night before, my sister's words. *Don't. Tell. Anyone.*

Aside from Rachel, Robin is the only person in the world who knows my true identity right now. I've already told him that much. I need to tell him the rest.

"Robin . . . I did something wrong."

His eyes are kind and concerned; there is not a trace of judgment in his gaze. "What did you do, Alice?"

I'm so ashamed that I can't look at him. "I stole some money."

" . . ."

"Robin, I stole a lot of money."

He stays calm, absorbing the information without much expression. "How much are we talking about, exactly?"

I close my eyes. "Ten thousand dollars."

I can tell he's trying not to react too strongly, but his body stiffens beside mine. "Jesus, Alice," he breathes, "why would you steal so much money? Where did you get it?"

"I found it." I unzip my bookbag and take out the money to show him.

"Oh my God." He shakes his head, like he can't believe what he's seeing. "Shit, Alice, you know whoever that belongs to is gonna miss it, don't you? Nobody just *loses* that kind of cash. Once they realize it's gone—if they haven't already—they're gonna want it back."

I nod. "I know. I tried to put it back, but I couldn't."

There is a hint of frustration in his voice. "How is that possible?"

"The door was locked."

He stares at the money, the thick pile of crisp hundreds in my shaky hand. I can tell he wants to touch it. I know I did, the first time I saw it. I couldn't help myself.

"Robin." I rest my hand on his forearm. "I took it for you. I was going to give it to you."

"For *me*? Alice, why the hell would you do that? I don't need any money."

"Of course you do! Robin, look around. This place is awful—it's practically falling apart. Nobody should have to live this way. This money could help you, couldn't it? You could buy a car, or get a new apartment, or . . . I don't know, do *something* to make your life better."

Robin shakes his head. "No. I don't need a better life. What I have now—this place, and you—that's the hand I've been dealt, you know? Nothing is going to change that, and even if it could, I don't want it to change."

My body slumps against the couch. "I'm sorry. You're right, I know, but I just wanted to help you. I thought that maybe if things were easier, we could . . . I don't know." I stuff the money into my backpack. "Forget it. It was a stupid idea."

"You thought the money would make it easier for us to be together, didn't you?" He looks at the painting of me hanging above the couch. When I posed for it over the summer, I took off all my clothes as I stood right in front of him. His gaze explored my entire body that day, but he never once tried to touch me. It has always been that way—it's like there's an invisible line between us that he won't allow himself to cross, and I have no idea why.

"Alice," he continues, "you have to listen to me. I don't care if the door to wherever you found this money was locked. You need to figure out a way to give it back. Has it occurred to you that whoever you stole this from might know what you did? And if they mistook your sister for you, they might have—"

"Yes," I say. I'm surprised by how flat my voice sounds. "I understand. That's what I'm trying to tell you. Whatever happens to Rachel is all my fault."

"So make it right," he urges. "Give the money back somehow."

From my purse, my phone begins to ring again. Somehow it sounds more insistent this time.

"Don't you want to get that?" Robin asks. "It might be Rachel."

"It's my uncle," I say. "I left the house without telling anyone. It's been a crazy morning."

He stares at his hands. He makes a halfhearted effort to pick at the paint beneath his fingernails.

I reach across the sofa and take the beer from his hand. He lets go of it easily enough. As I take a long swig, it occurs to me it's the first thing I've had to eat or drink since the sip I took from Holly's lemonade last night; my throat is parched and my lips are dry. The beer tastes fantastic. I can feel it moving down my throat, a rush of warmth spreading as it hits my stomach.

My phone rings again.

"Maybe you should answer that," he says. "It's the third time they've called."

I shrug. "It's just my uncle telling me to come home."

He tilts his head in question. "Do your aunt and uncle know where you are right now?"

"No. I snuck off. I took my uncle's car. They called the police right before I left. To report *Alice* missing."

Robin shuts his eyes. "Oh, man," he breathes. He stares at me, closing his hand over mine. "Alice, you should go home now. You need to talk to the police. I know it's going to be hard, but I think you should be honest with them. About everything."

"No!" I say. My voice rises as my words rush together. "Nobody can know who I really am, nobody except you. If I tell my aunt and uncle that I'm Alice and not Rachel, they're going to tell the cops. And if the police find out, then it's only a matter of time before other people learn the truth. Robin, please. If I tell anyone who I really am, then whoever took Rachel will come for me eventually." I swallow. "And if I don't figure out where she is, then whoever she's with might hurt her even more."

My phone rings again. I know that it's not going to stop ringing until I either answer it or show up at home.

The room goes fuzzy again as I stand up. The terror and dread that have spread within me seem to be alive, flowing through my veins, thriving on my worst fears. For so many years—since I was nine years old—I believed there was nothing in this world that could be worse than what I had already faced. Until now. "I'm leaving, okay?" I tell him.

Robin stands up and takes a step toward me. Carefully, like he's afraid he'll hurt me, he rests a hand on my shoulder. I am so overwhelmed with panic, so lost and alone, that I almost collapse beneath his grip. For a second, I'm afraid I'm going to throw up.

He brings his face so close to mine that I can feel the warmth from his breath. I lean closer, expecting him to kiss me, but at the last second he tilts his head away, his lips barely grazing my cheek before he whispers into my ear.

"Lang," he says.

I pull away. "What?"

"Lang," he repeats. "That's my last name."

"Oh." I try to smile, but the effort is weak. "Okay. Now I know."

There is a flash of something in his eyes—sadness, or maybe regret—as he takes a few steps backward, his hand slipping away from my shoulder. "Sure," he agrees. "Now you know."

I drive toward home in silence, the only noise the sound of raindrops pounding against the windshield as the Porsche sloshes along the wet streets. I think of my sister and her words in my dream. *Don't. Tell. Anyone.* Even in sleep, I trust her completely.

Rachel doesn't know about the money I took. Aside from Robin, nobody knows. At least, I don't think anyone does. The idea that someone might be punishing her for what I've done makes me feel so sick and panicked—so *guilty*—that I can barely stand to be in my own skin.

My sister has been the only constant in my life. If I lose her, I might as well lose everything.

The smell of turpentine clings to my clothing from Robin's touch, and for a moment my thoughts drift to last summer, when we met. It was a Monday afternoon in the first week of June. I was taking a painting class at the local community college. My easel was set up next to a large window that looked out on a grassy courtyard complete with a fountain surrounded by park benches. Each day as I worked, I sometimes found my gaze wandering outside. I watched students as they quietly studied in the grass, unaware of my stare. I watched a falafel vendor sweating over his cart at lunchtime, serving up pitas topped with condiments that had been sitting in the sun all morning. I saw mothers who let their toddlers run around in the fountain, ducking underwater and coming up with fistfuls of pennies from other people's wishes. And each afternoon, from sometime after one o'clock until my class ended at three, I saw Robin. He would stroll across the courtyard and sit down on a bench, spreading out the contents of his bookbag so he was taking up the whole space for himself. He'd pull out a sketchbook and he'd sit there beneath the sun for the entire afternoon, gazing down at the paper as he drew. Every once in a while he would glance up and look around, but it never seemed to me like he was looking at anything in particular.

From my place beside the window in my classroom, I watched him as he worked, day after day. It was like I could sense the energy coming from his body; even as I stood before my easel beneath the unpleasant fluorescent lights in the classroom, his proximity made me feel like I was bathed in sunbeams. After he'd shown up four days in a row, I spent Thursday afternoon drawing him with light pencil strokes, pausing every few seconds to glance out the window. He was a perfect subject: so still and beautiful, completely focused on whatever he was drawing.

From so far away, I didn't think he could possibly notice what I was doing. I'd seen him glance in my direction a few times, but I never got the impression that he was looking at me specifically. By late Friday afternoon, I had finished my sketch and wanted to begin painting over his faint likeness. I stayed late on campus to continue working as he remained on his bench, sketching away. Around four o'clock, immersed in the rhythm of my brushstrokes, I looked up and realized he was gone.

Thinking I could continue from memory—and wanting to continue so badly, to watch him as he became fully realized on paper—I kept going. I don't know how much time passed, or how long he stood in the doorway, watching me, before I noticed him.

We were alone in the room, maybe even alone in the building as far as I could tell. And here was this stranger who I'd essentially been spying on all week long, stepping into the room. Under any different circumstance, I might have been afraid. He could have reacted in so many ways. He could have been upset, even angry.

Instead, he seemed stunned. He looked from me to the painting, his gaze shifting back and forth, like he couldn't believe his eyes. Finally he said, "That's me."

I nodded. I felt heat rising in my cheeks as I blushed. "I'm sorry. You've been outside all week, so I just—"

"I see," he interrupted. He held his hand close to the paper, almost touching it. His hands were smeared with pencil lead. He'd been wearing the same clothing all week: a white cotton shirt, loose jeans, and paint-spattered Converse sneakers. He looked tired and disheveled—in other words, like a normal college student.

"I want to show you something," he said.

I should have been scared. Maybe he was a pervert, and he was going to flash me. We were alone; it would have been easy for him to overpower me. He was taller than I was by a good six inches. His arms were thick and muscular, stretching the fabric of his T-shirt around his biceps. And who knew what he might be carrying in his bookbag?

Yet I didn't feel the slightest bit afraid, even as he unzipped the main pocket and reached inside. Instead, I felt exhilarated.

He removed his sketchbook and flipped through the pages until he found what he was looking for. As he held it toward me, I stared down at the paper, blinking over and over again, convinced at first that I was seeing things.

It was a drawing of me, startling in its detail and accuracy. In it, I stood hunched at my easel, my hair tucked behind my ear to offer a clear view of my profile. He'd captured my likeness down to the last details: the splash of freckles across my nose; the slight wave to my hair; my big feather earrings that grazed my shoulders.

I reached out to touch the drawing, my fingertips barely brushing the paper, almost like I was afraid it would dissolve into thin air upon contact. "It's amazing." I paused. "How did you see all this from so far away?"

When he shrugged, I felt the air moving between us. I thought I could sense the warmth from his body. All week long I'd been drawing him . . . drawing me.

"I've always had a good eye for detail," he said. His breath smelled like cigarettes, but it didn't bother me. Instead, it was oddly pleasant and soothing, maybe because my parents had smoked when I was a kid—the smell sometimes made me think of that time in my life. I remember hearing from somewhere that smell is the most powerful trigger for memories.

I smiled at him. "I'm Alice Foster."

"Alice," he repeated. It was like he'd never heard the name before in his life.

"I like to paint," I added, and felt immediately embarrassed. *Obviously* I liked to paint.

When he didn't respond, I asked, "So are you a student here?"

He shook his head. "No. I'm just . . . hanging out." He shifted his gaze past my painting of him, toward the window. "I paint too. Oils, mostly."

"Oh yeah? Same here." I recognized that he was older than I was—probably a good three or four years older, if not more—but I didn't care a bit. At that moment, the only thing I cared about was making sure we kept talking for as long as possible.

"My parents were both artists," I continued. "It sort of runs in my family. I got my first easel when I was four years old. My mom let me use all her stuff—paints, pastels, everything. I even dressed up like Frida Kahlo for Halloween in the first grade."

He laughed. "You've got to be kidding me."

"I'm not!" I insisted. "I drew a unibrow on myself and everything."

"Did people know who you were?"

I shook my head. "Nobody. Just my family."

"Wow. In first grade, huh? That's pretty impressive." He leaned against a nearby desk as he rubbed the back of his neck, which I imagined was sore from gazing down at his sketchbook for the past few days. "I'd love to see pictures of that sometime."

I hesitated. I hated to ruin the moment, but the words came out of my mouth before I could stop them. Even as I spoke, I knew I was probably getting too personal, too fast. "I don't have any pictures." *Damn it, Alice,* I thought, *shut up.*

"Oh . . . okay." He got quiet. His gaze drifted around the room, silence filling the first awkward moment we'd shared since we started talking. The buzz of the fluorescent lights overhead was suddenly noticeable to the point of annoyance.

"I guess I should clean up," I said, nodding at my dirty brushes. I didn't want to leave him, not yet, but I couldn't stand the silence.

"Okay," he said, taking a step back, closing his sketchbook and slipping it into his bookbag. "I should probably get going too."

Before he left the room, he extended his hand for me to shake. His grip was warm and tight. He let it linger for a smidge longer than necessary as he smiled again. "It was good to meet you, Alice. Maybe I'll see you on Monday."

When he left the room, he pulled the door shut behind him. As I cleaned my brushes in the sink, I kept glancing at his painting on my easel. I didn't want to let go of how it felt to be alone with him. It was like being by myself, only better. The feeling was familiar to me; it was similar to how I felt when I was alone with Rachel. But she and I had known each other all our lives, and we were identical twins—our bond was to be expected. This was different. I barely knew this guy.

When I left the room a good ten minutes later, he was standing in the hallway. Right there, all by himself, his hands stuffed into the pockets of his jeans, backpack slung over one shoulder. Waiting for me.

Only then did it occur to me that our encounter this afternoon might be construed as creepy to an outsider. Here I was, in an almost empty building with a bona fide tall, dark stranger following me. Any girl with a good head on her shoulders would have been more cautious, I knew. But I also knew that caution rarely resulted in much excitement.

Without a word, he fell into step beside me, and as we approached the double doors leading to the parking lot, he asked, "So. Do you have a car?"

I grinned, nodding. "Yes." I was driving my aunt's car that day.

"Can you give me a ride home, Alice?"

Even a child would know this was a bad idea. I stopped walking, my keys dangling from my hand, and considered the possibility that I was being very stupid. There was nobody else around; even the parking lot was nearly empty. The phrase "nobody could hear you scream" crossed my mind.

But I wanted to do it so badly. Trying not to sound too eager, I said, "I don't even know your name."

The right corner of his mouth ebbed into a lopsided smile. "I'm Robin," he said. "And you're Alice." His face widened into a full grin. "Now we've been properly introduced."

In the months that followed, I replayed that afternoon over and over again in my mind, trying to rationalize the decision I made next. It could have ended so badly.

"Okay," I told him, "I'll give you a ride. Where do you need to go?"

And once I'd driven him home, taking him into the worst part of town and delivering him to a run-down duplex, I accepted his invitation to come inside and look at some of his other paintings. I stayed for two hours and drank four beers as we talked into the evening.

It wasn't until much later that night, as I lay in bed, giddy at the thought of him, that I realized he'd never told me his last name.

CHAPTER SEVEN

As I'm driving home, I try to concentrate, attempting to get some sense of where Rachel might have gone, but my thoughts are too jumbled. In the past, we've both snuck off to our grandma's house without telling our aunt and uncle, but that's only because they don't like us to visit her by ourselves. Depending on the day, her mood, and what medications she's been taking, her illness manifests itself in any number of unpleasant ways. My aunt calls her "emotionally toxic."

Despite Aunt Sharon's efforts to distance us from our grandmother, Rachel and I have managed to remain close to her over the years. It's not impossible that my sister could be at her house for some reason, but it's unlikely. Why would she sneak off without telling me? And why would she be in any danger? My grandma might be insane, but she would never dream of hurting either one of us.

It's late morning on a Sunday, so traffic is light as I drive, but there's construction on the highway, narrowing the road down to one lane a few miles before my exit. The cars move slowly in a messy, single-file procession. The Porsche is a stick shift. I'm okay at driving it, but not great; I know I could accidentally stall out.

Once while I'm stopped, I glance at my reflection in the rearview mirror. My bruises haven't gotten any worse, but they're definitely noticeable. How am I supposed to explain this to my aunt and uncle? To the police?

As soon as I get off the highway, I dig through my backpack for my makeup bag. I spend a good ten minutes applying foundation and concealer, followed by blush and powder. I have to be careful not to put it on too heavily, and I certainly can't wear eyeliner—Rachel never does. But the makeup looks good enough. I stare hard at my reflection. The bruises are all but invisible.

There is an odd, almost slow-motion quality to my street. Two police cars are parked outside my house, their blue-and-red lights flashing silently, making them seem innocuous somehow. My house looks so calm from the outside, so normal and wholly small-town America. The shrubs surrounding the front porch have been trimmed recently. The porch swing drifts gently back and forth, as though someone has just gotten up to go inside, leaving it to sway in the breeze.

Across the street, TJ is still working on his car, vacuuming the trunk with a hand-held Dirt Devil. He's shirtless, as usual. As he leans over, his muscles flex beneath his tan skin. There's a tattoo on his upper back that he must have gotten recently—I don't remember ever seeing it before. It's a phrase of some kind, but I can't make out what it says.

TJ and I have never talked much at all, but as I drive past, he stares at me, his gaze long and deliberate. He mouths something. I think he asks, "Where were you?"

The fact that he probably assumes I'm Rachel is not lost on me. What would he want with my sister?

His parents are sitting on their front porch. Mrs. Gardill—Trish—is a tall, heavy woman with short brown hair who almost never smiles. Her husband, Ray, is short and rail-thin. He keeps a large, carefully maintained vegetable garden in his backyard. He's a lot nicer than his wife; he's known on our street for giving out his surplus of tomatoes and zucchinis and peppers to his neighbors, often leaving bags filled with produce on our porches early in the morning. Every time I see the two of them together, I think of the nursery rhyme that goes, "Jack Sprat could eat no fat, his wife could eat no lean . . ." More than once, my sister and I have giggled at the idea of the Gardills having any kind of sex life.

Mr. Gardill raises his hand in a wave. Mrs. Gardill gives me a look of disapproval. They obviously see the police cars and are probably wondering what "Alice" did to get into trouble this time.

Farther down the block, a real estate agent fusses with an OPEN HOUSE sign in front of a brick Colonial that's been on the market, vacant, for over a year. About eight weeks ago, Robin and I broke into the house late on a Saturday night. We sat in front of the unlit fireplace in the master bedroom and shared a gallon jug of cheap white wine. We pretended the house belonged to us, that it was our bedroom, and that we were sitting before an actual fire. I held out a hand toward the imaginary flames and could almost feel their warmth spreading to my body. Much later that night, both of us tipsy and happy, we climbed the stairs to the attic and stared at the quiet, empty street, absorbing the silence all around us. Right before we left, Robin used his fingertip to write our initials in the thick layer of dust that had accumulated on the kitchen window.

The night was like magic. I remember every detail, right down to the silver hoop earring I lost at some point as we strolled around the house, unafraid of getting caught trespassing. Someone must have cleaned the house a few days later, because the next time I passed by, our initials were gone. I often wonder if my earring is still somewhere inside.

I turn into the alley that runs parallel to our street, behind our house. The garage door is open; I must have forgotten to close it this morning.

The garage is dark and silent, except for the low buzzing sound of a huge chest freezer against the far wall. I stand beside the Porsche for a few minutes, afraid to go inside my house and face the people who are waiting for me. Everything hung on the walls around me—gardening shears, an old saw, a neat row of screwdrivers, a throng of empty picture frames—seems angular and menacing, like they could come to life at any moment and attack me.

But I know it's all harmless. I know I'm safe for the moment. Wherever she is, Rachel is almost certainly *not* safe, and it's probably my fault. Any fear that I'm feeling, spurred by my anxiety and my imagination, is nothing compared to what she might be experiencing right now. As much as I'm dreading it, I know that I have to go inside and face the police. I have to find Rachel.

Once I'm outside, in the yard between the garage and the house, a calmness seems to settle across the landscape. Past the house and across the street, I can hear TJ's car radio still playing, notes of the Rolling Stones's "Wild Horses" in the air.

Everything seems so peaceful and ordinary. From all the way across the lawn, I notice a furry yellow caterpillar inching along the iron railing of the back porch. Through the picture window, I can see my aunt and uncle sitting at the dining room table. Two uniformed policemen are seated across from them. But since I can't hear what they're saying, and since it is such a bright, lovely day, I can almost pretend they're discussing something easy and relatively harmless, like an unpaid parking ticket.

From the yard next door, I hear a rhythmic swishing sound. I glance over to see our neighbor, Jane, sweeping leaves from the cement walkway that surrounds their in-ground pool. Her head is down, her long black skirt swirling around her full hips as she works, absorbed in her task. The smell of chlorine is unmistakable and powerful, but not unpleasant. In the upstairs of our house, I can see Charlie's tall silhouette through the translucent yellow curtains hanging in his bedroom window.

✑

My aunt has noticed me in the yard; she's left the dining room and is now looming in the doorway to the back porch. I don't know how long she's been there. She watches me, her expression worried and confused, as I stand in the middle of the lawn, staring at my surroundings.

From the street outside our house, TJ's radio plays David Bowie's "Young Americans." In the yard next door, the broom continues to go *swish, swish, swish.* I glance over and make eye contact with Jane, who stops sweeping for a moment to squint at me, probably trying to determine whether she's looking at Alice or Rachel. Thinking I'm Rachel, she gives me a smile that seems full of pity, as if to say, "I'm sorry your sister is such a mess."

Several months ago, only a few weeks after we met, Robin and I stripped down to our underwear and dove into the shallow end of Jane's swimming pool in the middle of the night. We'd been drinking for hours, sharing a bottle of high-end citrus vodka that went down quick and easy. By the time we had the idea to go swimming, I was so drunk I could barely walk, never mind swim.

When we noticed the police lights coming around the corner, we hurried out of the pool and took off into the dark, trying to hide. Robin got away; I didn't. I was still in my bra and underpants when the cops found me crouched behind a toolshed down the street; I'd left the rest of my clothes beside the pool. One of the officers wrapped a flimsy blue blanket around my shoulders and helped me to my front door while the neighbors looked on in stunned disbelief.

I called the cops assholes, screamed at Jane that she was a rotten bitch. It was a warm night; I didn't want the blanket. When my uncle saw me, he would barely look at me as I stumbled past him into the house. My aunt spoke to me in fierce, hushed tones in the dim light of the kitchen. I slumped against the wall and tried to drink a glass of water, spilling it everywhere. "What if your cousin wakes up?" she demanded. "Do you care about anybody besides yourself?"

"I'm sorry," I muttered.

She glared at me. "You think you're sorry now? You wait to see how sorry you feel tomorrow morning."

When I made it to the third floor and stumbled into our bedroom, I found my sister, Rachel, sitting calmly on my bed. She'd been crying. She watched for a while as I looked through a pile of dirty clothes on the floor, and finally settled on a wrinkled white button-down shirt. But I was too drunk to do the buttons. My sister slid off the bed to help me. Her breath smelled like black licorice. Her taste for it was one of our differences; black licorice makes me gag.

"Are you going to be sick?" Her small hands, identical to mine right down to the grooves in her fingernails, worked my buttons into place.

"No. I'm not that drunk."

"Sure you aren't. Look at me." She cupped my face in her hand. Her eyes were red and puffy. "I could see you from the guest room window, you know. You looked ridiculous."

I pulled away from her. "We were just having fun."

She paused. "We?"

The room was beginning to spin. I suspected that the vodka wouldn't taste quite as pleasant coming up as it had going down. "Yes, *we*. I was with Robin." I gave her a sharp look. "Don't tell Aunt Sharon." The last thing I wanted was a lecture on safe sex from my aunt, the woman who referred to sex as "intercourse" and virginity as "a special gift."

"Where did he go?" Rachel asked.

"Robin? I don't know. We ran in different directions."

"Alice . . . ," she began.

"What?"

Rachel looked ready to cry again. "Nothing. It's not important right now."

I stumbled to my bed, where Rachel had been sitting, rereading her dog-eared copy of *Little Women.* I lay down and closed my eyes for a moment, but it only made the room spin faster, so I sat up, wide-eyed, and began to take deep, steady breaths.

"You want a bucket?" Rachel offered.

"No. I'm fine."

"Like hell you are." And she put our wastebasket at my bedside. "They have a little boy, Alice." She meant our neighbors with the pool. "You probably scared him. You shouldn't have done that."

I ignored her. "Why were you crying?"

Too quickly she said, "I wasn't crying."

"Don't lie."

My sister crossed the room, the floorboards creaking beneath her bare feet. She crawled into bed beside me.

As we lay quietly together, she said, "I'll take care of tomorrow. We'll both sleep late. They'll never know the difference." She meant that she would take my place. She did that a lot when I got into trouble. I never asked her to, but she'd often insist. I'm not sure why.

"You don't have to do that." I stared out our window, across the street. The police were gone, but the neighborhood was still rippling from the excitement. Trish Gardill stood on her front porch, curlers in her hair, a bathrobe wrapped around her lumpy body, talking with Jane Summers. The two of them were undoubtedly rehashing my misbehavior.

"I want to do it. You need a break. Stay inside and rest. I don't mind."

My eyelids began to flutter closed against my will. "You want to get screamed at all morning? Aunt Sharon will probably be up here at seven a.m., banging pots and pans to wake you up. She'll probably make you go to church. You won't be allowed to talk to anyone. It'll be awful." I paused. "And what about Robin?"

"What about him?"

"I don't want you to see him. I don't want to trick him, okay? We're not doing that."

She was quiet for a minute. When I opened my eyes to peer at her, she was staring at me with the oddest expression, almost like she didn't recognize me anymore. "I don't think that will be a problem."

The offer was too good to refuse, even if I didn't understand her motivation. "All right. Have it your way."

"Good." She began to tug off her pajamas. "Sit up and give me your shirt."

∾

My aunt puts her hand on my arm. Two policemen, along with my uncle, stand behind her. I recognize the taller cop, whose name tag reads M. BALEST, as one of the officers who showed up the night of the incident in my neighbor's pool. "Rachel, honey," Aunt Sharon asks, "what happened to you? Where did you go?"

I lower my head. "I'm sorry. I was so scared. I went to look for . . . to look for her."

My aunt guides me inside to the dining room and helps me into a seat at the table. The adults hover around me. The police exchange a brief look of annoyance over my head, like we're all wasting their time.

With a tone that makes it sound like he'd rather be at home right now watching football, Officer Balest says, "Rachel. You need to tell us where you were."

I shake my head. "Nowhere. I drove around for a while. I looked for my sister."

"Uh-huh." I can tell he doesn't believe me. "So you stole your uncle's car just so you could—what? Drive around town? Did you look anywhere in particular for Alice? Do you have any idea where she might be?"

"I didn't steal my uncle's car," I clarify. "I borrowed it. And no, I don't know where my sister is. But I know she's in trouble. She didn't just wander away."

The other officer, the one I don't recognize, gives a little cough, like he wants to say something but doesn't quite have the nerve to interrupt my fascinating and productive exchange with his partner. His name tag reads R. MARTIN. He barely looks old enough to be out of high school. He's on the short side for a guy, maybe five nine or five ten, but he's not scrawny. He has cute, boyish features: a fresh-scrubbed face, big blue eyes, and rosy cheeks. Beneath his hat, I glimpse a few stray locks of straight, shiny blond hair. I notice a silver chain-link bracelet engraved with red lettering on his wrist. I can't make out what the words say, but I recognize the bracelet from a silly TV commercial—the one where the elderly woman has fallen and can't get up. It's a med-alert bracelet.

Our eyes meet, and I know he knows what I'm looking at. He probably thinks I'm wondering what's wrong with him. He flashes me a quick, uncomfortable smile. Then he puts his hand in his pocket, and the bracelet slips out of sight.

Officer Balest glances at him. "What's up?"

Martin seems surprised to be acknowledged at all. "Oh, nothing. I mean—well, I'm just wondering what makes Rachel so sure that her sister didn't run away." To me, he says, "You two are twins. I assume you know her better than anyone. Is that right?"

His gaze is kind and steady. He seems genuinely interested in what I have to say. For the first time since my sister disappeared, I feel like someone is tossing me a lifeline.

"Yes," I tell him. "I know that she's been in all kinds of trouble before, and I know it was mostly her fault. Believe me, I know. But this time is different. She just . . . vanished. We had plans last night. We walked to the fair together. She wouldn't have left on a whim without telling me where she was going."

"But she's done it before," my aunt breaks in. "You know that, Rachel."

Before I can respond, Balest begins to scribble something in the little notebook he's holding. "Tell us about that," he says. "When was the last time she disappeared? How long was she gone?"

"It was a couple of months ago." My aunt looks to my uncle for help remembering.

"July third," he supplies. "You remember."

She nods in agreement. "That's right. There were fire-works at Hollick Park, and we had plans to walk down and watch them. Like a family. But at the last minute, Alice didn't want to come along. She said she wanted to stay home and read." My aunt rolls her eyes. "We should have known better than to believe her. Anyway, we were gone for about an hour and a half, maybe two hours. We came home to an empty house. She didn't get back until late the next day, around dinnertime."

"Uh-huh." Balest continues to take notes. "And did you call the police?"

She shakes her head. "No, we didn't."

He stops writing to glance at my aunt. "Why not? Weren't you concerned?"

Aunt Sharon looks perplexed, sort of like even she isn't sure of the answer. She crosses her arms against her chest, hugging herself. "Alice has been having a lot of problems lately," she says, like that's a good explanation for her lack of caring.

"What kind of problems?" Balest asks.

My aunt glances at my uncle. "You tell them," she says.

I don't need to listen to this conversation. I know what I've been like for the past few months; hearing my uncle recite my adventures in delinquency isn't going to help me find Rachel any faster.

I'd been tuning them out for a few minutes, letting my

gaze drift in and out of focus on the Oriental rug beneath the table, when a hand clasps my shoulder, startling me back to attention.

It's my aunt, her grip gentle yet firm. I can smell the perfume on her wrists. It's called "Sweet Dreams," and it's the same fragrance she's worn her entire adult life. As a tradition, Charlie buys her a new bottle every year for Christmas. I have to admit that there's something comforting about her consistency, about the fact that she is steady and predictable right down to the smallest details.

Even though she's standing behind me and I can't see her, I can sense her gaze on the back of my head. My wound is covered with hair, but it must be noticeable to someone who knows what they're looking at. *How does she explain it?* I wonder. Does she think I did it to myself somehow? And if she believes it was inflicted by another person, why isn't she concerned that someone has hurt me?

I don't have any answers. All I know for sure is that my aunt isn't a big fan of introspection or self-examination. She tends to focus on superficial things instead of probing too deeply beneath any surfaces, particularly emotional ones. Maybe she doesn't want to think very hard about all the things she can't control. I know for certain that her life has turned out quite differently than she must have hoped. I'm pretty sure that, when she was much younger, she never wished her future would include staying home all day to care for her adult son or—surprise!—having to raise her sister's kids, one of whom turned out to be a juvenile delinquent.

That's the problem with life, I guess. The only thing a person can know for sure is that nothing in the world is certain, no matter how carefully they might try to plan the future.

"Rachel," Aunt Sharon says, "do you understand what the police are saying?"

I turn to look at her. "I'm sorry. I got distracted."

"Twenty-four hours," Balest says, shutting his notebook and tucking his pen into his breast pocket. "Your sister is an adult. If there's no real indication that she's in danger, we'll wait until she's been missing for twenty-four hours before we investigate any further."

I want to cry, but I know I shouldn't; my makeup might smear, revealing the bruises on my face. I fight back my tears with intense concentration, my eyes widened as I blink again and again, afraid that I won't be able to hold back. I can actually feel my cheeks growing hot and my chin quivering. I feel like such a stupid little girl, way over my head in a mess that I can't possibly clean up all by myself.

I stare at Balest, whose expression remains stony and cool. His dry lips are set in a straight line. He taps one of his shiny shoes against the floor, impatient, clearly anxious to leave.

"Why don't you believe me?" I plead, slumping away from my aunt's grasp, leaning toward him. "I know her. I know something's wrong."

With his mouth closed, Balest runs his tongue along the inside of his bottom lip. The gesture is creepy and vaguely sexual. "Tell me something," he begins. "Did you ever hear of Occam's razor?"

My gaze flickers to the far end of the room. Charlie stands on the opposite side of the doorway, the front of his body pressed close to the wall as he attempts to peek in on us while he eavesdrops. Linda McCartney is cradled awkwardly in his big arms. She wriggles halfheartedly, like she wants to get away from him but isn't feeling up to the task of escaping his grip. I notice that, sometime since last night, my aunt or uncle has purchased a rhinestone collar for her, with a small golden bell dangling from the buckle. As she shifts her weight around, the bell makes a soft *jingle, jingle, jingle.*

I pretend not to notice my cousin because I know he doesn't want to be noticed; he wants to feel like he's getting away with something. My aunt and uncle do the same. Officer Martin glances over his shoulder when he hears the bell, but it doesn't take him long to realize that something's different about Charlie.

But when Officer Balest notices the sound, he turns around and fixes his gaze on my cousin, who quickly ducks all the way out of sight. Balest's eyes narrow into small slits of focused judgment as he contemplates Charlie's existence. His expression makes me feel furious; watching him, I get the sense that he thinks he has more of a right to be here than Charlie somehow, like he's serving a meaningful purpose in our home, while my cousin is merely taking up space.

"Occam's razor," he continues, without waiting for my

response, "describes the law of succinctness. It's about simplicity." He pauses. "Do you understand what I'm getting at?"

Charlie pokes his head around the corner again. As Linda McCartney's bell goes *jingle, jingle,* I realize that my sister doesn't know about our new feline family member yet. The thought makes my stomach flutter with nausea; I remember having a similar realization years ago, a few months after our parents died. In an effort to bond with us, my aunt took me and Rachel to get our ears pierced, something our parents had simply never bothered to do. After it was done, I looked at myself in the mirror, admiring the shiny gold studs, and I thought, *I'm different now.* I understood that my sister and I would eventually grow into adults who barely resembled the Alice and Rachel who my parents had recognized. The fact made their deaths seem so final; it was like I could feel my entire life with them slipping away, its significance fading as time marched forward.

"I know what Occam's razor is," I tell Officer Balest. "It's the theory that the most obvious answer is usually the correct one."

He nods. "That's right."

I glance at Officer Martin, if only to avoid having to look Balest in the eye for a moment. Martin is looking at me with an intense expression, his brow wrinkled in thought. He seems unaware of the stray lock of blond hair that has fallen over his right eye. He's chewing gum, working it slowly with his jaw as he studies me.

"Alice has run away before," Balest continues. "What seems most likely to me, at least for now, is that she's done it again." He pauses. "Unless there's some other reason—aside from having a bad feeling—that makes you so convinced your sister is in danger? Maybe there's something you aren't telling us?"

I'm still looking at Officer Martin. I imagine that he would be understanding and receptive if I told him the truth about everything: who I really am, the money in my book-bag, even how it came into my possession. He would be concerned about Rachel. He would help me. For an instant, I consider blurting out the whole story. I imagine how different things would be once I'd explained everything to everyone, how light and relieved I would feel once the burden of all my secrets had been lifted away.

Don't. Tell. Anyone.

I shake my head. "No. There's nothing I'm not telling you."

All five of us are silent as my words dissolve and sink in. For just a moment, I think I see a flicker of doubt in Officer Balest's eyes. But it vanishes almost immediately, replaced by what seems like barely subdued relief at the fact that he finally gets to leave, to forget about the silly matter of my sister's disappearance that has taken up so much of his afternoon.

I go upstairs as my aunt and uncle walk the policemen to the door. As she passes Charlie, my aunt reaches out to muss his hair in a tiny, quick gesture of love that makes it impossible for me to hate her.

Upstairs in my room, I stare out the window as Officers Balest and Martin climb into their car. I'm startled to see that its blue-and-red lights have been flashing silently this whole time, as though alerting everyone who happens to pass by that something in our house has gone so wrong that we needed to reach out to complete strangers for help.

CHAPTER EIGHT

When I open the box that I keep beneath my bed, my intention is to replace the bundle of money without looking at any of the photographs. Sometimes I wonder why I keep them so close to me—they'd be just as safe somewhere else in the house, and maybe I wouldn't be tempted to take them out so often. Looking at the photos always hurts with a sharpness that can take my breath away, like I'm twisting the knife that's lodged in my heart, tearing open wounds that are almost healed. But sometimes I can't help myself.

Today is one of those times. I put the money back, and then I shut my eyes, trying to will myself to close the lid and slide the box under my bed. It's a weak effort; after a few seconds, I grab a stack of photos and settle into a cross-legged position on the floor.

Carefully, I spread out the photos, trying to look at all of them at once. Here we are: remnants of my long-gone family arranged in a semicircle, our glossy faces smiling, our bodies arranged in easy, candid poses as we gaze at the camera.

As I make my way through the pile, I come across one of my favorite snapshots, taken at my parents' wedding. I've looked at it so many times that the edges are bent and smeared with fingerprints. My mom and dad were married on a hilltop at my grandma's farm. It was a small, inexpensive wedding. My mom wore a dress that she'd sewn herself. My dad didn't even wear a suit—just a collared shirt and tie with khaki pants. In the photo, he's sitting at a picnic table, my mom on his lap, her arm slung around his neck. They're surrounded by friends, but they're looking only at each other in that moment, oblivious to everyone else. Both of them seem to be suppressing smiles, like they're sharing a secret, which they were: my mom was pregnant. I turn the photo over and trace her pretty cursive handwriting on the back with my fingertip, feeling the depressions from the ink on the paper, the words serving as evidence of her existence. *Wedding day, May 24.*

I still think about the day of the accident all the time, but not for the reasons a person might assume. I think about it because, up until the moment when everything went wrong, it was a lovely day. The four of us were happy together. And then, all of a sudden, it was over.

My parents died on March 15—the ides of March. Spring came early that year; the day was warm and sunny. In the afternoon, my dad got the Slip'N Slide out of the basement and set it up in our backyard. For hours, my sister and I played in our bathing suits while my parents stayed nearby. But they didn't pay much attention to us. We were nine years old, capable of playing in the yard without constant supervision. My mother sat in a reclining lawn chair, sipped a tall glass of Kool-Aid, and worked on a piece of macramé that she was weaving. My dad stayed mostly inside. We could see him through the sliding glass doors that led from the living-room to the yard. Like my mother, he was an artist. A few weeks earlier, he'd stripped the old wallpaper from the living-room walls, and now he was painting a mural on the one closest to the hallway that led to our bedrooms. He hadn't made much progress yet. His sketches showed plans to paint our house, my sister and me climbing a tree in the yard, my mother hanging laundry on the clothesline, and our cat, Nelly, sleeping in the shade. But so far he was only working on the sky above us, painting the clouds that blocked the sun. Our house, our family—we were only the lightest of pencil drawings, easily changed or erased.

It happened like this: Rachel was sitting in the grass, her wet swimsuit clinging to her skinny body. The grass had been cut recently, and the bright-green trimmings were caked onto her legs and feet.

"I'm too hot," she announced, shading her eyes as she squinted toward the bright sun.

"So go inside." I stood in front of her. We wore matching swimsuits covered in pink-and-white stripes. I could already

My mother had a similar tattoo on her right shoulder blade, except it was smaller, and it said my dad's name: *Steven*. Our parents had told us the story countless times. They'd met in college when they were eighteen years old. They hadn't even shared their first kiss when, a few weeks later, they got their tattoos. When my grandmother—my mom's mom—saw what her oldest daughter had done, she only laughed. She wasn't upset at all. The first time she'd met my dad, she shook his hand, smiled, and said, "Welcome back to the family." She was off her meds at the time.

My parents got married after their junior year ended; my sister and I were born a little over six months later. They never talked about it much, but I imagine having twins must have been overwhelming at the time. My dad finished college; my mom didn't. Even as a child, though, I remember being aware that she was the more talented one, despite her lack of a degree. She could do almost anything when it came to the visual arts: painting, sculpting, pastel drawing, pen and ink. My dad was strictly a painter, mainly with oils. He worked a day job as a high school art teacher. We were poor, but I never realized that fact when I was a kid. There were other things that never dawned on me then too—things I only understood once I grew older and got a better glimpse of how most other families function. My parents loved me and my sister, I know, but they often seemed far more absorbed in their own developments. It makes sense when you think about it; they were more or less still kids when we were born.

see the beginnings of a sunburn on her fair shoulders, knew that I would have one too. We weren't wearing screen. My mother thought it was silly, that people took c tion about sun exposure to such a ridiculous extent. Sh always ask, "How can something that feels so damn go possibly be bad for you?"

Rachel peered up at me. "You come inside too."

I shrugged. "Okay." When we walked past my mother she didn't even glance up at us. She was absorbed in her task, her fingers working the yarn with careful precision, slipping beads into place wherever she thought they belonged. She was using brown-and-yellow yarn, and as we walked by, I remember glancing down and thinking how ugly the project was, how the colors almost made me wince.

Inside, our dad was just as distracted. He stood on the highest rung of his stepladder—the one that says THIS IS NOT A STEP—and squinted as he drew careful, light outlines of the clouds. They were big and puffy—cumulus clouds. We were studying condensation in science class, and I knew all the different formations: cirrus, stratus, altostratus, and cumulus.

Nelly lay curled in a ball on a pile of my dad's sketches for the mural, purring as she slept. My dad wore paint-spattered jeans and a filthy white T-shirt. He was so young—only thirty-two years old, the same age as my mom. He had a silver stud in his left ear. On his upper right arm, he had a heart tattoo with my mother's name—*Anna*—on a banner going across it.

"Hot enough for you girls out there?" My dad wiped his forehead with a sleeve, leaning back to look at his work. The sliding glass doors leading to the yard were still open, and I heard the hiss of my mother's lighter as she lit a cigarette. She tossed the macramé onto the lawn and took a sip of her drink. It was her usual midafternoon cocktail: vodka and lime seltzer with plenty of ice, topped with three maraschino cherries. I remember her drinking all the time, but I don't remember ever seeing her drunk.

"Can I get a Popsicle?" Rachel asked.

"Did you ask your mom?"

"She won't care," I said. It was true too. My mom rarely cooked actual meals; domesticity wasn't really her thing. Even though she didn't have a paying job, she spent most of her time at home making art, leaving my sister and me pretty much to our own devices when we weren't in school. By the time I was eight, I was a pro at making any number of simple dinners: grilled cheese, tabouleh, homemade hummus with pita strips and black olives. My parents were strict vegetarians; I didn't taste meat for the first nine years of my life.

"Tell you what." My dad stepped down from the ladder and grinned at us. "How about we go for ice cream?"

"Yes!" I shouted.

"Yes!" Rachel echoed.

"Anna?" my dad called into the yard. "I'm going to take the girls for ice cream. You coming?"

I would replay the next words of conversation over and

over again in my mind for years. If only my dad had told my sister to get a Popsicle instead. If only my mom hadn't come with us. If only she'd been the kind of mother who kept the kitchen stocked with goodies for her kids, like ice cream. If, if, if. It can make you crazy after a while.

My parents only had one car, an old Ford Taurus with a rusty paint job and beat-up brown cloth interior. It was so ugly that, even at age nine, my sister and I were embarrassed to give our friends rides.

We lived in the middle of nowhere; the ice cream stand was along the side of a windy two-lane road, a good ten-minute drive from our house.

My sister and I were buckled into the backseat. We wore jean shorts over our bathing suits and plastic flip-flops on our feet. We put our windows down halfway, which was as far as they would go, and held out our hands to feel the warm wind rushing past. My mom turned up the radio and started singing along with "Me and Bobby McGee." A few wispy cirrus clouds hung in the late afternoon sky.

The ice cream stand—called, appropriately enough, "Mr. Ice Cream"—was crowded on such a warm day. As we stood in line, my sister and I read the menu out loud to each other. Going for ice cream was a rare treat. Like I said, even though I wasn't really aware of it at the time, my parents didn't have much money. Sometimes my mom would buy plastic gallon tubs of Neapolitan from the grocery warehouse in the nearest city. Within a week, all the chocolate ice cream would get eaten, leaving two dull stripes of vanilla and strawberry that would sit in the freezer for months, until it grew freezer burned and barely edible. Eventually, my mom would scoop out what was left and put it in a bowl for our cat. Ice cream always made Nelly sick; she'd spend the next few days throwing up gross, foamy piles of pink and white all over the house.

I think about things like that now, when I remember my mom. Why did she continue to buy Neapolitan, when she knew we only wanted chocolate? And why would she give the leftovers to Nelly, when she knew it would make her so sick? She could be careless like that. But what does it matter? She was my mother, imperfect and flighty. There was so much to love about her. She would often get up very early in the mornings, before my sister and I went to school, to put our hair into careful fishtail braids. She volunteered at the Humane Society one Sunday a month, changing kitty litter and walking dogs. She had a soft spot for the older animals and the ones with health problems, whose chances of getting adopted were low. Now and then she'd come home from the shelter in a bad mood—she'd be quiet and somber and spend more time than usual sitting on our patio, smoking cigarettes and staring at the woods like it had answers for her—and we'd know that one of the older, sicker animals had been euthanized since the last time she'd been there. She put salt on *everything*, even grapefruit and watermelon. She could sing "O Come, All Ye Faithful" in Latin—but she'd only do it once a year, on Christmas Eve.

As we stood in line at Mr. Ice Cream, a trio of older girls approached my family. All three of them sipped from tall, sweaty plastic cups that I guessed were filled with diet soda. Teenage girls, I knew, were always watching their figures. When my mom noticed them standing only a few feet away, giggling as they watched us, she nudged my dad.

"Hey, Mr. Foster," one of them said, her voice high and fluttery as they came right up to us in line. I realized that she must have been one of his students. The idea that my dad was in charge of so many kids during the day always struck me as somewhat ridiculous. It was like he had an entirely different life at work, where he had to act serious and wear clothes that weren't covered in paint stains and be a real grown-up.

"Hi, Claire." My dad seemed uncomfortable. The girls looked the four of us over. The tallest one—Claire—gazed at me with her wide, blue eyes. She was skinny and big-chested, a set of car keys dangling from her right hand. As she watched me, I took a step closer to Rachel. I felt so young and immature, like such a kid compared to these almost-women.

"Are these your daughters?" another of the three girls asked. She looked like she could be Claire's sister. All of them looked so similar: long hair, tanned skin, tight clothes.

Nodding, my dad reached out and took my hand. "Yep, these are the twins. This is Alice and Rachel." He and my mom never had any trouble telling us apart.

Claire and her friends smiled at us, but their expressions

didn't seem all that friendly. For some reason, I knew I disliked them. Who were they to approach my dad like this, in a public place? He was their teacher. We were his family. This wasn't school. I felt like they should have left him alone. He belonged to us.

But my mother obviously wasn't bothered by their interest. As she tugged her hair free from its ponytail, she wiggled the fingers on her right hand in a wave. She grinned at them like they were all sharing a secret. "So," she asked, leaning forward, "how's Mr. Foster in class?" She slipped her arm around my dad's waist. "Is he a meanie?"

"Of course I am," my dad answered. "I'm probably the meanest guy they know." And he winked—first at my mom, then at the girls. "Right?"

Rachel's gaze caught mine. I knew we were both thinking exactly the same thing about these girls. *Get. Lost.*

"I'm Anna Foster," my mom said. I don't think it occurred to her that it might be more appropriate if she introduced herself as *Mrs.* Foster. She smiled at the girls again, relaxed, almost bored. "I guess you probably figured that."

My dad rubbed his palm against his head, further messing up his hair in the process. "Good to see you, girls," he said. "You'd better enjoy the rest of your weekend. Midterms start tomorrow." He squeezed my hand. I watched with satisfaction as Rachel—usually so calm and sweet—shot daggers at the girls with her eyes. *Go away*, I thought, willing them to leave.

"We've been studying all day," Claire informed him. "Don't worry about us." And she gave another amused giggle. "So . . . are you here getting ice cream?"

Before our dad could open his mouth, Rachel interrupted to respond. "No," she said, sarcastic, "we're here to go ice-skating."

I laughed out loud, clapping a hand to my mouth.

"Rachel!" Our dad was embarrassed. But our mom, I could tell, was suppressing a smile.

Claire and her friends didn't know how to respond to my sister, her young face so snide and unfriendly for what probably seemed like no reason. They lingered for a few awkward seconds before saying good-bye and heading toward the grassy lawn surrounding the ice cream stand, where they settled at a picnic table and spoke to each other in hushed voices. Occasionally, one of them would look our way while we waited in line, and they would all start laughing. At that moment, I hated them so much. They didn't know my dad. They probably didn't even know his first name—he was just this other person to them, this "Mr. Foster" who my sister and I were unfamiliar with. Who were they to intrude? The day felt ruined.

Ice cream has a way of making everything better. My parents got milk shakes, and Rachel and I both got chocolate cones with rainbow sprinkles. We waited as my dad counted out exact change.

"Should we sit down?" he asked, squinting in the

direction of the picnic tables. Claire and her friends hadn't left yet.

My mom tugged on Rachel's hair. "Maybe we should just go home."

If only we'd stayed just a few moments longer. If only we'd never run into those girls. If only we'd sat down to finish our ice cream.

The road to our house was hilly, winding, so narrow in some parts that there was only room for one lane of cars. My mom put her bare feet on the dashboard and turned up the radio. She twisted the dial, searching for a clear signal, before stopping at "Space Oddity" by David Bowie. Her toenails were painted bright purple. I didn't think anything of it at the time, but in hindsight it seems like such a childlike, girlish color for a grown woman to choose.

In the backseat, I glanced over at Rachel. Our car's air conditioning didn't work, so even with the windows down, it was warm enough that our ice cream was melting quickly. She caught a few drops on her tongue, which had turned blue from the sprinkles. When I caught her eye, I mouthed *iceskating*, and we both started to laugh.

For whatever reason, our giggles seemed to annoy my dad. "Hey," he said, looking at us in the rearview mirror, "that's enough."

We were quiet for a few seconds as we suppressed our laughter. Then, so softly that only I could hear her, Rachel whispered, *ice-skating.* I lost it. Instead of reprimanding us again, our dad turned up the radio. He steered the car with one hand, the other one resting on my mom's leg, and rolled his eyes at her as he nodded at the backseat. My mom just shrugged and smiled. "Kids," she said.

The Taurus approached a tight, one-lane turn. We were in a small valley less than a mile before the entrance to Loyalhanna Lake. To our left, there was a steep hillside covered with trees and jutting rock formations. A sudden drop on our right led to a murky pool of still water littered with trash: a dirty mattress, a child's plastic rocking horse, a ripped garbage bag overflowing with clothes. Broken beer bottles. Old tires.

His hand still on her leg, I saw my father rub my mother's calf, the gesture tender and loving. I squinted at the garbage in the crevasse beneath us and noticed graffiti on the side of a huge gray rock. In orange spray paint, someone had written: DEAR KATE, I LOVED YOU MORE. Even at age nine, I felt a pang of heartache for whoever had scrawled those words. I believed them. I thought of how impossibly romantic it was that someone, probably a heartbroken ex-boyfriend, would profess such a private pain to the whole world.

It was a lovely day. Cirrus clouds drifted overhead like frayed cotton. The sun was beginning to descend, casting light and shadows across the wide surface of Loyalhanna Lake in the distance, beyond the trees in the valley below us.

I looked out the windshield in time to see a flash of bright green coming around the bend in the narrow road.

It was a pickup truck full of kids: three in the front, two in the bed.

Our vehicles hit each other head-on. After the initial impact, the truck spun out and rolled down the steep hillside. I heard it even though I couldn't see it anymore.

The whole thing seemed to happen in slow motion. The Taurus came to a stop at an angle, its body completely blocking the road. *That's it*, I thought to myself, *it's over. We're okay.* I felt my chest rise and fall. I stared down at my body, my arms and legs. Aside from a dull, deep pain across my torso, I was unharmed.

I glanced over at Rachel, assuming she'd be fine, just like me. But my sister was slumped in her seat, unconscious. Her window was splintered into tiny cracks where her right side had slammed against the glass. I could tell she was breathing, obviously alive, but a dim flicker of fear began to grow in my gut as I realized that everything was not okay, that maybe something had gone very wrong.

I looked over the edge of the road again and saw the green pickup truck resting upside down among the trash and shallow water, which rippled outward now from the impact, glinting in the sun. I saw a man in a white T-shirt lying facedown in the water, unmoving.

The radio was still playing "Space Oddity." What had felt like minutes had been only seconds.

I unbuckled my seat belt and climbed toward the front to check on my parents, who were silent. My mother was gone;

it was like she had disappeared, like it was all part of a night-marish magic trick. The windshield was shattered. My father sat in the driver's seat. If his eyes hadn't been open, I might have thought he was only sleeping, or that he'd been knocked unconscious like my sister. He stared off to one side, his head tilted at an odd angle. He was completely still. His nose was bleeding, dripping onto his white shirt. One drop. Then two. Then another, like someone slowly turning the handle of a faucet, until the drips became a trickle.

I'm not sure how anyone else might have reacted in the same situation. A small part of me understood what had happened, but it was like my mind wouldn't allow me to fully grasp the reality. Maybe I was in shock. I didn't cry or scream or get out of the car. I just sat back down, waiting for someone to find us. I stared at my sister, who was still unconscious, and it occurred to me that she wouldn't remember any of this once she woke up. But I would. And in those moments as I sat in the backseat with her, I thought of the plea: *I loved you more.* I could see it being written; I could imagine the heartache of that boy, because my heart was breaking too.

I pulled my legs close to my chest and rested my cheek against my knees, my head turned so I could continue to stare at Rachel. I sat there looking at my twin sister, one thought playing in my mind over and over again, long after a little red sports car happened upon the scene, after the police came with a whole slew of ambulances, after I watched them drive my parents away slowly, in no hurry at all, because there was nothing anybody could do to help them. Even that night, as

I lay in bed at my grandmother's house, I stared at the ceiling and mouthed the same phrase, until the rhythm of the words on my breath finally put me to sleep. I thought of Rachel in the next room, the fact that she hadn't woken up until an EMT held smelling salts beneath her nose. And I repeated the words like they were a prayer: *I wish I were you. I wish I were you. I wish I were you.*

And in a way, I *was* her. When I got up the next morning, my right side was throbbing from my head all the way down my arm; even my fingertips tingled unpleasantly. My flesh was swollen with vicious purple bruises. But my injuries weren't from the accident—not exactly.

I went into Rachel's bedroom, where she was still fast asleep, and nudged her awake. At first she looked up at me with a smile, and I knew that, in her sleep, she'd forgotten all about what had happened to our family the day before.

It only took a few seconds before she realized. I can't describe how horrifying it was to see her expression change, her body tensing up as her eyes filled and spilled over with tears before I had a chance to crawl into bed next to her.

I pulled the blanket aside to look at my sister's body and saw that her injuries were identical to mine. But the revelation didn't scare or upset me; instead I felt calm. I put my arms around Rachel, and for the rest of the morning we held onto each other with our eyes closed, and I remember thinking that we only had each other from now on, and how important it was that we never let each other go. No matter what.

CHAPTER NINE

It's still dark outside when the sound of the phone ringing downstairs ebbs me awake. It's the gentle, almost soothing *thrummm* of the house line, which my aunt and uncle keep connected in case there's an emergency. But nobody ever calls it; I didn't even know anyone had the number.

After a few moments, I hear footsteps coming up the stairs to the attic. From the sound, I know it's my aunt. I take a quick look in the mirror near my bed, checking to make sure the makeup that hides my bruises is still in place, which it is. Beside the mirror, the digital clock on my desk reads 5:17 a.m.

My aunt Sharon looks like she's been awake all night. Her face is typically drawn and tense, but this morning she looks much worse than usual. Her blond hair, which is usually shiny and styled, is pulled into a messy ponytail. She wears a long pink terry-cloth bathrobe that I don't recall ever seeing before now. She's in her bare feet, and I can see gauze wrapped around the side of her foot, to bandage her cut from yesterday morning.

"Hey, kiddo." I'm not used to hearing such a gentle tone to my aunt's voice; when she's speaking to me as Alice, our interactions are usually tense, her words clipped and frustrated. But right now, of course, she believes she's talking to Rachel. She sits down beside me in bed and puts a warm hand on my shoulder. "That was Susan Shields on the phone just now."

"Who?"

"Mrs. Shields." She stares down at me. "Kimber's mom," she clarifies.

"Oh. Sure . . . at five in the morning?"

"She was calling for Kimber," my aunt says. "She wanted to know if you needed a ride to school this morning."

At the mention of school, I feel a flutter of panic. How can my aunt expect me to go to *school* right now?

I sit up, shaking my head. The motion sends a sharp pain through the back of my skull and into my neck. I wince. As I brush my fingers across my wound, I'm startled to find that it's still damp, like it only happened a few moments ago. It should be scabbed over by now—shouldn't it?

"Aunt Sharon, I can't go to school today. Please."

She gives me a sympathetic look. "I know you're worried, Rachel. But you heard the police yesterday. She's been gone more than a day, so they're looking for her now. You know,

I'd be very surprised if she hadn't run off with Robin on Saturday. She'll be home soon." Aunt Sharon narrows her eyes and gives her head an angry little shake. "That jerk. Doesn't he have any human decency? What kind of a person refuses to meet his girlfriend's family? If Robin had any respect for Alice, he would have made more of an effort to get to know us. But all he's done so far is get her into trouble. If he truly cared about her . . ." Her voice trails off. "We don't need to discuss this right now. It won't bring Alice home any sooner." She flashes a quick smile. "Come on, get up. Get ready for school."

"But what about this?" I shove my hand beneath her face; my fingers are sticky with blood. "Something is happening to me because it's happening to Alice. She's in trouble. Why won't you listen to me?"

"I am listening," my aunt says, her tone so calm that I feel intense agitation, like I want to reach out and shake her. "Rachel, you know she's done this before—"

"This time is different! I'm sure of it!" I say, my voice rising as I fight back tears. I feel worn through, exhausted all over again; it's like the sleep I got last night never happened.

"What do you mean, Rachel?" My aunt narrows her eyes at me.

"You know what I mean. I can tell something's happened. I can *feel* it. And my head—"

"Stop it," she interrupts. "You hurt yourself somehow, but it has nothing to do with your sister. We're not going to discuss this, not now. It's nonsense."

"I didn't hurt myself! It just *happened*—it's like some-body grabbed a fistful of my hair and yanked as hard as they could. How do you explain that? How do you explain how I feel? She's my twin. I know her better than anybody." I pause, and then I add, "Better than you."

My aunt stares at her hands in her lap. She's quiet for a long moment. Finally, she says, "Rachel, what you're talking about is impossible."

"Why do you think so?" I glare at her. "Just because you've never felt that way? You know Alice feels things all the time. Grandma believes her. So did my mom. They both believed, because it's happened to them too. What about you, Aunt Sharon? You and my mother were twins. You never felt like you could sense her? You never knew when she was in some kind of trouble?"

"No," she says firmly. "Never."

"That doesn't mean it's impossible," I insist. "All it means is that you aren't the same as us."

My words make her flinch, and I know they've hurt her. But it's true; she isn't the same. She is concrete the same way we are intuitive. Instead of accepting the possibility that our feelings have meaning, that they come from somewhere beyond our own minds, she has convinced herself that we're all delusional.

My aunt doesn't respond for a while. Her shoulders slump within her heavy, shapeless robe. Finally, looking at me, she says, "I would expect this kind of thing from Alice. Not from you."

"Why?" I demand. "Why would you expect it from her and not from me?"

She flinches again. Her mouth opens, then closes, like she wants to say something but thinks it might not be the best idea.

"What?" I ask. "Tell me what you're thinking."

"You know exactly what I'm thinking, Rachel. You're different from Alice, and you know it. Alice is so much like your mother it isn't even funny. She's irresponsible and flighty and too emotional for her own good." She gives me a smile, like we're sharing a secret. "You're not like that. You're more like me."

The words feel like a slap. I blink at her a few times, trying to seem calm. "The police are looking," I say. "Right?"

She nods. "Yes. They're looking for Robin too." She gives me what's supposed to be a reassuring smile. "Please don't misunderstand me, Rachel. I'm concerned about Alice, but I believe we're going to find her soon. And when we do, we're going to get her the help she needs. Things will get better. I promise."

As we sit together on my sister's bed, staring at each other, I can hear the sudden noise of my uncle's alarm clock coming through the floor. The sound prompts a shift in my aunt's demeanor. She stands up, as though there's nothing more to discuss at the moment, and moves toward the stairs. "I told Sue Shields that you'd appreciate a ride to school," she says, without turning to look at me. "Kimber will be here at seven thirty. Go clean that head wound. Then, if you really want to, you can go back to sleep for a while. You have time. Maybe you'll feel more up to facing the day if you get a little more rest."

When I don't say anything, she turns to look at me. I stare at the ceiling, aware of her gaze, refusing to meet it.

"Rachel."

"Yes?"

"I love you very much. You know that."

My sister's bed is covered in her smell. Beneath the covers, I clutch her sheet tightly in my hands. I blink at the ceiling, with its odd, steep angles that follow the shape of the roof against the housetop. "I know you do," I tell her. "I know you love me."

Once she leaves my room, I crawl back underneath the covers and shut my eyes for a while, but it quickly becomes obvious that I'm not going to fall back asleep. My whole body aches, especially my arms—my wrists in particular.

I sit up. I'm wearing a gray sweatshirt; I push the sleeves back and see bright-red marks around the smallest part of my wrists; it's like my skin has been rubbed away.

First it was my head. Then it was my face. Now this. I don't care what my aunt thinks—or what anybody thinks, for that matter. What's happening to me is real.

❧

As I stare at my wounds, which are pulsing in pain now, I can hear my aunt talking to Charlie downstairs, the two of them laughing about something like they don't have a care in the world. I can forgive Charlie, who has no inkling of how concerned I am. My aunt is a different matter.

Things weren't always so strained between the two of us. When I was younger, we got along just fine. But one day something happened, and I've never been able to let it go. The truth is, I don't want to let it go.

Rachel and I were in tenth grade. We'd both been asked to homecoming that year; it was the first dance either of us had ever gone to. My aunt got us up early one Saturday morning and took us shopping for dresses. We drove all the way into Pittsburgh, to a fancy bridal shop that also sold semi-formal gowns, and my aunt told us to take our time picking out whatever we liked. Rachel and I spent over three hours trying on dresses, twirling in front of the three-way mirror to evaluate each outfit from every angle. The saleswoman brought us sparkling cider to sip from plastic champagne flutes. She and my aunt waited outside the dressing rooms as we changed, waiting for us to step out so they could offer their opinions. I was having so much fun. We all were.

Once we'd made our final selections, my aunt took our dresses to the register while Rachel and I got dressed. As we headed toward the front of the store to find our aunt, Rachel realized she'd left her purse in the dressing room and went back to get it.

As I approached the register, I could hear the saleswoman talking.

"Your daughters are so beautiful," she said to my aunt.

I froze. Neither one of them realized I was standing just a few feet away, my body hidden behind a mannequin dressed in a strapless silk wedding gown. My mom had been in the back of my mind all morning, and now the saleswoman's comment made it impossible for me to pretend we were just a normal family out for a day of shopping.

I couldn't see my aunt's expression; I could only hear her voice as she said, "Thank you. I think so too."

"They look so much like you," the saleswoman continued. "The resemblance is uncanny."

My aunt signed the sales receipt and tucked it into her purse. Her voice was pleasant as she said, "Oh, I know. People tell me that all the time." She laughed. "Although nobody has ever mistaken me for their sister, unfortunately."

The saleswoman slid our dresses into plastic garment bags and passed them across the counter. "Do you have any other children?"

My aunt only paused for a second. "No," she answered smoothly. "Just the twins."

It all happened so quickly, in just a few seconds. Their exchange shook me so badly that I broke out into a sweat; I was clammy by the time Rachel returned with her purse. I'm not sure what upset me more, the fact that she claimed us as her own daughters or the way she seemed to forget she had a son. Maybe it was both lies, and the way she spoke them with such ease, like she was slipping into another person's life— like she had any right to trade Charlie for us to portray a more perfect family.

I stayed quiet on the ride home. I could tell my aunt noticed the change in my mood, but she never asked me if anything was the matter. I don't know if she realized that I overheard her conversation. I never confronted her about it, and I've never told anybody what she said that day; not even my sister. But I've never been able to forget either.

⁕

To look at the two of them in the kitchen together—my aunt and Charlie—you'd think it was an ordinary Monday morning. At seven, Charlie is already fully dressed, sitting at the kitchen table, working on the last few bites of his granola cereal. Still wearing her bathrobe, my aunt stands at the kitchen counter with her back to me as she assembles a lasagna for tonight's dinner. She's like that: organized, prepared, deliberate. Every other Sunday, she makes a trip to the grocery store with a list of ingredients that she'll need to prepare our next two weeks' worth of meals. I don't remember a single evening, not in all the years I've lived here, when she hasn't had a hot dinner ready for all five of us at six o'clock. You'd think the predictability of her routine—the way her life is organized into lists and sub-lists and straightforward objectives—would be comforting. It's not. Instead, there is something sad and unsettling about her character. She has no patience for spontaneity. Everything is routine and order. It's like she's terrified of surprises.

This morning, for instance, my aunt has set a place for me at the kitchen table, across from Charlie. There's a tall glass of orange juice and a plate of scrambled eggs and toast waiting for me. The eggs are still steaming, but my aunt has already washed the pan she used to cook them; it sits on a dish towel, drying alongside a spatula and a big metal bowl.

I'm starving. I barely touched my dinner last night, and before that, I hadn't eaten in almost a full day. But I am Rachel today. Rachel never eats breakfast; it's another one of our differences.

It's like my aunt is reading my mind. "I don't care if you're not hungry, sweetie," she says. She doesn't look at me, and instead stays focused on her task of placing noodles atop a thick layer of ricotta cheese in the pan. "You need to eat something this morning."

"Mom made you eggs, Rachel. They look good, and I don't even like eggs. Hey. Did you know that kittens are blind when they're born? They can't see *anything*."

I smile at Charlie. He's dressed in a white button-down shirt and khaki pants, even though he doesn't have to be at work for hours. A few days a week, he buses tables at the Yellow Moon during the lunch shift. He's good at his job, and it makes him really happy to have a paycheck at the end of every week.

"How's Linda McCartney this morning?" I ask.

He shrugs. "I don't know. She's still pretty fat. All she does is lay around all the time."

"Well, she just had her kittens yesterday morning. She's probably tired." I sit down and begin to eat, grateful for the mandate from my aunt.

"Did Alice come home?" Charlie is in the habit of abruptly changing the subject. He has a hard time following the details of a conversation.

My aunt turns around quickly. "I just told you," she says to my cousin. "Alice isn't back yet. You don't need to ask Rachel." She doesn't say it in a mean way, not at all. Her tone is more weary than anything, even as she tries to be light and kind.

"Uh, I know what you told me," he says to his mom, rolling his eyes at me when my aunt turns away. "I thought maybe Rachel saw her, that's all."

"Rachel." My aunt's voice is sharp. "Can you do me a favor?"

"Right now?" I ask, in between mouthfuls of eggs.

"As soon as you're done eating." She glances at the clock on the stove, which reads 7:04. "I have to be at the museum for an early meeting. Can you walk Charlie down to Sean's?"

My aunt doesn't like to leave Charlie unattended. Whenever she needs to leave the house for any length of time, she often sends him down the street to stay with our neighbor, Sean Morelli. He's in his late thirties, unmarried, with no kids. He's a good friend of my aunt and uncle's. A few years ago, he volunteered to watch Charlie anytime my aunt needed the help. He's become like a part of our family.

"I can go by myself." Charlie studies his cuticles, embarrassed to be treated like such a child in front of me.

"No." My aunt holds up a single index finger and shakes her head. "We aren't going to have this argument right now."

"I'm an *adult*," he starts to insist, before my aunt cuts him off, saying, "You are *different*."

There's a long stretch of uncomfortable silence in the kitchen as Charlie glares at her. "I'm an adult," he repeats, more softly.

My aunt closes her eyes. She crosses her arms against her body and sort of hugs herself, fists clutching at her terry-cloth robe like she's holding on for her life.

I'm not hungry anymore, even though I've only taken a few bites of my breakfast. Pushing my plate away, I smile at my cousin again. He looks almost ready to cry. "Come on," I tell him gently. "It's not a big deal. We can walk over together."

As we stroll down the sidewalk, our street is almost silent except for the *whooshing* sound of dry leaves as the wind sends them tumbling along the curb. At nineteen years old, Charlie is six foot five and 270 pounds. He's a gentle giant. And even though he's my cousin—even though he's *different*, as my aunt put it—he's also very handsome. His red hair is so dark that it's almost more of a chestnut color. He has bright blue eyes and dimples. To look at him, without interacting, you'd think he was just a normal, good-looking guy, maybe a college kid. And he's right about one thing: he's perfectly capable of walking a block down the street by himself.

I know that my aunt only wants him to be safe, protected from harm at all times. But sometimes I think her caution isn't good for him, he should have the chance to do things on his own. If it were any normal day, if I were walking him to Mr. Morelli's house, I would send him on his way alone once we were out the front door.

That's what I would do. Me. Alice. And that's why, if she knew who I really was, my aunt never would have asked for my help in the first place. Rachel is much better at taking direction. Rachel is the responsible one.

Mr. Morelli opens the door before we have a chance to knock. My stomach flutters a little bit at the sight of him leaning in the doorway, sipping a mug of coffee. He might be thirtysomething, but he is *dreamy*: thick black hair, six-pack abs, piercing green eyes, and a smile that could make a girl melt.

When his eyes meet mine, he gives me a casual grin. I can feel my face growing hotter by the second, and am thankful that my foundation is thicker than usual in order to cover up my bruises.

"Hey, Rachel. Haven't seen you in a while." He takes a step back, opening the door farther. "Come on in, you two."

I see him all the time, but I never fail to get flustered around him. Today is no exception. "I can't, Mr. Morelli. I don't have time."

His grin widens. "Mr. Morelli is my dad's name, Rachel. Seriously, call me Sean." And he shifts his attention to Charlie. "Hey, Chuck." He nods toward the foyer behind him. "Go ahead in. Sheba's waiting for you." Sheba is Mr. Morelli's dog, a Labrador. Charlie adores her. He loves all animals.

Charlie hurries inside, barely bothering to nod good-bye in my direction. Mr. Morelli remains in the doorway, looking at me.

"So . . . how are you . . . Sean?"

"I'm well, Racquel." He pronounces the rhyme in a sing-song tone, still grinning ear to ear. He leans out the door and shades his eyes to gaze up at the clear sky, the sun already blazing. There isn't a cloud in sight, cirrus or otherwise. Looking me in the eye again, he gives me a wink. "Never better, actually. And how are you?"

I want to tell him the truth: I'm doing terribly. I should ask him if he's seen my sister. People need to know that she's missing, or they won't understand they should be looking for her.

Before I can respond, though, a maroon sedan comes around the corner and rolls to a slow stop in front of me. Kimber sits in the driver's seat, smiling and waving.

The idea that I'm supposed to go to school right now seems insane. I need to look for Rachel. I have no idea where to start, but there must be something I can do aside from sitting in classrooms all day, wasting time.

"I have to go," I tell Sean. "That's my friend."

"Oh, yeah?" He waves at Kimber. She waves back.

"Pretty girl," Sean says.

His comment strikes me as odd. I'm not sure what he expects me to say. "Um . . . okay."

He gives me another killer smile, but his expression shifts

when it's obvious I'm uncomfortable. "Rachel, hey. Are you okay?" He glances behind him, I assume to make sure that Charlie is out of earshot. "Is anything the matter?"

"No." I shake my head. I force a smile. "I'm fine. I just have to get to school."

"Where's Alice? Is she home sick today?"

From the street, Kimber has rolled down the passenger window of her car. "Hey," she calls. "Are you coming? We'll be late." She pauses. "Where's your bookbag?"

My bookbag. Or rather, Rachel's bookbag. Shit. I can picture it on the floor of our bedroom.

My vision tunnels. I need to get away, to go anywhere else but here. I feel like I'll suffocate if I get into Kimber's car.

"Rachel. Are you okay? I asked you if Alice was sick today." Sean studies me, concerned.

"She isn't sick," I blurt. "She's missing."

He pauses, mid-sip of his coffee. "What?"

"We can't find her." Saying the words out loud brings a warm rush of relief to my body. "Mr. Morelli—I mean, Sean—Alice disappeared on Saturday night. While we were at the carnival. We don't know where she is."

"Okay." He nods. "Calm down, Rachel. I'm sure Alice is fine." He puts a hand on my shoulder. "Don't worry," he says, smiling. As quickly as it surfaced, his concern seems to vanish. "This is what Alice does, isn't it? She gets herself into trouble. She probably ran off with her boyfriend again."

"No." I shake my head. "No, it's different this time."

"Did your aunt and uncle call the police?"

"Yes." I nod.

"Rach!" I turn my head to see Kimber holding up her hands in an expectant shrug. "Come on!"

"And what did the police say? Are they looking for her?"

I don't have time for this. Even though it's chilly, the wind strong enough that it blows my hair across my face, I feel hot and clammy all over. "I think so. Listen, I have to go now. Just . . . will you keep an eye out for her? Please?"

"Of course I will. Sure." He pauses. "Don't worry, Rachel. They'll find her. They always do."

I don't say anything else. I turn away, toward the street. I need air, space, to get away.

Kimber stares at me as I approach her. "You look horrible."

"Thanks."

"I mean it, Rachel. You don't look like yourself at all."

I almost laugh out loud. Instead, I look right into her eyes. A small part of me hopes she'll realize who I am.

But it doesn't happen. "Meet me in front of my house, okay?" I tell her. "I need to run in and get my bookbag."

My aunt's car is still parked on our street. She's probably getting ready for her meeting. Maybe she's in the shower or blow-drying her hair. It doesn't really matter. I have an idea.

As Kimber's sedan idles in the street, I take a few steps closer to it. "You know what?" I say. "You can go ahead without me. My aunt will give me a ride."

She frowns. "You don't need to do that. I'll wait."

"No." I give her a pleading look. "You're my friend. Right?"

She's confused. "Sure. Of course I am."

"Do something for me then. Go."

"Rachel . . ." She shakes her head. "You're being really weird."

"If you're really my friend, you'll do this for me. It's important."

She stares at me, then sighs. Finally, she shrugs. "All right. Whatever."

She pulls away as I walk toward my house, and I watch as her car disappears around the corner. I take a quick look up and down the street, checking to make sure none of my neighbors are outside. I don't see anyone. Then, slowly and as quietly as possible, I open the front door a few inches to peer inside.

I don't see my aunt anywhere downstairs. I slip into the house without making much sound, and I take off my shoes. Holding them in my hand, I hurry on tiptoe in my socks down the hallway, toward the kitchen.

In a single, practiced motion, I press on the edge of the hidden door. It springs open without so much as a creak. The stairway within is completely dark. Once I shut the door behind me, I might as well have my eyes closed for all I can see.

My plan, for the moment, involves waiting here until my aunt leaves the house, so I'll have a chance to collect a few things after she's gone. I count the steps in my mind as I go up: one, two, three, four, five, six, then there's a small landing as the stairway curves toward the front of the house. I can hear water running upstairs. My aunt is in the shower.

In the darkness, I sit down on the landing and pull my knees against my chest. The air is cool and stale. I take deep, calm breaths. I cannot see a thing, not even my hand in front of my face. When I was younger, I used to love being all alone in the darkness. Somehow, it seemed full of possibilities.

Today, though, I feel afraid. For my sister, wherever she is. For myself. For my family. For everything. I feel more helpless and alone than I have in years.

CHAPTER TEN

It was Rachel's idea to switch places the first time, when we were in the ninth grade. Even though we were in the same year at school, my sister was on an accelerated schedule by then. Always the smarter of the two of us, she'd been advanced enough the previous year to take biology, while I struggled my way through earth science with the rest of the mediocre minds in our class. So when we got to ninth grade, Rachel went on to chem, while I finally had a crack at bio.

For most of the year, things went pretty much the way I expected. I did as little work as possible for the class and managed to scrape by at the bottom of the curve with a C minus, which was fine by me, while Rachel brought home straight As and seemed to genuinely enjoy studying.

In early spring, we started a unit on dissection. Our first project was an earthworm. I sat at my desk, ready to get started, with a piece of cardboard, a small kit that included a probe and scalpel, and two dozen pins. Mr. Slater was our teacher; he teaches every section of bio at our school and also a couple of chemistry classes. He put a detailed transparency on the projector, illustrating exactly what we were expected to do to our worms. He called them "specimens."

And there they were, in a clear glass jar of fluid on his desk: gray and dead, their outsides patterned with endless smooth ridges. They were only worms, and I'd never had a weak stomach. What was there to be afraid of?

But as Mr. Slater made his way around the room doling out worms to my classmates, who were giddy with excitement to see the real-life insides of a once-living thing, I got a whiff from the stagnant jar in his hands. The smell was like watered-down alcohol. It was so different from the smell I'd always associated with earthworms until that day. After a hard rain in the warmer months, our street would often be littered with them. The odor of their flesh as they crawled along the side-walk, fat and glistening, was definitely unpleasant, but it was also something else. To me it was lime green, almost pulsing. It was bright and busy, the smell of countless lives thrum-ming along just as they should be. Everything around us is alive, from the sky to deep inside the ground. The earth-worms on the concrete outside my house, and the smell of their bodies as they wriggled along under the sun, was a reminder of that. But now here they were in biology class: gray and colorless, almost odorless except for the dull smell of preservative.

For the remaining forty minutes of class, I sat at my desk, staring at my worm on its piece of cardboard. I couldn't even bring myself to pin it down, much less make the first cut.

Holly Willis and Nicholas Hahn were both in class with me. Holly sat directly to my right, and Nicholas was on her other side. They were already a couple by then, both of them intermittently giggling and groaning as they probed the insides of their worms. Our instructions had been to make a single cut down the center of their bodies. Then we were supposed to flay them, pulling back the skin on either side and pinning it to the cardboard in order to get a perfect view of their internal workings.

For the first time since we'd been given our specimens, Holly glanced in my direction and noticed that I hadn't touched my worm. She and I were still pretty good friends back then.

"What's the matter, Alice?" She seemed genuinely concerned. "Are you grossed out?" She'd wrinkled her nose and nudged her desk a few inches away from mine. Frowning, she said, "Whatever you do, don't puke on me."

I forced a smile. "I won't puke on you."

Nicholas leaned across his desk and said, "If you're not grossed out, then what's the matter? It's just a worm."

"You three." Mr. Slater clapped his hands at the front of the room. "Is there a problem?"

"Alice doesn't like her worm," Holly explained. To me, she said, "It's not bad. They're just, you know, *guts*. And you only have to make one cut."

By then Mr. Slater was at my side. He seemed weary and frustrated, as usual, like he'd rather be anywhere but in a classroom full of teenagers. I couldn't bring myself to look at him that day; I was so embarrassed by my odd behavior, so frustrated that I couldn't force myself to make a single incision in a dead thing.

In a rare moment of kindness, he knelt beside my desk and put a hand on my shoulder. "Are you okay? Do you feel nauseated?"

I shook my head, staring past my desk at a scuff mark on the white linoleum floor.

"All right. I'll help you then. Here." He placed his hand over mine and began to guide me. Together, we pinned the worm to the cardboard. It wasn't as bad as I'd expected. Then he helped me pick up the scalpel. He pressed it against the dull, tough flesh of the worm until it broke, and a bubble of clear fluid burst from the incision.

I jerked away so quickly that the scalpel in my hand went flying. It landed on the floor a few feet away from my desk, only an inch or so from Nicholas's bare toes, which were poking out from his sandals.

By then we had the whole class's attention. Even as I covered my face with my hands, I could feel them staring at me.

"Okay. Everyone calm down." Mr. Slater reeked of cigarettes, as usual, as he knelt by my side; I tried to concentrate on his smell, desperate for some relief from the stink of formaldehyde and dead worms. "Stand up," he whispered. "Go get a drink of water. Calm yourself down."

I couldn't get out of there fast enough. I slammed the door shut behind me, leaving my things behind. I ran down the empty hallway to the girls' bathroom and locked myself into a stall, sitting on a closed toilet lid with my knees pulled against my chest. The smell from the classroom lingered all over me: it was on my clothes, in my hair, like an invisible layer of sludge. I stayed in the bathroom until the end of the period, and I didn't go back to the room for my things until the end of the day.

That night in our bedroom, my sister and I sat quietly at our desks. We were supposed to be doing our home-work. Rachel chewed absently at a string of black licorice as she worked on a sheet of algebra equations. My bookbag was on the floor across the room, untouched since I'd come home that afternoon. I had no plans to do any actual school-work. Instead, I concentrated on a sketch. It was a pencil drawing, the same one I'd been doing over and over again for months by then. My hand gripped my pencil as I drew the features of a young girl's face. She was pretty, probably in her late teens. She had long, straight hair, wide-set eyes, and a smile—like she was sharing a secret. Her appearance was marked by a gap between her two front teeth; that, and the fact that she wore earrings made from tiny blue feathers, like something you'd find in a Native American store.

I had no recollection of ever meeting the girl in my sketch. I didn't even know if she was real. But she was in my head almost every day, her image so clear that she might as well have been standing right in front of me, begging to be drawn over and over again.

"I heard what happened in bio class today," Rachel said, still doing her homework.

I felt a flutter of embarrassment at her words. "You did? How?"

"Holly told me." My sister put down her pencil, pushed away from her desk, and pulled her legs against her chest. "Why were you so upset? Was it because of the worms? They're already dead. They don't feel anything."

"I know that. I know." I shook my head, frustrated. "I'm not sure what happened. I just couldn't do it. I felt awful. It was like . . . like a violation. I don't know how else to explain it."

She squinted at me. "Like a violation," she echoed. "A violation of what, exactly?"

I stared at the hardwood floor of our bedroom. It was dark and shiny with lacquer-filled grooves in the thick planks of wood. More than a hundred years ago, when the house was new, the third floor used to be the servants' quarters. That fact never bothered Rachel or me in the least; we knew we had the best spot in the house. Servants should be so lucky. We'd been begging to move up here since we were ten years old, once we'd grown comfortable enough around our aunt and uncle to start asking for the things we wanted.

"I'm not sure," I told her. "Life? Their dead bodies? Cutting them open seemed . . . oh God, I don't know. It felt wrong, okay?"

Absently, she reached into her open mouth with an index finger to probe a piece of licorice stuck in her back teeth. Then she nibbled at the end of the same finger. She knew how much I hated black licorice—she thought it was funny. "It's because you're so sensitive," she said, wiping her hand on the back of her jeans. "Isn't it?"

I shrugged, pretending to brush away the label with indifference, but Rachel and I both knew better; by then we had plenty of evidence that I was most definitely *sensitive,* at the very least.

"You're like Mom," she continued. "You're like Grandma too. It runs in the family, but not with me."

I shook my head. "Aunt Sharon doesn't think so. She thinks Grandma's just crazy."

Rachel gave a dismissive wave. "Maybe she is. So what? That doesn't mean she can't be special too."

I couldn't help but feel a little bit proud. I loved knowing that I was similar to our mom and grandma. It made me feel like I belonged somewhere, like I was a part of something bigger than myself. Our gift was something that couldn't be explained, but it was real, and it bound us together permanently—nothing could take it away. Even then, I felt an urgency to hold it close, to nurture it as much as I could. I felt like I'd been entrusted with our family's legacy, and it was my responsibility to preserve it.

Rachel's gaze drifted to the sketch on my desk. I knew she'd noticed that I'd been drawing the same girl over and over again for weeks, but she hadn't mentioned it yet. She didn't mention it now either. Instead, she said, "I have an idea. I can help you with bio class."

I could hear strains of the *Jeopardy* theme song playing from downstairs, the sound drifting through the kitchen and up the secret stairs. My uncle watched it every week-night. He was good at answering the questions—even better than most of the contestants. I imagined the three of them sitting together on the living-room sofa with all the lights dimmed, captivated. It was like that sometimes, no matter how much they tried to include us. The three of them were a family. My sister and I were mere interlopers.

I shrugged at Rachel's idea. "You don't need to help me. I'll probably still pass with a D."

"But you can do better." She took another big bite from her licorice stick. I could smell her breath from a few feet away. "You could get a C. Maybe even a B."

"No, I couldn't. I'm not smart like you."

"Stop it. Don't say that." She continued to chew. She was still squinting. Our room was only lit by a few floor lamps in the corners, a small light on each of our desks, and a night-light beneath the front windows. The night-light's cover was a pink-and-gold butterfly, hand-painted onto a translucent ceramic cover by our mom. It had been in our bedroom ever since we were infants. "What if you let me help you?" she asked.

"What do you mean? Like, with my homework? I don't care, Rachel. It's not important to me. It's just school."

"That's not what I'm saying. What if . . . what if we switched?" There was a glint of excitement in her eyes as she spoke the possibility out loud.

The idea seemed ridiculous to me. Twins switching places was something that happened in movies and on TV—not in real life. "Come on, Rach. We'd never get away with it."

She took another bite of licorice, chewing with enthusiasm, leaning forward in her chair as she spoke. "Yes we would. We could do it. I know how you are—how you walk, how you talk, everything. All I'd have to do is wear some more makeup. And you could be me. Alice, it would work. I'm certain it would."

"I don't know." I stared at the drawing of the gap-toothed girl in my sketchbook. Maybe I'd meet her someday. Maybe I'd be walking down the street, and our paths would cross. It wouldn't be the oddest thing that had ever happened to me. And then what would I do? Take her to my house, show her all my drawings of her? She'd think I was insane.

"Why would you want to do that, Rachel?" I asked. "It won't matter if I get a C or a B in bio. My grades are still awful. And you'd have to pretend that you hadn't studied too much, and that you didn't care about school, or people would figure it out. So why even bother? What do we have to gain from it? We'd just be deceiving everyone for no good reason."

"No." She shook her head. "That's not true. There are good reasons."

"Oh yeah?" And I pulled my knees to my own chest, in a movement identical to what Rachel had done just a few minutes earlier. It sounds like a cliché, but it's true: sometimes being with her was like staring into a mirror. It wasn't something I ever got used to, not completely. "What are they, these reasons?"

"You suffer all the time," she said. "You remember everything that happened that day. Don't you?"

Her words gave me the shivers. She didn't have to explain what she was talking about; we both knew she meant the accident that killed our parents. As close as we were, neither one of us ever brought it up directly.

I stared past her, gazing at the night light glowing just above the floorboard, the paint in the butterfly's wings flaking from so many years of proximity to the heat of a tiny bulb. "I'm fine."

Her tone was gentle and understanding. "But you're not, are you? You weren't fine today in class. And what about next week, when you dissect a pig's heart? How are you going to feel? Will you be able to stand—"

"Let's say we do it," I interrupted. "Say we do it, and it works, and nobody figures it out. Maybe it helps me some. You're right, I don't want to dissect a pig's heart anytime soon." I looked at her. "Why bother, Rachel? What does it do for you? Why would you want to be me, even for a little while?"

Her eyes—which had sparkled with excitement only a moment ago—seemed to deepen in color as she shifted her gaze toward the floor. "Because I love you."

I shook my head. "That's not a good enough reason."

"Yes," she said firmly. "It is."

". . ."

". . ."

"Okay," I said. "I have bio fifth period. What do you have?"

She let go of my hands and pushed herself away. Finally, I could look at her again without having to smell the licorice on her breath. She gave me a wide grin. Giggling, she said, "I have study hall."

☙

So we did it. And it was amazing. The first time I became my sister—even though it was only for a few hours—it felt like so many years' worth of pressure, coming from somewhere deep within me, had finally been released. I forgot who I was for the day. Obviously, I was still myself physically, but it was like parts of me that were usually illuminated, at the forefront of my mind's stage, suddenly went dark. They were there, in the background, but they didn't rule me like usual. Not while I was Rachel.

My sister was happy to do it too—at least I always thought so. There were plenty of times when she volunteered without me even having to ask, whenever I was faced with something she thought might be unmanageable. Dissection. Punishment. Rachel seemed to feel like it was her duty to protect me from myself, to do whatever she could to ease my suffering. My gift, she believed, was too much of a burden for me to shoulder on my own. Rachel could help me carry it; allowing me to become her offered me some temporary relief. She did it for me all the time. She never said no, not once. She never showed any sign of reluctance, but somehow I knew that it must be draining her. How could it not?

She did it because she loved me, and for so long I believed that was a good enough reason. I let it keep happening, because after we'd done it once, I was hooked. I should have known better. It's the kind of thing everyone hears over and over again, about any act or substance that alters your mind: it's never as good as it was the first time. Maybe I under-stood that from the beginning, maybe not. It didn't stop me from trying. And Rachel kept giving herself over to me, again and again, because she knew how desperate I was to escape from myself. I took so much from her, I realize now. Maybe it was too much. And even if it wasn't, the fact remains: I never gave her anything in return.

CHAPTER ELEVEN

I've been sitting in the stairwell for what feels like hours, waiting, listening to the sounds of my aunt getting ready upstairs. It's almost impossible to tell exactly how much time has passed, but I know it can't be as long as it feels. She told me at breakfast that her meeting was at nine a.m. My aunt is always on time, which means she'll have to leave the house by 8:45 at the latest to drive to the museum uptown.

Faintly, I can hear her moving between her bedroom and bathroom, her steps on the carpet muffled and barely audible. I don't worry for a second that she'll decide to take the secret stairs into the kitchen; my sister and I are the only ones who ever use them.

As I wait, I go over my plan for the day in my mind. Obviously I'm not going to school; instead, once my aunt leaves, I'm going to walk to the police station. It's probably at least two miles away, but I don't care. Once I'm there, I'll demand to speak to one of the officers from yesterday, and I'll find out what they're doing to look for my sister.

I hear footsteps on the stairs. The sound of my aunt's heels against the hardwood floor, her light steps heading down the hall, toward the kitchen. She moves around, going back and forth, coming close to the wall nearest me and then walking away, doing—what? There is the sound of glass clinking, probably a dish or cup, followed by water running. I'm holding as still as I possibly can, barely breathing, so afraid she'll sense my presence behind the wall.

It dawns on me that she's probably making herself a cup of coffee before she leaves. For her birthday last summer, Charlie saved up the money he earned working at the Yellow Moon to buy her one of those single-cup coffee makers that are so popular. I can hear it whirring to life as the heater kicks in, followed by the steady drip of water being forced through the machine, filling her cup. She sighs, waiting, and I imagine her leaning against the counter in one of her typical poses: tired but ready for the day, well dressed and smiling, with only a hint of weariness to her features.

The phone rings. It's the house phone again—and like I said, almost *nobody* ever calls that line. It's only for emergencies, and also to provide a connection for the security system that's wired throughout the house, hooked up to all the outside doors. Every so often, Charlie will wander away. He never goes far—he usually ends up in one of the neighbors' yards or at Mr. Morelli's house, which isn't a big deal—but my aunt and uncle try to keep the alarm set all the time now, so they'll know if he leaves.

My aunt sighs again. Taking slow steps, she walks to the phone and answers it on the ninth ring. We don't have an answering machine.

"Yes."

"..."

This isn't the first time I've hidden in the stairs, so I'm used to listening in on my family's conversations when they don't know I'm there. Eavesdropping is always an odd feeling, but listening to her one-sided conversation is even stranger.

"I have a meeting this morning, Mom. I can't talk long." She's speaking to my grandma.

"..."

"I know I called you at ten o'clock last night. I thought you'd be awake."

"..."

"Well, I'm sorry. I didn't mean—"

"..."

"Mom, it's fine." Her tone is impatient and strained. She and my grandma aren't particularly close. She lives just a few miles outside town, in the same farmhouse where my mom and aunt grew up, but we only visit her a few times a year.

My aunt is silent, listening to my grandmother. After a while, she interrupts with: "We don't know where Alice is— that's why I called you. If she shows up at your house, you need to let me or Jeff know immediately." Another sigh. "Because she's not *well*, Mother. She needs help."

Not well? She's talking about me. Alice.

"I have to go, Mom. Please promise you'll call if you hear from her."

"..."

"Yes, we called the police. She's eighteen years old. They're looking, but they can't do much. Not yet, anyway."

"..."

"Of course Rachel's worried. It's not that we aren't worried. Please don't be this way."

"..."

"Why would you want to do that?" she demands, her voice rising. "What do you have to tell Rachel that you can't tell me? You'll make things worse than they already are."

"..."

"I need to get going, Mom."

"..."

"I'm not doing that. I'll let you know when we find her, but that's all."

"..."

"Stop it, Mother. I'm not having this conversation. She doesn't need your help. She needs a professional."

"..."

"I said I'm not doing this."

"..."

"Great. Is that what you think?" My aunt's tone is

suddenly much quieter. In an instant, her voice shifts from anger to . . . what?

"I'm sorry, Mom. I'm not Anna."

It's sadness. She's talking about my mother.

". . ."

"Don't tell me how you feel. I know how you feel. I've always known."

". . ."

"I'm hanging up now. Good-bye."

There's a sharp *beep* as she turns off the phone. I expect her to do something else—to call my uncle maybe, or even start crying after such an unpleasant conversation—but she doesn't do either of those things, at least not that I can hear. There is the sound of her keys jingling, followed by her footsteps leading to the front door, and four quick electronic beeps as she sets the security alarm. She pulls the door shut so hard that I can feel the whole house vibrating around me; the action is the only sign at all that she might be upset.

I wait. I close my eyes and slowly count to thirty in my head: *one Mississippi, two Mississippi, three Mississippi* . . .

Once I'm sure she's gone, at least for the rest of the morning, I nudge the secret door open and step into the kitchen. The room is neat and orderly. The only sign at all of anything amiss is my aunt's cup of coffee, which rests beside the phone on the countertop, untouched, no trace of lipstick anywhere on the rim, the contents still steaming.

I stand in the middle of the kitchen for a few seconds,

still breathing lightly, almost as though I'm afraid someone might burst into the house and discover me at any moment. What did my aunt mean when she said that I needed a professional? What kind of professional? I'm not *well*?

She thinks I'm crazy, just like my grandma. She thought my mother was crazy too. Despite the occasional nagging doubt—and the fact that my intuition is sometimes wrong—I don't need any help, that's for damn sure. Rachel is the one who needs help right now. Rachel needs *my* help; she needs everyone's help. How much longer can I lie to everybody about who I am? How long until the deception makes me responsible for whatever might happen to her?

Okay, Alice, I tell myself, *you need to get out of here.* I go upstairs to our room and grab my bookbag. I start to fill it with supplies: a notebook and pen, a change of clothes, my sister's phone. I fish through her oversize purse—the same purse I was carrying on Saturday night at the fair—and find her wallet. Among other things, it contains her ID, her debit card, and twenty-seven dollars in cash. There are other random items floating around in her purse too: a fun-sized box of Good & Plenty candies, which are black licorice flavor. There's a tiny French-to-English dictionary, its pages tissue-paper thin, the words so small I can barely read them. French is Rachel's foreign language at school; she's been taking it for years. (Not me; I did two semesters of Spanish to fulfill my foreign-language requirement, and I was done.) In the side pocket, I find a used tube of strawberry-flavored lip gloss, a handful of gum wrappers (but no gum) . . . and something else. At first I think it's just garbage, the kind of stray papers and junk that tends to hide out in the bottom of bags that have seen plenty of use. But it's something more. I tilt the purse onto her desk and shake out the contents of the pocket. A little pile of what looks like grass clippings falls out. I lean forward, peering at them, and pick one up.

They aren't grass clippings at all. They're tiny flowers. Even though their color has long faded away, I can tell they used to be yellow buttercups, the kind that spring up in droves on people's lawns every summer. Each stem is tied into a little loop, which is knotted at the base of the flower. There must be a few dozen of them here.

It's a weird discovery. I've never known Rachel to have an interest in . . . whatever the flowers are supposed to be. And it's almost like they were hidden away in her purse, an entire collection of dried-up loops. What reason would she have to keep them? I scoop them into my hand and put them back into the pocket. Even if they're garbage to me, they were obviously important to her. There's no way I can throw them away.

Just as I'm pulling a gray hooded sweatshirt over my head, I hear a rustling sound coming from downstairs. I stop, listening.

Maybe it's the mailman on the porch. But the mail doesn't usually come this early.

It could be Charlie. Maybe he's forgotten something he needs for work.

The rustling grows louder, more insistent. I freeze.

The security alarm goes off, the sound shrill and deafening. I can't move. There's nowhere to run—nowhere to go but down, and by the time I could make it to the secret stairs, whoever's inside the house might find me. Even if I got there, what if he or she knew where to look? What if it's the same person who took Rachel? It's like the whole world is being drowned out; I can't even think straight. After something like sixty seconds, if the four-digit code isn't punched in, the police will be notified. The security company will call my aunt and uncle. They'll have to come home.

There's another option, though. I was here when the alarm was installed a few years ago. The tech the company sent out was a hulking, three-hundred-plus-pound guy with sleeves of tattoos on both of his arms. As his big fingers worked to adjust the alarm settings, he explained to us that our system came with a feature called a "hostage code."

"It's different from your regular alarm code," he said. "Basically, it's another four-digit combination of your choosing. Let's say somebody breaks in while you're at home. The alarm goes off, and they order you to punch in your code. Instead of using your regular code to turn it off, you'd use the hostage code. The alarm will turn off as usual, but the system immediately alerts the police that there's a hostage situation at your residence." He gave us a stern look. "Cops take this seriously. It's only for emergencies."

"How do we program it?" my aunt asked.

He'd smiled. "I already did it for you. I used your street address—4606. Because here's the thing: if somebody breaks in and you're *not* home, they're probably gonna take their best guess at the code. What do you think they'll try? Something easy, right? Like your house numbers."

"It makes sense," my aunt said later, explaining the new system to my uncle. "But Jeff, you should have seen this guy. He was . . . uh . . . *imposing.* Maybe we should switch the code."

I remember the events so clearly, but I don't remember if they ever actually reprogrammed the alarm. If they did, they never told me. As far as I know, they never told Rachel or Charlie, either.

I could try it now. 4606. I repeat the numbers over and over in my mind, terrified that I'll forget them in my panic.

Too much time has passed already; I don't have the opportunity to think things through any further. I run downstairs, toward the front door where the keypad is mounted on the wall, adrenaline rushing through my body, ready to push past whoever has broken in. As I'm running, though, I lose my footing. I fall. And when I hit the hardwood floor, landing flat on my back, I get the wind knocked out of me. I can't speak or scream or move as I lie there, staring up at the figure hovering over me.

The face is familiar, concerned, and looks just as panicked as I feel. She takes me by the hands and pulls me to a sitting position. I struggle and struggle, trying to breathe, until something inside me releases and I find air again.

I'm not going to need the hostage code. "Two-five-one-one," I gasp, pointing at the alarm panel beside the front door. "Two-five-one-one-*stop*. Go punch it in. Do it now! Two-five-one-one-stop."

I press my face into my hands. I'm still dizzy from the fall. How long has it been since the alarm went off? Twenty seconds? Thirty? More?

Just as suddenly as the noise erupted, it goes silent with a final, meek *chirp*. I stare across the room, breathing hard, watching her with a combination of relief and confusion.

"What the hell are you doing here?" I ask, standing up.

She looks ready to cry. "I don't know. I was worried about you."

"So you break into my house?"

She leans against the front door and slides her body downward until she's sitting cross-legged on the floor. She pulls her knees close to her chest and tilts her head so her long blond hair falls across her face, like she's trying to hide behind it. "I'm sorry. I didn't know what else to do. I don't think anybody saw me. We can leave now, okay? Let's go to school. It's okay if we're late." She looks up at me suddenly, pushing her hair away from her face, pouting. "I was going to have perfect attendance this semester."

Perfect attendance. I almost laugh out loud at her. Instead I say, "Oh, Kimber. That's so typical of you."

Kimber shrugs. In a small voice, she says, "Attendance is important."

"I need your car," I respond. "I need it for the whole day."

She blinks, confused. "For what?"

"To talk to the police. To look for my sister."

"No." She shakes her head. "It's my mom's car. She'll go crazy if I let you use it."

I should have known I would have difficulty convincing Kimber to hand over her keys. "Then come with me," I tell her. "You can drive. But you have to go where I tell you."

Her pretty green eyes widen. "You mean, like, skipping school?"

I nod.

"I can't . . . Rachel, no."

"Yes," I insist. "Please. It's important, Kimber."

"Skip school," she repeats, pronouncing the words like she's saying something much, much worse. *Commit a felony. Hijack an airplane. Steal the Declaration of Independence.*

"Make up your mind," I say. "If you won't do it, you need to tell me now."

She nods to herself. She's thinking about it, I can tell.

"We won't get caught," I assure her.

"The school will call our houses."

"Is your mom going to be home?"

She brings her thumbnail to her mouth and begins to nibble at the edge. I notice that all her nails are bitten down so far that some of them are bright red around the cuticles. She shakes her head.

I give her a tentative smile. "Kimber, come on. I need your help today. Please."

She swallows hard, still chewing. Then she pulls her finger away from her mouth and stares at it, appraising the damage with an unsatisfied expression.

"Okay," she says, climbing to her feet. "I'll do it."

We both stand there for a minute, staring at each other, our breathing shallow; hers with nervous excitement, mine with a more troubled feeling of anxiety.

"Thank you," I tell her. "You're a good friend."

She gives her head a small shake. "You don't have to thank me. You know, 'Do unto others,' and all that. You need help, right?"

"My sister needs help," I correct, moving toward the door. I peer outside to make sure none of the neighbors are around. It's all clear.

"Alice needs help?" Kimber echoes. She laughs. "Yeah, Rachel. Everybody knows that. She needed help before she ever ran away. She needs more than *help*."

I pause with my hand on the doorknob. "What do you mean?"

She gives me a blank look, her smile fading at my serious expression. "You know exactly what I mean, Rachel. We've talked about this plenty of times."

They have?

"I don't mean to upset you. I'm sure she's okay. She's just . . . well, it's like you said. Her reality is different from everyone else's. One of these days she'll stop knowing what's real, and then . . . she'll be gone."

CHAPTER TWELVE

So where are we going?" Kimber asks, fiddling with the radio settings on her dash, settling on a country station. Glancing at me, she says, "Sorry. I know you don't like country. This is classic country, though. You should give it a chance."

I don't even want to dignify her suggestion with a response. I *hate* country—thank God Rachel does too. "Drive to the police station," I tell her, rummaging through my sister's backpack. "Make a left at this stop sign. Then go down to Pennsylvania Avenue and make another left. You'll be going parallel to the trail."

"I know where the police station is," she says, an edge to her voice. "I've lived in this town my entire life." She glances at me. "What are you looking for?"

"My sunglasses. I could have sworn I put them in here somewhere." As we're talking, I keep glancing out the window, afraid that someone will spot the two of us skipping school together. I've done it plenty of times before, but I don't know that Rachel ever has. And Kimber obviously hasn't. What kind of a person—what kind of an eighteen-year-old teenager—is concerned with having perfect attendance?

"Why do you need sunglasses?" Her hands are at ten and two o'clock on the steering wheel, just like we were taught to do in driver's ed class. She's clearly nervous, hunched low in her seat to avoid being seen, gripping the wheel so tightly that her knuckles are white. She takes slow, deep breaths in and out through her mouth, like she's trying to keep herself calm.

It's a bright day, but the sun is behind a patch of cumulus clouds as we drive. That's not why I need the sunglasses, though. "I don't want people to recognize me," I tell her.

"Yeah, me neither. My mother would kill me. I'm not kidding." She nods toward the glove box. "I think there might be a baseball cap in there. Take a look."

When the door to the compartment falls open, a whole mess of papers and pens and, yup, a hat spills onto the floor of the car, which is otherwise spotless. Once I've put it on, pulling the brim down to hide my face, I start poking through the stuff on the floor. If Kimber minds my unabashed snooping, she doesn't say anything; she just stares straight ahead, concentrating on the narrow road as she drives. The speed limit is thirty-five, and she's going twenty miles per hour. The walking trail is on our right, clearly visible as it runs parallel to the road for the next few miles. It's the only trail in town, an extension of the same one that goes through my neighborhood and curves down into Hollick Park; the same trail where Rachel and I last stood alone together, preparing to play our game on Saturday night. Right now there are quite a few people on it, out for bike rides or morning jogs. Unless my sister left the fair in somebody's car, she would have had to use the trail to go anywhere else; the only road leading out of Hollick Park is a windy two-lane that leads directly to the highway.

"Hey, there's Homeless Harvey," Kimber says, pointing with her index finger. She draws a tiny loop in the air, as though she's circling his face. "I've never seen him out this far before." She gives her car's horn a light, friendly *honk*. Before I have the time to realize that we're being awfully conspicuous, we both wave at him.

Homeless Harvey has been a constant fixture on the trail in Greensburg for months now. Nobody knows his real name, or where he came from, or where he goes when he's not walking along with his dog, a huge filthy mutt with a red-and-white bandanna tied around its neck. Nobody even knows for sure that he's actually homeless, but it sure seems that way. He always wears the same outfit, no matter what the weather is like: faded jeans and a plain black T-shirt. He carries the same navy-blue backpack with him everywhere. His dog doesn't have a collar. They both look like they could really use a bath.

As soon as they're out of our sights, Harvey and his dog slip from my thoughts, and I find myself focusing on Rachel again. We're almost to the police station. I'm trying to rehearse what I'm going to say in my head, but I'm having a hard time focusing. As a rule, cops make me nervous. Most of my encounters with them have been less than pleasant.

Kimber pulls into a parking space on the street, more than a block away from the station.

"What are you doing?" I ask. "Why are we so far away?"

She gives me a dubious look. *"Duh,"* she says. "I'm a criminal. So are you, for that matter. I don't know why you even bothered trying to disguise yourself if you're going to walk right in there and present yourself to the police."

I roll my eyes; I can't help it. "What the hell are you talking about, Kimber?"

"We're *truant,*" she says. "It's illegal."

I take off the hat I'm wearing and toss it into her lap. "Right. By all means, then, stay in the car. Wear the hat. Do you have any additional means of concealing your identity? Because it's almost ten o'clock, you know. I'm sure the authorities have organized a search party to look for us by now."

"That's not funny," she says, digging around in her purse.

As I'm getting out of the car, she says, "Wait. How long do you think you'll be gone? I only have two quarters."

"Why do you need quarters?"

"To pay the meter," she says.

"But you're waiting in the car. If the meter maid comes down the street, just drive away. I'll find you."

She stares at me like it's the most ridiculous idea she's ever heard. "It costs money to park on the street, Rachel. I'm not going on a crime spree with you today."

I shake my head. "Sorry. I don't have any quarters. I'm going now, okay? Text me if you need anything. I'll be as quick as I can."

As I'm walking away, she puts down the passenger-side window, leans over, and shouts, "Society depends on its members to do the right thing in order to preserve our morality! Otherwise there would be anarchy!"

She yells loud enough to attract the attention of a few nearby pedestrians. Apparently her desire to lecture me on the finer points of social order outweighs the importance of keeping a low profile.

༨

The police station is dingy and depressing. As I walk in, there's a small reception area to my left. A drab-looking middle-aged woman sits at the desk, chatting on the phone as she stares at her computer. She's on the website for the Home Shopping

Network. It only takes me a few seconds of listening to understand that she's placing an order for a porcelain Marie Osmond doll.

I stand in front of her, waiting as she chatters away. She's either so absorbed in her task that she's oblivious to my presence, or else she's deliberately ignoring me. I help myself to a handful of Hershey's kisses sitting in a bowl on the counter, then I cough a few times, trying to get her attention. All she does is glance at me, like I'm nothing more than a minor distraction, and go back to her conversation. Yes, she would like the extended two-year warranty. Yes, she would like two-day shipping for an additional $18.99. *To hell with work,* I think to myself. *Gotta get that Marie Osmond doll before the weekend.*

She finally hangs up. "Yes?" she asks me, giving me a doubtful once-over with her heavily made-up eyes, their lids caked with green shadow, her lashes so thick with mascara that I immediately think of tarantulas. "If you're here to pay an outstanding parking ticket, you need to go to the third floor."

"I need to talk to someone," I tell her. I give her a quick explanation of who I am and say I need to speak with Officer Balest or Officer Martin.

Before I can finish, she starts shaking her head. "Balest isn't in today," she says, cracking open a can of soda that she produces from a mini-fridge beneath her desk. "He's on a hunting trip up north. Bow and arrow, I think."

Her indifference makes me want to scream. My fists are clenched so tightly at my sides that my fingernails dig into my palms.

"What about Officer Martin?" I demand. Despite my best efforts to stay calm, I can feel tears welling in my eyes. "Is he here, or did he go hunting too?"

She gives me a long, blank look. I return the stare. Finally, she picks up her phone's headset and punches a few numbers into the dialer. "Hey, Cindy, it's Larraine," she says, making no effort to disguise her irritation with me. "Can you tell me if Ryan's in the building?" She pauses. "Yeah. Uh-huh. . . . Okay, then. . . . What? No, I use a Crock-Pot instead of a double boiler. . . . I don't know, eight or ten hours. Or you can put it all together the night before. . . . That's right, three cans of chipped beef. Four if you've got a crowd to feed. . . . All righty. Good luck, honey. Bye, now." She hangs up and gives me a frown. "He'll be right down," she says, obviously disappointed that she doesn't get to turn me away.

Within a couple of minutes, the elevator doors beside me open, and Officer Martin steps out. He's accompanied by a big long-haired dog whose breed I can't identify.

"Rachel Foster." He smiles, shaking my hand, his med-alert bracelet gleaming beneath the harsh overhead lights. "Follow me," he says, pointing. "We can talk somewhere more private."

He leads me into a small windowless room. The walls are painted cinderblock. The only furniture is a small metal folding table and two wooden chairs. The dog follows him inside, then he shuts the door. As we take our seats, the dog lies down at Officer Martin's feet, resting its head on its paws.

"This is Cookie," he says, nodding at the pile of fur. He gives an embarrassed shrug. "The name wasn't my idea."

I couldn't care less about the dog's name, or what it's doing in here with us. "Are you looking for my sister?" I blurt out. "She's been gone for two days. Why aren't you trying harder to find her?"

"Calm down, Rachel," he says, opening the folder he's been carrying beneath his arm. Inside is a short typewritten note, only a few paragraphs long, and a photo of me. It's last year's school photo. My aunt and uncle must have given it to the police before I got home yesterday.

I wait as he takes a moment to read over the notes. "Tell me about this boyfriend," he says. "Robin Lang."

I stare at my hands, which are shaking in my lap. I feel guilty for having given the police Robin's full name in the first place, but I didn't feel like I had much of a choice. "I don't think he would hurt my sister."

"How well do you know him?"

For some reason I can't look at him. "I don't. I've never met him."

"Then what makes you so certain he's not dangerous?"

"I don't know. I just am."

"Okay . . . Rachel, I know you're concerned about Alice. I

need you to be honest with me right now. Is there anything you haven't told us that might be relevant to her disappearance? It could even be something little, something that only seems odd in hindsight. Had she been acting strange lately? Has she participated in any illegal activities, maybe something that could get her in trouble? Take your time. Think hard."

The room is silent except for the dog's light snore as I pretend to contemplate the questions. In reality, I'm thinking about the money underneath my bed, and the likelihood that whoever has Rachel is really after me. Robin was right about one thing—if the police are going to be any help at all, I have to tell them something resembling the truth about the money I stole. But I'm not sure how to do it, not without revealing who I truly am. If I admit that we switched places, Officer Martin will have to tell Officer Balest—that is, once he returns from his hunting trip. The police will tell my aunt and uncle, who will surely tell *someone*, and then who knows who might find out? Our town is pretty small. There has to be a way around explaining the whole story. I need to figure out how to give him just enough information to motivate him to search harder for my sister, without revealing everything.

Before I can fully organize my thoughts, he says, "Can I ask you something, Rachel?"

I nod. "Sure."

"Look at me. Let me see your face."

I go cold. But I raise my head, my eyes meeting his gaze. He seems kind and concerned, not nearly as harsh and intimidating as Officer Balest. I feel like I can trust him.

When he speaks, his voice is gentle, not accusing. "You have a lot of makeup on today."

I nod again. "Yes."

"Are you trying to conceal something? When I saw you yesterday, your face looked puffy. I can see it now, too, underneath your makeup. Do you have bruises?"

I don't answer him; my silence is enough of a response.

"Tell me how they happened," he presses.

Above us, one of the fluorescent lights flickers a few times. Cookie raises her head and whimpers.

"Officer Martin—" I begin.

"You can call me Ryan," he interrupts. He glances at the lights, then down at the dog and says, "Cookie, settle," in a firm tone. To me, he says, "I'm sorry. Go on."

"Ryan." Addressing him by his first name makes me feel more relaxed; I imagine he knows that.

I take a shaky breath. I can't *believe* what I'm about to tell him. "Have you ever heard of something called twin phenomenon?"

"Twin phenomenon," he repeats. "I don't think so. Why don't you tell me about it?"

I take another breath. I'm not sure where to start. No matter how I begin, I have little doubt that Ryan is going to think I sound crazy. But I have to try.

I spend the next twenty minutes or so talking almost nonstop, explaining the idea that twins can be connected by an invisible link, that their bond can be so powerful they're able to sense things about each other, even when they're not together. I tell him the story about my sister choking on gum when she was a child, about the hornet's nest in her bike pouch. I tell him about my feelings of dread at the fair on Saturday night, trying to explain how distinctly I sensed her presence vanish.

Once I start, it's like I've broken through an invisible barrier and I can't stop. I tell him everything I can think of that might strengthen my argument. I explain how these abilities seem to run in my family, that my mother often had strong intuitions of her own, and so does my grandmother.

Then I show him the back of my head. I face the wall as he leans close to me, his fingertips almost touching the wound. When I turn around, his expression is uneasy.

Before he can say anything, I reach up and smear away the makeup beneath my eyes. Then I push up my sleeves and show him the marks I've been hiding all morning. "Do you see?" I ask.

He gazes at the bright-red lines encircling my wrists, which have an angry, aggressive look to them. "Yes," he says, "I see."

"Someone's hurting my sister, Ryan. That's why these things are happening to me."

He leans forward, resting his elbows on the table. He

presses his hands together in a gesture that makes it look like he's getting ready to pray.

The lights flicker again, then again.

"Shit," Ryan says, pushing back his chair. "Don't move, Rachel."

Cookie seems to awaken instantly from her sleep; she stands up, tilts her head back, and howls softly, tapping her front legs against the floor in a demand to be noticed.

"It's okay, girl," Ryan says. "Sit down." He stares at the lights. "I think it's over for now, Cookie. Good girl."

The dog doesn't seem convinced. She tilts her head, puzzled.

"Cookie. Sit."

"What's going on?" I look around, intending to glance outside to see if it's storming or something, before I remember that the room has no windows.

Ryan sits very still, thinking, like he's calculating his next words. "It's odd," he says. "That's what it is."

I squint at him. "What's odd? The lights flickering?"

"Yes." He leans across the table and lowers his voice, like somebody might be eavesdropping on us. "Do me a favor, okay, Rachel? Don't make any loud noises or sudden moves. Try to stay calm."

"Okay. Why?"

Ryan shuts his eyes. He places his palms flat on the desk, his med-alert bracelet clinking against the table.

"I shouldn't be talking to you about any of this," he tells

me. His eyes are still closed. "This is so unprofessional," he murmurs.

He seems so . . . so *human*. So ordinary and approachable, despite the authority that his uniform suggests.

"It's okay," I venture, trying to put him at ease. "Professionalism is overrated."

He opens his eyes, gives me a little grin. "I believe what you've told me," he says. He nods slowly, then a little harder, like he's growing more certain by the second. "I believe all of it."

My relief is instantaneous; it's like the bubble of doubt and anxiety that has been swelling within me all day has popped. I have to stop myself from reaching across the table to touch his hands, to let my relief flow into him; that's how strong it feels. It's almost overwhelming.

He taps an index finger against his lips, thinking. "Energy is a funny thing," he begins. "People think they understand how it works, but nobody fully comprehends it."

I don't say anything. I just listen.

"Why haven't you asked me why I brought my dog with me today, Rachel?"

I shrug. "I didn't think about it much."

"Do you know why I wear this?" He holds up his wrist.

"It's a med-alert bracelet."

"Yes." He nods. "I wear it so that, if I have a medical emergency, the EMTs—or whoever helps me—will know all about my condition."

"Your condition?" I echo. "What kind of condition?"

"Epilepsy. Seizures." He nods at the floor beside him. "Cookie is a service dog. She's been trained to help me manage it. She can sense subtle changes in my body that I wouldn't necessarily be able to detect myself. Things like increased heart rate, different breathing patterns, the way I smell—anything that might indicate I'm about to have an episode. She lets me know if something's not right. Dogs are amazing creatures."

I look at Cookie. She's breathing with her mouth open, her tongue hanging out, a few drops of saliva making the beginnings of a puddle on the dirty linoleum. She doesn't seem to be paying any attention whatsoever to Ryan. "Is she actually helpful?" I ask.

"Yes. She's amazing."

"But she freaked out for no reason a few minutes ago. When the lights flickered, both times, she started barking and yelping. Why did she do that? Was she trying to warn you?"

He shakes his head. "I don't think so, not exactly. I've never been sensitive to light patterns. They're not a trigger for me, at least not yet."

I shake my head, fidgeting with irritation. "So what then? She was wrong? She was scared of the dark?"

He smiles, revealing a dimple that I hadn't noticed before. "Now it's my turn to sound crazy."

I smile back. "Go ahead."

"I'm not sure where to start," he begins. "Nobody fully understands what causes epilepsy. There are lots of theories. And some people think it has to do with higher functions of the brain, with things we aren't able to study just yet. Our brains give off electrical impulses, and they're more power-ful for some people—for people like me. When the lights flickered, both times . . . that was me, Rachel. I did it." He pauses, gauging me for my reaction. "What do you think about that?"

I bite my bottom lip, trying to suppress my spreading grin. "I think it sounds insane."

He leans against the table, closer to me; the gesture is intimate without being uncomfortable. I can tell that we both understand we are alike somehow, less alone in the world as we sit together in this little room, sharing our secrets with each other, basking in the comfort of acceptance.

"I've never been able to wear a watch," he tells me, "because the battery goes dead almost instantly. I've gone through five cell phones in the past *year*. Every one of them has malfunctioned, or else they don't keep a charge, or they just burn out."

The thrill humming through me is so strong that I almost can't breathe.

"Energy takes all kinds of different forms in ways that we don't understand," he continues, echoing his words from a few minutes earlier. "There's so much we don't know yet. The mind is a powerful thing."

"You're right," I agree. But as much as I'm enjoying talking with him, feeling so comfortable, I haven't forgotten what brought me here in the first place. "If you really believe everything I've told you—if you believe that my sister is in danger—then help me find her. Please."

"I will." And he inches his fingers across the table, bringing them closer to mine but not quite touching. "You know she's in trouble, Rachel. You must have some idea of what happened, even if it's just an inkling. Think," he urges me. "What does your gut tell you?"

My thoughts flash back to my conversation with Officer Balest the day before. I remember what he said about Occam's razor: the most obvious solution to a problem is usually the correct one.

I'm not ready to tell him the whole truth, but I need to tell him the closest thing possible.

"My sister stole some money from an empty house on Pennsylvania Avenue."

He doesn't react much. He reaches for his pen and paper. "How much money?"

"Ten thousand dollars."

He gives me a quick, startled glance, and I can tell he wasn't expecting such a huge amount. "Besides you, who else knows that she took it?"

"I didn't think anybody else knew. But someone must have seen something. Maybe he was watching her. Maybe he has a camera set up somewhere, and he saw what she did. I don't know. But it makes sense, doesn't it? If he wanted his money back, he might have taken my sister. It's the only possibility I can come up with."

Ryan's pen goes still. Looking at me, he says, "You keep saying 'he.' Does he have a name?"

I nod. "Yes, he does. His name is Marcus Hahn."

CHAPTER THIRTEEN

Once we've finished our conversation, Ryan walks me down the hall in the station, Cookie trotting faithfully at his side the whole way.

"You said she goes everywhere with you. Why wasn't she at my house yesterday?" I ask, nodding at the dog.

"My partner doesn't like to take her on calls." He glances at Cookie with a look of adoration. "Isn't that right, girl?"

"Why not?" We're near the receptionist's desk, which is a few steps away from the door to the women's restroom. Larraine is on the phone again. She seems oblivious to our presence.

"He thinks it makes us seem unprofessional." Ryan shrugs. "I think it would seem more unprofessional if I had a grand mal seizure in the middle of a stranger's living room, but what do I know?"

Larraine shoots us a look of annoyance. She brings a finger

to her lips in a shushing gesture. "Do you have a nice, fancy punch bowl?" she asks whoever's on the other end of her call. "Okay, then. You're gonna need four parts lemon-lime soda, two parts orange juice, and five cups of orange sherbet. I like to add a fifth of peach schnapps, too, but that's optional."

"Larraine," Ryan says, "I need your help with something."

She holds up her index finger and mouths, "Wait."

Ryan rolls his eyes. Then he raises his voice and asks me, "Have you ever thought about working as a receptionist part time, Rachel? We could really use some help around here."

I giggle. Larraine scowls at both of us. "Patty, let me call you back in a few minutes. . . . Sure, you can use generic. . . . Well, if you've got a good coupon, then by all means. . . . Okay, sweetie. Bye now."

After she hangs up, she crosses her arms against her chest—she's wearing a yellow sweater embroidered with big maple leaves and smiling chipmunks—and asks, "Yes?"

"I need Balest," Ryan says. "Can you get him on the phone?"

She gives us a doubtful look. "He's up in the mountains. I don't think there's cell reception."

"Try him. If you don't get through right away, keep calling until you do. It's important."

She's obviously put out at being charged with such a monumental task. "All right," she says, tucking a pen into her shellacked hairdo. "I'll do my best."

According to the clock on her desk, I've been at the station for over an hour. I hope Kimber is still waiting for me.

"Thank you," I say to Ryan. And even though I know I shouldn't, I reach out and put a hand on his arm. He doesn't seem to mind.

"Of course. We'll be in touch." He takes a step backward, and my hand slips away. He nods at the door to the restroom. "Go clean yourself up. Then go to school."

℗

I take my time working on my makeup in the bathroom, reapplying foundation and powder until the bruises beneath my eyes are all but invisible. When I leave, Ryan is gone and Larraine isn't at her desk.

Kimber is studying SAT vocabulary flash cards when I climb back into the car. "How'd it go?" she asks, not looking up, her gaze focused on "trepidation."

"It was good. Really, really good."

"That's great," she says without enthusiasm. She tucks the cards into her purse and adjusts her rearview mirror, studying her reflection for a few seconds. "Where do you want to go now?"

"My grandma's house," I tell her. "She lives out past the Shur-Save plaza. The one on the north side of town."

Kimber gives me a blank look. "What street?"

"Go straight," I say. "I'll explain how to get there."

As Kimber drives, I try to convince myself of the possibility that my sister is at my grandma's house, that maybe she slipped away on Saturday night and got hurt somehow.

In my gut, though, I know it's not likely. I'm reluctant to admit it to myself, but the truth, I realize, is that I just want to see my grandma, to tell her in my own words what's happening. She probably won't be any real help, but she might be able to offer some comfort at the very least. And on the minuscule chance that my sister *is* at my grandma's, it's actually plausible that she would help Rachel hide out, even going so far as to lie to my aunt, her own daughter.

But if Rachel were there, I would know. I would feel her. Her pull on me would not have simply disintegrated the moment she left my sight at the fair.

"Here," I direct Kimber, nodding as we approach a four-way intersection that crosses the trail. "Make a right. Then make a left onto Route 119. You'll go for about a mile, and then you'll turn right again onto Foxtail Road. She lives back there." My grandma's farm is close to town, but Greensburg is surrounded on all sides by woods and country. You only have to drive for a few minutes in order to feel like you're in the middle of nowhere.

As we travel down Route 119, we pass restaurants: there's a Denny's, a Cracker Barrel, and a McDonald's. There's a strip mall containing a Shur-Save discount grocery, a consignment store, a do-it-yourself pet grooming salon, a notary public, and a methadone clinic. Meth clinics are for heroin addicts who are trying to clean up their act; I guess the methadone keeps them from being able to get high somehow. The clinic went in last year, despite rampant protests from the community, who objected to its placement so close to the trail. Apparently, thanks to the overall mismanagement of their lives, lots of heroin addicts don't have cars—so they walk to the clinic instead. You can always spot them on the trail; usually they're in groups of three or four people, shuffling along, chain-smoking, and keeping their heads down. They know nobody wants them around. It's not even eleven a.m. and already there's a line of about a dozen people, both men and women, going all the way out the door.

Kimber has been quiet for the past few minutes. As we approach the turn onto Foxtail Road, she brings the car to a rolling stop at the red light. Then she nods to the left, her eyes narrowing as she stares at the huge brick building complex situated on the hillside. The buildings are surrounded by high metal fencing, topped with shiny loops of barbed wire. It's the state prison.

"Wave to my daddy," she murmurs. Her tone is both sad and sarcastic.

"Oh, yeah." I lower my sunglasses to peer at the structure. If it weren't for the barbed wire, the gated entrance, the guard-occupied security booth, and the huge sign that reads STATE CORRECTIONAL INSTITUTE, the place could almost be mistaken for something less menacing, like a college or a hospital.

"Has he been there ever since . . . ? I mean—"

"Ever since he tried to kill me and my mother?" she asks, her voice bitter. "Yeah. It's lovely that we still get to be neighbors, isn't it?"

She makes the right turn onto Foxtail Road. This is the

first time I've ever heard Kimber say anything about her dad. Until now, everything I knew about the incident came from other sources. It happened years ago, but people still talk about it. After the fire, Kimber's old house was leveled down to the foundation, but nobody has done anything with the lot since then. It's just *there*, only a few blocks from Kimber's new house that she shares with her mom, a constant reminder of what happened.

"Have you ever thought about going to visit him?"

She gives me a sharp look. "No."

". . ."

". . ."

"Sorry," I tell her. "I didn't mean to pry. It's just . . . I don't know . . . I can't imagine what it must feel like."

"It feels fantastic. How do you think it feels?" The prison slips out of sight as we continue down the narrow, curvy road. We are surrounded by tall pine trees on both sides. *Over the river and through the woods, to Grandmother's house we go . . .*

"I'm sorry," I say again.

She shakes her head. "It's okay. It's funny that you asked, though. I'll probably see him later this week, as much as I don't want to." And she nods toward the floor of the passenger side, where the items that spilled from the glove box a few moments earlier are still in a messy pile. "Can you put that stuff away?"

I lean over and start placing things back inside the compartment. The door has been hanging open all this time. As

I'm doing so, Kimber tells me, "It's not like I ever stop thinking about him. All I have to do is look in the mirror. Every
morning when I get dressed. Every time I take a shower."

I've seen the scars on her back a few times before. They're
horrible. And I know now how she must feel, at least to some
extent: every time I look in the mirror, I am reminded of my
sister.

"So why are you going to see him now? I mean, after all
these years?"

She snorts. "Because the district attorney called my house
a few months ago. My dad is up for parole in November—
there's going to be a hearing on Friday. I might have to testify."
She blinks a few times, staring straight ahead. "I'm going to
try and keep him in jail."

And without any warning, she reaches into her shirt,
into her bra. In a swift, practiced motion, she tugs at each
side of her chest. Then she hands something to me: two flesh-
colored, rubbery half moons, which are sticky on one side
and warm all over from being so close to her body.

I stare at them in my hands, shocked. Kimber is a private, shy person; never in a million years would I expect
her to hand me something from her bra.

"Put those in the glove box, too," she instructs me. Her
voice is cold, but it wavers with the slightest hint of embarrassment, as though even she can't believe what she's just
done.

I can't stop looking at them. "What are these?"

She continues to stare straight ahead. "They're my breasts, Rachel. The fire ruined me. It killed so much tissue that I'll never have normal ones, so I wear these instead."

I don't know what to say. How am I supposed to respond? All I can think to do is rest the inserts carefully on top of the driver's manual and close the door to the glove box.

We are approaching my grandmother's long gravel driveway. "Pull in here," I tell her quietly.

She brings the car to a stop outside the house. She shuts off the engine, turns to me, and places a hand gently on my arm. "Hey. I'm sorry. I wasn't trying to freak you out back there. I'm not sure what I was thinking. I didn't mean to make this about me, either. I shouldn't have said anything."

"It's fine. You can tell me whatever you want." *Oh, Kimber.* I feel a pang of guilt for my recent dismissive attitude toward her.

"Those things—my mom calls them cutlets—they get all hot and sweaty. I hate wearing them every day." And she shrugs. "I don't know why I bother, anyway. I guess I just want to look normal, from the outside at least. I'm not trying to attract attention from boys or anyone. I don't want you to think that."

I shake my head. "That isn't what I thought."

"It's not like I'm going to fool anybody into thinking I'm beautiful." She tosses her keys into her purse. "Not that it matters. Nobody wants to date a freak, right?"

"Kimber . . ."

She shakes her head. "Stop. Don't say anything else. I'm sorry I brought it up at all."

There is a silence, not so much awkward as it is filled with unspoken thoughts; I can tell we both have plenty of them.

Kimber looks at our surroundings, like she's noticing them for the first time. Just beyond the gravel driveway, in a wide clearing on a hillside, there is a big brick Colonial house covered in dark-green ivy. A crooked wooden porch wraps around the entire first floor. Beyond the house, there's a large red barn. This place hasn't been a working farm in decades; in the field beside the house, a rusty, broken tractor rests on the ground, surrounded by tall grass. It's like somebody, many years ago, decided to take his lunch break in the middle of working the land and simply never returned.

"Your grandma lives here?" she asks. "This is beautiful. I never knew this place even existed."

"Yep. This is our family's old farm." I open my door and climb out of the car, sliding my purse onto my shoulder. "Come on."

"You think Alice might be here?" Kimber steps gingerly on the uneven ground, large patches of dirt and rocks mingled with the grass beneath us.

"I don't know," I say, staring at the house. I cannot set foot in this place without thinking of my childhood and all the times we used to spend here as a family: my parents, my sister, and myself. We visited as often as once a week, mostly on Sundays. Even when my grandma wasn't here, away on one of her many stints at the state hospital, we still came by to check on the place all the time.

My mother never seemed to resent my grandma for her problems. She was always gentle and loving and patient, even when my grandma was out of control. I remember arriving one Sunday morning, years ago, to find her—she was in her fifties—up on the roof, still in her nightgown. She was painting the eaves of the house bright green for no particular reason. Once my parents coaxed her down, she admitted that she hadn't slept in almost four days.

When we were kids, my parents never explained much about my grandma's condition. They simply told us she was sick. "Sometimes people's bodies get sick," my mom would say, "and sometimes our minds get sick."

As a child, I was confused by the explanation. "But she has a gift," I said. "She knows things other people don't. You've told me so yourself. How does that make her sick?" To me, it only made her extraordinary.

The question didn't faze my mother; I realize now that she'd probably given the matter plenty of thought herself. "It's a fine line," she told me. "Sometimes it can be hard to tell the difference. And sometimes the line is . . . blurred."

ᏆᎧ

My aunt has never been nearly as tactful. She throws around words like "crazy" and "delusional" and "destructive." She only references her childhood in terms of neglect and unhappiness. My grandma first started to show signs of illness when my aunt and mom were toddlers. After their father died, there were times when my grandma wasn't able to care for them, and they ended up in and out of foster care until they were teenagers. My aunt can't let it go.

My mother and her sister dealt with their upbringing in very different ways. My mom threw herself into art, using her creativity to disguise whatever hard feelings might have lingered inside her, turning her suffering into beauty. But she was also a little unstable, maybe never quite as invested in reality as she should have been. I didn't understand that as a child, but I do now.

My aunt is the polar opposite of her mother and sister. She clings to order and logic and facts, like they're somehow more reliable than emotion, which can get so out of control if it comes unhinged. She's afraid of ending up like my grandma; that much is obvious. But what she doesn't seem to understand is that you can't make something go away simply by ignoring it.

That's why my aunt will never accept that I have any special connection to my sister. The idea is too close to the insanity that she grew up with for her to acknowledge that it might be real.

"Are you okay?" Kimber is staring, waiting for me to move toward the house so she can follow. She squints at me. "Rachel?"

At the sound of my sister's name, an achy wave of guilt

ripples through my body. It should have been me who disappeared on Saturday.

If I pretend hard enough, could I make it true? Could I make it happen by simply ignoring the truth? I could almost be her right now. I could fool everyone. And would they even miss me—would they miss Alice? Would they wish I hadn't disappeared? Or would they be content for the rest of their lives, believing my sister had been spared whatever happened to her twin?

Because I could do it, if I wanted to. If I put my whole self into it, I could become Rachel—I know I could. I could make Alice disappear forever. And maybe everyone would be happier that way.

Chapter Fourteen

After our parents' deaths, my sister and I came to understand certain facts that no nine-year-olds should ever have to contemplate. We learned, for instance, that our parents had been desperately broke: living on a single teacher's salary, struggling to keep up with student-loan payments and a mortgage, while still supporting themselves and their daughters. We learned that there had been no life insurance to speak of—and while we might not have understood exactly what life insurance was at the time, we could pick up enough meaning from our relatives' tones to know it was pretty important.

We learned that neither one of them had bothered to draft a will. Our grandmother covered the cost for our mother's funeral; our father's parents, who had lived in Las Vegas all our lives and who we rarely saw, paid for his casket and burial. It was sort of like the way a bride and groom's parents divvy up costs for a wedding, except it wasn't like that at all.

We learned by listening. Eavesdropping, really. My sister and I began staying with our aunt and uncle almost immediately after the accident. When they gave us our tour of the house, they made a point of not showing us the secret stairwell. It makes sense that they wouldn't want us to know about it; the stairs are steep and could be dangerous for a child. And the doors—especially the one that leads into the kitchen—tend to stick. Of course they didn't want us crawling around in the darkness alone either.

But after we'd been living there for a week or so, Charlie found a quiet moment when we were watching television together downstairs to bring up the subject. He was only thirteen back then. My sister and I understood that he was slower than we were, but the difference didn't seem nearly as pronounced at the time.

We were watching *The Price is Right*, the three of us sipping soda from plastic cups, uncomfortable, staring at the screen, pretending to be engrossed in the game show. Up to that point, Charlie had been extremely shy around us.

"Hey," he'd said, brightening, looking around to make sure his parents weren't anywhere they could hear us. "Do you guys want to see something cool?"

Rachel and I exchanged a wary glance. We didn't answer him at first.

"I mean it," he said. "It's awesome. You guys aren't supposed to know about it. I'm breaking a rule."

Even at that age—and even in the wake of my parents' deaths—I was drawn to breaking rules. I nodded at Charlie. "Okay."

Rachel was more hesitant. "I don't know," she said, weaving her fingers through mine. "I don't want to get into trouble." She shifted her gaze to our cousin. "How do your parents punish you, Charlie?"

All three of us had neon-green straws in our cups. Distracted, Charlie blew air bubbles into his drink. "What do you mean, *punish*?" he asked. "Like when I get into trouble?"

Rachel nodded. "Yeah. Do you get sent to your room? Or do they do something different?"

It seemed like a fair enough question. We might have been related to them, but we'd only known these people for a week. Who knew what they might do if they caught us snooping around their house without permission?

But Charlie only shrugged. "I'm not sure," he told Rachel. "I hardly ever get into trouble." He paused. "Are you gonna let me show you?" His eyes were bright and warm. I barely knew him, but I loved him already. "You'll like it. I promise."

So we followed him to the guest room. We watched as his chubby fingers pressed against an ordinary-looking part of the wall, and together we gasped as the door swung open, almost like it had materialized from out of nowhere.

"See?" Charlie asked, obviously pleased with himself. "It's a secret passage. It leads into the kitchen. There's another door down there, in the wall next to the fridge."

My sister and I peered inside the dark stairwell. "It's cold," Rachel said.

We could hear voices lilting up from the kitchen. It was our aunt and uncle, along with our grandmother, the three of them having a heated discussion about something.

"Don't tell anyone that I showed you. I wasn't supposed to," Charlie said.

I glanced back at him. He gave me a shy, sincere smile. I pulled my thumb and index finger across my lips, like I was zipping them shut. Then I pretended to toss the key across the room.

⚭

After that day, my sister and I began to spend hours in the stairwell, listening. It was how we learned that my aunt and uncle refused to let my grandmother—who Rachel and I adored—take custody of us. My aunt claimed that our grandmother was unstable. Even though a part of me suspected she was right, at the time it seemed cruel that we weren't allowed to stay with the relative we were closest to, instead of having to move in with people who were basically strangers. But even though Aunt Sharon and our mom hadn't spoken for years, she explained to our grandma in hushed, angry tones that she would be *damned* if she'd let her raise us.

"You think I'm incompetent?" our grandma had asked,

sounding more amused than upset. "You turned out just fine, didn't you? Here you are, a nice house, good family—what are you so worried about?"

Although I couldn't see my aunt, I pictured her so clearly in my mind: her eyes shut, fists clenched in frustration, genuine fury in her voice—yet I was certain that if I could have seen her right then, she wouldn't have a single hair out of place. "Mother, you need to let this go. We will take you to court, and we will win. You cannot raise these girls." She'd paused. "Not like you raised me and Anna. Especially Anna."

My sister nudged me from her place beside me on the stairs. I could barely see her in the dark, but I understood immediately what she was feeling. Her breath was ragged. A warm dampness seemed to rise from her body: sweat combined with flushed panic, the rapid heartbeat of someone who felt helpless and trapped. She didn't want to listen anymore, I knew. And from that day on, I went into the stairwell alone.

❦

Today, Kimber and I find my sixty-year-old grandmother standing in her kitchen, her clothing covered in blackberry juice, her hands stained a deep shade of purple. Her countertops are lined with empty mason jars. A huge silver pot filled with dark-purple goo simmers on the stove. The room smells so sweet that it's almost overwhelming. She's making jelly,

I'm guessing, which is an extremely uncharacteristic thing for my grandma to do. She barely cooks at all; even though she never stays to visit, my aunt usually brings her over a casserole or something every Sunday, and it lasts pretty much all week. My grandma is rail-thin, and I've heard her complain more than once that her medication takes away her appetite. It could also have something to do with the fact that she chain-smokes and drinks coffee all day.

"Hello, ladies," she says, smiling graciously, almost like she was expecting us. She's wearing an apron, which is also out of character; I'm surprised she even owns one. Underneath it, she's wearing a pale-pink nightgown, which is really more of a slip. Her feet are bare. Her hair, which she's been dyeing red ever since it started going gray, falls past her shoulders in gentle waves. It's the hair of a much younger woman, and it might look ridiculous on anybody else her age, but somehow she pulls it off. Her face is wrinkled but still beautiful, her eyes sharp and deep blue, her makeup subtle except for her lips, which are painted a bright red. In her right hand, she holds a lit cigarette between her index and middle finger. Every few seconds she takes a dainty puff, blowing smoke rings into the air. I've never heard her say anything about wanting to quit.

After I've made the introductions between my grandmother and Kimber, I take a harder look around the kitchen. It's a huge mess; she'll be working for days to get it cleaned up, if she bothers to clean it up at all. She might just wait for my aunt to come over, notice the mess, and take care of it for her.

"I know what you're thinking," my grandma says, dragging on her cigarette, "but I had no other choice. I had all these berries in the basement freezer. Jack Allen's wife, Louise, grew them in her garden." My grandma gives a little snort of amusement. "Louise passed away two weeks ago. Jack is moving to Pine Ridge—that's an assisted-living facility—so he's cleaning out their house. Now here I am, stuck with a dead woman's berry stash. How the hell am I going to eat them? I'm not a bird. So I thought, well, I'm an old lady. Aren't we supposed to do things like this?" She winks at Kimber. "But it's my special recipe. Medicinal jelly. I should put up a stand outside the senior center downtown. What do you think I could charge—forty dollars a jar? Fifty? I won't go lower than thirty-five. I need the money. I'm on a fixed income, you know."

Kimber is confused, and I'm not surprised; I didn't say anything to prepare her for my grandma's . . . personality. "Why is it medicinal?" she asks.

Without any hesitation, my grandmother replies, "Why do you think? It's pot jelly."

Kimber gives me a panicked glance. I giggle.

"She's kidding," I explain. "It's just regular jelly." At least I hope she's kidding. I'm fairly certain that reefer jelly won't complement my grandma's pharmaceutical regimen too well.

"Bullshit." My grandma grinds out her cigarette in a clay

ashtray. "That's the thing about being older. You can get away with anything. Even shoplifting!"

"Grandma—" I begin, but she interrupts me.

"I know why you're here." She fans the smoke in the air. "You're looking for your sister."

Kimber and I both nod. I open my mouth, ready to launch into an explanation of recent events, but my grandma doesn't seem interested in listening at the moment. She has other ideas. She turns abruptly, collects half a dozen sealed jars of jelly, and presses them into my arms. "Before we discuss this," she says, "take these into the barn real quick for me. Put them on the shelves."

"Here," Kimber says, leaping at the opportunity to get away from my grandma, who I guess must seem downright creepy to someone as wholesome as Kimber. "Let me help you, Rachel."

"Oh, please. Stay with me, would you?" My grandma's voice becomes falsely meek and pathetic. "It's so rare for me to get company . . . especially now that Louise is gone."

There is an uncomfortable pause as Kimber—who seems torn between the polite thing to do and what she obviously wants to do (avoid being alone with my grandma)—presses her rosy, full lips together, doing her best not to pout.

With my arms full of jars, I begin to back away. "You know, Kimber is a Girl Scout," I tell my grandma.

Kimber shoots me a desperate look. I shrug apologetically. "I'll be right back," I tell her.

As I'm going down the hall toward the front door, I hear Kimber ask, "Was the woman who passed away—Louise—a close friend of yours?"

"Not really," my grandma says. "She was a Republican."

"Oh." Pause. "How did she, um, can I ask—"

"How did she die? Well, she was eighty-four, so that should be obvious, shouldn't it?"

"Uh . . . you mean because she was very elderly? So I take it she was in poor health?"

"No," my grandma replies, "she was in fine health." I hear the distinct hiss of a match as she lights another cigarette. "It was a waterskiing accident."

ॐ

The barn sits at the bottom of the hillside, a few feet from the driveway and Kimber's car. Although my grandma doesn't use it much, my aunt and uncle make sure the building stays in decent repair. A few summers ago they had it repainted and had the roof replaced. Still, it's only a barn: it has a dirt floor, plenty of spiderwebs (and spiders), and no heat. Inside, the only source of light comes from a few bare bulbs scattered around the walls, their wiring exposed, simply stapled to the wood.

Since my arms are full, I nudge one of the wooden doors with my hip. There is an immediate blast of cold as I step into the dark, damp space. A long, narrow triangle of light illuminates the dirty floor, the air filled with thousands of tiny specks of dust, as the door drifts all the way open.

I feel like a child. I feel afraid. There are rustling sounds in the darkness, but I can't tell exactly where they're coming from. There could be all kinds of creatures hiding in here. I gather the jars in one arm, and then I use my free hand to feel along the wall for the light switch. Directly behind me, outside, it is a bright and lovely day; yet standing in the barn makes me feel like I've stepped into another world. The daylight over my shoulder seems to be getting farther away with each second, like I'm being pulled against my will through a dark tunnel, leaving the light behind. There is a musty, unpleasant odor in the air, but I can't quite place the smell. I consider setting the jars down on the ground right in front of me and leaving, not bothering to put them on the shelves, which are on the opposite end of the barn. The light coming from the burning bulbs is dim; the exposed wood beams in the walls look like hovering figures all around me. The rustling sound persists. It is quiet enough that I might not have noticed it if I weren't alone in here, if my senses weren't heightened by my anxiety and the darkness.

I squint, looking around, trying to focus on the noise, to stay calm, to steady myself. There is a sudden loud snapping sound, like somebody or something has stepped on a twig. And then I realize: the noises are coming from the hayloft.

Behind me, the door creaks back and forth in the light breeze. The noise could be anything. It could be something as innocent as a squirrel or the wind coming through a crack in the wall. The smell, so pungent and unpleasant, is probably just the smell of an old barn: wood chewed away by insects from the inside out, piles of who knows what stacked against the walls, my grandmother's random stuff collected over the decades and stashed away, unused but still wanted. She likes to hold on to things. It's not so much a matter of being sentimental as it is a matter of her being sort of insane.

The smell is stronger now. It might as well be seeping from the walls. All of a sudden, I recognize it, plain as anything: it's the smell of rotting apples, the odor sweet and damp and rancid. There are several crab apple trees on my grandma's property. When my sister and I were younger, our parents used to keep us occupied during visits here by giving us paper grocery bags and sending us into the field to collect the apples that had fallen onto the ground. Usually they were rotting, chewed by bugs in places, obviously not fit to eat. But I remember the way my hands would smell after an afternoon spent gathering apples. They smelled like this place, right here and now. Back then the smell didn't bother me; I was so happy to be outside with my sister, just the two of us alone, the rest of the world a distraction that we could simply ignore. Today, the smell is overwhelming, so unsettling that my skin feels electric with fear.

I need more light. I walk along the wall, running my hand against the wood, until my fingers find another switch.

I turn it on; a bulb a few feet ahead of me glows to life in its socket, crackles loudly, and burns out almost before I have a chance to get a better look at the inside of the barn.

Almost. In the few seconds that I can see more clearly, my gaze shifts toward the hay loft, where the rustling sound seems to be coming from. And I see something: hunched, waiting, watching me: it's a person. A girl.

As my arms go limp, the jars I've been carrying fall to the floor, shattering at my feet. But I don't care; I barely even notice. Standing in the darkness, I don't have to see the person above me in the light to know exactly what she looks like.

It's Rachel.

CHAPTER FIFTEEN

Something is wrong. As I rush toward the hayloft, frantic, my sister tries to crawl toward the edge on her hands and knees, but she's having trouble; she shuffles forward a few inches and then stops, pulls herself into a tight ball, and rocks gently back and forth. She's wearing the same outfit from the night she vanished: denim skirt, tank top, leggings—but her feet are bare, their soles black with dirt, and her clothes are filthy. But she's here. She's alone. If I can only get to her somehow, I can bring her home.

"Where's the ladder?" My voice is high and scratchy, echoing off the walls. She doesn't speak, responding instead by shaking her head and pressing two fingers to her lips. Her hands are clasped, like an invisible cord is binding them together.

"Say something!" I plead, pacing back and forth beneath the periphery of the loft, searching for a way to reach her. I don't see the ladder anywhere; I have no idea how she could have gotten up there by herself.

She presses a hand to her throat, her eyes wide and frightened, and shakes her head.

"What's the matter? Why can't you talk to me?"

Her fingertips flutter against her neck; she's lost her voice.

"Rachel, what are you doing up there? Where have you been? Why did you leave me?" She's so close to me, but I feel an oppressive sense of urgency, like if I don't find some way to get to her *right now*, it might be too late.

Her gaze shifts back and forth across the barn, like she's searching for an answer. She gives me another helpless look as she points toward the door.

"Does Grandma know you're in here?"

Another shake of her head.

"Can you get down? Kimber's with me. We have her car, Rachel. We can take you home right now. Everything will be okay." I reach upward, extending my arms as far as I can, standing on my tiptoes, urging her to come closer, even though the distance between us is too far to make contact.

"I have to get a ladder. I'll be right back," I tell her, stepping away, preparing to run toward the house for help.

She doesn't want me to leave; that much is clear. Her gaze is pleading, desperate, as she falls onto all fours again and scrambles along the edge of the loft. I can hear her knees scraping against the old wooden boards, the heels of her hands dragging across the dull, splintered surface as she struggles to crawl closer to me.

"I'll be back in five minutes," I tell her, "I promise." But I can't bring myself to leave her alone. I glance toward the door again, at my grandma's house on the hill. Why do I feel so afraid right now? Why do I feel like I shouldn't go, like she'll be gone when I return?

Sitting back on her heels again, my sister opens her mouth wide and gestures to her teeth, tapping her fingernails against her incisors. With her thumb and forefinger, she begins to wiggle one of them. I can tell the tooth is already loose as she tugs it back and forth, but the act is still hard to watch.

"What are you doing?" I shriek. "Stop it!"

I can't believe what I'm seeing; it's almost like I'm watching a movie play out on a screen. Her form seems to flicker right before my eyes; the light, which is already dim, recedes further, until I can hardly see anything at all. In the darkness, I can only make out her teeth now; they seem to glow as she pulls, twisting her fingers back and forth until her mouth is smeared with blood.

Rachel yanks out her tooth. My stomach curdles. I clap a hand to my mouth, muffling my scream as I gag.

She reaches into her mouth, peeling her upper lip back to expose the newly formed gap between her teeth. The act is so grotesque, so unbearable to witness, that my steps stutter backward as I turn away, running toward the door.

The tip of my shoe catches on something bumping up from the dirt floor, and I trip, falling hard. I don't have enough time to brace myself against the fall; my body hits the ground with a hard *thump*, knocking the wind out of me for the second time today. As I struggle to pull a breath into my lungs, bursts of blackness appear like inkblots in my line of vision.

Finally, I find air. But I remain crouched on the ground for a moment longer, waiting for the black dots and my dizziness to dissipate, blinking as I try to regain my sense of balance. Climbing to my feet, I look around in confusion that quickly tunnels into stunned disbelief.

The barn—so dark and unsettling just a moment ago—is brightly lit now, the atmosphere cheerful and innocuous; I look up to see two rows of fluorescent bulbs running along the highest point in the ceiling, buzzing softly as they glow.

I'm still a little dizzy and confused from my fall, but I'm not *that* confused; I know what I saw before the lights somehow came on. I know Rachel was here. I glance toward the loft, which is bare except for several piles of hay.

What just happened? Rachel was here; I'm certain of it. But where did she go? The only explanation I can come up with is that she's crawled behind the hay, that she's hidden herself from me for some reason.

"Rachel!" I shout, hurrying toward the edge. "Rachel, where are you?"

But there's no answer. Everything is still. She must be up

there, I know, but she doesn't want to come down. It doesn't make any sense.

I should get help. As much as I don't want to leave my sister alone in here, I have no way of getting to her on my own. Leaving the lights on—I can't bear the thought of shutting them off and abandoning her in the darkness—I run outside, up the hill toward my grandma's house, barely pausing to regain my footing even as I stumble through the doorway, rushing down the hall and into the kitchen.

My grandmother leans against the counter as she takes leisurely puffs from a cigarette. Her clothing is covered in blackberry juice, her hands stained a deep shade of purple. Empty mason jars are lined up against the wall behind her. A huge silver pot filled with dark-purple goo simmers on the stove. The room smells so sweet that it's almost overwhelming. She's making jelly.

Something isn't right; I can tell. Neither Kimber or my grandma seem the least bit startled by my breathless appearance, even as I gaze back and forth at them in confusion.

"I know it's not like me to cook," my grandma says, dragging on her cigarette, gesturing to the mess all around her, "but what was I supposed to do? Jack Allen's wife, Louise, passed away a few weeks ago, and Jack is already moving up to Pine Ridge—that's an assisted-living facility—so he's clearing out the house, including everything from Louise's gardens. He told me he thought Louise would want me to have the berries. Ha! I took them—just to be polite, you know—but how the hell am I going to eat them? So I figured I'd make jam." She pauses, frowning. "Or maybe it's actually jelly. I don't know the difference." She gives us a conspiratorial giggle. "I have a special recipe, though. This is medicinal jelly. I'm thinking about selling it at the senior center. I could make a killing." She pauses. "Well—so to speak."

"What makes it medicinal?" Kimber asks, glancing at me. All I can do is stare at them. Their words sound hollow and tinny, like there's an echo in the room.

"You don't know? You're a teenager, aren't you?" my grandma replies, grinning. "It's pot jelly."

What the hell is going on? Why is this happening again? It's like the record has skipped, and I'm the only one who noticed. Even as I speak, trying to sound calm and normal despite how disturbed I feel, the words seem like they're not mine as they're coming from my mouth.

"You're kidding, Grandma," I say weakly. "It's not pot jelly."

"Fine. Believe what you want." My grandma grinds her cigarette out in an ashtray. "But I'll tell you both, that's the wonderful thing about being old. You can get away with just about anything."

"Grandma—" I begin, but she interrupts me.

"I know why you're here, kiddo." She fans the smoke in the air. "You're trying to find your sister. Isn't that right?"

This is impossible. It's like some kind of sick joke. Why would they do this to me? But what other explanation could there be? Don't they realize we just had almost the exact same conversation?

Before I can continue, my grandma presses half a dozen jars of jelly into my arms. "We'll talk about this soon," she says. "But first I want you to take these into the barn real quick for me, okay? Find some room on the shelves."

"Here," Kimber says. "I'll help you, Rachel."

"Oh no. Stay here with me, would you?" my grandma asks. "I love having company. I get so lonely all by myself here, day after day."

Kimber presses her lips together, doing her best not to pout. *I have to go back to the barn,* I think. *She'll be there.*

"You should stay," I tell Kimber, backing out of the room with my arms full of jars. "I'll be quick."

Kimber shoots me a desperate look. She can't possibly be messing around with me, could she? Maybe my grandma convinced her it would be funny. But I'm obviously not laughing—so why are they continuing to act this way?

As I'm walking down the hall, I hear Kimber ask, "So this woman who passed away—Louise—were the two of you close?"

"I wouldn't say that," my grandma says. "She was a bore."

"Oh." Pause. "May I ask how she . . . ?"

"How did she die? Well, she was in her eighties, so it should be obvious, shouldn't it?"

"I see," Kimber says. "Was she in poor health?"

"No," my grandma replies, "she was fine." A match hisses

to life as she lights another cigarette. "Her parachute didn't open."

⤴

The barn is fully illuminated, the bright fluorescent lights buzzing overhead. It seems empty. As I place the jars on a shelf—there is no trace of the shattered ones from just a few moments earlier—they feel oddly heavy; I have to tighten my grip to keep them from sliding out of my hand.

I stare up at the loft, expecting to see Rachel. She isn't there. But she *was*—wasn't she? Why can't I think straight? I'm *exhausted*; I almost feel like I could curl up right here on the dirt floor and go to sleep.

There's nobody here except me, I know. I can feel a goose egg forming on the side of my head; I must have bumped it when I tripped and fell earlier. Maybe I blacked out for a few seconds.

There was no ladder before, but there's one now: silver and sturdy, leading toward the loft. I rush toward it and climb two rungs at a time, so rushed and shaky that my feet slip a few times on my way up.

She isn't here. Not anymore, at least. But where could she have gone so quickly? How did she get the ladder? Was there someone else here, helping her?

I squeeze my eyes shut, struggling to recover my memory. In my mind, I see Rachel crouched in the loft. It's dark. I see her pulling her tooth, twisting it back and forth before she finally yanks it out, the look on her face pleased and hopeful even as I back away, horrified.

She was here; it really happened. Why would I imagine something like that?

I take another long look around, waiting, hoping she'll step out from behind a corner in the barn beneath me or somehow materialize in the loft, but I'm so *tired* all of a sudden—all I can think about is going home and getting some rest. Even if she's still in here, hiding somewhere, she obviously doesn't want to come home yet. Maybe I should leave her alone, give her some time. At least I know she's safe for the moment.

✍

Before I climb down, I crawl around on my hands and knees, studying the patterns on the dusty floor, searching for any sign of her.

"Please come home, Rachel," I say out loud. "I miss you. Everyone is worried about you. I love you. We all love you so much."

Silence.

I breathe a shaky sigh as I bring myself to a sitting position, frustrated by her lack of response, grudgingly accepting of the fact that she isn't ready to leave yet, for some reason. "I love you," I repeat, trying not to cry. "Whatever's going on, you can tell me. I'll understand."

No response.

I bite my bottom lip hard. I'm still disoriented and incredibly tired, my fatigue so overwhelming that I almost feel like I've been drugged. The loft feels so much higher than it did just a second ago; the simple act of climbing down the ladder seems dangerous and intimidating.

As I'm crawling toward the edge, I feel something small and rounded beneath my right palm. I pull my hand away, expecting to see a pebble or a piece of glass in the dirt.

I look down. My body twitches with a jolt of adrenaline as I stare, leaning over to pluck the object from the floor. It is shiny and white in my palm, bigger than I would have expected, its pulpy roots fresh with life, their edges rough and bloody.

It's a tooth.

More than that, though, it's *proof*: Rachel was up here. And she's still around somewhere hiding, unwilling to answer me. For some reason, the fact brings me little comfort.

Before I leave the barn, I slip the tooth into my pocket. As I pull the heavy wooden door shut behind me, I wince at the sunlight, which feels almost painful on my skin. I have no energy; it seems to take effort just to breathe, to walk back up the hill to my grandma's house. I know she and Kimber are inside, waiting for me; I know my grandma expects to talk about my sister. She claims she wants to help me, but I'm not so sure now. She must know that Rachel is out here. Maybe this is all entertainment to her. It's possible, I think, that her mind has deteriorated to the point that she's nothing but crazy now, bored and alone here in this big house, desperate for a way to keep life interesting. It doesn't make much sense to me, but it's the best explanation I can come up with at the moment.

CHAPTER SIXTEEN

At first I can't find my grandma or Kimber anywhere. The farmhouse is huge—it has sixteen rooms in total—but the ceilings are low and my grandma doesn't clean much, so the house tends to be cluttered and dark. After I wander around the downstairs for a minute, listening, I finally hear snippets of Kimber's voice coming from somewhere upstairs.

I find them standing in the hallway outside the only bathroom in the house. Kimber's face is pale, her expression horrified, as my grandmother leans against the wall while she pets an enormous Saint Bernard sitting beside the bathroom door.

"There she is." My grandma winks at me. "I was just introducing your friend to the Captain." She means the dog. I wince, shooting an apologetic glance at Kimber. The Captain belonged to my grandma years ago. After he died, my grandma had him stuffed and placed in the hallway like it was the most normal thing in the world. She still pets him, talks to him, tells him good night and good morning every day. The fur between his shoulder blades is worn thin from so many years of her touch. Even I know that it's creepy, but I've gotten used to it over time. I can't imagine what Kimber must be thinking right now.

"Did you take care of the jam?" My grandma asks the question like it's important.

"Yes," I say. I tug Kimber's arm. "We should go, Grandma. I feel bad showing up out of nowhere. You're in the middle of . . . something." My tone has a harsh edge to it. I don't want to play this game anymore. I could confront her about what's just happened, but I get the feeling she'd only lie to me.

"Right. You girls really interrupted my day." My grandma scratches the top of the Captain's head. "Kimber asked how the Captain died. Do you want to tell her?"

"She asked how he died?" I echo. First it was what happened to my grandma's friend Louise, and now this?

"Go ahead," she says, examining a strand of her red hair for split ends. "Tell her."

I press my lips together, trying to suppress my agitation. There's no way I'm telling this story.

"What's the matter?" my grandma asks.

"Nothing. I don't remember, that's all. It was natural causes, right? He was old."

"Old and sick," my grandma agrees, her eyes sparkling with amusement.

"It's getting late," Kimber interjects. "Rachel is right. We should probably go."

"All right. Go ahead." My grandma stands up straight, and the three of us start to walk toward the stairs. As Kimber moves past her, my grandma reaches out in a quick motion and grasps her by the arm. Her eyes narrow. The hall seems to tunnel. I stop breathing for a second, staring.

She gets like this sometimes. The person I've known all my life slips away and is replaced by someone completely different. I've seen it happen countless times, but I never get used to it. Her typically bright eyes take on a thick glassiness, making them seem almost cloudy. When she speaks, even though her voice has the same tone and pitch, it is somehow different. It seems older. I don't know exactly how to explain it, and I'm not sure if it's more her madness than it is her gift.

Maybe it's both. Like my mom said, it's a blurry line.

Kimber is frozen, staring at my grandmother. I can tell she's scared. She looks ready to cry.

"You're hurting me," she says, the words coming out in a whisper.

The edges of my grandma's mouth curl upward in a slight smile. "There are things much worse than death," she says. "You remember that. Things much worse."

Kimber yanks her arm away. She stands there, rubbing her skin where my grandma took hold, speechless with horror, her breathing shaky and shallow. I wasn't expecting anything like this to happen, but considering everything else that's going on right now, I should have known better than to bring her here. Even though it's been a long time since my grandma has slipped away like this—months, maybe close to a year—it's always a possibility.

And then, all of a sudden, Kimber breaks away from us and runs down the stairs. From the window in the landing, my grandma and I can see her as she rushes toward her car and climbs inside.

"Why'd you do that?" I demand. "You scared the hell out of her."

My grandma gives a shudder. She shakes her head, coming back into herself. "I'm sorry. I didn't mean it. What did I say to her just now?"

I pause. "You don't remember?"

She shakes her head. "I never do, sweetie."

"You said, 'There are worse things than death.'"

"Oh my." She feigns embarrassment, but I can tell she's half amused by all the fuss over what is, to her, a normal occurrence. "I'm sorry. Go after her, then. What a thing to say."

I stare at her. "Grandma, are you okay? Are you taking your pills?" I regret the question immediately. I sound exactly like my aunt.

But my grandma doesn't seem to mind. She simply ignores it, glancing down at the Captain. She gives him a pat on the head. "I think I'll take a nap, sweetheart. We can talk more later. Okay?"

Again, I feel the urge to confront her, but it feels like the wrong time. As weird as it sounds, I'm just too *tired*. "Okay," I agree. "We'll talk soon."

She stands in the hallway, watching as I move down the stairs. Just as I'm reaching the front door, she calls out to me. "Rachel?"

I pause. "Yes?" I ask, not turning around.

"It's true, sweetie. There are worse things. You know that."

What is that even supposed to mean? Does it mean anything at all? Or is it just the ramblings of an old woman, her brain misfiring to form thoughts that make no sense at all, insanity in action?

There is so much that I want to say to her right now, so many questions to ask. But I don't; I'm too afraid of what her answers might be, of where they might lead me. It's like I've got a loose thread, and something is tugging at it, pulling just hard enough to make me certain that one good yank could make everything unravel, and I'd never be able to put things back together again. Not the way they were.

❦

Kimber sits alone in her car, hands gripping the wheel at ten and two, staring straight ahead at my grandma's house. Except she isn't really looking at it; her mind is obviously elsewhere.

"Are you okay?" I ask.

She nods. "I'm fine." She turns her head so quickly that her long hair whips through the space between us. "What's the matter with her?"

I don't have the energy to explain my family's history of mental illness right now. I am so exhausted that all I can think about is getting some sleep. My body is so weak that I can barely pull my door shut. "She's old," I say. "She gets confused sometimes, that's all. We should leave." I glance at the barn, resting wide and still against the horizon, and picture my sister inside, alone, maybe peeking out one of the windows, watching us. Why wouldn't she speak to me? Why won't she come home?

Kimber won't let it go. "No," she says, shaking her head. Her hands, I notice, are gripping the steering wheel tightly. "It was like she became somebody else. I've never seen anything like that, not in my whole life."

"She's sick," I say. "You know, emotionally. She takes medication for it. It makes her strange." All of this is sort of true. Except that it's not. The medication is supposed to make her normal, not the other way around.

Kimber stares at me. "Sick," she echoes.

"Yes."

"Mentally ill."

"*Yes.*"

Kimber starts the car. She nudges the gearstick into reverse and begins to back down the long gravel driveway.

With her head turned, almost nonchalantly, she says, "That kind of stuff runs in families, Rachel. Doesn't it?"

We're sitting at the intersection of the driveway and the road. I know what she's getting at. Has my sister talked to her about this, or is it something that everyone is talking about behind my back?

"I guess so," I say. Even my voice is weak; the words come out like they've been rolled in gravel.

"Okay. So maybe Alice is having similar problems. That's what you think, isn't it?"

She's wrong. Maybe my grandmother slipped over the edge at some point, but I'm not even close. What does Rachel think, though? The idea that she might doubt my sanity is a stinging possibility. She's never said anything like that, not to me, and the thought that she might choose to confide in Kimber, of all people, feels like a betrayal. If she had concerns, she should have told me directly. She would have told me.

✑

As Kimber drives slowly through town, I have to fight to keep my eyes open. When we reach my house, we see that my aunt's car is parked outside on the street, but I can't even muster the energy to care that I'm going to get in trouble.

"Do you want me to come in with you?" she offers, even though it's obvious she'd rather not.

"That's okay." My legs are shaky as I get out of the car; I would almost rather crawl inside than have to stay upright.

Kimber seems oblivious to my fatigue. "Will you be at work tonight?"

Work. Shit, shit, shit. I'd totally forgotten about work. Mr. Hahn is hardly ever at the restaurant in the evenings, but what if he shows up tonight? How am I supposed to act around him? If I don't go at all, will that seem even stranger? The idea of having to remain conscious, waiting tables and chatting with customers, seems impossible. I feel like I could sleep for days and still be exhausted.

"Sure," I manage, even though I'm anything but certain. "I'll be there." Kimber works as a server at the Yellow Moon too.

"All right. Then I'll see you later." She looks at my house, then at me. She gives me a bright smile. "Good luck in there."

Chapter Seventeen

The house is oddly quiet as I step inside. All the downstairs lights are on, and the television is turned to the midday local news, but the sound is off. From the hallway, I can see my aunt's purse sitting on the kitchen counter. The rhythmic ticking of the grandfather clock is the only sound breaking the silence, but even its noise is overwhelming; the room throbs with each passing second. I feel so weak that even climbing the stairs seems unmanageable.

"Hello?" I call, startled all over again by how soft and hoarse my voice is. Before I can sleep, I have to give my aunt some explanation as to why I'm home so early. It won't be difficult to pretend I'm not feeling well. As I stand in the foyer, I summon every remaining shred of my strength, trying to muster the energy to find her. From the corner of my eye, I see Linda McCartney—the cat—taking deliberate steps down the stairs. Overnight, she has become so skinny that

I can make out hollows near her rib cage beneath her long orange fur. I can see the outline of her spine. It's probably because she's nursing her kittens so much; they're sucking everything out of her.

My aunt is sitting on the floor of my bedroom. She's looking through one of my old sketchbooks, which sits open in her lap. Beside her, there's a whole stack of them, probably going back at least a few years. She's crying.

My aunt is not my friend; we have never gotten along well. But in all the years I've lived here, she has quietly encouraged my art, even when things between us have been particularly rough. Every birthday and Christmas brings new paints, canvases, pencils, and brushes. It's not cheap, I know, and since my parents didn't leave us any money, she and my uncle are under no obligation to indulge my interest. In return for this kindness, I have treated them terribly; I know this. There is a part of me that understands how much I owe them. They fought to raise Rachel and me when our grandmother wanted us, because they believed they could do a better job. They have been strict but fair. They love me. Yet in the past year, I have done little else but put them through endless troubles.

I have my reasons. Good ones. To my aunt and uncle, though, I'm just a brat.

But as I stand here, watching her cry, her eyeliner and mascara smudged, foundation worn away beneath her eyes to reveal fine wrinkles, I feel nothing but sorry for her.

Maybe I'm just too tired to waste what little energy I have left being angry and resentful.

"Rachel," she says, surprised, "what are you doing here?" She glances at her watch. "It's barely twelve thirty."

"I feel sick," I say, slumping against the wall, out of breath just from climbing the stairs. "The nurse sent me home."

She sniffles. "They let you walk? It's over a mile."

I nod. "I guess it was okay because I'm eighteen."

It's a flimsy explanation at best, but she doesn't question it.

"What are you doing up here?" I ask. "You're going through Alice's things?"

She shakes her head. "No. I mean, I didn't mean to. I came home from my meeting and sort of wandered up here, and before I knew it I was looking at her sketches." She stares down at the open book. "They're so good. She really has a gift. You already knew that."

The book in her lap is open to a portrait of the gap-toothed girl I've been sketching for so long. Because of the way her eyes are drawn, no matter where you're standing in the room, she's always looking at you. I didn't plan it that way, not at first, but for some reason that's how most of my drawings of her have turned out.

"Come here," my aunt says. "Sit down with me."

As I take a seat on the floor beside her, it almost feels like an unseen hand is tugging me downward, like I don't have control over my own body. I lean against her, still catching my breath, grateful for the moment that she believes I'm Rachel; I can rest my head on her shoulder without it seeming too odd.

My aunt runs a finger along the jawline of the gap-toothed girl. "Do you know who this is?" she asks me.

"No." My eyelids flutter. I could fall asleep right here. "Do you?"

She doesn't answer the question. Instead, she says, "There are pages and pages of her in these books. It's the same face, over and over again." She gives me a sideward glance. "Alice must know her somehow."

Despite my exhaustion, my lips tilt upward in a slight smile. "Alice says she's never seen her before in her life."

Aunt Sharon shakes her head. "She's wrong. She must be."

"Oh?" I yawn.

"Yes," Aunt Sharon says. "She must have met her somewhere, at some point. Maybe just crossing paths on the street, but still. Her face didn't come from thin air, Rachel." And she pauses, glancing down at the portrait again. The girl stares up at us, and even though she's half-smiling, there is something incredibly sad about her expression.

"You know, I recognize her from somewhere myself," my aunt says.

The information surprises me; a jolt of energy ripples through my body. This isn't the first time she's seen one of these portraits, and she's never mentioned that the girl looks familiar until now.

"Where do you know her from?" I ask, sitting up a

little straighter. There's an edge to my voice, and my aunt senses it.

"I didn't say I knew her. I said I recognized her. And I don't know how. But I could swear I've seen her before."

She touches the drawing again. Then, abruptly, she closes the sketchbook and sets it aside, on top of the others. The redness around her eyes has faded somewhat; it's like she was never upset at all. "Anyway," she continues, "that's not important right now. You look exhausted, Rachel. You should take a nap."

She stands up, extending a hand to help me to my feet. I'm too tired to think about anything right now, even my sister. All I want to do is fall asleep.

My aunt pulls the covers aside and helps me climb into bed. I feel like a small child as she tucks the blanket beneath my chin and presses her hand to my cheek, checking for a fever.

"You're warm," she murmurs, but my eyes are already shut, and her voice sounds far away. I feel her hair brush against my face as she leans down to kiss me on the forehead.

"Get some rest, sweet girl," she whispers. But I barely have time to process her words before the room slips away—slowly at first, and then all at once—like someone is reaching out from the darkness to yank me toward them, and there's nothing I can do to stop it.

⌒〰⌒

The dream is vivid and bright: I'm on the trail again, but this time Rachel is walking a few steps ahead of me. She's in her outfit from Saturday night, but her feet are bare as she navigates the stone-covered path, stopping every few seconds to kneel down and peer at the ground.

I try to walk faster, but my legs won't move as quickly as I need them to; no matter how hard I struggle to catch up with her, she remains a few paces away, just out of reach. The wound on the back of her head is nearly identical to mine, the shiny, damp circle of bare flesh oozing fluid, refusing to heal.

She glances over her shoulder, looking at me. "Can you help me, Alice?" she asks. There is almost no expression to her face; it's like she doesn't understand who I am, even as she says my name.

"What are you looking for?" Again, I try to get closer, but it's difficult to walk. Each step is a struggle for me, like I'm wading through a layer of sap.

She shades her eyes from the bright light all around us, which is harsh and blinding, even though I don't see the sun anywhere. The bruises on her face are much worse than mine; her left eye is swollen shut, and she has a split lip. There is blood smeared around her nose, dripping from her nostrils. When I look at the ground, I see that the droplets have been falling onto the stones, leaving bright-red bursts of color every few paces as she moves along, like a grisly trail of bread crumbs marking her path.

She doesn't seem like she's in pain, though; instead, she's preoccupied by her search, oblivious to the way she looks. "I'm so thirsty, Alice. I've never felt so thirsty before in my life." She pauses. "Will you help me look? I could swear I just had it a minute ago."

"You could swear you just had *what*, Rachel? Tell me," I plead.

My desperation has no impact on her. "I got it at the fair," she continues, "from an old man. It's the most amazing thing, Alice. It's a little monkey carved out of a peach pit." She frowns, biting her bottom lip, a blossom of blood appearing as her teeth sink into the flesh.

"Rachel, you're bleeding! You're hurt!" I try to reach for her again, without success. If anything, the distance between us seems to be growing wider, even though we're both standing still.

She gives a dismissive wave of her hand; her wrist is encircled by a thick line of dried blood. "That's not important right now, Alice. Help me find it, please? I was going to give it to Charlie."

"I have one too," I say. "Don't worry about it—I'll give mine to Charlie. Just come home."

"No," she says, shaking her head. "That's not good enough. We need to find this one."

"Why?" I demand.

"Because it doesn't belong to him. It belongs to me."

"What do you mean?"

She pauses. She tilts her head, listening. "Be quiet," she whispers. "He'll hear us."

"Who will? Rachel, who is it?" I try to take a step forward, but I cannot even lift my feet off the ground; it's like I'm glued in place.

"I have to leave," she says, looking around, a trace of worry in her voice. "Promise me you'll keep looking, okay?"

Paralysis begins to spread through my body, starting at my feet and creeping upward, until I can't even move my arms. I try to speak, but I can't open my mouth. All I can do is stare at her.

"Promise me," she repeats.

Even as I nod, my neck begins to stiffen.

"Good." She smiles. "I knew I would find you, Alice. I knew you would help me."

She begins to walk away, more quickly this time, hurrying along without stopping to look for the monkey anymore. As she recedes into the distance, her form starts to blur, until she is so far away that I can't even recognize her. I watch, helpless, until she disappears, her body slipping out of sight like she's been swallowed by the horizon.

When I look down at the path again, I see the long, crooked trail of blood that she has left behind, a horrifying series of connect-the-dots, their color throbbing beneath the light, threatening to burst at any moment. If I could only *move*, I could follow them. I'm certain they would lead me right to her.

But I can't do anything. I can't even blink anymore. All I can do is stare straight ahead, hoping for another glimpse of her even as the light begins to fade all around me.

As the darkness grows, there is a brief flash of white light at the horizon, and another form appears. I can tell immediately that it's not Rachel, though; it's a man. At first I feel afraid as he approaches me slowly, seeming to take his time, almost like he knows I can't go anywhere, that I have no choice but to wait for him.

As he gets closer, even in the near-darkness, I can see that it's Robin. His body radiates a soft, eerie glow from within; I can see his veins mapped out beneath his flesh, the textured fibers of his muscles; I notice that the hairs on his arms are flattened against his skin, curled into continuous swirling patterns, like they have been smoothed carefully into place. By the time he reaches me, as he stands just a few feet away, I realize that he's soaking wet. His clothing clings to his body. His form ripples against the dark background, like there's a wall of water separating us.

As he reaches toward me, his hand breaks through the wall, and the water comes splashing down in a foamy wave, soaking the ground all around him. Somehow I remain completely dry.

"I want to help you, Alice," he says to me, putting a hand on my arm. His hand is cold. Even though I can't shift my gaze to look downward, I can feel that his fingers are shriveled, like they've been soaking in water for a long time.

I give him a desperate look, still unable to speak or move.

"It's too late for me," he continues. "I would do anything to take it back, Alice, but I can't. I have to keep going. It's the way things are. A person can't hold still forever."

He brings his face close to mine, so our noses are touching. "It's too late for us, but it's not too late for her. I promise."

I want to hold him so badly, to warm him with the heat from my body. But I can't do anything. Even as he begins to back away, my body is so paralyzed that I can barely breathe.

"I'll see you soon," he says. They are his last words to me. He turns, begins to walk into the darkness, the light around him receding as he moves forward, growing dimmer by the second like a flame deprived of oxygen, until it finally slips away completely. The last things I see before everything around me goes black are his footprints on the path, their indentations filled with muddy water, one after another arranged in a meandering line that runs parallel to Rachel's trail of blood.

The air grows very cold all around me as I stand in complete darkness, frozen in place. My mouth is dry, but I can't swallow. As I stand there, I am aware of someone lingering close behind me. I don't know how, but I'm certain it's a man—I'm also certain it isn't Robin, not this time.

I can hear him breathing as he watches me; I can sense his gaze at my back. He has been observing me the whole time, I know, even though I've only become aware of him now. I don't know who he is, but I understand that he's stay-ing close for a reason, reassuring himself of my immobility, keeping watch in the dark, ready to pounce if I get too close to her.

CHAPTER EIGHTEEN

My room is warm and dim when I wake up after sleeping for over five hours. At least I'm not exhausted anymore; instead I feel bursting with energy. I have a vague recollection of my dream—or was it more of a nightmare?—but I can't remember all the details now; the only thing I remember clearly is my sister's insistence that I look for her monkey. She said it was important, I know, but I can't recall if she told me why. There are blank spaces in my memory; even as I try to go over the day's events, I find myself struggling to remember the simplest things: what I had for breakfast, whether or not I went to school. Every time I start to grasp on to something, it slips just out of reach.

The only thing I know for sure is that Rachel was in the barn this afternoon. I remember my encounter with her clearly, right down to the moment she pulled out her front tooth. I slip my hand into my pocket, expecting to grasp the tooth again, to reassure myself of our interaction.

It's not there. I check my other pocket, but that's empty too. I tug my sheets back, searching, trying to stay calm and convince myself that it easily could have fallen out somehow, that it could be anywhere. But where?

The more I try to focus on specific events from the past few days, the more confused and frustrated I become. Even the details of Rachel's disappearance are hard to recall. As I replay the events of Saturday evening in my mind, I feel uncertain that I'm remembering them correctly. We were in our room, getting ready for the fair. I was reluctant to go see our friends, since I'd recently grown apart from them so much. Rachel tried to reassure me that everything would be fine, and when that didn't work, she offered to switch places, to make things easier for me.

But maybe I'm wrong. Is that the way it happened? She had her back to me as she spoke; she was staring out our front window, looking at something, preoccupied. I couldn't see her expression. The more I try to remember our conversation, the more scrambled it seems.

She offered to take my place. She wanted to help me.

It was her idea, not mine. I didn't ask her to do it. I didn't have to convince her.

I didn't.

⁓

Just from glancing out my window, I can tell that it's cold and damp outside. Even though it's the last thing I want to do tonight, I know I have to go to work. After I told Officer "call me Ryan" Martin about the stolen money, he told me it was important that I try to act as normal as possible around Mr. Hahn. "If he does have something to do with Alice's disappearance," he'd told me, "then you don't want to upset him or make him feel alarmed for any reason." But I know now that the money didn't have anything to do with Rachel's disappearance. It couldn't have; I just saw her, and she was safe. I can't shake my confusion, though; pieces that fit together so perfectly in my mind just a few hours ago seem disjointed now; nothing makes sense the way it should. I try to concentrate, clinging to the things I know for sure: My sister is in my grandma's barn. My body is falling apart. My thoughts are unclear and disjointed—maybe I'm actually getting sick. Maybe I'm exhausted, even though I slept all afternoon. I have to go to work, though. I promised Ryan. I'm not sure why I care so much about keeping my word to him; I just do.

I decline a ride from my uncle; for some reason I prefer to walk, despite the lousy weather. As I approach the restaurant, I quickly scan the parking lot. Sure enough, Mr. Hahn's black Mercedes—complete with tinted windows and a vanity license plate that reads YOURBOSS—is in its usual spot. The best I can do tonight is try to avoid him as much as possible.

Mondays at the Yellow Moon are always slow. Since it's more of a bar than a restaurant, the patrons who come early in the week tend to be regulars. When I get to work it's

6:12, and there are a total of six customers. One of them is Holly; she's sitting at a high-top table with Nicholas, where they're deep in conversation, both of them eating french fries dipped in mayonnaise. Nicholas isn't on the schedule to work tonight, but he tends to hang out here quite a bit anyway.

Two of our regulars, a young married couple named Matt and Katie Follet, are alone at the far end of the bar, drinking beer and giggling, their heads close together. A well-dressed couple who I don't recognize are eating dinner at a corner table. Kimber is folding silverware into napkins at the servers' station outside the kitchen doors. The bartender, Doug, leans against the wall while he reads a worn copy of *The Hitchhiker's Guide to the Galaxy.* Charlie must be here somewhere, too, but I don't see him.

When Holly notices me, she nudges Nicholas, who waves me over to their table.

"You're late," he says. "You were supposed to be here almost fifteen minutes ago." He pauses. "Where's Alice? She's still gone?" There's a map of Greensburg sitting in front of him, its margins scribbled with notes. Nicholas's handwriting is like chicken scratch; I can't make out what any of it says, but I assume it all has something to do with geocaching. He and Holly are obsessed.

"Kimber told you already," Holly says to Nicholas. She squeezes more mayonnaise onto the plate of fries. *Gross.*

"You're eating french fries? With mayo?" I ask. For as

long as I've known her, Holly has been on some kind of diet.

She nods. "The fries are baked. And the mayo is low-fat. You can't tell the difference, though." She shoves a fry toward my face. "Try it."

I turn my head away. "Ugh, no." When I look at her again, I notice that she has a plastic silver star pinned to the front of her shirt. It looks like it came out of a Cracker Jack box. I point to it. "What's that?"

Holly beams. "It's my prize. I found it this afternoon."

I lean in to take a closer look. "A prize for what?"

"Geocaching." I should have known. "It took me all week to track this down," she tells me. "I finally found it taped to the bottom of a bench at the bus station." She smirks at her boyfriend. "Nicholas is jealous."

I feel like I'm missing something. "But it's plastic, isn't it? What kind of prize is that?"

Holly and Nicholas exchange an amused look. "It's not the prize that matters," Nicholas explains. "It's the search."

"The *quest*," Holly clarifies.

Nicholas nods in agreement. "Yeah, the quest."

"Oh." I frown. "So you don't actually win anything valuable?"

Nicholas is impatient. "Rachel, you're not getting it. It's the *experience* that counts. That's what's valuable."

Holly nods vigorously. "The quest," she repeats. She picks up another mayonnaise-covered french fry and pops it into her mouth. "I can't believe you don't want to try this," she says as she chews. "I'm telling you, it tastes exactly the same as regular mayo."

"It doesn't taste the same. It tastes like shit." Nicholas grins. "She hasn't had anything full-fat in years, so she doesn't know the difference. The mayo tastes like . . . I don't know, like paste or something."

Holly sticks out her bottom lip in a pout. She bats her eyes at her boyfriend. "I don't want to fight."

It's like I'm not even here anymore. Nicholas puts an arm around her shoulders. "We aren't fighting. Don't worry, baby." He brushes his fingers across the silver star. "I'm a little bit jealous. But I'm proud of you too."

She brings her face close to his, until their noses are touching. "I love you."

"I love you too."

And then—as I'm standing *right next to them*—Holly picks up another fry, puts it in her mouth so a few inches are sticking out, and leans close so Nicholas can take a bite, his lips touching hers in a greasy kiss that continues as they both chew on their respective mouthfuls.

"Hi," I say. "I'm standing right here. It's not awkward at all."

They ignore me for a few seconds. Finally, Nicholas pulls away. "My dad wants to see you in his office. He said to send you in as soon as you got here."

Fabulous. I try to act calm, but I can feel every muscle in my body tensing. "What does he want?"

Nicholas rolls his eyes, oblivious to my anxiety. "I don't know. He doesn't tell me anything." He pauses. "Just . . . be nice to him, okay? He's had a tough day."

⁂

Mr. Hahn's office, which is at the end of a long hallway toward the back of the building, is thick with cigar smoke. I can smell it before I even knock on the door.

"Yeah." He doesn't say "who is it" or "come in." His voice is like oiled gravel. He clears his throat every few seconds, an act that produces sounds that I'd much rather not hear—especially not in the context of a restaurant. Mr. Hahn is wearing a white dress shirt that fits a little too tightly over his big belly. The rest of him is rail-thin. There's a glass of scotch on his desk, which I can smell as soon as I walk into the room. I *hate* the smell of scotch. I try to breathe through my mouth as I take a seat in the chair across from his big mahogany desk, but it doesn't help much.

"I didn't tell you to sit down, Rachel." He's doing some kind of paperwork. He doesn't bother to look up at me. The scotch is so stomach-churning that it reminds me of the smell of black licorice, which reminds me of my sister.

I stand up. "Sorry. I didn't mean—"

"Don't worry about it." Mr. Hahn finally looks at me. "You're late."

"Yes." I brush a few stray hairs from my face. "I got stuck at home. I'm sorry. It won't happen again."

He takes a sip of scotch. "Where's Alice?" He crosses his arms against his belly, still clutching the tumbler.

Just breathe. Don't gag. If you throw up in his office, he'll definitely fire you. Although I ordinarily wouldn't mind getting the ax, I'm sure my sister won't be too pleased if I've lost her job by the time she comes home.

"Alice isn't here, Mr. Hahn."

He sticks his pinky finger into his left ear and wiggles it around, like he's trying to scratch a deep itch. "Yeah, I know. Nicky told me she ran away again." He means Nicholas. His dad is the only person who calls him Nicky.

Mr. Hahn studies my face as he swirls the scotch around in his glass. "Can I ask you a question, Rachel?"

I'm too nervous to look at him. I stare at my hands instead. "Okay."

"Why would the police want to ask me about your sister?"

The room seems to have an echo all of a sudden. Even though he's right in front of me, Mr. Hahn's voice sounds far away. I feel like I'm shrinking into myself, like I might be able to disappear if I concentrate hard enough.

I try to focus on taking deep, even breaths as I repeat exactly what Ryan told me to say if this situation came up. "My aunt and uncle called the police yesterday to report her missing. They're talking to everyone who knows her."

"I see." He takes another swig of scotch. "They asked me

some pretty personal questions. About things that are none of their goddamn business."

I don't say anything. I still can't look at him, afraid my face will give something away.

"Where do you think she is, Rachel? Do you have any idea?" Before I can answer him, he waves a bony hand through the air and says, "You know what? I don't care. She was supposed to work tonight. She's on the schedule until ten. Doesn't matter where she went; she should be here."

He stands up. Finally, I force myself to meet his gaze. He gives me a sharp look as he continues to swirl his oily drink in the glass. "Your sister's a little brat. You know that?" He peers into his glass, like he's giving the matter deep thought. "Shows up late. Doesn't show up. Always getting into trouble. Rude to customers." Now he's talking more to himself than he is to me. "Little brat," he murmurs. Swig. "Little freaking brat." It's like I'm not even here anymore.

"Is there anything else you want to talk about?" I ask. I'm doing my best not to say something I shouldn't, but I know that I'm going to burst if I don't get out of here soon. I feel claustrophobic, almost like I can't breathe. I want to tell him off, to grab his drink and throw it in his face like a little brat should, but I know it would be a big mistake.

"Oh. Right." He shakes the ice in his glass before taking one last drink. As he's chomping on the ice cubes, he lets out a low belch. I have to look away and hold my breath, or else I'm going to puke all over his office.

"Tell Alice she's fired the next time you see her, okay? I've had enough of her shit. I'm trying to run a damn business here."

I nod. I take a big step backward, trying to pull deep breaths; I need fresh air so badly. The walls seem to ripple when I look at them. I want to go home.

Out of nowhere, I am acutely aware of the pain in the back of my head. The bald spot is hidden by my partial ponytail, but I can feel the dull throb with every pulse of my heart. My wrists hurt, too, their marks covered by the cuffs of my shirt. Every time I move my arms, the fabric brushing against my skin sends tiny shivers of pain through my body.

I can't stop myself. "You're a joke," I blurt. Just as quickly, I clap a hand to my mouth. *Shit.*

He pauses midswig, surprised, staring at me. "What did you say to me?"

I reach behind myself, feeling around for the doorknob.

"You're not going anywhere yet. Say that again."

The façade of my sister has slipped away. It's just me now. He's a fool if he doesn't recognize me as Alice.

"I said you're a joke. Everyone in town knows it. People laugh behind your back. They know you cheat on your wife. You're an embarrassment to your family, especially your son. If I had a father like you—"

"But you don't," he says calmly. He shakes his head, almost like he's disappointed in me. "I'd expect this sort of shit from your sister, but not from you. I guess I shouldn't be surprised, though, since you *are* twins." He leans back in his chair and laces his fingers together behind his head. He seems to be enjoying himself. "The poor little orphan girls. Right? That's what people say about you two, if you're interested. There's Rachel, the sweet one, and Alice, the screwup." He laughs. "I guess you're more alike than I thought."

I turn around, fumbling at the doorknob. I don't want to start crying, not now, not in here.

"Go ahead and leave," he says, laughing again. "I don't give a damn. Come back and apologize when you've calmed down. Your sister's a different matter, though. She's not welcome here at all. She's done. If she ever comes home at all. That's another thing people say, Rachel. They say that one of these days, Alice is going to get herself into some real trouble if she keeps screwing up—"

I spin to face him so quickly that my hair whips the side of my face. My vision is blurry with anger. I can feel my heartbeat behind my eyes.

"Shut up about my sister."

He gives me an amused look, sips his drink, and turns his attention back to the paperwork sitting on his desk. He waves a hand carelessly at me. "Get the hell out of here, Rachel."

∽

As I leave his office, I slam the door behind me with enough force that pretty much everyone in the bar is looking in my direction once I come rushing down the hallway.

"Hey," Kimber says as I hurry past her, "what's the matter with you?"

I ignore her. I ignore everyone. I take a quick look around the restaurant, searching for my cousin, until I catch a glimpse of him through the window of the swinging kitchen door. He's back there washing dishes, smiling to himself, his iPod headphones on his ears.

I want to go back and get him, to bring him home with me. He shouldn't be working at a place like this, not with a boss like Mr. Hahn. But as I'm standing at the door, watching him, something stops me.

He looks so happy. He loves this job. And as far as I know, nobody—not even Mr. Hahn—has ever been unkind to him.

"Rachel."

I jump. Kimber's hand is on my shoulder. I turn around to find her frowning at me. Her waitress uniform—a long-sleeved white dress shirt and black pants—is clean and perfectly ironed, her red bow tie knotted in such a way that its center curves into a dimple. Her long hair is pulled into a high ponytail, and for the first time in as long as I've known her, I notice that her ears aren't pierced. When she turns her head, a wispy cluster of scarring is visible just above her collar, near the bottom of her neck.

"What is it?" I'm out of breath from running down the hallway.

She wrinkles her forehead in concern. "What happened back there? Did you get into trouble?"

I ignore the question, turning to look at Charlie again instead. He notices me, his smile widening as our eyes meet. He waves with a hand covered in soap bubbles.

"I quit," I tell her.

"What?" she almost shrieks. "Why? What did Mr. Hahn—"

"Mr. Hahn is an asshole," I interrupt, tugging at the corner of my bow tie until it comes undone. "I hate this job anyway. Screw it." I'm so frustrated that I could cry. I turn away from the kitchen door so that Charlie won't see me. "Screw it," I repeat, under my breath.

Kimber presses her lips together, a hint of disapproval clouding her typically serene expression. But she doesn't seem angry, not exactly—she seems sad. "Do you mean that?" she asks.

Now that I'm out of his office, I feel like I can breathe again. I take deep breaths, grateful for the feeling of air spreading through my lungs. My face is sweaty and flushed. I lean forward and rest my elbows on my knees, nodding.

When I stand up, Kimber's arms are crossed against her chest. "Rachel," she says in a loud whisper, "what's the matter? We're friends; you can tell me."

The truth seems so obvious. I'm barely even trying to act like my sister; how can she not realize who I am?

When I don't answer her, she continues, asking, "Is that it? You're just going to leave?"

I nod. "Yes." After a pause, I add, "He fired Alice. I don't want to work here without her."

She wrinkles her eyebrows. "Come on, Rachel. I know

she's your sister, but Mr. Hahn had every right to let her go. He could have fired her a long time ago. She's been stealing liquor for months—you know that."

Did Rachel know? I'm surprised by all of this shared knowledge about my theft; my sister has never mentioned to me that she was aware of it, and I always did my best to hide it from her. I didn't want to get her in any trouble. Too late for that now, I guess.

"Charlie will be upset that you're leaving," Kimber says.

I nod. "I know. I'm sorry. Just tell him . . . tell him I got a headache, okay?"

She frowns. "All right. Are you sure you don't want to talk, though? I'm really worried about you."

"Not now," I say, shaking my head. "I have to go home." I pause. "Call me later, okay? We'll talk then."

She presses the heels of her hands against her eyes. As her arms fall limply at her sides, she sighs. "Fine." After a few seconds of silence, the two of us staring at each other, she nods at the door. "Go. You'd better leave before you get into even more trouble."

I start to walk away, but then I have second thoughts. Without a word, I walk behind the bar and lean past Doug, who's mixing a drink, to grab a bottle of tequila.

"Rachel?" He stops midstir. "What are you doing?"

I grab a tumbler and pour a few shots into the glass. I swallow it in one gulp; it tastes so foul that my eyes water, and I have to hold my breath for a few seconds just to keep it all down. Once I'm finished, I press the glass into Doug's free hand. He takes it, stunned. Everyone in the bar is stealing glances at me, even as they pretend to be minding their own business. I can still feel their gaze at my back as I walk out the door.

✍

I've only taken a few hurried steps outside when I hear a low whistle coming from somewhere behind me. Before I have a chance to turn around, someone calls, "Rachel, stop. What's your hurry?"

It's my friendly neighborhood policeman, Ryan Martin. He stands beneath one of the bright floodlights in the parking lot, his hands shoved into his pockets. Instead of his uniform, he's wearing jeans, a long-sleeved gray shirt, and loafers without socks.

"What are you doing here?" I ask.

He gives me a lopsided, shy smile. "I guess I'm following you."

In a matter of seconds, it has begun to rain. I step beneath one of the green canvas awnings attached to the building. Ryan joins me, but right away it becomes obvious that there's not quite enough covered space for both of us to stand comfortably; our bodies are only a few inches apart, draped in shadow as we stand beyond the reach of the lights that shine down on the parking lot.

"You're following me?" I repeat, trying not to breathe on him, afraid he'll smell the liquor on my breath.

He doesn't respond at first. He looks past me, toward the parking lot, and smiles. "I think you made a friend."

"What?"

"Cookie." He nods. "Look."

I glance over my shoulder. A red compact car is parked maybe fifty feet away. The passenger-side window is down; Cookie is looking at us. She sits with her paws resting on the edge of the door, her furry head sticking out into the rain. "She's going to get soaked," I tell him. "So is the inside of your car."

"Meh." He runs a hand through his hair, mussing it up. "They're both washable."

There is a loud crash from inside the restaurant; it's obviously the sound of somebody dropping a tray of dishes. I wince, thinking of Charlie, and how devastated he'd be if he lost his job.

"Actually, Rachel, I do have a question for you. Do you have a minute?"

I nod, keeping my mouth closed.

"It's about your sister's boyfriend, Robin. I did some research after you left the station today, and I couldn't find an address for him. You said his last name is Lang, correct?"

I nod again.

"Can you spell it for me?"

It seems like a silly question. How many different ways

are there to spell Lang? I do it anyway, though, turning my head slightly, hoping he won't notice that I reek of booze. "L-A-N-G," I say slowly. "Just like it sounds."

"Huh. Okay." He scratches his forehead. "You're sure?"

"Yes, I'm sure. Why? What's the matter?"

"We couldn't find any record of somebody with that name in Greensburg."

It doesn't surprise me that much; Robin never even got a driver's license. He's always claimed he prefers to stay under the radar. I shrug. "Sorry. That's all I know about him."

"Rachel . . ." Ryan's voice trails off. He stares up at the underside of the awning; its corners are thick with cobwebs. A big black spider dangles from a single thread, its legs pulled close to its body as it hangs in the misty air, waiting for who knows what.

Ryan lets out a deep breath. "Look, you seem like a nice girl. I don't want you or your sister to get into any trouble. But things aren't adding up. Not the way you've explained them to me."

I wrap my arms around my body, shivering in the chilly night air. My memory has grown clearer since I got to work; I was probably just too tired to think earlier tonight. I remember everything about the day now, including my visit to the police station. "What do you mean? I told you everything I know this morning. You said you believed me. You told me about your epilepsy. I thought you understood how sometimes things happen that we can't explain." I know

I should tell him that I saw Rachel this afternoon, but I'm afraid of what might happen to my grandma if I reveal that she's been helping my sister hide out. I can't do that to her.

"I know what I said," Ryan answers. "I remember. And I did believe you."

I take a step backward, into the rain. "You *did*? You mean you don't believe me anymore?"

"Come on. Don't do that." He reaches out and tugs my arm, pulling me back under the awning. "I talked to Marcus Hahn today. He swears up and down that nobody has stolen anything from him."

I shake my head. "He's lying."

"I don't know about that. He was very cooperative." Ryan pauses. "He was in Philadelphia on business all weekend. He can prove it."

"So what?" Regardless of why Rachel ran away, Mr. Hahn *is* lying about the money.

Another pause. "Rachel, does Robin own a car?"

". . ."

"You never met him, did you? How would you know where he lives? How would you know he didn't hurt your sister? Do you know anything about him aside from what she's told you?"

"Stop it. I know enough."

He softens his tone. "Rachel, you can trust me. I only want to help you. Both of you."

I'm so cold that my fingertips are numb. All I want is to

He cups his hands around his mouth. "You'll catch a cold!" he yells.

I'm almost to the end of the street before I realize what a ridiculous warning it is. The understanding makes me laugh out loud. *I'll catch a cold*, I think, unable to suppress my giggles. *What a tragedy.*

go home. Squeezing myself more tightly, I ask, "
come here tonight? Just to accuse me of lying?"

He doesn't miss a beat. "No. I came here to cl

I stare at him. "Why would you need to do t

"Because it's my job," he says simply. "To
serve. You've heard that before, I assume?"

Instead of responding, I look beyond him a
Greensburg spread out all around us, the rain
heavily by the minute. I'll be soaked by the time

"I have to go," I say.

He frowns. "You're not walking, are you?"

"Yes. I'll be fine."

"No way." He shakes his head vigorously.
me. I'm giving you a ride."

"I don't want a ride." It's not true; I'd a
one. But if I get in his car, he'll definitely smell n

"I don't care if you *want* one," Ryan press
letting you walk home in the dark, especially not

I give him a steely look. "I'll be fine. I can do v

He seems disappointed. "You're sure?"

I force a smile. "I'll be fine," I repeat.

As I walk away, the rain is coming down in t
that feel like a million needles hitting my skin;
almost immediately.

Even with my back turned, I can tell Ryan is
ing under the awning, watching me. Before I cros
I look over my shoulder. Sure enough, there he is

CHAPTER NINETEEN

The rain remains constant and heavy as it pours from the low, thick stratus clouds overhead, hitting my cheeks as I walk toward the center of town, to the path that will take me home. My shirt is soaked all the way through to my skin. I have goose bumps. The days are growing shorter, and it's completely dark right now, at barely seven o'clock. In a few weeks it will be dark by five. I've never liked autumn much. A person can go for what feels like forever around here without seeing the sun.

The path, once I reach it, appears to be empty. And even though it's eerie to see it so still and quiet when it's usually pretty crowded, it doesn't surprise me. Who would be out for a stroll on a night like this? The rain comes down harder by the minute as the sky grows darker, and the evening gives me such an uncomfortable, unsettled feeling that I find myself walking faster, almost trotting in my dress shoes as I hurry to get home.

A faint noise sounds behind me in the almost-darkness, pebbles tumbling along and falling against one another, a low scuffle of motion. I pause for a second, listening.

Swoosh, swoosh, swoosh, swoosh.

I glance over my shoulder. After maybe fifty feet, the trail curves to my left, preventing me from seeing anything beyond a certain point. Maybe all I'm hearing is the rain hitting the ground or trickling down from the leaves on the trees surrounding me.

I keep walking, a little faster now. *Swoosh, swoosh, swoosh.* The sound is rhythmic and constant. It's not the rain.

Swoosh, swoosh, swoosh. It's a person. I can sense him before I see him. But then, as I hurry forward, I look over my shoulder again and make out a tall figure wearing a dark raincoat—camouflage, maybe?—and sweatpants. It's a man, a jogger. He's heading right toward me, trotting along with his head down, hood pulled tightly around his face.

I don't know why, but I'm scared. I'm sure whoever's behind me is just a random person out for an evening run. And even though the trail is otherwise empty right now, I'm sure that lots of people go running on it in all kinds of weather. There's nothing for me to be afraid of. Right?

Still, I speed up, trotting a bit, my feet aching with every stride as my shoes hit the loose gravel. I'm starting to wish I'd accepted Ryan's offer for a ride.

Swoosh, swoosh, swoosh. The runner is getting closer. I speed up a bit more, my adrenaline flowing, and finally I see the break in the path that leads to the road near my house.

"Rachel!" I hear from behind me. "Rachel, wait!"

It's Sean Morelli. I stop, catching my breath as my panic subsides. He trots closer to me, puts a hand on my shoulder. "What are you doing out here?"

"I'm going home." My teeth chatter as I smile. "You scared me."

"I did? Aww, I'm sorry. I was trying to catch up with you. I thought something might be wrong." He looks up and down the path, which is still deserted. "Anyway," he continues, "you shouldn't be out here by yourself, not at night. Come on—I'm going home too. I'll walk with you."

For a little while, both of us are quiet as we head toward our street, rushing to get out of the rain even though we're already soaked. I've known Sean for six years, but it's still an awkward silence. I'm not used to being alone with him.

"Wish I had an umbrella for you," he says. "Why did you have to walk home? Couldn't someone pick you up?"

My steps grow slower as we trudge uphill. It's tough to walk quickly on the pavement in these shoes, which are uncomfortable under the best of conditions.

"I got fired," I tell him, my tone apologetic. I give him a quick explanation of the night's events so far. He listens, eyes wide open in attention, nodding his head as I tell him everything that Mr. Hahn said about Alice. By the time I'm finished, we're standing on the front porch of his house.

"You ever been fired before?" he asks, fiddling with his keys as he goes to unlock his front door.

"Never." I hesitate as he steps into the foyer. "Um, I should probably go home. Thanks for walking with me."

He looks me over. "You're drenched. I'm not sending you home like that. Come inside and dry off first." Smiling, he adds, "You don't want to catch a cold, do you?"

∽

I wait in the kitchen, taking a seat at the table while he goes upstairs to get me a towel. His house is sparsely decorated, clearly lacking a woman's touch. As far as I know, he doesn't date much. I remember him having a girlfriend a couple of years ago—Adrienne? No. Her name was Alexis. She was a teacher too. I think she taught chemistry or biology— something like that. Anyway, they lived together for a few months. Charlie adored her. She and Mr. Morelli adopted his dog together from the Humane Society. But after a while, something went wrong between them and she moved away. It happened quickly. She came to our house early one morn- ing to say good-bye to Charlie, and her car was parked down the street, already packed up and ready to go. She drove away and never came back. Poor Mr. Morelli—I remember my aunt and uncle talking about how heartbroken he was when it happened.

The house is almost quiet except for the sounds of his

footsteps upstairs as he walks around his room. I imagine him changing out of his wet clothes and getting dressed again, and can feel heat rising in my cheeks, embarrassed by my own thoughts. His yellow Lab, Sheba, is asleep on the living-room carpet. She's the calmest dog I've ever encountered. All around me, I hear small sounds that would otherwise blend into the stillness of the room if I weren't paying attention to them: The hum of the refrigerator. The sound of the faucet dripping, all the way down the hall in the first-floor bathroom. The rain outside hitting the windows. Sheba's heavy breathing, the air in her lungs creating a light wheezing sound.

As I'm sitting there, my gaze catches something sticking out from behind the refrigerator. I recognize the shape right away: it's a canvas stretched across a square frame, the fabric pulled tightly over the corner and held in place with a small row of staples. I can tell immediately that it must be a painting. But what is it doing behind his fridge?

Weird. Mr. Morelli isn't an artist, but anybody with half a brain should know that you can't store art behind a fridge; the heat from the coils will warp the painting, eventually destroying it. It's almost like storing it behind a radiator.

I listen for a moment, paying attention to the noise upstairs. I can hear water running. Maybe he's taking a quick shower. For a brief instant, I imagine him like that—in the shower—and I feel embarrassed all over again. *Get ahold of yourself, Alice. He's just a guy.*

I walk to the fridge and tug at the corner of the painting. As it falls out from its place against the wall, I stare at it, confused.

It's one of mine, a painting I did over the summer. It's sort of a throwaway piece, only half-finished. I barely remember working on it at all; I think it was part of a three-day exercise in my art class at the college. As I tug it free from the space, I recognize the brushstrokes as my own; I recognize the glint in the subject's eyes, the curve of her jawline, the wave in her hair. I recognize her playful smile, those eyes looking at me from every angle, and the small gap between her front teeth.

The painting feels oddly heavy in my hands. It's just a thin piece of canvas, plus a few staples and nails to keep everything in place, but I can barely hold it up for more than a few seconds. My arms begin to tingle; the feeling starts at my shoulders and moves all the way down to my fingertips. I shift my weight, trying to steady myself as I hold on to the painting, but the weight quickly becomes too much to bear; I have to put it down.

As I'm resting it on the kitchen table, my vision goes fuzzy. I grab the edge of the table with both hands, afraid I might pass out. I squeeze my eyes shut for a moment; when I open them, everything is in focus again.

Everything except the painting.

At first the girl is only a blur, the brushstrokes so muddled that I can't even make out her face anymore. But then, right before my eyes, her image begins to multiply. It's the same effect that happens when a person stands in front of a three-way mirror: a hundred blurred faces fading into infinity, pulling apart as I watch, astonished by what I'm seeing, until they stretch across the entire room. The farther outward they go, the fainter her face becomes; it's like a little more color is lost with each copy. Then, just as rapidly as they expanded, they begin to collapse, folding in on themselves from either side until there are only two faces in front of me. They both look completely real, like I could reach out and feel the grooves in the paint.

But they aren't identical, not anymore. The image on the left is the same one I've been seeing this whole time: it's the gap-toothed girl, with her long golden hair and feather earrings, smiling up at me.

The face on the right belongs to my sister. Rachel holds the same pose as her blond counterpart. She wears the same expression. She has the same glint in her eyes. If it weren't for her hair and teeth, the subtle difference in the shape of their mouths, they could almost be twins.

"Hey."

I scream, yanking my outstretched hand away from the faces like I've touched something hot. I can smell Mr. Morelli before I turn around to look at him. He smells soapy, damp, freshly showered. But there's something else: the smell of autumn, dirt, wet leaves. It's an earthy smell.

"Rachel, calm down! What's the matter?" He tugs at my

arm, glancing down at the table. "Oh. I see you've found her."

"What?" I stare, expecting to see both faces still gazing back at me. But my sister is gone; there is only the gap-toothed girl now, her expression still and unchanging.

"The painting," Sean clarifies. "You found her. I mean, you found it."

"Huh?" I press my palm to my forehead, which is cold and sweaty. "Oh, right. Yeah."

"Are you okay?" His hand is still on my arm. "I'm sorry if I scared you."

"I'm fine," I tell him, blinking again and again as I look around the room. *She was right there,* I think to myself. *I saw her.*

But now she's gone. What is the matter with me? Am I hallucinating? Regardless, I know I shouldn't say anything to Sean about what happened; he'd probably insist on walking home with me to tell my aunt and uncle.

"I'm sorry," I say, trying to seem calm. "I didn't mean to snoop. I saw the corner sticking out, and I was just curious—"

"Rachel, relax." He hands me a clean towel. Then he leans past me, bends over, and picks up the painting. We both look at it as I blot my hair dry.

"She's beautiful, isn't she?" he asks. He has changed into loose-fitting jeans and a red-and-white-plaid button-down shirt. His sleeves are rolled up to reveal tanned forearms. There are small bursts of dark hair on each of his knuckles.

He holds the painting with his right hand, and he places his left hand gently on my back. I get goose bumps from his touch.

"Alice painted that," I say.

"She sure did," he agrees. "I can't believe she didn't take it with her. I was walking past the art studio a few weeks ago, and there it was, perched on an easel." He teaches English at the community college; I used to see him there all the time last summer.

He takes a step away from me, letting his hand linger on my back for just a second before he walks across the room and rests the painting on a windowsill. "I've been meaning to tell her it's over here. I'm guessing she doesn't want it, though." He glances at me and flashes a smile. His teeth are so white that they almost seem to glow. "Do you think she'll mind if I keep it? I've been thinking of hanging it some-where." He pauses. "What am I saying? I should offer to buy it. She does such great work; it's hard to believe she's only eighteen."

"..."

"..."

"Hey, Rachel." He peers at me. "Are you sure you're okay? You look pale."

I force a smile. "Yes, I'm fine. It's getting late, that's all. I should go home." The clock on his stove says that it's seven thirty already. I have to come clean to my aunt and uncle about what happened at work tonight; it's what Rachel would do.

Mr. Morelli nods. "All right. Why don't you let me walk you, though? Here, take my umbrella. I'll get another one. It's still raining out there."

"No," I blurt. "I'm fine. I mean, I'll take an umbrella, but you don't have to walk with me." I smile again. "I'm a big girl."

He stares at me for a long moment. Then he scratches his head, like he's puzzled about something, but he finally smiles back. "I know you are."

Before I get the chance to say anything else, he starts toward the hallway. I can tell from his movements and his expression that he knows I'm uncomfortable, but his smile is unwavering. "All right," he says, gesturing with his hand. "Go ahead. Get out of here."

CHAPTER TWENTY

My feet feel unsteady on the pavement as I hurry along, holding the umbrella at an angle against the rain, which stings my cheeks as a few stray drops hit my face. Farther down the street, TJ is climbing out of his car, holding a newspaper above his head to protect himself from the downpour. His headlights are still on, beams of light slicing through the darkness, and I consider crossing the street to avoid having to say hello to him.

As I'm passing the still-vacant house that Robin and I broke into so many months ago, I glance up at the third-floor dormer window. There's a dim light shining from somewhere in the room.

For an instant, everything goes red. It's like a translucent curtain has been draped across my eyes. I stop dead, staring, unable to believe what I'm seeing. Again.

It's my sister. She stands in the window, staring down at

me. Robin is beside her. The two of them are so close together, they're almost touching. I get a sick, lurching feeling in my stomach. As I let the umbrella fall to my side, indifferent to the fact that I'm getting soaked for the second time tonight, I see swirls of red and crimson. I feel so dizzy that I wonder who might find me if I pass out right here on the street in the pouring-down rain.

I look up at the window again. The light is still shining, dim yet steady, but my sister and Robin are gone. They must have ducked out of the way. The thought of them together seems impossible, but I know what I saw. Could they have met without my knowledge at some point? Could they have been seeing each other secretly? Is it possible—it *can't* be—that everyone is right, and my sister *did* run off with Robin on Saturday? That she hasn't been at my grandma's house this whole time?

Without thinking much about what I'm doing, I drop the umbrella on the street and rush toward the vacant house, onto the porch. I try the heavy wooden front door, leaning on it with all my weight, not caring that anybody who might be looking out their window right now can see me. It's locked. Deadbolted.

I run around to the side of the house, find another locked door. In the backyard, it's the same thing. Kitchen door: locked. Basement door: locked. I return to the front porch, where I ring the bell over and over again. I pound on the door with both of my fists, crying, so angry and confused and hurt all at once. *God, what is happening to me?* And just behind that, there's another thought, one that I'd much rather not consider, not now or anytime: *is this how it feels to go crazy?*

I saw them. Then I didn't see them. It happened so fast, but I could have sworn they were looking right at me, like they wanted to make sure I caught a glimpse of them, even if only for a second. Why would they do this to me? They are the only two people in the world who really know me—why would they want to hurt me? I'm crying so hard that I can barely catch my breath.

"Shh. Shh. Stop it, Rachel. Rachel! Stop it!" There are arms around my shoulders, trying to pull my hands close to my body. I struggle with whoever is behind me, trying to break free. When I turn around to get a look at the person, I almost can't believe who I'm seeing.

Staring back at me, his brown eyes warm and full of concern, is my neighbor, TJ. He is out of breath from our struggle. Beneath the dim light of the front porch, I can see that his forearms are red and scratched.

"Let me go," I say, still trying to wriggle away from him. And he does, releasing me so quickly that I almost fall backward. As I steady myself, I sneer at him, demanding, "What the hell are you doing?"

"What am I doing? What are *you* doing? You can't try to break into an empty house, Rachel. It still belongs to someone. Are you trying to get yourself arrested?" His tone is defensive and a little harsh, but he doesn't sound angry; it's more like he's simply freaked out. But what does he care? He's never exchanged more than a few words with Rachel. And now he's watching her? Following her down the street?

TJ takes a step toward me; I take a big step away from him. He holds out his arms; I turn my head away, embarrassed that the former dork from across the street is seeing me cry.

"Go away," I say, choking on the words. "Leave me the hell alone, would you?"

"Of course I won't leave you alone. Where have you been the past two days? Have you been avoiding me?"

I almost laugh. "Avoiding you? TJ, what are you talking about?"

"Sunday morning," he says, "we were supposed to meet at our place."

"Our place?" I sputter. "What?"

"The house on Pennsylvania Avenue," he says. "I waited for over an hour, but you never showed. What happened to you? And what were you doing down at Sean Morelli's house just now? Why didn't you get in touch with me?" His tone softens a bit. "And don't call me TJ. You never call me TJ."

I can feel my pulse quicken as a sick feeling washes over me. There are things going on here that I have no idea about, I realize. Things that Rachel never bothered to tell me. That's what she was doing at the house all the times she slipped away last summer—she was meeting TJ. But she didn't tell me. Why didn't she want me to know?

I can't think straight. I have to leave. As I step forward,

preparing to shove past TJ and run home, he grabs me by the arm and holds on tight. He pulls me close to him and slides his hands around my waist. His breath smells of peppermint gum. His lips are smooth and wet as he kisses me, hard, backing me toward the outside wall of the house.

No. *Nonononono.* This cannot be happening. My sister would *never* let TJ kiss her.

But I have no idea what else to do besides go along with it. If I push him away again, he'll know that I'm not Rachel. I let him press me lightly against the brick, his hands sliding from my waist down to my sides as he laces his fingers through mine. After a few more seconds, he pulls away and smiles at me.

"There," he says. "That's better."

His gum is in my mouth now. *Ew.* I have to actively resist the urge to spit it back in his face.

"I'm sorry," I tell him. "Things are all messed up right now."

He squints at me. "What's wrong? Why were you trying to break into this place?"

What am I supposed to tell him? I guess the truth—sort of. "I thought I saw my sister in the window." I remove his gum from my mouth with my fingers and toss it onto the lawn. "I made a mistake. It couldn't have been her. All the doors are locked."

"She ran away again," he says, "didn't she? Your aunt told my mom about it yesterday."

I nod. "I think so."

"Rachel," he whispers, shaking his head and grinning, "don't worry about her. You're here. You're fine. And just think—in less than a year, this will all be over. We'll be alone together. You won't have to worry about what kind of trouble Alice is getting into anymore."

His words feel like a punch in the gut. Surely he's mistaken. My sister would never do . . . whatever it is he thinks they're doing together.

But she is. And she's been doing everything she can to make sure I don't know about any of it.

As much as I don't want to cry, I can feel my eyes growing damp at the possibility that I have no idea what's going on in my own home, with my own twin. Why would she keep something as big as a relationship from me? We make fun of TJ all the time, sure, but she could have told me if she'd gotten to know him, or even if she liked him. I would have listened. I would have understood.

"Think about it," he continues, "next August we'll pack up my car and drive down to Asheville together, just you and me. No more Aunt Sharon or Uncle Jeff. No more high school. No more waitressing at the Yellow Moon. No more sneaking around and lying to everyone . . ." His voice lowers to a whisper again. "And no more Alice."

He kisses the tip of my nose. I want to throw up.

"Just you and me," I echo.

TJ nods. "That's right." He leans in so close that our foreheads touch. "I love you, Rachel."

He loves her. He loves my sister. Well, then, I suppose the feeling must be mutual.

"I love you," I repeat, amazed that he doesn't seem to notice the hollow sound of my voice.

"Come on," he urges, leading me toward the street by tugging my arm, far more gently this time than just a few seconds ago. "We're being stupid. Someone will see us if we aren't careful."

He steps onto the sidewalk before me, picks up the umbrella, and waits for me to join him beneath it. Once I'm beside him, we walk down the street together, our arms brushing against each other.

We stop a few feet from my house. "I'll see you tomorrow morning, right?" he asks. Of course, I have no idea what he's talking about. I'm good at pretending, though.

"Yes," I agree, "tomorrow."

"Okay." He smiles again. He gives me another quick kiss on the lips. "Till tomorrow." As he backs away from me, he presses his right hand to his chest. "I'll be counting the minutes."

❀

The security sensor on the front door beeps as I step quietly inside the house. I cringe, waiting for the inevitable talk with my aunt and uncle about why I'm home from work so early.

"Rachel," my aunt calls from the kitchen, "is that you?"

I close my eyes and lean against the front door. This day has been too much. All I want to do right now is talk to my sister about everything that's happened, to confront her about what she's been hiding from me.

My uncle is in the living room, watching *Jeopardy!* He barely glances at me as I walk past; his gaze is fixated on the Daily Double. "Charlemagne," he says under his breath. "Charlemagne. It was Charlemagne."

"Who was King George?" the contestant ventures.

"Oh, I'm sorry, that's incorrect. The response we were looking for is 'Who is Charlemagne?'" Alex Trebek says.

My uncle finally glances at me, a silly, satisfied grin on his face. "I'm pretty smart, huh?"

I can't help myself; even though the gesture is definitely more Alice than Rachel, I give him a slow, patronizing nod. "Pure genius," I tell him. "Consider my mind officially blown."

He frowns at me. I shrug and continue past him, into the kitchen.

My aunt is seated at the table, drinking beer from a frosted mug and rifling through a stack of bills. "You're back early," she says, not looking up.

I take a deep breath. "I left. I guess I quit."

She still doesn't look at me. "I know. Charlie told me all about it when I picked him up. He's worried."

"I'm sorry. I didn't mean for it to happen. I got into a fight with Mr. Hahn."

She sighs, then takes a long sip of her beer. Leave it to my aunt to use a frosted mug in the privacy of her own home; I suppose drinking from the bottle would be far too common for her. "Are you feeling any better?"

I pause, confused by the question at first. Then I remember: I told her I came home sick from school this afternoon. All the lies get difficult to keep track of after a while. "I'm okay," I say. "Better. Not great, though."

"Did you take something? You should try ibuprofen."

"I did," I lie. "But it didn't help much."

She sighs again. She finally looks at me. "You should go upstairs and talk to Charlie."

I shake my head. "Is that all? Aren't you going to yell at me for losing my job?"

Another sip. Her shoulders slump a little bit. She's tired. "We can talk about it tomorrow, Rachel. I can't do it right now."

I don't move for a few seconds. I just stand there, looking at her, waiting for her to say something else. I'd almost rather she yelled at me. Her weary indifference is more unsettling than anger would be; at least I know how to deal with her when she's angry.

But she only continues to gaze at me with an odd, sad look on her face. Her life, I realize, has not turned out the way she expected it to, not at all. But then, none of ours have.

"Aunt Sharon?" Even as I'm pronouncing her name, I'm not exactly sure what I'm going to say next, if she lets me say anything at all. I can almost see her trying to summon enough emotional strength to respond.

"Yes?"

The words come out before I have a chance to think them through. "Do you remember the day you took us shopping for homecoming dresses? We were sophomores. We drove into the city early in the morning. Remember?"

"Sure I do. Why?"

I never thought I'd be telling her what I overhead that day, but I can't stop myself. Bringing it up right now seems cruel. She's tired. She's upset. I do it anyway, though. It's like I can't stand to go one more day without knowing why she said those things.

"While you were paying for our dresses, the saleswoman asked you if we were your daughters. You said yes. She asked if you had any other children, and you said no. I heard you."

My aunt looks at her hands. She fiddles with her wedding band, twirling it around her finger in a worried gesture. For a second I think she might cry.

She doesn't. She presses her hands against her frosted beer mug. "I poured this the wrong way," she says. "See how there's so much foam on top? When we were in high school, at parties, your mom always had this method for dissolving it. She'd rub her finger on her face, and then she'd stir it around in the foam."

"You went to parties in high school? With my mom?" I can't imagine my aunt surrounded by fun or laughter. I can't imagine her approving of a party full of high school students, much less attending one.

The question seems to upset her far more than my revelation of what I overheard at the dress shop two years ago. "Of course I went to parties. That surprises you, doesn't it?"

"Maybe a little," I admit.

"I even had a nickname." She glances into the living room, where my uncle is still watching television. "I had this boyfriend named Anthony, but everyone called him Tony. He moved here from New York City at the beginning of our senior year. He drove a red Camaro." She laughs. "Can you imagine? Me riding in a red Camaro with this beautiful, sophisticated boy? At least, we all thought he was sophisticated. He sold a lot of pot, I remember." Her eyes crinkle at their corners in a reflex of disapproval.

"What was your nickname?"

"What? Oh, right—it was Sherry. Sherry Baby." And she starts to hum softly. I recognize the song: it's "Sherry Baby" by the Four Seasons.

"What happened to him?"

She stops humming. She seems lost. "What happened to whom?"

"Your boyfriend. Tony."

"I have no idea. We broke up after a few months, and we graduated shortly after that. I went off to college and met your uncle. A couple of years later, we had Charlie. You know the rest. I don't think I'd recognize Tony if I passed him on the street tomorrow. It's funny, because at the time, I was so in love with him. I thought we'd get married after high school, and the rest of our lives together would be perfect." She sips her beer. "I was stupid back then, Rachel. I didn't know anything about life. Someday you'll understand what I mean."

My aunt has never talked much about her youth until now. I'm still not sure I believe anything she's saying; maybe she's making it all up, trying to convince me there was a time when she was cool. She's right about one thing, though: the idea of her riding around town in a Camaro with a cute boy from New York City seems impossible.

"I remember the day I took you shopping," she says. "We had so much fun, didn't we? You and your sister tried on all those dresses . . . you both looked so beautiful."

"You let us buy Wonderbras that day too," I say. My sister and I were giddy over them. For an instant, my thoughts shift to Kimber and her cutlets, and I feel almost ashamed by the fact that I got to own a Wonderbra despite already having perfectly adequate breasts.

"I remember what I said to the saleswoman too."

I'd expected her to deny it, or insist that I misheard their conversation. "You do?"

"Yes."

" . . . "

" . . . "

"Why did you lie, Aunt Sharon?"

She leans her elbows on the table and rests her chin in

her hands. "Don't you ever wish you could be someone else, Rachel? Even for just one day?"

When I don't answer her right away, it's like the spell she's been under is suddenly broken. She sits up and shakes her head a little bit, like she's coming out of a daze. "Well. I have to finish these bills before I go to the post office tomorrow." Her voice is crisp again. "Tell your cousin to get some sleep."

৵

When I reach the second-floor landing, Charlie's bedroom door is closed most of the way, but not completely. I can hear the soft mewing of kittens within. I nudge the door open and see my cousin curled up on his side in bed. He's already asleep, snoring softly, his sheets pulled up to his chin, a pair of bulky headphones over his ears. The headphones are attached to his iPod, which is clipped to the collar of his white undershirt. The music is turned up so loud that I can hear it from across the room. I can't help but smile. The song is "Rocky Raccoon" by the Beatles.

As I'm looking at him, I notice something moving beneath his sheet, near his stomach. Taking careful, slow steps so as not to wake him—although he's always been a deep sleeper—I lean over the bed and tug back the sheet. There, nestled at his side, are all four of the kittens.

They're asleep. At least, I think they are—they're probably

not old enough yet for their eyes to have opened. They lay in tiny gray balls, so close to one another that I can barely tell them apart, each of them no bigger than my cousin's fist. They don't even look like kittens, really—more like some kind of unknown, furry creature, sort of like a tiny squirrel crossed with a miniature rabbit. They are far too small to have climbed up here by themselves, I know. Charlie has brought them into bed with him. He wants to keep them close.

At the other side of his room, Linda McCartney is awake and watching me. She sits on her side, her fuzzy tail beating against the beige carpet. She's skinny all over, except for her belly, which is fat and distended, swollen with milk. It looks like she's nursed recently; the fur around her nipples is wet and shiny.

Charlie's breathing is deep and even. He looks incredibly peaceful right now, his serene expression so different from how I'm feeling inside. As I watch him, I can only think of one thing: I want to sketch him like this.

So I go up to my room, find a sketchbook, and hurry back downstairs. I shut his door behind me and sit on his bedroom floor with my legs crossed, trying to work quickly so my aunt or uncle doesn't catch me in here, but still trying to enjoy the act of drawing, which I haven't done in days.

My mother taught me how to draw and paint. When I was four, my dad built me my own miniature easel. He set it up beside my mom's, and she and I would spend hour after silent hour that way, eyes focused on the blank spaces as we filled them in, trying to breathe life into our subjects on paper.

When I was thirteen and living with my aunt and uncle, I completed my first oil painting. It took me seven months. It was a painting of my late grandfather, who I never had the chance to meet; he died long before I was born. I worked from some photographs that my grandmother had provided for me. Sometimes my aunt told me stories about him. She remembered the tiniest details: once, she described to me how he used to brush her hair when she was a little girl. "He was so gentle," she told me. "Your grandma was always in a rush to get me ready. She'd tug a comb through my knots, yanking so much that I'd cry sometimes. Your grandpa had these big, rough hands that looked clumsy and intimidating, but when he'd brush my hair, he was so gentle that he barely touched me. I'd go to school with knots all through my hair. I didn't even care."

Once the painting was finished and framed, I presented it to my grandma for her birthday. She wasn't taking medication at the time, and it showed. She was disoriented. She'd stay up for five days straight and then sleep for three. She moved the Captain into her family room—he was already stuffed by then—and she'd watch soap operas with him in the afternoons, carrying on long, one-sided conversations, pausing after she spoke, pretending to listen to his responses.

When she saw the painting, my grandma stared at it for a long time without saying anything. Her expression shifted out of focus, and she started to sway on her feet, almost like she was going to pass out. My aunt grabbed her by the elbow. "Mom, are you all right?" Her tone was a shade harsher than concerned. "Mother! Answer me!"

My grandma smiled at me. "I see him," she said.

I stared at her, listening, trying not to reveal how scared I felt. "Who do you see, Grandma?"

"Oh, I don't know his name. He's a looker, though. A young man, Alice. A young man guides your hand."

"Mom!" my aunt barked again, genuine anger in her voice. "Stop it!"

It was like she'd slipped into a kind of trance. When I was thirteen, I wanted to believe so badly that my grandmother had a special ability to see things others couldn't. But my aunt had no patience for her mother's displays. She'd been putting up with them her whole life. To her, there was nothing special about it at all. It was just simple lunacy.

I lose track of time as I sit, sketching Charlie. Maybe it's been twenty minutes, or maybe it's been two hours. That's what happens to me when I draw: I go somewhere else. It's the most amazing feeling.

As I'm finishing up, I stare at the kittens, my hand working to draw their wispy, almost invisible whiskers. The four of them are completely still, except for the faint rise and fall of their rib cages as they breathe. When the drawing is complete, I set aside the sketchbook and approach the bed. They can't stay here with him all night. They have to be with their mother.

One by one, I pick them up and move them to the floor. Immediately, they find Linda and burrow close to her, their tiny mouths opening as they search for milk in the darkness.

But when I pick up the last kitten, it feels oddly heavy in my hand. It is warm and limp. It's not breathing.

Charlie will be devastated. I consider taking it down-stairs, giving it to my uncle and letting him worry about it. These things happen, I know; the kittens are weak and small. Things die all the time, every day, but that won't matter to my cousin. He'll be heartbroken.

I take the kitten to its mother. Before I set it down beside her, I hold it against my chest with both hands. I take long, deep breaths with my eyes closed. I don't know what I'm doing. I'm not expecting anything to happen. But it feels right to hold it close, my hands cupped so tightly around its body that, if it were alive, I'd be worried I was going to hurt it.

After a minute or so, I lay it gently on the floor. I pull Charlie's sheet up to his neck again. I turn down the volume on his MP3 player, the sounds of "Hey Jude" receding until I can barely hear them.

∾

The day feels like it has lasted forever. Despite my long nap earlier, I feel exhausted all over again. I can't concentrate either; when I try to focus on the night's events, they are nothing but a blur, and for a second I almost convince myself that I've been asleep this whole time, that I haven't woken up from my nap yet, and everything that's happened to me—at work, with Sean, with TJ—is a bad dream.

Right now, what I want is to sleep *without* dreams. To do so, though, is going to require a healthy dose of pharmaceutical assistance. Rachel doesn't even like to take NyQuil because she says it makes her feel fuzzy the next day. I, on the other hand, seem to have a natural affinity for self-medication.

I guess it runs in the family. When we were kids, Rachel and I grew to recognize the distinct smell of marijuana that used to come from our parents' closed bedroom door some evenings. We didn't know what it was at the time, of course, but I'll never forget my first teenage encounter with it, at a party a few years ago, and the instant recognition of its odor. Rachel was at that party, too, and she got *so* upset when it became clear that our parents had been toking up while their daughters played in the next room.

The realization that my parents were far from perfect came slowly to me over the years. I've never held it against them, though. If they had been different in any way, then everything else would be different, too, in ways I can't begin to imagine. I don't love them because they did everything right. They were my parents; I would have loved them regardless. Perfection is subjective, especially when it comes to people. To me, they were exactly what they were supposed to be. Until they died.

❦

My aunt and uncle, despite all their outward squareness, are not so different from my parents. My uncle's side of their walk-in closet is neat and orderly; everything about it screams normal. But on the very top shelf, behind a row of neatly folded sweaters, there's the motherload: it's a metal safe built right into the wall. Just the sight of the thing, all mystery and possibility, gives me a shiver of excitement.

I pull out one of the dresser drawers and stand on the edge in order to reach the safe. Two years ago, when I first stumbled upon its existence during a routine snoop session while I was home alone one afternoon, I guessed the combination on my second try: 04-17-91. It's Charlie's birthday.

Even though I already know what's inside, I still get a thrill every time the door swings open. There are a few file folders containing legal documents: my aunt's and uncle's wills, birth certificates, social security cards, that kind of stuff. There are the keys to the Porsche, which will have to stay put as long as they're in here; I can't take anything too obvious or my aunt and uncle will realize I've found their best hiding spot. There are several bottles of prescription painkillers, leftovers from a triple root canal that kept my aunt in a foul mood for pretty much all of last winter. And way in the back, pushed into the corner, there's a Ziploc baggie of primo dope and a package of rolling papers. The pot is actually mine; my aunt "accidentally" found it while "cleaning" my room a few months ago. Why she was cleaning underneath my mattress remains a mystery. In any case, my stash got confiscated, and I got grounded. Good, upstanding citizens that they are, my aunt and uncle claimed to have flushed the pot. I never believed them, not for a minute. And I don't feel the slightest bit guilty helping myself to a small amount from time to time—that, along with a few of the papers and a couple of painkillers that my aunt will never miss.

I go into my room, straight to my bathroom, and wash down the painkillers with a glass of water. Then I curl up in the oversize window seat facing the backyard. Slowly and carefully, I roll a small joint. When I light it up, I lean out the window as far as possible, trying to prevent the smoke from coming into the room.

Once I've finished, I leave the window open and change into my pajamas. My stomach is empty; the pills should be kicking in soon.

But just as my surroundings are starting to blur, I remember my sketchbook. It's still in Charlie's room, open to the drawing of him and the kittens. As tired as I am, I know I can't leave it there. I'm supposed to be Rachel, and Rachel doesn't draw.

I rush downstairs to retrieve it. The TV is on in the living room; my aunt and uncle are still awake, which means they probably haven't checked on my cousin yet. I crack his door open and lean over to pick up the sketchbook from the floor.

I stop. I stop moving, stop breathing, stop thinking. I stare across his room, astounded by what I'm seeing. It's impossible.

Linda is still on the floor with her kittens beside her. They are nursing.

All four of them.

CHAPTER TWENTY-ONE

My sleep is hard and dreamless until my alarm jerks me awake after what feels like only seconds of unconsciousness. My room is dark. I'm freezing, and the air all around me feels cold and damp; it's because I slept with my window open. I'm covered in gooseflesh as I climb out of bed and patter across the floor in my bare feet, fumbling with the buttons on our alarm clock, trying to shut it off, to hit snooze, to do *something* to make it stop beeping. But nothing works; not the buttons, not the volume dial, not even a good, hard smack. Finally, I lean over to unplug the damn thing. That's when I notice the time. It's two a.m. I have no recollection of setting the alarm at all last night, much less programming it to go off right now.

My throat hurts. My mouth is so dry that my tongue feels like it's been coated in sawdust. Suddenly I'm so thirsty that all I can think about is getting some water. I go into my bathroom and cup my hands beneath the faucet, drinking from them again and again, but it doesn't seem to help; I might as well be downing salt water for all the good it's doing, each sip somehow less satisfying than the last. Even after I lean over to place my mouth directly on the flow of water, unable to gulp fast enough to keep up with it, soaking the front of my shirt, it's not enough. I need a glass, something that can be refilled. I go downstairs, into the kitchen, wincing with every creak of the floorboards. My aunt has always placed an over-the-top emphasis on maintaining proper sleep habits. Even when Rachel and I had sleepovers at our house, she insisted that we go to bed at a decent hour. She claims it has to do with the underestimated importance of circadian rhythms, that the body is thrown completely out of whack without a consistent routine, but that's not really why it bothers her so much. It's because my grandma goes for days without sleep sometimes, slipping deeper into the funhouse of her mind with every passing hour, until she has no choice but to shut down. She used to do it all the time when my aunt was young, alternating between a manic alertness and total exhaustion that required days of sleep in order to recover. By the time she was twelve, my aunt claims she was basically running the household for my grandma, who rarely knew what day it was.

I drink three full glasses of water, one right after the next, until my thirst begins to diminish. As I'm refilling my glass for the fourth time, I hear a soft tapping against the kitchen window. I look up to see Robin standing on the back porch, his face so close that each breath creates a small circle of fog against the glass as he exhales. It's obvious that he wants to come in.

The security alarm is set. When I type in the code to shut it off, every button I press is accompanied by a loud beeping sound, and I'm terrified that someone will wake up and discover us down here together. But they don't.

The sensor on the back door beeps as I let him in. He's never set foot in my house until now. He's not wearing a jacket, just his usual jeans and a white T-shirt. "You must be freezing," I say, rubbing my hands along his bare arms, trying to warm him up. "What the hell are you doing here, Robin? It's the middle of the night. I was dead asleep."

His eyes crinkle at their corners as he smiles. "You look awake to me."

I frown. "How did you even know I'd be down here?"

"I got lucky. I was out for a walk. I was going to throw stones at your window, but then I saw you."

A small part of me feels disappointed that he spotted me in the kitchen. Nobody has ever thrown stones at my window in the middle of the night. The idea is so impossibly romantic; does it actually happen in real life, and not just in the movies? It would have made such a lovely memory. It could have been my red Camaro moment. But it didn't happen.

It wouldn't have mattered, anyway. Not after what I saw

earlier. "You're lying to me," I say, letting my hands fall away from him. "You weren't out for a walk."

"What?" He starts to smile, but then he realizes I'm not kidding. "Alice, why would I lie?"

"Because I *saw* you with her!" I hiss, struggling to keep my voice low. "And you saw me too. Tell me what's going on, Robin. What were you doing with Rachel?"

"You think I was with Rachel? Alice, I swear, I've never even met your sister. I wasn't with her. Not tonight, and not any other time." He pulls me toward him, taking my hands and pressing them flat against his chest. "I'm right here," he whispers. "I'm with you."

I want to cry, but I'm so parched that I can't even bring tears to my eyes. "But I saw you," I murmur.

"No, you didn't."

I look up at him. "Then who was it? Who did I see in the window with Rachel?"

"Alice," he says, smoothing my hair, careful to avoid the back of my head, "you're upset. You're not thinking straight." He's right about that much.

I turn my head, leaning against him with my whole body as he wraps his arms around my waist. "I don't know what to do," I whisper.

"Then don't do anything. Just be with me tonight."

"I can't. My aunt and uncle will go berserk if they wake up and find you here." I've always hated having to say "my aunt and uncle" instead of "my parents." The former is such a mouthful, five syllables instead of only three, not to mention the necessary explanation every time I discuss them for the first time with someone new. Over the years, I've gotten good at keeping it short. "My aunt and uncle. I live with them." End of story. People usually don't pry beyond that, at least not to my face. They wait until I'm not around to get the full story from a third-party source. As annoying as those five syllables can be, I've never once considered referring to them as my parents to avoid the hassle of an explanation.

"So let's go somewhere else." Robin waves an arm around the room. "The night is ours."

I bite my bottom lip. "I don't know." But I do know, and so does he. I'm only faking hesitation. "You want to drive somewhere?" My aunt's car keys, I'm sure, are in her purse, which is just an arm's length away on the kitchen table.

"Sure." He steps back, looking me over. I'm wearing boxer shorts and a tank top. "You'll need a jacket, though. It's chilly out there."

❦

There are hardly any other cars on the road as we drive away from town, heading east on the highway, our destination still unclear. I didn't bother to bring a jacket. I didn't even bother to put shoes on before we left; I'm driving barefoot. Robin leans his seat back and rests his shoes against the dashboard. He isn't buckled in. "I love this time of night," he says, closing his hand over mine. He's done it plenty of times before, but it always thrills me just the same. There's something about him that makes me feel so protected when we're together, especially when we're doing something so irresponsible. "Everyone is asleep right now," he continues, giving me a sideways glance. "Even the criminals."

The windshield is fogging up. I should turn on the defroster, but I don't want to pull my hand away; his touch feels too good to let go. "So then what does that make us?" I lean forward, squinting to see the road.

"It doesn't make us anything. It's almost like we don't exist right now. Nobody knows we're out here."

"You shouldn't have come over tonight," I say, unable to dismiss my worry. "The police are looking for you."

"I figured. That's why I wanted to see you." He rubs his index finger across my knuckles. "I'm gonna have to leave for a while, Alice."

"What?" I lose my grip on the wheel; the car drifts to the right, onto the rumble strips. In a smooth motion, Robin leans over and uses his free hand to help me steer us back onto the road.

"You can't do that," I say. "You can't just *leave.* Where will you go?"

He doesn't answer me right away. We drive past a sign that says FOREST HILLS – 7 MILES, and our destination tonight suddenly becomes clear. Maybe I've known it all along.

"I'll go home," he says. "I've been gone for too long."

"Home," I repeat. My voice is flat. "I thought this was your home."

He stares out his window. "You know it's not."

The fog on the windshield is so thick that I can barely see the road. I finally turn on the defroster. Robin lights a cigarette. The smoke fills the car, burning my eyes. We'll have to drive home with the windows down to get rid of the smell. I could tell him to toss it, but I don't. I'm not sure why.

∽

In the past nine years, I've only taken the Forest Hills exit three times. The first time was less than two years ago, right after my sister and I got our drivers' licenses. We never discussed where we were going that day; we both knew without having to say it out loud.

Our old house was really more of a cottage, a single story built on a few wooded acres, our yard basically part of the forest. You had to know where you were going in order to find the place. It was on a dead-end gravel road in the middle of nowhere; our closest neighbor growing up was a fifteen-minute walk away, a tiny run-down A-frame occupied by an elderly guy named Ed Shandy. Rachel and I used to visit him sometimes when we went for walks without our mom or dad. Ed kept a refrigerator in his basement stocked with Red Chief cherry soda. As far as we could tell, it was the only thing he ever drank. Our mom never bought soda, so it was a treat we looked forward to with ridiculous anticipation every time we went to see Ed. Rachel only ever drank one, sometimes two, but I couldn't get enough of it. I was maybe seven or eight, already hard-wired with an appetite for excess. One time I drank so much soda that I ended up puking on the walk home.

I was the one driving the day Rachel and I visited our old house. "Don't park," she instructed, once we were almost there. "Just slow down while you drive past."

But I couldn't help it; I had to stop. I hadn't come this far just to get a glimpse. I pulled to the side of the road and shut off the engine.

"It looks so much smaller than I remember," I said. "Was it always this tiny?"

Rachel flattened her hands against the passenger side window, like it was a barrier that could not possibly be breached, and peered at the house. "*We* were smaller. Of course it seemed bigger at the time." She leaned back in her seat. "I'm ready to go."

"Are you kidding? I don't think anybody's home. Come on, let's get out. We can look in the windows."

"No." She grabbed my arm. "I want to leave now."

But once I'd voiced the idea, I couldn't let it go. "I'll only be a few minutes," I said, wriggling free of her grasp as I climbed out of the car.

"Alice, come back." She was pleading with me, her eyes

wide with panic, like I might disappear onto the property and never return. I felt a rare twinge of annoyance. This was her home too. How could she not want to peek inside, to compare the way it looked now to the fossilized version in our minds? To me, the house served as proof that we'd existed as a normal family once. *We slept in this room. We ate in this room. We played in these woods. We were here. It was real.* My aunt and uncle have never made much of an effort to preserve the memory of our parents. Maybe they think it will be too painful for us. What's more painful, I think, is trying to ignore the past, to pretend it never happened.

Another family had moved in. A new wooden playset—the fancy, expensive kind—had been installed in the back-yard. A neat rectangle of land had been cleared to make room for a tidy vegetable garden, the plants arranged in symmetri-cal rows, the whole thing surrounded by low wire fencing to keep out small animals. A newish central A/C unit hummed away beneath the living-room window. My parents used to claim they didn't believe in air conditioning—they said it was better to just wear fewer clothes and keep the windows open—but now I wondered if they only said that because it was a luxury they never could have afforded.

I took my time circling the house, looking into every window. The roof had been replaced, three skylights in-stalled where there used to be nothing but rotting shin-gles, the glass squares spilling light into the formerly dim foyer. The sliding glass doors leading to the side patio were now french doors. The kitchen was almost unrecognizable: ceramic tile instead of linoleum, granite countertops instead of chipped laminate. It was the same thing in the bathroom; everything was new and clean and beautiful. There were no wet towels on the floor beside the shower, no toiletries cluttering the sink, no visible ring around the tub (which my mother used to swear was impossible to get rid of). I don't know why whoever lived there even bothered to leave the house standing; they'd changed so much they might as well have torn down the place and started from scratch. Somehow, I think I would have preferred that. The way things were, it was like the new owners wanted to destroy all traces of us, to lift away every impression we'd ever made and replace it with something newer, something *better*, like the remnants we'd left behind weren't good enough. I had no idea who these people were, but I knew I disliked them, even as I understood how irrational the feeling was. They'd bought the house. They had every right to do whatever they pleased to it.

I only looked around for five or ten minutes before returning to the car. "They changed everything," I said. "Are you sure you don't want to see for yourself?"

"I'm sure." She folded her legs, pulling her knees against her chest, and turned the radio up so loud that it was impossible to hold a conversation. As we drove away, I slowed down when we passed the spot where Ed Shandy's A-frame used to sit, but it was gone. In its place, someone had built a two-story Colonial with ugly beige siding. They'd cut down all the trees and installed an in-ground swimming pool.

I turned off the radio. "I wonder what happened to Ed? It seems strange that he would move away, don't you think?"

My sister looked at me sharply. "He was ancient, Alice. I'm sure he's dead by now."

For some reason, the possibility hadn't crossed my mind. In the months after the accident, I used to imagine Ed sitting in his house, watching game shows on his old TV with its crooked wire antenna, an overflowing supply of Red Chief cherry soda waiting for us in his basement. I used to think that, no matter how long we were gone, Ed would always be there when we finally returned. For a while, I used to ask my aunt to buy us cherry soda when she went grocery shopping. She was happy to oblige me, but it never seemed to taste the same; the syrupy flavor seemed artificial (which I'm sure it was) and overwhelming; I felt sick after just a few sips.

When we got home that day, I felt sorry that I'd forced my sister to wait while I snooped around outside our old house. But she had wanted to go as much as I did—at least I'd assumed she had. "I thought you wanted to go," I told her. "Didn't you?"

She didn't answer me.

"Don't be mad at me because you were too afraid to leave the car," I said. The words came out harsher than I'd intended.

"I'm not mad. And I wasn't afraid." She glanced at our front porch, where Charlie was sitting with Sean Morelli, helping him brush Sheba. She was shedding like crazy; wisps of loose fur drifted through the air as they worked, floating away in the breeze like miniature tumbleweeds.

"Then what's the matter? Why are you ignoring me?"

She held very still as she spoke. "I thought being there would feel different. I thought I'd be sad, or angry, or . . . something."

"But you weren't?" Charlie and Sean were watching, waiting for us to get out of the car.

"No."

"Well, then, what *did* you feel?"

Rachel didn't move. She didn't even blink. "I didn't feel anything. All I could think about was that we didn't belong there, that we were trespassing. None of it is ours anymore, Alice. Do you know what I mean?"

"We used to live there," I insisted. "We had every right to look around."

"You're wrong." She seemed certain of the fact.

"I'm not wrong. That place was a part of our lives."

"No, it wasn't. It was part of a different life. Not the one we have now." She got out of the car and started toward the house. When she reached the porch, she sat down on the swing and slipped into conversation with Charlie and Sean, the three of them laughing about something while I stayed in the car, trying to wrap my head around the idea that a person could simply wipe away the past and start all over again. We hadn't had much of a choice, true, but Rachel seemed to have let go without a struggle. It wasn't nearly as easy for me; I was leaving claw marks, resisting with all my strength, desperate to combine all those memories into something that felt whole. It wasn't working.

⌒

Robin and I are parked in front of my old house now, at almost two thirty in the morning, my headlights switched off so we won't look too suspicious, even though it's unlikely anyone will notice us this late at night.

"Rachel never came back after that," I explain. "Not that I ever invited her."

"But you did come back," he says. "Didn't you?"

"Yes. I came back twice by myself. The second time was just like the first. Nobody was home. I looked around for a while, and then I left. It was no big deal."

He rolls down his window to toss out his cigarette. "And what happened the third time?"

"I saw them. I saw the people who live here now." I try to swallow, but it's difficult; I'm still so thirsty that I can barely stand it.

"I drove up just as they were leaving," I continue. "I watched them get into their car, the mom and dad and their daughter."

"Did they notice you?"

"Yes. I pretended I was pulled over to make a phone call. They didn't pay much attention."

He lights another cigarette. "That's because you look so innocent." He grins. "But I know better."

I know he's trying to be flirtatious, that his comment was innocent, but I'm not in the mood for flirtation right now—not when he's just told me he's leaving soon. "They looked normal," I say, trying to pretend his words have no effect on me. "They seemed happy. They drove away, and I waited for a few minutes before I got out of the car, and then I did the same thing I'd done the other times."

"You looked in the windows?"

"Yeah." I pause.

"What?" Robin asks, sensing my hesitation. "What else did you do?"

"Nothing," I say quickly, which is a lie, and he knows it.

"Tell me." When I turn my face toward him, he cups my chin in his hand. "You can trust me, Alice. Don't you know that?"

But I don't trust him, not like I used to. He just told me he's leaving. He doesn't care that I'll be alone. He's looking out for himself.

I tell him anyway. "I threw a rock through the french doors. The glass shattered everywhere."

He exhales a ribbon of smoke, staring as it dissipates in front of us. "Why did you do that?"

"I don't know." That's not true, either; I'd done it because I wanted to hurt them, the new owners with their perfect, happy life and their renovated house filled with expensive things.

"I went inside, Robin."

The whites of his eyes flash as his gaze widens. "Jesus, Alice. Did you steal anything?"

"No." The question seems ridiculous. Why would I want something of theirs? "All I wanted was to see my dad's mural. Before the accident, my dad was working on a mural in the living room. It took up a whole wall. He never got to finish it."

Robin crinkles his forehead in surprise. "And it was still there? They didn't paint over it?"

"Oh, sure," I say, "they repainted the whole room. It's sort of a beige color now. It's boring."

"Alice, you're not making sense. If they painted over the mural, then how could you see it?"

I close my eyes. I remember standing in the living room, shattered glass surrounding my feet, staring at the blank wall, trying to remember what the mural had looked like. And then it just . . . appeared. It seemed to emerge from beneath the new layers of paint, the lines bleeding through gradually at first, and then all of a sudden, until I could see every last detail. It was as clear as anything, every bit as real to me as Robin is right now, sitting beside me in the car.

And then it was gone, just as quickly as it had appeared. It simply dissolved, the colors bleeding together until there was nothing left. But it was real. I'd seen it and touched it, and I knew that it would always be there, no matter how many new layers of paint were applied. As long as the house was standing, the new owners could do whatever they wanted to make it their own, but the mural would remain. To me, it was proof: we were here once. Nothing could change that.

∽

It's almost four a.m. by the time we get back to my house. All the lights are out. Everybody is still asleep. Nobody will know I was ever gone.

We stand together on the back porch. Robin wraps his arms around me, and I rest my face against his chest, trying to commit his smell to memory. "Please don't go." I'm crying, getting his shirt damp.

"I have to, Alice. I'm sorry."

"I wish I'd never met you," I say, even though it's not true. "This isn't fair."

"I know. I'm sorry. I never meant for all this to happen. I just wanted to meet you, just once. I didn't mean to— Never mind."

"You didn't mean to what?" I pull back a little. "What didn't you mean to do?"

He kisses my forehead. I want him to kiss my mouth, the way a real boyfriend would, but I know he won't do it. He's leaving. It's over.

I can't prolong the inevitable, not anymore. I'm tired. "Be careful," I tell him, reaching for the doorknob.

He smiles. "Don't worry about me. Good-bye, Alice."

"Good-bye." I want to get upstairs before I lose it, and spend the rest of the night sobbing into my pillow like a silly teenager with a bad crush. But just as I'm about to close the door, I turn around to look at him one last time.

"Robin?"

"Yeah?"

"I loved you."

His shoulders slump a little bit. He looks small and sad as he backs away, one step at a time. "I loved you too, Alice." He takes a few more steps, and his body fades into the darkness, until I can barely see him at all. "I loved you more."

CHAPTER TWENTY-TWO

I want to stay up for the rest of the night, wallowing in my heartache, but I'm too exhausted even to cry. Sleep comes over me almost immediately, yanking me into unconsciousness. There's not a thing I can do to stop it.

All night long, I dream of the girl with the gap-toothed smile. We jog along the trail together, sweating, our breath labored, but our legs don't take us anywhere; we remain in the same place, unable to move forward.

"He's back there," she says to me, smiling, nodding over her shoulder.

"Who?" I ask, trying to run. The sense that I need to get away from something—that we both need to escape—is overwhelming, and makes me feel so helpless as my legs carry me nowhere.

"You know him." Her voice, which is sweet and high, becomes singsong. "He's gonna get us . . ."

I look behind me. There's a figure in the distance, walking at a leisurely pace, catching up to us little by little. I recognize him immediately: it's Homeless Harvey and his dog.

"That's just Harvey," I say, relieved. "He won't hurt us."

She continues to smile at me as we jog in place. "He'll catch up eventually, Alice."

I frown. "How do you know my name? Who are you?"

Her eyes flash beneath the bright sunlight. We are both sweating. She smells horrible, like rotting flesh. "You know who I am."

"No, I don't," I insist. "Tell me your name."

"What do you mean?" Her grin fades. "We're sisters. It's me, Alice. It's Rachel."

I stop. I take a closer look at her. "You aren't Rachel."

"Yes I am. I'm Rachel." And her face starts to go fuzzy, blurring out of focus until I can't recognize her at all. Behind us, Homeless Harvey gets closer, his dog strolling along by his side.

"You aren't Rachel," I repeat.

"I have lots of names. Jamie. Jennifer. Susan. Rebecca." She pauses, so blurry now that I can hardly make out her face at all. "He's coming," she says again. "Do you want me to keep going? Amy. Shannon. Melissa. Rachel." I can barely see her; it's like she's disintegrating right in front of me. "Alice," she says.

"What?" I ask, starting to feel panicked. "What do you want?"

"My name is Alice," she tells me. "Alice Foster. Rachel Foster."

"You're lying." Harvey is closer now, maybe fifty feet away. He raises his right arm in a friendly wave when I look back at him.

She's gone. I'm alone on the path. I try to run again, but I can't. My legs pump, my chest aches with each deep breath, but I don't move. He gets closer and closer. I remember what my uncle told me once: *Homeless Harvey is harmless.* It sounds almost like a nursery rhyme. I realize that I'm holding something in my left hand. I glance down, my body electric with fear and panic, and see the peach pit monkey clutched in my fist.

"Wake up." It's her voice—the gap-toothed girl, even though I can't see her.

"Wake up," she repeats. Harvey is maybe ten feet away. He's grinning ear to ear as he approaches.

"Wake up, Rachel."

I squeeze my eyes shut and try to scream. A hand covers my mouth.

"Rachel! Wake up!"

But as hard as I try, I can't seem to make any sound.

The sky goes dark. Rain begins to pour. Before I know it, I'm soaked, and there is blackness all around me.

"Rachel."

My whole body feels heavy. My eyes are still closed, but I'm awake; I'm sure of it. Someone is shaking me.

My eyelids flutter open, and I see Kimber leaning over me, a concerned look on her pretty face. I sit up. "Kimber. What the hell are you doing in my room?" I'm out of breath, still shaking a little bit from the nightmare. "Oh God. I just had the weirdest dream." It occurs to me that I'm freezing again, despite the fact that my body is beneath the covers.

"Get up," Kimber says. "Get dressed. I'm driving you to school."

Super-duper. I look at my alarm clock; it's already 7:40. I've slept in, which doesn't surprise me, considering last night's substance abuse and subsequent joyride. I'm groggy, and the inside of my mouth feels like it's covered in wet moss. I didn't bother to brush my teeth or wash my face last night, but maybe this is a good thing; with any luck, there's still enough makeup to hide my bruises. I'd pulled on a sweatshirt just before bed, so my wrists are hidden by the sleeves.

Unlike me, Kimber appears to be feeling great; it's like she spent her morning on a coffee IV drip. When I don't crawl out of bed right away, she claps her hands twice and rises onto the balls of her feet in a little jump. Her glossy hair, which has been styled with a curling iron, bounces over her shoulders. She wears a pink polo shirt and white capri pants with a slim silver belt. There are no traces whatsoever of her awkward discomfort at my grandma's house yesterday, or her persistent curiosity from our exchange at work last night.

Tossing the covers aside, coughing a few times, I ask her, "What the hell are you so chipper for?" Immediately, I regret my snide tone. It's so very "Alice" of me.

But Kimber doesn't seem to notice. She twirls a piece of hair around her finger, looking at the room, her gaze lingering on my drawings fastened to the walls. "I'm an early bird," she says, staring at Robin's portrait on the easel. "If I sleep past eight, I feel like I've wasted the day."

Her perkiness is irritating as hell; I could slap her. Instead, I get up and stroll toward the bathroom to start getting ready, shutting the door behind me without another word, leaving her to wait alone in my bedroom.

I check my reflection and feel instant relief: my makeup is still pretty much in place. If Kimber looked close enough, she would definitely notice the bruising, but I don't think she was paying attention. I wash my face and reapply my makeup, double checking it before I leave the bathroom.

I can tell Kimber is impatient as I'm getting dressed. Once I'm ready, she whisks me downstairs. I barely have a chance to say good-bye to my aunt and Charlie before she tugs me out the door. I don't realize until we're driving away that the money I stole is in my sister's bookbag, right here in the car with me. I'd put it there last night in my drug-and-alcohol haze, thinking I would give it back to Nicholas at school. Once I sobered up, I realized it was a terrible idea, but I forgot to replace it under my bed before we left this morning.

∽

High school. I've never particularly liked it, but I don't hate it either. Before today, having Rachel around made things bearable. Even when the rest of our friends began to avoid me, and even after I'd gotten a reputation as a Bad Influence, I always had my sister. And when things got too tough to manage, I could *be* my sister: Popular. Kind. Smart. Slipping into her life used to give me such a sense of peace and normalcy in what otherwise felt like a constant state of internal chaos.

But something feels different now, today, especially after yesterday's confrontation with TJ. I can't wrap my head around the possibility that Rachel has actually been seeing him behind my back. Why wouldn't she tell me? She and I tell each other everything. We always have.

Our lockers are in alphabetical order, so hers is next to mine, in the hallway on the second floor. For her morning classes, I'm going to need her texts for English, French, and calculus. She has study hall fourth period, which will be easy, but I'm not sure exactly how I'm going to make it through the morning prior to that. When we've switched in the past, we've always gone to great lengths to prepare each other: going over homework together, making sure we know exactly what's going on in each other's classes. But without Rachel's prep, my confidence is growing shakier by the minute. I can probably get through English and French okay, as long as there aren't any quizzes. Calculus, though, will be nearly impossible. I'm still in algebra II, and I'm barely getting by with a C.

I spin the dial on her locker, trying to think. I could fake a headache and go to the nurse. I could skip class altogether and hide out in the library. Or I could ditch the whole day and do something else entirely. But what? I don't have a car on campus, and it's a long walk home; someone could easily recognize me in town.

I lift the latch on Rachel's locker. It doesn't open. I jiggle it a little bit—these things tend to stick—but it still won't budge. Weird.

The hallway is starting to empty as students make their way to homeroom. I feel a small twinge of panic, and a thought crosses my mind for just a second before I push it away. *Impossible.* I try the combination again. No luck.

We get to program our own combinations at the beginning of each year. Most people, including me and my sister, just keep the same numbers from one year to the next. The only way Rachel's would have changed is if she'd reprogrammed it herself.

But why would she do something like that? I'm the only other person who knows her combination. Why wouldn't she want me to be able to open her locker?

The three-minute warning bell rings.

Mr. Slater—who is Rachel's homeroom teacher, in addition to teaching bio and chem—comes strolling into the hallway. He's usually in a foul mood, and today is no exception. As he approaches me, the reek of cigarette smoke on his body and clothing is so powerful that I have to breathe through my mouth to avoid feeling sick. His outfit, a button-down white shirt and khaki pants, appears wrinkled and disheveled, almost like he slept in his clothes the night before. There is a small square of toilet paper blotting a shaving cut on his blotchy neck. He's balding and overweight, his soft belly hanging over his belt a little bit. His skin has a grayish, unhealthy color. And he looks . . . empty. He looks defeated, like life has beaten him down over the years. Despite the fact that he gave me a failing grade on my diorama of a molecule last year, which blew my strong C-minus average for the semester, I find myself feeling sorry for him.

"Rachel," he says, "you're going to be late. What's the problem?" He's trying to be stern, but he sounds more indifferent than anything, like he can't be bothered with anything beyond going through the motions.

I shake my head, staring down at my sister's locker, fumbling to try the combination. And once again, it doesn't work.

Could she have possibly . . . no. No, no, no. She would have told me if she'd changed her locker combination. She would have told me if she were seeing TJ. She would have told me all of it. She's my best friend.

"What's the problem?" Mr. Slater repeats, taking a few steps closer to me, looking annoyed. There are half moons of papery skin beneath his eyes, which makes his face appear frail and droopy. And sad. He just looks so incredibly sad. I've never noticed it until now.

"I can't—It's not—" My words falter. What am I supposed to tell him? That I've forgotten my own locker combination?

"Rachel?" He tilts his head to one side. The square of toilet paper on his neck falls away and goes drifting to the floor, unnoticed by him. A small dot of bright-red blood bursts onto his skin.

"Come on," he says, beckoning with his hand, turning to walk toward his room, oblivious to my panic.

I follow him. At least I have Rachel's backpack; inside are a few spiral notebooks and her copy of *Our Town*, which we're reading in English. Maybe nobody will notice that I don't have the right books. Or that I'm totally unprepared. Or that I'm not Rachel.

My sister and I have homeroom together, but none of our good friends—that is, none of Rachel's good friends—are in here with us. This morning, it's just me and three other students, none of whom I know well at all. The four of us sit at our desks, absently listening to the morning announcements. Tacos and enchiladas for lunch. No cross-country practice after school today. The cheerleaders are holding a car wash this weekend in the parking lot of Dunkin' Donuts to raise money for new uniforms.

Throughout the announcements, Mr. Slater shoots glances at the empty desk beside mine, the one I'd normally be sitting at if Rachel were here. Every few seconds, he shifts his gaze to me, then back to the desk. I notice him sweating a little bit at his hairline, at the sides of his face. When the bell rings for first period, everyone stands up at once and heads toward the door. For a second, I think he's going to stop me as I'm leaving, but he doesn't. When I glance over my shoulder, I see him continuing to sit at his desk, hands balled into fists in front of him, his body held still. He almost looks like he's going to cry.

∽

English passes without incident; we have an in-class discussion on *Our Town*, which I haven't read a word of, but I manage to avoid getting called on by nodding along with everyone else's comments and pretending to listen attentively, even though my mind keeps drifting back to my inability to open Rachel's locker. I remember Kimber's comments yesterday, and my aunt's one-sided phone conversation with my grandmother. My mentally unstable grandmother. My aunt and uncle are convinced that her abilities are not separate from her illness; they think they go hand in hand. That's why I've never tried much to explain what I sense to my aunt and uncle; they'd only think I was crazy too.

But Rachel has always known. And she's always believed me. Is it possible that she was starting to doubt our connection? My own twin sister. She must understand the way I am. She has to. If she doesn't, then who will? Our grandma, I guess, but lately she's been drifting away, like she did yesterday, her thoughts slipping into nonsense while she was talking to Kimber and me.

There are worse things than death.

No, there aren't. Not as far as I know.

✍

French class is a breeze. We spend the entire period watching a foreign film without the subtitles. All I have to do before lunch is make it through calculus and study hall.

I stop to use the second-floor bathroom before calc. I've just locked the door to my stall when someone else comes in behind me. I peek through the crack and see that it's Kimber.

Before I have a chance to make myself known, she goes into the handicapped stall. Instead of sitting on the toilet, though, she takes a seat on the floor and pulls her legs close to her body. Her breath is shallow and quick for a few seconds. Then she begins to cry.

As I leave my stall, her cries turn into choked sobs; I can tell she's struggling to be quiet but unable to control herself. I should leave and give her some privacy. She'd probably be mortified if I spoke up now.

But as I stand there, deliberating about what to do, it's like the pain she feels is seeping from her body and filling the room. I want to help her. She and I used to be good friends, before I started getting into trouble so much last summer, before Kimber's mother decided she shouldn't spend too much time around someone like me. Rachel and I used to have sleepovers at Kimber's house on lots of weekends in elementary and middle school. She had this old record player in her bedroom, but she only had one record for it, a single of "Celebration" by Kool and the Gang. As little girls, we'd get all dolled up in her mom's old dresses and high heels, and we'd pretend we were at a fancy party together, all three of us dancing like fools to "Celebration."

I was drawn to her back then because she was damaged by what her father had done, sort of like Rachel and I were damaged by our parents' deaths. The three of us never talked about it at all, but there was always a sense of defiance to our fun, our laughter loud and alive, proof that we still existed, and that we mattered to one another.

I can't leave her alone in here to cry. I lean against the door and tap gently on it with my fingertips. "Kimber? Hey, it's me. It's Rachel."

Her crying stops abruptly. "Shit," she murmurs. I don't think I've ever heard her swear before. Her voice is so smooth and lilting that the word actually sounds pretty coming from her. "Shit. Shit. Shit." There's a rustling sound as she gets to her feet and opens the door to stare at me.

"What do you want?" she asks flatly. Her face is streaky with makeup. Her lips are chapped beneath a layer of gloss. She looks so different from her usual, chipper self. She seemed fine this morning—better than fine. So what happened between now and then to make her go to pieces?

I'm not sure why I think of the little carved monkey at this moment, but all of a sudden it springs to my mind. I put it in the front pocket of my sister's bookbag this morning; for some reason, I wanted to keep it close to me throughout the day. Silly. I have the strongest urge to feel it in the palm of my hand right now, to hold it in my closed fist. But I don't reach for the bookbag slung over my shoulder; instead I step closer to Kimber and place my hands on her arm. Her skin feels hot, like she has a fever.

"It's okay," I tell her. "You can talk to me. We can lock the door and stay in here if you want. Or we could go to the library." The librarian, Mrs. Dodd, is about a hundred years old and pays absolutely no attention to the comings and goings of students throughout the day. She'll never notice us if we stay in the back of the room and keep our voices down.

Kimber shakes her head, blond hair whipping against her face. "No. I should go back to class. We both should. We'll get in trouble if we skip." She narrows her eyes at me, a twinge of resentment in her expression. "I mean, if we skip *again*."

"Forget about class. It doesn't matter."

"Maybe not to you." She tries to push past me, toward the door, but I stop her. I put my arms around her torso and feel the scars in her back, deep and warm and grotesque, even as I'm struggling not to think of the wounds as gross in any way. But they are, no matter how I try to pretend otherwise. They're horrifying. And Kimber has to live with them for the rest of her life.

I want to help her right now. She thinks I'm one of her best friends. I know I shouldn't be deceiving her, but I don't have much of a choice.

She breaks away from me, but she doesn't move closer to the bathroom door. She leans against the shiny pink wall and presses her hands to her face, rubbing her eyes with the heels of her palms, smudging her mascara all over the place. As her arms fall limp at her sides, she lowers herself toward the floor again. She sits cross-legged, staring at the dirty beige octagonal tile.

"Do you know what it feels like to hate somebody?" she asks. She is suddenly calm, but as her words move into the space between us, I feel like all the air has been sucked from the room. I close my eyes; in my mind I see the wreckage of the green pickup truck in the ravine, still bodies floating in filthy water, the heartbroken plea scrawled in spray paint on the side of the boulder: *I loved you more.* The same thing Robin said to me last night.

"Yes," I tell her. "I know what that feels like."

She looks up at me. "Who is it? Who do you hate?"

Saying the words out loud makes me feel like something raw inside me is cracking open, seeping everywhere, suffocating me from within. "I hate the man who was driving the truck that killed my parents."

She's quiet. Her breathing is even and slow. "Of course you do."

"My aunt and uncle are Christians," I tell her. "They believe in forgiveness. They used to try to bring it up some-times, a few years ago. They'd take me to church with them on Sundays. They must have told their pastor the whole story about what happened, because he used to look at me sometimes like . . ." I stop. I'm sweating, thirsty, suddenly drained.

"Like what?" Kimber prompts, tilting her head. I can see her scars climbing up the left side of her neck, near her spine. With her right index finger, she draws a slow figure eight around two of the tiles in the floor.

"Like I was hopeless," I finish. "And he was right. I never wanted to forgive that man. I never even considered it, not really. I just . . . it's a part of me now, the way I hate him. It's like something inside me that I keep feeding, every time I remember my mom and dad." I swallow. My heart goes *thumpety-thump* in my chest, which feels hollow. "Sometimes I wish he hadn't died in the wreck, just so he would have spent the rest of his life living with what he took from us."

Kimber nods. I know she understands. She probably always has.

"What was his name?" she asks.

The question surprises me. Nobody has ever asked me before. And the truth is that I don't know the driver's name;

I don't know the names of any of the other passengers in the truck either. I'm sure my aunt and uncle do, but they've never told me, and I've never asked. I could go online and find the newspaper archives from the accident, but I've never felt any desire to do so. I never felt the need to know what other people called the man behind the wheel, or his friends; to me, he'll always be the man who killed my parents, his friends the ones who helped it to happen. It's the only information about any of them that I need.

"I don't know," I tell her. "I don't want to know."

Kimber is quiet. She pulls her knees against her chest and hugs her legs.

I let Rachel's bookbag slide to the floor, and then I sit down beside Kimber. I unzip the bookbag's front pocket and reach inside. My hand closes around the monkey.

"Raymond Shields," she says. "That's who I hate." She sits up a little straighter and gazes at the opposite wall, where one of the sinks is dripping without making any sound.

"He's my father," she continues, "and I hate him." Her expression remains calm but steady as she looks straight ahead. "He used to play the guitar for me before I went to sleep at night. I was born in April. You know that song by Simon and Garfunkel? 'April, Come She Will'? He used to sing it to me. He was good on the guitar too. His fingertips were callused from practicing all the time. He called me Kimmy. I loved him so much."

I let out a breath I didn't realize I was holding. "Kimber,"

I say, "I'm sorry." I roll the monkey in my hand, feeling the grooves in the pit against my fingers. They feel like the scars on her back.

"Don't be," she says. "It's not your fault. My parents used to fight all the time. Then, when I was six years old, my mom kicked my dad out." She pauses. "He was gone for a while, and my mom seemed happy about it. But he came back a few months later, on the Fourth of July. Mom had taken me to see the fireworks in Hollick Park that night. We came home and went straight to bed. And while she and I were sleeping, my father came inside our house and poured gasoline all over the downstairs. Then he went outside, into the front yard, and he lit a sparkler. My neighbors were watching him. They thought he was drunk. They didn't know what he'd done already." She closes her eyes. "He stood in the grass and spun around, watching the sparkler burn down. When it was almost out, he threw it inside our front door."

"Have you seen him?" I ask. "I mean, since he got arrested?"

"No. But he writes me letters sometimes. He says he's sorry, and that it doesn't matter where he is—whether he's in prison or not—because he'll regret what he did for the rest of his life. He wants me to forgive him." She laughs. "To *forgive* him," she repeats. "He's my father. My father tried to kill me. I'll probably never get married, Rachel. I'll never wear a strapless dress or go to the beach in a bikini."

"You could get married," I tell her. "They're only scars. If someone loves you, he won't care."

She doesn't respond to the comment, like the possibility that someone could look beyond her flesh is unimaginable. "My mom says she forgives him," Kimber continues. "It makes me so angry every time she brings it up. But my mom says that you can't hold on to your hate forever. She says that hating my father won't change anything that happened; all it will do is eat me from the inside out, like cancer. She says that if I forgive him, I'll be free. I'll be able to get on with my life, instead of wasting my energy on things that can't be changed. What do you think, Rachel? Do you think she's right?"

"Maybe," I say. "I never really thought of it that way."

"Well, I think she's right," Kimber says.

"You do?"

"Yes. I know she's right." She pauses. "But sometimes I feel like I need to hate him. Like it's become so much a part of who I am. If I let it go, then what do I have left?"

"Jesus," I say. "God. Kimber, you've never told me all that before." I've heard the general story plenty of times, of course—people at school still talk about it—but we've never discussed it in as much detail as we are right now.

Finally, she looks at me. She smiles. "I never told you," she repeats.

I nod. "Yes."

She *laughs* at me. She shakes her head. "You're right. I never told you."

Her gaze locks onto mine. The room is so still.

"But I told your sister all about it, a few weeks ago."

The room deflates. "You told my sister."

"Yes." Her smile widens. "I told your sister. I told Rachel."

CHAPTER TWENTY-THREE

As the weight of Kimber's words sinks in, the room seems to shrink around us, leaving little space for me to breathe, let alone think. My first instinct is to lie to her, to deny everything and insist that I *am* Rachel. I only have to pretend for a few more days. Maybe it won't even take that long. Maybe everything will work out, and Kimber will never have to know any different. I could pretend to be disoriented, like I'm getting a headache. I could claim to have forgotten what she told me about her father, and the night he started the fire that almost killed her.

Except who could forget a story like that? As Kimber stares at me, waiting for a response to her accusation, I know that I can't lie to her anymore. I don't have the energy. And she deserves to hear the truth.

My voice is suddenly hoarse, my throat dry. "When did you know?"

She leans her head back and stares up at the ceiling. Just above us, there's a circular brown stain on the paint. It's probably from a water leak. The discolored area is puffy, its paint beginning to chip and peel away, the faintest layer of condensation glistening on the surface of the mark. I wonder how long the leak had been there, seeping through the plaster, before the ceiling showed any external signs of a problem.

"I knew something was weird the night of the fair," she begins. "When Rachel wandered off, I knew from the way you panicked that things weren't right. If it were really Alice who'd snuck away, why would you be so worried? Alice runs away all the time, right?"

I nod.

"But this time was different," Kimber continues. "You were so upset, like you knew it didn't make any sense for her to disappear. But even when I first had the idea, I thought it was ridiculous. I mean, the two of you? Switching places? It's crazy. Twins don't actually do things like that, not in real life." She pauses. "And then when you made me skip school, and we went to visit your grandma, it was all so . . . I don't know, so surreal. It wasn't the kind of thing Rachel would do. It didn't make sense. So I paid closer attention. And you know the funniest thing? I almost believed that you were her, and that I was just imagining things. Because you're so good at being her. I mean, Alice, you look *exactly* like her. The way you move, the way you talk, everything."

As she's speaking, she gets up and crosses the room. She turns the lock on the door, and as it clicks into place I feel a sense of finality combined with the urge to tell her everything. Maybe she knows far more about Rachel's life in the past few months than I do. Maybe she knows about TJ. The question is whether or not she'll be willing to tell me anything. My best shot, I know, is to be honest and see where it gets me.

She leans against the sink and crosses her arms, waiting for me to explain my side of things.

Where am I supposed to begin? If I tell her the whole truth right away, she'll only think I'm crazy, if she doesn't already.

I grip the monkey in my hand. I feel so alone, so completely out of control. It's unlikely that she'll believe what I'm about to tell her, but what do I have to lose?

So I begin in what seems to me like as good a place as any. "You want to know how my grandma's dog died?" I ask.

She shrugs. "Not really. Aren't you going to admit the truth? You've been lying to me for days."

"I know." The space still feels impossibly small, like there's not enough room to breathe. It's like my tension is weaving a cocoon around my body, closing me off from the rest of the world.

"Then tell me why," she says. "Please."

"I will, Kimber. But first you need to understand how things are between me and Rachel. If I tell you what happened to the dog, it will make more sense." I pause. "Will you listen? Please?"

For a second I think she might refuse to hear me out. But she doesn't protest; she just gives a reluctant nod and waits for me to keep talking. Apparently she isn't concerned about being late for study hall anymore.

"Our grandma owned the Captain ever since before Rachel and I were born. He was a really good dog. Every time we'd go to visit her, we'd spend most of our time playing with him in the yard. We both loved him, but Rachel was always a little more timid than I was. When we were younger, like five and six years old, he was so much bigger than we were. He was always gentle, never mean at all, but our parents still used to warn us to be careful around him.

"Anyway, this one afternoon we went to visit my grandma. She'd been in the hospital for a while, and she'd just gotten home a few days earlier, so my parents brought over a cake and we had a picnic outside. Afterward, Rachel and I were running around the yard, playing with the Captain, trying to keep him from catching this tennis ball we had. We were throwing it back and forth between the two of us, over his head."

"How old were you?" Kimber asks.

"We were about to turn seven." I stop, shutting my eyes. It's like I can see everything happening right in front of me, almost like I'm living it again: My parents are sitting at the picnic table behind my grandma's house, deep in conversation, barely paying attention to me and Rachel. A nearly empty pitcher of sangria sits on the table, along with the half-eaten cake. My grandma looks like she's lost a ton of weight in the last few weeks; she seems weak and frail and not like herself at all. That day was the first time I realized she'd been dyeing her hair for as long as I'd known her. It was naturally red once, but now her roots were coming in gray. She must not have had time to touch it up in between her return from the hospital and our visit, and it made her look so much older than usual.

The Captain ran toward my sister. Just before he reached her, she threw the tennis ball high overhead, in my direction. Every other time we'd done this, the dog would quickly change direction to continue chasing after the ball. This time, though, he kept heading toward Rachel. When he reached her, he jumped onto his back legs and tackled her to the ground.

"He bit her. She was wearing shorts, and he bit her on the calf. Our parents didn't realize what had happened at first, but I did. I ran over to her and started screaming at the dog. His teeth were still in her leg. He started to drag her body downhill. I threw the tennis ball as hard as I could, and he let go and went running after it. The whole thing happened in less than ten seconds, and then it was over. By the time our parents got to us, I had my arms around Rachel; she was screaming, and I was crying. She was bleeding all over the place. There were deep bite marks in her calf. My parents took her to the hospital right away. She needed sixteen stitches."

"Okay," Kimber says, "so the dog bit your sister. What does that have to do with anything, Alice?"

I've never told anyone this story before in my whole life. The only people who ever knew what happened were the ones who were there. What I'm about to tell Kimber is going to sound impossible, I know. She probably won't believe me. But I have to try.

"My parents left me at my grandma's while they drove Rachel to the hospital," I continue, "and my grandma took me inside and gave me some lemonade. She left the Captain outside, in her front yard." As I'm speaking, I begin to roll up the left leg of my jeans to expose my bare calf. "I was sitting at her kitchen table and I felt something running down my leg. I thought it was sweat. I leaned over to wipe it away, and when I looked at my hand, there was blood all over it." I extend my leg, showing Kimber. "Here. See it? I was sitting in her kitchen, and it just appeared. Bite marks identical to the ones in Rachel's leg. You can still see the scars."

Kimber crosses her arms against her chest and kneels down to take a look. She stares hard at the scar, which is so faint that you wouldn't even notice it unless you knew what to look for.

She stands up. "I don't know what you want me to say. It's a scar." Her voice wavers. "Everybody has them."

"Kimber," I beg, "please believe me. Rachel and I aren't

ordinary twins. We're different." I take a deep breath, ready to spill more of the unbelievable truth. "I know things about her sometimes. Things I shouldn't know, things she hasn't told me yet. I can even sense things before they happen to her sometimes. I know it's crazy, I know, but please listen. On Saturday night, I had this terrible feeling that something bad had happened to her. Then the feeling just vanished, and I was so afraid, and that's why I made you skip school, so we could look for her. But then I saw her in the barn at my grandma's house, except I couldn't talk to her. I don't know why. She wouldn't tell me anything. I don't know why she's doing this. I don't know what's happening to me. And the more I try to figure it out, the more confused I get." I pause. "Maybe she hates me. Maybe all she wants is to get away from me forever."

Kimber's eyes are filled with pity. "That's not true. She's worried about you, Alice."

"No," I say, shaking my head. "I don't believe you. Why would she be worried? I'm right here. I'm fine."

"Alice," Kimber says gently, "I know you're upset. I know things don't make sense. But has it ever occurred to you that these abilities you think you have—your connection to Rachel, and the things you sense about her—are just part of your imagination?"

I stare at the scars on my leg. They're concrete proof of our connection—can't Kimber understand that? And why would Rachel ever doubt it? "I'm not imagining them," I insist. "Just because you don't believe me doesn't mean it's not really happening. You can't prove that."

She takes a sharp breath inward. She steps toward me, kneels down again, and places a hand on my shoulder. "What if I *can* prove it, Alice?"

I am crying. Kimber was my only hope—someone who might be able to help me right now, who might believe me— and she obviously thinks I'm losing it.

"If I can prove that you've imagined some of these things," she continues, "then will you tell your aunt and uncle the truth? That you're Alice?"

I give up. Let her try, I think. See how far it gets either of us. I nod in agreement.

"Good," she says, smiling. "And we'll figure out where Rachel is. You'll tell us what happened on Saturday night. Right?"

At the sound of her words, I feel like I've been punched in the stomach. I stare up at her in disbelief. Suddenly, I under- stand: she thinks I know exactly where Rachel is, because she thinks I did something to Rachel.

"I already told you everything I know," I lie.

Kimber is cool as a cucumber. "Okay. Fine. I believe you." I can tell she's lying too.

"I would never hurt my sister, Kimber."

She nods. She doesn't respond.

"How are you going to prove anything? I know what I feel. I know what I've seen."

"We'll go after school," she says. "I'll show you something. Then you'll understand what I mean."

"Where are we going?"

She doesn't answer me.

"Where are we going?" I demand, my voice rising a little bit. I'm still crying, the monkey clutched in my fist. Everything is falling apart, and there's nobody who can help me.

Kimber sighs. She stands up and unlocks the bathroom door, and she gives me a long, sad look.

"We're going to Friendship," she says. "We're going to see your friend Robin."

CHAPTER TWENTY-FOUR

If Kimber's reaction tells me anything, I don't think I'll be able to get away with pretending to be Rachel for the rest of the school day. There are a couple of obvious factors against me: the wrong locker combination and the fact that I'm totally unprepared for her more advanced classes—but there's more to it than that.

In the past, it's like she and I have been able to slip into each other's skin. It was so easy for me to be Rachel, and vice versa. When I played Rachel, it used to feel like a valve had been turned from somewhere within myself, and there'd be this blissful release in pressure when I got to hide behind her calm kindness for the day. It was like a time-out in life, like pressing pause on all the chaos and volatility I usually feel. I used to love it so much.

And while Rachel usually seemed to enjoy being me, it occurs to me now that I never thought much about what it did for her. I was far too preoccupied with what it allowed me to do: relax. Could it have had the opposite effect on her? The burden of my personality, all my problems with school and authority and our friends—was it too much for her? Did she decide that she finally couldn't take it anymore? And if so, why didn't she just tell me how she felt? I would have listened.

I'm pretty sure I would have listened.

∞

After my conversation with Kimber in the bathroom, I go straight to the nurse's office and fake a headache. The nurse, Miss Weaver, offers to call my aunt to pick me up. I tell her she's not home, and I get to lay down for the rest of the day. I'm not sure what to do about Wednesday and Thursday if Rachel doesn't come back by then. I guess I'll have to keep pretending to be sick.

When the final bell rings, signaling the end of the school day, I go to my locker—my real locker—to collect a few things. Then I give Rachel's combination one more try; it still doesn't work.

The school janitor, Mr. Smith—everyone calls him Smitty—walks by as I tug at the handle on my sister's locker. He stops to watch me. We're the only two people in the hallway.

"What's the matter?" he asks, suspicious. "Is that your locker?"

He's been here for years, but I've never had a reason to speak to him until now. "Yes," I say. "It won't open."

He looks annoyed. "Did you try the combination?"

"Of course I did. Four times. It's not working."

He lets out a long sigh. "Okay. Move over." And he unhooks a huge circular ring from his belt. There must be fifty keys dangling from it, but somehow he knows exactly which one to choose. In a few easy seconds, he opens my sister's locker. "There you go," he tells me, stepping aside to give me access. "She's all yours."

There's nothing out of the ordinary in Rachel's locker, at least not that I notice right away. Her books are stacked neatly on the top shelf. A maroon sweater hangs from one of the hooks. Her gym clothes are folded at the bottom. *Why the hell would she change the combination? What is here that she doesn't want me to see?*

And then I find it. Or rather, I find *them*. A small black drawstring bag is tucked into the back corner. I tug it open and dump the contents into my hand. A slew of tiny dried-up flowers, each one knotted into a circle, falls out. There must be at least two dozen. They're the same as the ones I found in her bookbag.

All together, there are probably more than a hundred of them. It doesn't make any sense; why wouldn't she want me to see them? And where did she get them?

∽

I don't have time to stand around and think about it. Kimber has instructed me to find her car in the parking lot immediately after school. As the building empties for the day, I move away from the students who spill from the building in groups of two or more, walking alone around the edge of the parking lot, keeping my head down, hoping that nobody will approach me to talk.

There's a car behind me. I don't turn around to look at it, not at first. But as I move along, it continues to creep behind me, so close that I can hear the music coming from its radio. As "Hotel California" winds to an end, the singsong voice of DJ Dave breaks in to announce that I'm listening to the afternoon rock block on KRVC, all classic rock, all the time.

I stop. I still don't turn around. The car behind me stalls, waiting for me to do something, to acknowledge it somehow. I don't have to turn around to know that it's TJ, following me in his car, assuming that I'm Rachel.

I remember his words from last night: *See you tomorrow.* So here we both are.

For a few seconds I just stand there, trying to think, to figure out what to do. This isn't going to work. If he and Rachel have really been seeing each other secretly, there's no way I'll be able to fool him into believing I'm her in the light of day. Last night was different. It was dark and rainy, and I was upset, and our exchange happened quickly. Now, though, he'll expect me to have a normal conversation. He'll probably try to kiss me again. Our contact last night was sloppy and rushed; I was so shook up that he probably didn't notice if I kissed differently than Rachel, which I'm assuming I do.

If he knows her like he says he does, all it might take is the wrong tilt of my head, or the touch of my foreign hand, to realize who I really am. And then he'll freak.

But I don't really have a choice, do I? I can't ignore him—he'll probably just continue to follow me. And I can't exactly tell him what's going on. That would be an interesting conversation, to say the least. *Well, your real girlfriend disappeared on Saturday night at the fair. I'm just standing in for her. At first I thought something terrible had happened, because you see, I'm totally psychic when it comes to Rachel. She's okay, though—I saw her yesterday. She was hanging out in our grandma's barn. What was she doing there? I have no idea. I don't know where she's staying either. But I have reason to believe she might be hanging out with my boyfriend, Robin. Lord knows what those crazy kids are up to right now!*

The driver's side window is already rolled down as I approach TJ's car. The inside has obviously been cleaned recently; I can even see faint vacuum marks in the floor's shaggy beige upholstery as I glance around the inside. I have to stop myself from groaning out loud at the fuzzy dice hanging from the rearview mirror. The backseat is empty except for a small cooler resting on the floor. An open box of Good & Plenty—black licorice candy, the most repulsive taste sensation known to man—sits in the change tray behind the gearshift. While I've met other people who can tolerate black licorice, Rachel is the only person I know who actively seeks it out; when we were kids, she used to hoard loose change from around the house in order to buy fistfuls of five-cent ropes of the stuff every time our mom took us to the grocery store. As soon as I see the pink-and-black box of candy, I know that my sister has been in TJ's car recently.

I rest my hands on the edge of the open window and lean down to look at my neighbor. Pee-Wee. We called him other things behind his back too: The Uber-Geek. Mommy's boy. The stay-at-home son. Never once did I get even an inkling that my sister felt anything but amused derision toward him. If she's been lying to me for however long they've been seeing each other—weeks? Maybe months?—then she's a much better liar than I thought. Maybe even a better liar than I am.

She did live her days as me plenty of times. And when Rachel took over as Alice, she was always so good at it. Maybe our personalities are not so different. Maybe our shared qualities—all the less-desirable ones that I can't seem to conceal within myself, no matter what the circumstances— maybe she's just better at keeping them hidden most of the time.

"Hey, beautiful," he says to me, closing one of his hands over mine. "How's high school?"

His smile is genuine, deep and radiant. He is thrilled to see me. Looking at him up close, I see features of his that I've never noticed before. His dark hair is full and thick, his hair- line curves into a slight widow's peak at the center of his forehead. His eyes are an electric shade of blue beneath contact lenses. A faint line of scar tissue, light as can be, runs from just beneath his nose down to the edge of his upper lip, the telltale mark of someone who's had surgery to correct a cleft palate. In addition, there is an odd patch of white discoloration, another scar of some kind, just above his left eyebrow.

I'm not sure why Rachel and I have made fun of him so much over the years. I guess he's an easy target; he's seemed like such an odd guy, out of college and still living with his parents, always mowing the lawn with his shirt off, showing off his newly buff physique for the whole neighborhood. But I've never really talked to him before now. I don't know anything about him beyond what I've observed. Looking at him up close, I realize that, despite his slight build, he's not a bad-looking guy at all. His scars don't do anything to diminish his looks; instead, they make his face more interesting.

"What are you waiting for?" he asks, still grinning. "Get in."

I give him a timid, regretful smile. In a deliberate gesture that is pure Rachel, I begin to wind a strand of my hair around my index finger. "I'm sorry, TJ. I can't. Not today."

He seems confused. "Rach, what are you talking about? We've been planning this for over a week."

"It's Kimber," I tell him. Wait—does he even know who Kimber is? "My friend Kimber," I clarify.

"Yeah, sure." His hand is still over mine on the edge of

the window. He weaves his fingers through mine, holding on tight. "You have to come," he says. "I left work early." His grin wavers just a little, but I can tell he's trying to maintain it, to hide his disappointment. "Come on," he says. "I bought a forty-dollar bottle of champagne. You aren't going to make me drink it all by myself, are you?"

I nod. "I'm really sorry, TJ. Kimber needs me right now. It's important."

He squints at me. The small wrinkles at the corners of his eyes are papery, almost translucent. "Right." His voice is flat. "Okay. I get it." There's a pause. He loosens his grip on my fingers. "Want to tell me what's so important that Kimber can't take care of it herself? She's a big girl."

I hesitate. "I can't tell you. Not right now."

He tugs his hand away. "Oh."

"TJ—"

"No, that's okay," he interrupts. "Don't worry about it." He is suddenly so cool and detached that I feel a twinge of worry. I'm pretty certain this isn't how a conversation between him and Rachel typically goes. "Go ahead, then, if it's such a big deal. I'll see you later."

I nod, trying to remain warm and apologetic. "Of course."

He's still squinting at me. Without looking down, he shifts the car into drive.

"Okay, then. Bye, Rach."

I force another smile. "Bye, TJ."

I watch him as he pulls away. When I swallow, I could swear that my mouth tastes like black licorice.

Kimber's car is waiting right where she said it would be: in the parking lot of Rita's Pizzeria, across the road from our high school. As a rule, Rita's serves lousy food. One time last year, Holly found a rubber band in her salad. The staff is made up entirely of miserable-looking middle-aged men who look like they're on work-release programs from prison. On most weekday afternoons, Homeless Harvey can be seen sitting alone at his corner booth, which is right next to the swinging kitchen door. He never talks to anyone; he just sits there, quietly observing, sipping coffee while his dog rests at his feet beneath the table. I guess the employees must feel sorry for him.

Despite the horrible atmosphere, the almost inedible food, and the constant presence of our town's resident Creepy Homeless Man, Rita's is always packed with teenagers. There's an old cigarette vending machine in the basement that any-body can use without having to show ID. I don't know how they've gotten away with catering to underage kids for so long, but it seems to make for a pretty successful business model.

It's only about 3:15, but the parking lot is already full. A cluster of four giddy girls who can't be older than thirteen or fourteen are huddled in a semicircle beside the front door, looking absurd as they puff on long, skinny cigarettes. Three of them are hacking away as they attempt to take drags, while their remaining friend puffs like a pro, blowing a rapid succession of tiny smoke rings in my direction as I pass by.

Inside, the place is already swarming with high school kids. Across the crowded room, sitting alone at his booth, Homeless Harvey chews on a piece of bread, putting it in his mouth with one hand, his other reaching under the table as he feeds the crust to his dog.

As I'm looking around, Harvey's gaze catches mine for a second. He opens his mouth, sort of like he's about to yawn, but instead he wiggles his lower jaw back and forth a little bit, like maybe it's sore or something. And it's funny—of all things, I notice that he has a perfect set of teeth. They're straight as can be, two neat rows of gleaming white chompers visible behind his dry, chapped lips. Strange.

I spot Kimber right away. She's sitting at a booth with Holly and Nicholas. She gives me a shaky smile and waves me over.

"Don't sit," she says as I approach them. "We're leaving in a minute."

Nicholas is looking down at a paper menu, staring at it like he's thinking hard about what to order. Aside from soda and beer, the menu offers five items: pizza, with or without pepperoni; salad; french fries; onion rings, and—inexplicably—pickled eggs, which are sold for twenty-five cents apiece, although I've never seen anyone actually order one.

Holly is eating a basket of onion rings. Carefully, like

she's performing surgery, she picks up one of the rings and begins to peel away a portion of its fried outer shell with her manicured fingertips. After she has completely extracted the cooked onion from inside, she tilts her head back and places the slimy, translucent ribbon gently into her open mouth.

"That's disgusting," Kimber says, scrunching up her face. "I wish you'd stop."

Holly smiles as she chews. "It's delicious."

"You're wasting the breading," Kimber insists. "The breading is the best part."

Nicholas continues to stare at his menu on the table. Holly glances at him for a second before shifting her gaze to Kimber. I can't tell what the two of them are thinking, but there's obviously something more going on here beyond Holly's repulsive eating habits.

As the three of us look around, silent, Nicholas stands up. Without a word, he slides out of the booth and heads toward the bathroom.

Holly stares at him. She pushes out her bottom lip in a pout. "I feel so bad for him."

"Why?" I ask. "What's the matter?"

She and Kimber exchange another glance.

"It's okay," Holly says. "You can tell her." She gives me a half smile.

But Kimber doesn't explain. Instead, she nudges Holly to stand up. "We have to leave," she says.

"Right now?" Holly takes a sip of her soda as she scoots out of the booth. "Why?"

"I have to give Rachel a ride somewhere." Kimber clutches her purse to her side. Her car keys dangle from her right hand.

Holly isn't paying attention. She stares into her drink, frowning.

"Tell Nicholas good-bye for us," I say.

"Uh-huh. I will." And she shoves her drink at my face. "Taste this, Rachel. Does this taste like diet to you?"

I take a sip. "Yes, it's definitely diet." It's definitely not.

Holly breathes a sigh of genuine relief. "Oh, good. Okay— go ahead, then. See you both later."

✍

As we're pulling out of the parking lot, I tell Kimber to make a right and head toward the highway. The afternoon is bright and sunny. The sky is clear, except for a few stray stratus clouds. Far above us, an airplane crawls across the sky. It seems impossible to think that it's actually moving at hundreds of miles an hour, carrying all those passengers.

"I know where to go," she says, sliding her sunglasses onto the bridge of her nose.

"You do?" I ask. "How?"

She sighs. "Alice . . . your sister and I followed you one day last summer."

I feel stunned. "You followed me."

"Yes."

"Why the hell would you do that?"

"Because Rachel was worried about you. You'd been sneaking off to meet this guy Robin for weeks, but you wouldn't introduce him to anyone. Rachel wanted to know where you were going with him all the time, to make sure you were safe." She pauses. "And she wanted to see him for herself."

I don't know how to respond. In the space of a few days, my whole reality has shifted out of focus. I stare out the window as we glide down the highway, trying to keep my breathing steady and calm.

Kimber doesn't try to make conversation. She switches on the radio and tunes in to the local oldies' station. As she drives, keeping her speed at a constant fifty-three miles per hour in a fifty-five-mile zone, she hums along to "Me and Bobby McGee" by Janis Joplin.

We exit the highway after a few miles and begin to make our way along the dingy main drag lined with run-down storefronts. Since it's the middle of the afternoon, there are plenty of people out. But this is a bad part of town; at one stoplight, there's a guy who looks homeless selling crude colored-pencil drawings of birds for ten dollars apiece. Behind him, on the sidewalk, a grown man in a white track suit rides a child's bicycle, his knees bumping against his chest as he pedals clumsily along.

Kimber turns onto Willow Circle. She parks on the brick-paved street in front of the white duplex where Robin lives.

"Alice." Her voice is soft and sympathetic.

"Yes?" As Kimber removes her sunglasses, I'm startled to see that her eyes are red and glossy, like she's trying not to cry.

"What's the matter?" I ask.

She shakes her head. "Nothing. I don't know." She folds her glasses and slips them into her purse on her lap. "This is hard for me, that's all."

I stare at her. "Why is it hard?"

She bites her bottom lip. "Because you're not going to like this."

I glance out my window at the duplex. There's a pink piece of paper covered in writing taped to Robin's door, but we're too far away for me to make out any of the words. I notice that the yellow curtain that normally hangs across the front window is gone.

A sense of discomfort begins to creep over me. Something isn't quite right here. I know it, and so does Kimber. I feel reluctant to get out of the car. At the same time, sitting inside with all the windows up gives me a suffocated feeling. The air is suddenly cool, like I've been hit with a blast from the air conditioner. But the car isn't running; there's nothing coming out of the vents.

Still staring at the duplex, I say, "You didn't tell me yet why Nicholas was so upset at Rita's."

"It's not a big deal. Don't worry about it." I can feel her looking past me at the house. Her breathing is quick and shallow. Even though it's an older model, her car still has that new-car smell, which I find comforting for some reason. Kimber knows how to take good care of things.

"Tell me," I press. My bookbag is in my lap, the money stuffed into a paper bag at the bottom.

She shrugs dismissively. "Oh, I don't even know. Something about one of the houses his dad owns. The one on Pennsylvania Avenue, I think. His dad took away his key. I guess Mr. Hahn went over there a couple of days ago and found the door hanging wide open."

I wince. "Did Nicholas get in trouble?"

"No, but he was freaking out at school today. So was Holly."

"Do you know why?"

"Nope. Wait—maybe. They were whispering about it in study hall. Something about a geocaching tournament. I don't really understand it. Anyway, it's not important."

But it is. Could the money have belonged to Nicholas? Was it some kind of prize, maybe?

Before I can say anything else, Kimber nudges me. "Look."

As I glance at the duplex, the door to the apartment on the left—not Robin's apartment—swings open. A cute guy in his mid-twenties steps onto the porch. He gives us a smile as he walks toward Kimber's car, like he's been expecting us.

I don't have a chance to ask her anything else about

Nicholas. Before I know what's happening, Kimber is getting out of her car to greet the man, who's standing on the sidewalk now just a few feet from us, a set of keys dangling from his hand. "Come on, Alice," she says to me. "Get out of the car."

So I do. I stand there as Kimber and the man shake hands and exchange friendly small talk. The guy introduces himself as Michael. He seems eager to be meeting us, almost hopeful. I don't say anything; I just stand there, trying to hide my confusion. This guy lives next door to Robin? I've never seen him before in my life. As far as I knew, the other side of the duplex was vacant.

"This is my friend Alice," Kimber says. She grins. "We're going to be roommates."

Startled, I look at her. She stares back at me, her gaze steady and calm. *Play along,* it says.

"Great." Michael turns to look at the house. "I hope you like it. Pretty much everything is new. I did all the work myself. You've got new carpets, new paint, new flooring in the kitchen, new fixtures in the bathroom." He lets out a low whistle. "You wouldn't believe what the inside of this place looked like when I bought it. What a disaster."

What is he talking about? My whole body feels cold. I need air. I need to think. As we approach the house, the familiar smell of turpentine seeps into the air, so powerful that my eyes start to burn. If Kimber or Michael can smell it, they don't say anything.

Michael uses his keys to unlock the door. The three of us step inside. He switches on the lights.

As I look around the room, I reach for Kimber's arm, trying to steady myself. The turpentine smell is overwhelming. I can taste the vapor in my throat. As my vision adjusts to the indoor lighting, tiny black dots swim in rapid circles before my eyes.

I stare. I see, but I don't see. I don't understand.

The apartment is completely empty: no furniture, no television, and no paintings. The walls themselves are freshly painted a light shade of beige. The ceiling and baseboards are still covered in bright-blue painter's tape. The old shag carpet has been pulled up to reveal smooth, shiny hardwood floors. I look past the living room into the kitchen, where the old fridge and stove have been replaced with stainless-steel appliances.

There is simply no way that anybody could have gutted and renovated this entire place in less than three days. It's not possible.

The wound on the back of my head, hidden by a ponytail, throbs in time with my heartbeat.

Michael begins to walk toward the bedroom, talking to us as he moves. "So the rent is six hundred a month, and I'm asking for the first and last month's rent as a security deposit," he says, flipping on light switches as he passes them, pausing in the hallway to glance back at us. "If that's going to be an issue for you to come up with all at once, you can split it over a few months."

Every time another light comes on, it feels like a blow to my senses as the apartment is further illuminated to reveal its emptiness. Kimber squeezes my hand. My palm is clammy and damp. There is a dull, low ringing sound in my ears.

"Hey," she whispers, flashing me a worried look, "are you okay?"

I am too stunned to answer her. She's brought me here to show me—what? That Robin is gone? But he was *just here* on Sunday. I was just here. The two of us sat on his sofa together. I spoke to him. He knew who I was immediately, even though anybody else would have assumed I was Rachel.

Somehow, I find my voice. "This is a joke," I tell Kimber. "Why are you doing this to me?"

Her gaze searches my face. She seems to be struggling to figure out if I'm serious. Her expression shifts from concern to sadness to pity. Whatever she was trying to accomplish by coming here, I can tell that my reaction is not what she expected.

"We thought you knew," she says.

"You thought I knew what?" The sunlight coming through the window beside us casts a purplish hue throughout the room. My toes have gone numb in my shoes.

"We thought you were lying to us. We followed you here. We watched you go inside. You were alone, getting drunk all by yourself. Smoking cigarettes."

I shake my head. "I don't smoke. Robin smokes."

"Alice." Kimber seems to shrink, her posture slumping

as she lets go of my hand and takes a step away from me. "There was nobody here with you."

My throat burns, dry and raw. Every breath hurts. I have to get out of here. "You're wrong," I say, keeping my voice low.

Kimber's hand moves to the small golden crucifix around her neck. She holds it between her thumb and index finger, rubbing them together in tiny, circular motions. She glances down the hallway, where Michael has disappeared into the bedroom for the moment.

"A few months ago, they hadn't started renovating yet," she says. "The apartment was empty. You sat on the floor for the longest time. You had this look in your eyes, like your mind was somewhere else." She looks ready to cry. "We could see your lips moving, but you weren't making any sound."

I don't think Kimber would lie to me on purpose, but the alternative is too upsetting to consider. What Kimber is describing—that faraway gaze, the silent mouthing of nonsense—I've seen it before when my grandmother slips into confusion. But it's never happened to me. Besides, I've talked to Robin countless times. I've touched him. I've felt his hands on my skin, the familiar calluses on his fingertips. He was here with me. He's real.

Michael has returned from the bedroom. He stands in the kitchen, leaning against the new refrigerator. "If you girls want to think about it, that's fine. I can get you a copy of the lease to look over." He shrugs. "To be honest, you're the only interest I've had so far. If you want the place, it's yours."

"Thanks." Kimber smiles at him. "Before we go, can I ask you a few questions?"

He nods. "Shoot."

"How long have you owned this apartment?"

"Uh . . . let me think. My wife and I bought it this past May, so that would be . . . almost four months now."

"Do you know anything about the previous owners?"

"Not really," Michael says. "The place had been in fore-closure for years. We bought it from the bank. It was in pretty awful shape. The neighborhood's seen a lot of reno-vation lately, but there's still some riffraff. The locks on the doors were broken. Local kids probably used this place to hang out and party." He laughs. "Looks like their fun here is over. I put three-inch deadbolts on the doors yesterday. Nobody's getting in now without a key."

Kimber nods. "Okay. Good to know." She looks at me. "Alice? Is there anything you want to ask? We should prob-ably get going soon."

I can hardly breathe, let alone speak. I shake my head.

"Okay then." Michael taps his fingertips against the white kitchen wall. "I'll go grab you that lease. Meet you out-side in a few minutes."

⁋

Once we're in the car again, I don't say anything for a long time. My nerves are so frayed that the click of my seat belt buckling makes me cringe. The turpentine smell from the apartment clings to my clothing. Even after I put down my window, I have to breathe deeply, inhaling through my nose and exhaling through my mouth, to keep my nausea at bay as Kimber drives.

"Don't take me home yet," I say, as she's approaching my street. "Go to Nicholas's house first."

"I don't have time, Alice. I have Girl Scouts at six thirty." I get the feeling she might be lying to me, that she might not have Scouts at all, but she just wants to get away from me as soon as possible. I don't know if I blame her. But I have to do this now. If she won't drop me off, I'll walk.

"Please, Kimber." I hug my bookbag to my chest. "It won't take me long."

"Mr. Hahn just fired you. He won't like you showing up at his door." But once we reach the next intersection, after a long hesitation at the stop sign, she turns onto Walnut Street, where Nicholas lives.

The only car in the driveway is Holly's little blue Subaru. "See?" I tell Kimber. "His dad isn't even home." I hop out of the sedan before it comes all the way to a stop. "Stay here, okay? I'll be back in a minute."

I ring the doorbell and wait, still clutching my bookbag tightly, until Holly opens the door. She leans against the frame as she takes a large bite from a bagel smeared with hummus. "Hey," she says, her mouth full. "What's up?"

"I need to see Nicholas."

Holly continues to chew. Without a word, she turns and walks back inside, gesturing for me to follow her. Nicholas is in the sunroom attached to the back of the house. He's lifting free weights and watching a rerun of *Family Feud* on a huge flat-screen TV.

"Rachel is here," Holly announces. Nicholas nods at me, struggling to complete a bicep curl.

I glance at Holly. "Can I talk to him alone for a minute?"

She bristles. "It doesn't matter if I'm here or not. He'll just tell me what you said as soon as you're gone."

"She's right," Nicholas says, grunting. He drops his free weights on the floor.

"Fine." I take a deep, slow breath. "Remember the party you had a few weeks ago? At the house your dad bought?"

He shrugs. "Sure. What about it?"

"Nicholas . . . I was in the basement. I was alone. I found something hidden down there." I start to unzip my bookbag. "I took it. I'm really sorry, okay? I tried to put it back, but the door was padlocked." I remove the paper bag and shove it toward him. "Here. It's yours, right? I don't know where you got it, and I don't care. I'm sorry," I repeat, so embarrassed that I can't look him or Holly in the eye. "I don't know what I was thinking. I wasn't thinking at all, I guess. Anyway, it's yours."

I expect him to snatch the paper bag from my hands, to start screaming at me, to do *something*. But he only glances at it with mild interest. "Okay. Thanks, I guess. But I don't need it anymore." He sticks out his bottom lip in a pout. "The tournament has been put on hold indefinitely. My dad doesn't want us using the house anymore. I have to make a new map."

I have no idea what he's talking about. My thoughts are a jumbled mess.

"My dad will be home any minute," he continues. "You should probably leave. You're not exactly his favorite person right now."

"Nicholas." I press the bag into his hands. "I don't want it. It's yours."

He shoots Holly a goofy grin. "It's not a big deal, Rachel. I can get more."

My mouth falls open. "What are you talking about?"

"I'm talking about the prize." He pauses. "What are *you* talking about?"

"The money! Nicholas, I stole it from you! Come on, take it!" My hands begin to shake as I clutch the bag, suddenly afraid to look inside.

Holly laughs. "Rachel, relax. He just told you it's not a big deal." She cracks open a Diet Coke and takes a long sip. The two of them look at me, bored, mildly amused.

"Is that all you wanted?" Nicholas raises a single eyebrow. "To give it back?" He takes the bag from my hands, turns it upside down, and shakes the contents onto the coffee table.

All three of us look at it. "You know what you should

do?" he says to Holly. "You should spread it out on my mattress and roll around in it."

She giggles. "You're so bad."

"Okay, well, thanks," Nicholas says to me, strolling away from the table. "You want something to eat? My stepmom is taking a cake-decorating class. We've got, like, three sheet cakes in our fridge."

I don't answer him; I can't. I can't do anything but stand there, staring down at the contents of the bag, trying to keep my knees from buckling as it slowly dawns on me what I'm looking at.

It's impossible. I *saw* it. I counted it over and over again. I held it in my hands.

But I saw Robin too. I felt his breath on my face. I touched him. He was real, just like the money was real.

Except they're not. Neither one of them, I realize. There's no money on the table. There was never any money. It's a geocaching prize, just as worthless as Holly's silver medal. At a glance, the bills on the table seem like they could be real, but it only takes one good look to recognize how flimsy they are, their coloring slightly off—and then there's the face in the middle. It's not Benjamin Franklin.

It's Elvis.

"Rachel?" Holly starts to seem concerned. "Are you okay? Do you want some Diet Coke?"

I shake my head, still staring. How did I not see it? "I have to leave," I say, backing away. "I have to go home."

"Rachel, wait." Holly reaches for me. "Something's wrong with you, I can tell."

Yes, I think to myself, *something's definitely wrong with me.* I once heard someone say that the definition of insanity is when the reality inside a person's mind doesn't match up with the reality everyone else sees. The description, I realize, fits me perfectly. There's no Robin. No money. It was all in my head.

"I have to go home," I repeat. I think of the mural on the wall at my old house. All the time I spent with Robin, and the way he seemed to know me so well, almost better than I knew myself. How long has this been happening to me? For months? Longer than that?

I run toward the front door, ignoring Nicholas and Holly as they call for me to come back. When I climb into the car, I lean against the seat and take quick, shallow breaths with my eyes closed. For a second I imagine that I'm a kid again, riding in my parents' car on that pretty day nine years ago, when everything seemed perfect, until it wasn't. I keep my eyes shut as Kimber starts to drive again, afraid to open them and look at the world around me, preferring not to see anything at all, clinging to the knowledge that at least the darkness is real.

❧

Kimber doesn't speak to me until we reach my house. She pulls up to the curb and puts her car in park, but she leaves the engine running. Then she slips off her sunglasses, sliding them up her forehead to use them as a headband.

"I have to go home," she says. "I don't want to be late."

I stare past her, at my house. All I want is to go inside and find my sister there, waiting for me. I want her to explain everything that's happened over the past few days. I want someone to confide in, someone who understands me and doesn't think I'm crazy. I used to think Rachel was the only true friend I had, aside from maybe Robin. I'm starting to believe that I don't have anyone, that even my bond with my own sister has been a figment of my imagination.

"You have to tell your aunt and uncle what's going on," Kimber says. "They need to be looking for Rachel."

The night at the fair seems like it happened so long ago. Who knows if my memory of the events that evening is even accurate? I'm not certain of anything. I thought I was different, that I was special, just like my grandma. Now I realize, what's most likely is that neither one of us is special at all. We're just crazy.

"Kimber?"

She sighs. "Yeah?"

"When we were talking earlier today in the bathroom, I started to tell you what happened to the Captain, but I didn't finish the story. I never told you how he died."

She doesn't even bother to feign interest. "You can tell me some other time."

"No. I want to tell you now."

"Alice," she says, frustrated, "it's not important."

"Yes it is," I insist. "Something happened that day after they took Rachel to the hospital." I bite the inside of my cheek, hard, until I can taste blood. "Something happened to the Captain."

"Okay," she says, obviously humoring me, "what happened?"

"After my parents took Rachel to the hospital, and after my grandma bandaged up my leg, she put the Captain on the back porch. She tied his leash to the railing so he couldn't get away. We could see him from the kitchen door. My grandma cut me a slice of angel food cake with strawberries, and then she went upstairs to change her clothes. I was alone in the kitchen."

I pause, waiting for Kimber to give me a sign that she's listening. She opens her purse and removes a stick of gum. Then she puts it in her mouth and starts to chew loudly, making it clear that she wants me to hurry up and finish so she can get the hell out of Crazytown.

"I sat there eating my cake, getting more and more angry with the Captain. My leg was throbbing. I was thinking about my sister at the hospital; I was worried about her. I started wishing that something terrible would happen to the dog. After a few minutes, I went onto the back porch where he was lying down, asleep. I put my hands on his body. I could feel him breathing. I hated him so much at that moment— I know it was wrong, and that he was just being a dog, but I was only a little girl. Kimber, I stood there touching him for what felt like an hour. He was twitching in his sleep, like he was having a dream. Then he stopped. It happened all of a sudden. One minute he was breathing, the next minute he wasn't. I could feel the life leaving his body. I know that sounds crazy." I pause. "I thought I could feel the energy leaving his body. I thought I was taking it from him."

Our next-door neighbor walks past with her dog. She flashes us a suspicious look, leaning down to peer inside the car. Kimber wiggles her fingers in a friendly wave, like nothing in the world is the matter.

I stare out my window at TJ's house. His front yard is neatly manicured, the lawn recently mowed, the flowerbeds free of dead leaves or other debris from last night's hard rain. At the edge of the property, there is a round burst of tiny yellow flowers peeking up from the frays of the lawn. They are the same kind of flowers, I realize, that Rachel has been collecting for who knows how long.

"Alice," Kimber says, once my neighbor is farther down the street, "I can't listen to this anymore."

I nod. "I understand. I know it wasn't real, Kimber. I know he just happened to die, and that it was all a big coincidence. But my grandma believed me. She told me it would be our secret. And I trusted her, you know? I wanted to believe her so badly."

Kimber closes her eyes and leans back in her seat. She presses her palms against her face and takes a few deep breaths. "You need to go home," she whispers.

"Kimber, what if none of this is real? What if *you're* not real? What if this is all—"

"Just stop," she interrupts, shaking her head. "I mean it, I want you to go. This is too much for me right now. I can't do it, Alice. I'm sorry."

She turns away, waiting for me to get out of the car. I'm having trouble fighting back tears. My world, I realize, does not make sense to anyone but me.

I get out of the car. Once I'm on my front porch, I turn around to watch her pull away without another glance in my direction.

When I walk into my house, I freeze. I drop Rachel's bookbag onto the hardwood floor.

My aunt and uncle are sitting on the living-room sofa with Sean Morelli. TJ is with them.

My aunt is crying. She's holding a sheet of sketch paper in her lap. It's the drawing I did yesterday of Charlie, asleep with the kittens.

Sean Morelli won't look at me. TJ is glaring. My uncle's whole face is bright red.

"Alice," he says.

I nod. "Yes. It's me."

He puts his head in his hands. My aunt's cries turn into sobs. "What did you do?" she demands, staring at me. Her expression is pure heartbreak, a combination of anger and horror directed at me alone. As she stands up, the drawing of Charlie and the kittens drifts to the floor. My uncle reaches toward her, trying to pull her back into her seat.

"What did you do?" she repeats, screaming now, struggling to get away from my uncle, trying to lunge at me.

What did I do? I cannot find my voice. I open my mouth to speak, but the words won't come out. In my mind, I hear them over and over again: *I don't know. I don't know. I don't know.*

CHAPTER TWENTY-FIVE

My aunt and uncle seem almost paralyzed with anger and disappointment. After a long silence, it is Sean Morelli who finally takes me gently by the arm and guides me toward the oversize chair in the corner of the room. As we walk past TJ, I stop, even as Sean tries to pull me farther along.

"What are you doing here?" I demand. "You don't know either of us. You might think you know Rachel, but you're wrong." I pause. "I know her. Better than you ever will." But my words sound hollow, even to me. Maybe I don't know my sister at all. I think of the flowers in TJ's front yard, and I understand that he must have been giving them to her for a while now, as some kind of small romantic gesture. And Rachel kept them close to her, but she made sure to hide them from me.

TJ leans forward until our heads are only a few inches apart. He stares right into my eyes. "I knew it was you today after school. Want to know how?"

I don't blink. I don't flinch. "How?"

"Because Rachel never calls me TJ. She calls me by my real first name. Tom."

I shrug in careless defiance. "That doesn't mean anything."

His breath, so close to my face, smells like peppermint bubble gum. "Maybe not," he agrees. "But I can tell you one thing, Alice. I've been seeing Rachel for almost a year. Really. Almost a whole year, and she never even told you. She couldn't stand the idea of you knowing, because she thought you would ruin it."

I feel like I've been punched in the stomach. I take a step backward, closer to Sean's arms. "That's not true," I say.

"It is true. And you know what else?" He leans closer to me. I cannot back away any farther; Sean's arms are all the way around my shoulders now. "She couldn't *wait* to get away from you."

"Hey," Sean interrupts, "come on. You don't need to do this right now."

TJ closes his mouth and takes a step backward, but he continues to glare—first at Sean, then at me.

Still holding my arm, Sean leads me all the way to the chair, holding on to me as I sit down. I look up at him, desperate for a hint of sympathy or understanding. His expression is glazed and empty, like he cannot believe I'm standing right here in front of him.

"What?" I ask. "What is it?"

He blinks a few times. His eyes are damp. His neck and

cheeks have turned a deep shade of blotchy red. "You're really Alice," he says.

"Yes," I say.

I can actually see him, right now, breaking into a sweat. Tiny beads gather like shiny sand in the hollows beneath his eyes, on his forehead, at his temples. He lets out a deep breath. "Holy shit," he murmurs. "You sure as hell fooled me."

"Alice," my uncle says, "we need some answers, and we need them right now. Where is Rachel? We know she's not with Robin."

That's right, I think, *because Robin isn't real.*

"Alice," my uncle repeats, more firmly now, "answer me. Where is your sister? When was the last time you saw her? Was it last Saturday? At the fair?"

I shake my head. "No. I saw her yesterday."

"Yesterday," he repeats. "Okay. Where did you see her?"

I try to swallow, but my mouth is so dry that it feels like I'm going to choke on my tongue. "At Grandma's," I say. "I saw her in Grandma's barn."

My aunt glares, first at me, then at my uncle. "My mother. My own goddamn *mother.* Are you hearing this, Jeff?"

He nods. "Yes." To me he says, "Does Grandma know Rachel's there?"

My aunt stands up. She stomps her foot against the floor with such force that the heel of her shoe breaks off, tipping her balance so she has to grab my uncle's arm for support. "Of course she knows!" she shrieks, leaning over to yank off her shoe without missing a beat. "Get the phone. I'm calling her. No—wait. Get the car keys. We're going over there right now."

My uncle nods. He heads toward the kitchen.

As the four of us sit there, waiting, there is a sudden loud knock at the front door. Nobody moves to answer it. After a few seconds, the doorbell rings.

My aunt crosses the room, taking off her other shoe as she walks. Once she opens the door, I can only make out the low murmur of her voice, but not her actual words.

I look at Sean. "Where's Charlie?" I ask.

"At work. I'm supposed to pick him up in a little while."

"Oh."

". . ."

". . ."

". . ."

"Mr. Morelli?"

This time, he doesn't tell me to call him Sean. "Yes?"

"What were you doing over here?"

"What? Oh." He shakes his head, like he's distracted by something. "I, uh, came down for a beer. I wasn't here five minutes before TJ came banging on the door, insisting you weren't Rachel. Your aunt didn't believe him at first. She went upstairs to take a look around your room, and she found the drawing you did of Charlie." He pauses. As he glances toward the door, he lowers his voice. "Tell me the truth, Alice," he whispers. "You didn't see Rachel at your grandma's house yesterday, did you?"

"Yes." I nod. "I saw her." But did I? I can't be sure. I can't be sure of anything anymore.

He narrows his eyes. His lips curl into a slow smile. When he speaks again, his voice is so low that I can barely make out his words. But I could almost swear that he whispers, "You're a little fucking liar."

I don't have time to react. My aunt comes into the room, followed by—oh God. Just when things were going so well.

It's Mr. Slater.

"Alice," my aunt says, "Mr. Slater stopped by to drop off your homework assignments. When I told him you were here, he said he had something he wanted to ask you."

I stare at my aunt. "Really? Now?"

She shrugs. "He insisted."

"Oh." Right away, I can smell the reek of cigarette smoke all over him. As usual, he looks sad and disheveled.

"Alice?" he asks. "Are you sure? You look just like Rachel."

I shake my head. "I'm Alice."

"Oh." He pauses, stares at the pile of papers in his arms. "I feel silly asking this. I'm sure it doesn't matter. You must have seen her picture somewhere and used it to work from. I hope you'll understand. I—I—don't want you to draw her anymore. If it's all the same to you."

And as he stands in my living room, my teacher begins to cry.

"Mr. Slater?" I ask, startled. I've never seen one of my teachers cry before. The sight is unsettling, to say the least. "I don't know what you're talking about."

My uncle has returned with his car keys. "What's going on?" He looks at Mr. Slater. "Who are you?"

"My homeroom teacher," I explain.

"Alice has done something to upset him," my aunt says drily.

"No, no she hasn't. I'm sure she didn't mean to. I wouldn't even have known, but I was collecting her assignments today, thinking I'd give them to Rachel to bring to her. I went to the art room, because I know how Alice loves to draw—I thought maybe there was something she'd like to work on from home. And her teacher gave me this."

His hand is shaking so much that he can barely grip the sketch paper. He's still crying. He shoves the drawing toward me, almost like he can't bear to hold on to it for even a second longer.

It's one of my portraits of the gap-toothed girl.

"Oh my God." In an oddly intimate gesture, my aunt reaches out toward my uncle and laces her fingers through his. "I recognize her now. I can't believe I forgot." She stares at Mr. Slater. "Was she your daughter?"

He nods. He wipes at his eyes with his free hand. "She *is* my daughter. She is my daughter. She is."

My fingertips are going numb. The room feels fuzzy, like I'm not getting enough air. Sean Morelli gazes at Mr. Slater with a mixture of confusion and fascination.

Even though I'm sitting down, I'm lightheaded. "Mr. Slater, what are you talking about? What do you mean, she's your daughter? I didn't even know you had a daughter."

"Jesus," my uncle interrupts. I can almost *see* the light bulb above his head. "You're Jamie Slater's father."

He's still crying. Without saying anything, he places my homework on the coffee table. He takes his wallet out of his back pocket. It falls open to display a photograph of the face I've come to know so well over the years, even if I didn't know who she was. I lean forward, barely breathing, and stare into her eyes.

It's like she's looking right at me. It's like she's been waiting all this time for me to discover her identity.

The room begins to fade away. Nobody notices as I struggle to breathe, to remain conscious. The last exchange I hear is Sean Morelli asking, "Who is Jamie Slater?"

"It was years ago." It's my uncle's voice. "She just disappeared one day."

Then my aunt says, "Alice, are you okay? Alice?"

Against the blackness, I see the back of a young woman as she jogs into space. Her long blond hair is wound into two braids that bounce against her back with every step. She turns around to look at me, raises one hand in a friendly wave. She smiles, like she's been waiting for me, like she's never been so happy to see somebody in her entire life. Her name, I know now, is Jamie Slater.

She looks forward again and continues to jog, her steps light and carefree. The lines of her body blur into the darkness. Then there's nothing at all.

CHAPTER TWENTY-SIX

When I come to, I am lying on the hardwood floor in the living room, surrounded by my aunt, my uncle, TJ, and Sean Morelli. As their faces come into focus, I feel something cool and damp on my forehead. I try to sit up, but my uncle puts his hand on my shoulder, pressing me gently downward.

"What happened?" I ask, blinking and blinking, turning my head away as my aunt wipes my face with a wet washcloth.

"You passed out," Sean says. "You slid right out of your chair."

There is a hissing sound in the back of my brain as I remember his words from a few minutes earlier. *You're a little fucking liar.* Why would he speak to me that way?

As my aunt is wiping my cheeks, she stops. She lowers the washcloth and leans closer to me. "Alice," she says, "your face. What happened?"

She's talking about the bruises; she hasn't seen them until now.

I thought I knew exactly where the bruises came from, but I don't. I don't know anything. All I have is a name—Jamie Slater—and a banged-up face, and a sister who's been trying to get away from me for over a year, if there's any truth to what TJ says. I'm guessing there's at least some. I have been wrong about so many things. Robin. Rachel. The money. The Captain. And the kitten the other night, the one that came back to life—surely that was all in my head, too. *Crazy*, I think. *I'm crazy.*

I brush away my uncle's arm and manage to bring myself into a sitting position. "I don't know what happened," I tell my aunt. "Where did Mr. Slater go?"

"He left," my uncle says. He and my aunt exchange a glance. "Alice . . . what happened to you? Did somebody hurt you? Did you get into a fight?"

"She's upset," Sean says. "Give her a minute. She just woke up. She's probably still dizzy."

I shake my head. "I'm fine. Nobody hurt me, okay?"

"But your face—" my aunt begins.

"I know what my face looks like!" I don't mean to yell at her; that's just how the words come out. So much is happening so quickly, and I don't have control over any of it. What I want right now, more than anything, is to find my sister. Regardless of what she might tell me, I know that she'll have some answers. Even if they aren't the ones I want to hear.

"I'm sorry," I say, trying to calm myself with deep breaths.
"I'm just . . . confused, I guess. I don't know." I frown. Tears
come to my eyes without warning. "I want you to find Rachel.
I want her to come home."

"We are," my uncle says. "We're going right now."

TJ stands up straighter. "I'm coming with you."

"No, you're not. This is a family matter."

TJ frowns. He shakes his head, but he doesn't argue.

My uncle hesitates. "Alice, I don't think you should come
with us either."

"Uncle Jeff, I'm not going to sit here alone and wait for
you."

"He's right," my aunt agrees. "It's not a good idea, Alice.
We're going to have a talk with Grandma. I don't think you
should be there." Her lips stiffen into a straight line. "It's not
going to be fun."

"Go ahead," Sean says. "I'll stay with her."

I stare at him. He still smells like damp earth: wet leaves,
dirt, like the debris that's left in the gutter after a heavy rain.
You're a little fucking liar.

"I want to come with you," I insist, trying to climb to my
feet.

"Alice, no." Sean helps me stand. He gives me a worried
look. He's so *cute.* It occurs to me that it's an odd observa-
tion to make at a time like this, but it's true; he's just such a
charming, good-looking guy. When Rachel and I were maybe
ten or eleven years old, he used to do these cheesy little

magic tricks for us. It was simple stuff: making a handker-
chief disappear into his fist, or pulling a quarter out from
behind our ears. We always looked forward to seeing him.
Even as little girls, we were drawn to his charisma. Everyone is.

"I have to pick up your cousin in fifteen minutes," he
says. He nods at my aunt and uncle. "I'll take Alice with me
to get Charlie, and then we'll come right back here. I'll stay
with them for as long as it takes you to find Rachel and do
whatever else you need to do." He looks at TJ. "You should
go home now."

My aunt and uncle glance at each other, communicating
with their eyes. I can tell they're hesitant to leave me alone,
even for a little while.

"We might be gone for a long time," my uncle says.

"It's fine, honestly. I don't have anything else to do." Sean
pats my uncle's shoulder. "Really, you should go. I'll take care
of everything here. That's what neighbors are for, right?"

My aunt begins to massage her own neck, tilting her head
back, sighing as she stares at the ceiling. She must be exhausted. "Jeff? What do you think?"

My uncle rubs his forehead. "I don't know . . ."

"*Go.*" Sean is friendly but firm. "We'll be fine. Maybe I'll
teach Alice how to play poker while you're gone." He winks
at me. "I bet she's a great bluffer."

✑

Even though I've known Sean for years, I've only been alone with him a handful of times. Given the events of the past hour or so, I'm more than a little uncomfortable with the still silence that follows once my aunt and uncle head out the door, followed by an obviously reluctant TJ.

Sean doesn't say anything at first. Without a word, he leaves me alone and walks into the kitchen, where I hear him rifling around in the cupboard. There is the sound of running water, followed by the low electric hum of the microwave.

The smell of earth is everywhere, all over the downstairs. I almost feel like I'll look down to see dirt and leaves strewn across the floor.

"Are you just going to stand there?" Sean calls from the kitchen. "Come in and talk to me, kiddo." There is no trace of the sinister undertones in his voice that I detected just a few minutes ago. He is calm, casual, almost like this is any other day.

I sit at the kitchen table, watching him as he finishes making a cup of tea. He sets it down in front of me and says, "Drink." But when I take a sip, it's too hot. The water burns my tongue. Immediately, I feel a blister rise on the roof of my mouth.

He gets a beer from the fridge and leans against the wall for a minute, trying to twist off the cap, which won't budge.

"It's not a twist-off," I say.

"Oh." He frowns at the bottle, almost like he's embarrassed. "Well, excuse me." And he starts digging through the drawers, looking for the opener. With his back to me, he says, "You know, I remember that girl. What's-her-name, your teacher's daughter. She's the same one from the painting you saw at my house, isn't she?"

The steam from the tea is dampening my face. "Yes."

"It happened right after I moved here. It was a big deal on the local news. They had search parties out looking for her for weeks. She was home from college for the weekend, and she went out running one day and just never came home." He turns to face me. "You and Rachel would have been about ten. Do you remember when it happened?"

I can hear the kittens mewing upstairs, the grandfather clock ticking in the hallway. Looking out the window behind Sean, I can see the sun setting. It will be dark in a few minutes. "No. I don't remember anything about it."

He tilts his head back and takes a long swig of beer. He drinks over half the bottle in a few gulps. He takes another sip, then another, watching me the whole time. Once there's only an inch of beer or so left in the bottle, he pours the remainder into the sink. He gets another one, opens it, and drinks it just as quickly.

"Then why did you draw her? You drew her over and over again, didn't you?" His voice is soft, almost gentle.

I nod. The house feels suddenly smaller, the earthy smell more potent than ever.

He finishes his second beer. Glancing at the clock on the stove, he says, "Oh, man. We need to go get Charlie. We're late."

I blink at him. "You just drank two beers."

He laughs. "Relax. Come on."

I leave my tea on the table, where it will go cold by the time we return. I don't want to go anywhere with him. At the very least, I should insist that he let me drive, I know. But it's less than a mile to the Yellow Moon, and he's only had two beers. Maybe he's right, and I should relax. My intuition is telling me that something isn't right—not at all—but if there's one thing I've learned by now it's that my intuition isn't good for much of anything.

Just as we're leaving the house, he stops next to the front door. He smiles at me. "It's incredible," he says, shaking his head in disbelief.

He's standing too close to me, invading my personal space. I get the feeling he's doing it on purpose.

"What is?" I ask.

"How much you look like your sister. I bet I couldn't tell the two of you apart right now if my life depended on it."

I feel like screaming. I feel like running outside and banging on our neighbors' front door and insisting that they call the police.

"Except for my bruises," I say.

He pauses. Still grinning, he asks, "What?"

"You couldn't tell us apart if it weren't for the bruises on my face."

He doesn't miss a beat. "Yes. Right."

Sean walks out the front door, but I don't follow him. I wait until he's on the porch, until he's looking at me impatiently, before I give him my sweetest smile and say, "Hold on. I have to set the alarm."

ॐ

It's only 6:03, but it's dark. "Late, late, late," he murmurs, more to himself than to me.

He seems tipsy from the beers, steering his car with one finger as we drive through town. He turns up the radio, which is tuned to the same classic-rock station that TJ is so fond of.

The Yellow Moon's parking lot is packed. Sean doesn't even try to find a space; he just pulls up in front of the double doors and shifts the car into park, letting the engine idle.

He switches off the radio; silence swells all around us. "You okay waiting here for me?" he asks, climbing out of the car. He wasn't wearing a seat belt.

"Sure." I smile at him again through gritted teeth.

"Okie-dokie. Be right back."

I watch him disappear into the restaurant. Through the glass doors, I can see Holly sitting at a high-top in the corner, eating an enormous pickle. Doug the bartender is mixing a drink, chatting with Matt and Katie Follet, who have taken their usual seats for the evening.

Everything is fine. Rachel is coming home. It will be all

right. Everyone is where they're supposed to be, doing what they're supposed to be doing.

I sigh, bored despite my nerves, looking around the car as I wait. There's a small book wedged in between my seat and the center console. I tug at the edge, struggling to read the title in the darkness. As my eyes adjust, I can see that it is called *Trails of Southwestern Pennsylvania.* Of course; he's a runner. It makes sense that he would have something like this.

I pick up the book with the intention of paging through it as I wait, but there isn't enough light. My gaze drifts across the dash. Even in the dimness, I can tell this is a *really* old car; it still has a cassette player and even a cigarette lighter.

A glint of moonlight hits my eye as the keys swing gently from the ignition. It seems weird; all the windows are up, and the air conditioner is off, so there's no breeze in the car.

There's a soft drip as something hits Sean's book of trails, which is resting in my lap. I look down. *Drip, drip, drip.*

It's my nose. It's bleeding.

I stare at the keys as they move back and forth somehow, propelled by an invisible force. I count five of them attached to a silver loop.

Beneath the loop, a tiny object dangles from a chain. I squint, trying to get a better look.

My gaze snaps into focus like a key turning in a lock.

I scream, but I don't make any sound. I want to run, but I

cannot move. All I can do is watch as it swings back and forth, back and forth. If I reach out to touch it, I know it will feel damp in the palm of my hand. *Drip.*

It's a peach pit. Carved into the shape of a monkey.

Chapter Twenty-seven

Hey, Rachel! I didn't know you were here too!" Charlie greets me with his usual enthusiasm as he lumbers into the backseat. He's been washing dishes all night; I can tell because he smells soapy and clean. As I press my sleeve against my nose, trying to hide the bleeding from my cousin, my instinct is to shout at him to run back inside, to call the police . . . but what would he tell them? I imagine the conversation in my mind as Sean pulls away from the restaurant:

"My cousin has a bad feeling about our neighbor."

"And?"

"And that's it. She gets feelings sometimes. They're usually wrong, though."

Click.

It's too short of a drive back to our house; I don't have enough time to think. Right now, my aunt and uncle are at my grandma's, looking for Rachel. I want her to be there so

badly. I want to come home and find all three of them waiting for us. I want them to yell at us, to ground us and take
away our after-school privileges and look at us with disapproval. I don't care what they do; I just want Rachel to come
home and fill in all the blanks that have accumulated over
the past few days. Let her go away with TJ and leave me
behind after high school. I don't care. All I want is to know
that she's safe.

Sean is almost giddy. He turns up the radio, singing along.
If he notices that my nose is bleeding, he doesn't mention it.
He hiccups a few times, shifting gears jerkily as he drives
uphill toward our end of town. He's going way too fast, over
fifty miles per hour in a thirty-five zone. He speeds through
a yellow light and only makes it halfway through another
before it turns red, turning onto our street without pausing
at the stop sign. I can feel Charlie's buckled-down weight
shifting in the backseat with every reckless maneuver, but he
doesn't seem to notice that anything is amiss. Maybe Sean
drives this way all the time.

He doesn't even slow down as he approaches our house;
instead, he keeps going until he reaches the end of the block.
He veers sharply to the right, pulling up in front of his own
house, his wheel hitting the curb as he comes to an abrupt
stop.

It's so dark now. A few of my neighbors' porch lights
glow in the thick dusk, but the street lights won't come on
for another hour or so. The wind carries dead leaves along

the sidewalk in a gentle stop-and-start rhythm, a few stragglers catching in the edges of people's lawns to get chewed into bits by mowers tomorrow or the next day. As I look at Sean, all I can make out are the whites of his big eyes, staring at me. I can feel the warmth from his breath on my face; it smells like decay.

Rotting leaves. Dirt. Decomposition. Death. I am so afraid of him that I can barely put my thoughts together; they're all singular ideas like *run, scream, fight, protect,* but I'm too frantic and uncertain to actually *do* any of it.

He smiles at Charlie and me. His teeth are bright white. The word *chompers* comes to mind.

"What's wrong?" he asks, pulling my hand away, staring at the blood on my sleeve.

"Rachel?" Charlie leans forward to look at me. "Aww." He makes a face. "You've been picking your nose!" he exclaims. "That's why it's bleeding! Gross!"

"We'll go down to your place in a few minutes," Sean says, climbing out of the car. "Sheba needs to go out first."

"Can I walk her, Mr. Morelli?" Charlie pleads, pressing his palms together as we approach Sean's house. "I'll only take her in the yard. You know I won't go anywhere else. I'll do a good job, I promise."

"Sure, buddy." As Sean unlocks his front door, I cannot bring myself to look down at the monkey on his keychain again.

Am I being hysterical? Panicking for no good reason? He

could have gone to the fair just as easily as anyone else in our town. He could have bought one of the monkeys from the old man. It might mean nothing at all; it probably *does* mean nothing at all. I'm not thinking straight. Maybe it's not even there, like Robin wasn't really there. Maybe it's all in my crazy, screwed-up head, and my nosebleed is just a coincidence.

You're a little fucking liar. The look in his eyes as he whispered those words to me. He meant something. It was as though, for just an instant, his mask slipped off, and I saw the man behind it.

The three of us go into his kitchen. Immediately, Sean gets a can of beer from his fridge. He snaps Sheba's leash onto her collar, hands her off to Charlie, and lets the two of them out the back door before my cousin has a chance to take a good look at me and notice my bruised face. Sean's backyard is lit by floodlights. Through the window, I can see Charlie as he waits patiently for Sheba, talking to her, smiling, taking enormous pleasure in such a simple act.

Sean doesn't offer me a rag for my nose; he just continues to let me use my sleeve. "Come here," he says, strolling past me. "There's something I want to show you. It's back here, in the hallway."

I don't move. I try to think, struggling to figure out what to do next. I need to get away from Sean somehow.

"Alice?" He cocks his head at me. "What's the matter, sweetie? You seem spooked."

When I don't answer right away, he leans his head back and laughs. "Come on. It's fine. There's no bogeyman, I promise." He gives me his signature wink. "It's just you and me."

What else am I supposed to do? I follow him through the living room, around the corner, and into the hallway. For a few seconds, we're surrounded by darkness. Then he switches on a light, and before I know what's happening he puts his arm around me, pulling me close, and says, "Well? Do you like it?"

It's my painting of Jamie Slater. He's hung it on the wall outside his bedroom.

He takes a few gulps of beer. He burps. Then he continues to speak, still holding me close, digging his fingernails into my bare arm until it hurts.

He sighs. "She was so pretty. I always liked women who were a little odd looking, and that gap between her teeth made her seem really special. We only talked for a few minutes, but she was a sweet girl." He pauses. "Well, she was nineteen, so I guess she was more of a woman."

All I can do is stare into her painted eyes as she gazes back at me. I can't move; he won't let me. He wants me to listen.

"It was so long ago, I'd almost completely forgotten about her. There have been a few, you know. A guy gets bored over the years. Everyone needs a hobby. I was *so* careful, Alice. Everything would have been fine. But then you came along. Painting her. Drawing her. I've seen her in your sketchbooks. Why would you do that to me? How did you even know who she was?"

As I finally force myself to speak, my voice is hoarse, like I've been screaming. "What did you do to her?"

He seems surprised by the question, as though the answer should be obvious. "I killed her, stupid."

We hear the kitchen door open. "Good girl, Sheba," Charlie says, his heavy footsteps echoing through the downstairs. "You're a good girl." I imagine him looking around the kitchen for us. "Hello?" he calls. "Mr. Morelli? Rachel? Where'd you go?"

Finally, I summon the will to scream. "Charlie, run! Run away and call the police, Charlie!"

"Shut up," Sean hisses, his bright teeth gritted, yanking me closer to him. His breath is foul and rancid. "Shut your mouth, Alice."

I struggle to get away from him, kicking my legs, trying to wriggle free. It doesn't work.

Charlie's huge frame appears in the hallway. He's confused and frightened by the sight of us, I can tell. He takes a tentative step backward. Sean pastes on a wry smile, slides a hand over my mouth, and says, "Hey, buddy. Your cousin and I are having a little talk. Everything's okay. She was only kidding. Weren't you, dear?"

With his palm against my face, he forces me to nod yes. Blood drips from my nose onto his hand.

Charlie's smile loses its gleam. "Rachel?" he asks doubtfully.

I give him a pleading look. I need him to run away. I cannot let him get hurt.

"Here's what I want you to do, buddy," Sean explains, keeping his voice slow and calm. "I want you to go ahead and walk home by yourself. Go inside and turn off the alarm. Can you do that? Do you know the code?"

My cousin hesitates for a second. He glances back and forth between me and Sean. "No," he admits, "I don't remember." His whole face trembles. "I'm sorry."

Sean nudges me hard. "Tell him the code. Now."

I stare at my cousin, pleading at him with my eyes, knowing he won't comprehend what I'm about to do. It's the only chance we have at getting away.

"Charlie," I say slowly, keeping my voice steady, my words deliberate, "you must remember the code. It's easy. 4-6-0-6. You just punch in 4-6-0-6, and then you press the button that says *stop*."

He's confused. "But 4606 is our address."

"Right," I say quickly. "That's why your parents picked it. So it would be easy to remember."

His gaze searches mine. I can tell that things aren't adding up in his mind. If that really were the code, he knows he wouldn't have forgotten it. I recognize the doubt in his eyes.

"Charlie," I say, "that's the code. Do it."

He wipes the sweat from his forehead. His breathing is shallow and quick.

"Charlie, buddy, listen to your cousin," Sean says. "Go."

But he doesn't move, at least not yet. "Rachel?" he asks me. "Is it true? Is everything okay? Your nose is still bleeding."

Sean grows a twinge impatient. "I already told you it's fine, buddy. Come on, now. Don't let me down. Do what I'm telling you."

Charlie takes another step backward, and for a second I think he might turn and run out the front door, just like I screamed at him to do. But then he stops. He closes one eye a little bit, like he's zooming in on the two of us, thinking hard, trying to determine what he should do.

"I want Rachel to tell me everything's okay," he says. "I'm not leaving until she tells me."

Sean's breathing is shallow and rapid, his chest rising and falling against my back. He's trying so hard to stay calm, I can tell. Any second now he could lose it.

"All right," he says. He takes his hand away from my mouth. He loosens his grip on my body—not completely, but enough that I can breathe freely again. "Go ahead, Rachel. Tell him yourself."

I force myself to smile, pressing my sleeve to my face again, trying to act like it's no big deal that my nose is gushing like a faucet. "Charlie," I say, keeping my voice low and even, "everything is okay. I want you to go home now. I want you to wait for us. Don't be afraid. Everything will be fine." I pause, trying to think, desperate for him to comprehend my meaning. "After you turn off the alarm, find a spot to wait for us. You can wait anywhere you want in the whole house."

He nods slowly. "Okay."

"Anywhere," I repeat. "You won't get in trouble. I promise."

"That's enough," Sean interrupts.

The three of us stand in near silence. All I can hear is the sound of our breathing.

Sean nods in the direction of the door. "Go ahead, buddy. Go now."

Taking careful, wide steps, Charlie backs down the hallway. Once he's in the doorway to the living room, he turns and walks quickly. I hear the front door open and shut. Then it's just the two of us, alone in the house with pretty Jamie Slater, whose face appeared in my mind years ago and demanded to be drawn.

Seconds after Charlie leaves, Sean hooks his arm around my neck, covering my mouth with his hand again. He wraps his other arm around my body and begins to drag me toward the back of the house.

"I could have sworn it was you," he murmurs, his mouth pressed close against my ear. "She could have told me I had the wrong goddamn sister. She could have told me a hundred times, but she never said a word."

He opens the door to his bedroom, shoves me onto the floor, and drags me in by my hair. When I scream, he kicks me hard in the stomach. "Shut up," he says, kicking me again. The act seems to give him intense satisfaction; his eyes are glazed with pleasure as he steps away from me, shaking his arms as he hops from one foot to the other like he's loosening up, getting ready for a good fight. He goes to his nightstand and switches on his clock radio, which is tuned to a classical station. "How about some music?" he asks, stretching out his arms, weaving his fingers together to crack his knuckles as he approaches me again. "I've always"—*kick*—"loved"—*kick*—"Vivaldi." *Kick, kick, kick, kick.*

He pauses for a second, reaches into his dresser drawer, and removes a pack of cigarettes and a book of matches. As he lights up, blowing a few large, wispy rings into the air, I'm certain that he's the reason I felt so uncomfortable on the trail with my sister last Saturday night. He was there, watching us, waiting for his opportunity.

After a few more drags of his cigarette, he tosses it onto the floor, grinding it out with the heel of his boot, before he resumes my beating. The next blow, delivered right to my gut, knocks the wind out of me. I clutch my hands to my stomach, trying to block him; it only makes him pummel me harder, his boot crushing my fingers as he shifts his weight onto me, leaning over to stare into my eyes as my body buckles beneath him. Then he straightens up, cracks his knuckles, and begins to kick me in the head.

The pain is explosive; it's like fireworks are going off inside my skull. I try to scream again, but the sound comes out in a pathetic gurgle, and I taste blood in my mouth. If he doesn't stop, I'll be unconscious soon.

His doorbell rings. Sean freezes, but only for a second. He crouches beside me, smoothing my hair, which is wet with fresh blood. He's sweating so much that beads of perspiration drip from his forehead onto my face. When I try to turn my head away, he grabs me by the chin, forcing me to look at him.

"Don't get too excited," he purrs as the doorbell rings again. "It's just gonna be the two of us here. I'm not in the mood for any more company tonight."

But whoever's outside isn't giving up yet. A few seconds go by, and then they start knocking—pounding, really—pumping insistently at the door. *Please don't let it be Charlie*, I think, struggling to breathe, unable to swallow the blood and spit that has pooled in my mouth. *Let it be anybody but Charlie.*

Sean grabs me by the hair and begins to drag me into the hallway. My eyes are so swollen from his beating that I can barely see. My jaw is throbbing so badly that I can't even force my mouth open wide enough to attempt a scream. I'm limp, helpless, on the verge of passing out, either from the pain or all the blood I'm losing.

He kicks the basement door open, grips me beneath my arms, and pulls me down the stairs. Every step creates an explosion of agony as my body bumps along, the two of us descending deeper into the darkness. The only light in the basement comes from a bare bulb screwed into the ceiling near the foot of the stairs. After what feels like an eternity, we finally reach the bottom. Sean drags my body to the center of the room and leans over me, catching his breath as the pounding continues on the front door.

"Excuse me for a moment," he says, planting his boot against my chest, pressing so hard that I can feel my ribs splintering beneath his weight. "I'm going to see who's at the door. Can you behave yourself while I'm gone?" He pauses. "I hope so, Alice. Otherwise this will be very unpleasant for you."

I don't respond. I just lay there, feeling more afraid than I ever have in my life, certain that I'm going to die tonight. My immobility seems to give Sean immense satisfaction. He grins at me as he smooths his hair with the palm of his hand, then wipes the sweat from his forehead. He delivers another hard kick to the side of my head. My blood is all over his boots.

Sean coughs, rearranging the contents of his chest cavity, then he spits onto the dirt floor, his saliva landing just a few hairs from my face. I can see it; I can smell it, too. I give a pathetic, barely audible choke of disgust as I gag.

"Don't go anywhere, beautiful," he says with a laugh. "I'll be back in a jiffy."

As he moves toward the stairs, there is a giddy skip to his step. Once he reaches the top, he doesn't even bother to close the basement door.

❧

I can hear everything going on upstairs, right down to the sounds of Vivaldi lilting down the hallway. When Sean answers the door, I recognize his visitor's voice immediately.

It feels like a miracle. As Sheba barks loudly, Ryan—Officer Martin—says, "It's okay. She must smell my dog."

"What can I do for you?" Sean's voice is smooth and cool. "Is anything wrong?"

"No, not really. I don't want to interrupt your evening, but I'm looking for one of your neighbors. Her name is Rachel Foster."

He's been following me, I know. Maybe he saw me come in a few minutes ago. Maybe he's talked to Charlie. If Sean lies, tells him I'm not here, he'll know something's wrong. He'll find me.

"Sure, I know Rachel. She isn't here, though. I haven't seen her all day."

My eyes have adjusted to the dimness of the basement, but they're too puffy for me to make out much of anything in the room, and I'm in too much pain to turn my head and look around. Instead, I have no choice but to stare at the dirt floor.

"You haven't?" There's a definite hint of doubt in Ryan's voice.

I notice something odd in my line of vision. There are several grainy, rust-colored circular spots on the floor. Struggling to focus, I realize the color is familiar; it's blood. And even though I'm bleeding profusely, I know the stains I'm looking at didn't come from my body. They're older; I can tell because the color is dried into the floor.

"Uh . . . I don't think so, Officer. I've been home all night."

As my vision sharpens, I make out three, four, five spots—maybe more. They create a trail that winds down the center of the room, a droplet distributed every few inches, one right after another to create a crooked line, almost like a path. I've seen something like this before.

"Do you have any idea where I might find Rachel?" Ryan asks. "Nobody's answering the door at her house. I have a few questions for her."

I stare at the blood, trying to comprehend why it's so familiar. It's like a game of connect the dots.

"No, I don't," Sean says. "I'm sorry I can't help you more. I'll certainly keep an eye out for her."

Like a trail of bread crumbs.

"Actually, I've been meaning to speak with you, too. Mr. Morelli, would you mind stepping outside for a minute?"

There is a long pause. Finally, Sean says, "Okay. I only have a few minutes, though. I'm in the middle of a little project."

My gaze follows the trail all the way to the opposite wall of the basement, to a low, narrow doorway. I know immediately that it leads to a sub-basement, just like the one in the house on Pennsylvania Avenue.

As soon as Sean is out the door—I hear him pull it shut behind him—I struggle to crawl across the room. My chest throbs in pain; each inhalation feels like a series of explosions going off inside my lungs. I hurt too much to stand up, but I don't let that stop me; I summon every bit of my remaining strength to drag myself along on my forearms until I reach the doorway, and somehow I manage to reach up and turn the knob.

I don't stop to think about my options; I know I have to get down the steps somehow. Any minute now, Sean is going to come back downstairs; if he finds me like this, I know he'll kill me. The pain is almost too much to bear as I turn myself around so I can slide down the stairs feet first, my ribs bumping against each step, my bones screaming in protest as I force myself farther and farther until I land in a heap on the floor. My body curls in surrender, as though it's trying to recede into itself, to escape the pain that radiates from every pore.

A single light bulb hangs from the ceiling, casting a dim light throughout the tiny room. The walls are gray cement block. There are no windows. The floor is packed dirt.

My sister, Rachel, rests on her side on the ground, in the far corner of the room. She faces the wall, so I can't see whether or not her eyes are open. Her hands are tied behind her back with a thick plastic cord. It is pulled so tightly around her wrists that her surrounding skin is swollen and purplish. She's wearing the same outfit from our night at the fair: a white tank top and denim miniskirt. Her feet are bare, their soles black with filth from the basement floor. Her shoes are nowhere to be seen.

There is a bald, bloody circle on the back of her head, near her neck. The wound hasn't healed properly; it is a painful shade of bright red, oozing fluid. It's like she was walking along and somebody grabbed her by the hair, yanking it so hard that it was torn from her scalp by the roots. She isn't moving. I can't tell if she's breathing.

I try to scream, but all I can manage is another weak gurgle. I spit out a mouthful of blood and try again; the sound is louder this time, but I know it's nowhere near loud enough for Ryan to hear me all the way outside.

"Rachel," I gasp, struggling to drag myself closer. As soon as I reach her, I turn her onto her side to face me.

Her right eyelid flutters open; her left eye is swollen completely shut.

"You found me," she breathes.

"Yes," I manage, my voice barely audible.

"I hoped you'd come."

"I'm here, Rachel."

"I'm so thirsty, Alice," she murmurs.

I lean closer, bringing my mouth close to hers, my body finally coming to rest as we lay there together. I struggle to pull quick, shallow breaths into my lungs. I can feel the warmth of her breath on my face; the pain in my body slips away, replaced by numbness as I bask in the peace of knowing I've found her.

My aunt and uncle, I know, will not discover any signs of Rachel at our grandma's house. What I saw in the barn yesterday was not really my sister, at least not physically. In my dream, she told me about the monkey because she knew

Sean had taken it from her; she knew that I'd understand what had happened as soon as I saw it on his keychain. She waited for me down here. She suffered in my place, never revealing who she was, hoping I would unravel the truth on my own somehow. I have felt so alone in her absence, but I was wrong. She has been with me all along.

As my pain continues to subside, I manage to sit up and pull her close to me. I hold her body against mine until our skin pressed together grows damp. I cry onto her shirt. I kiss her forehead. She remains still and limp, barely moving at all. Her breath stutters out of her unevenly, as though there's a kink in her windpipe.

"Rachel," I say, "breathe. Just breathe."

She tries to speak, but she can't. Her eyes roll back in her head as her lids flutter shut. Her lips move, but she doesn't make any sound.

"Rachel, he's coming back soon. You have to get up. *Please.* We have to go now."

"I can't," she manages to whisper. Her lips are so dry that they're cracked around the edges.

"Rachel," I plead, "we have to leave right now. He'll kill us. You need to get up. You need to try. Please."

But she doesn't move, and I know that she truly can't. She's too weak.

I know I'm not strong enough lift her on my own, but I think I can make it up the stairs. If I'm going to get help for us, I have to do it *now*.

"I'm going to go get the police," I tell her, easing her body back onto the floor. I am crying. The last thing in the world I want to do is leave her, but I don't think I have a choice.

She doesn't say anything else. Her eyelids flutter as she slips into unconsciousness.

✍

Somehow, I climb to my feet and make it up the stairs into the basement. I lean against the wall, listening for footsteps above, but I don't hear anything. Sean is still outside with Ryan. All I have to do is get to them, and I'll be able to rest, knowing I've saved Rachel.

Once I'm at the top of the stairs, I get a surge of strength and energy that feels electric, and I begin to run. On my way out, I pass the painting of Jamie Slater in the hallway. Even in my panic, pure fear screaming through my body, pushing me forward, I feel her blue eyes at my back, watching me, her smile wide and constant as she stares.

CHAPTER TWENTY-EIGHT

When I reach the street, there are no signs of Ryan or Sean. Stumbling across his lawn, I manage to find my voice and scream as loud as I can. The surge of strength I felt just a few moments ago is still with me, but it's fading fast. I start to run toward my house, but I only make it a few feet before I have to slow down; my whole body buckles in pain, my knees threaten to give out, and I feel like I'm going to throw up any second now. Still, I manage to make it down the street. Once I'm almost to my house I pound on my neighbors' doors with my fists, ringing their bells over and over again before I move on, so that when I reach my porch there are a handful of people outside, wanting to know what all the noise is about. I trust that at least one of my neighbors will assume that I've finally gone crazy and call the police to haul me away.

Our house is locked. The inside is dark. There is no sign of Charlie.

I turn around to face the street. As soon as I lean against the front door, my legs give out completely; when my body hits the floor of the porch, the impact causes so much pain that I can't even summon the strength to scream; it's a challenge just to keep myself from keeling over. Fuzzy black dots burst like tiny explosions in my line of vision, each one its own separate wavelength of agony as I look up and down the sidewalk. There are three of my neighbors, peering down at me, their faces alarmed at my beaten face and body. Regardless of the way I look, I'm sure they're assuming it's me, Alice, who is in trouble.

Rachel never causes trouble. Not for anybody.

As I look around, my vision grows increasingly blurry. The stragglers outside are growing in number, gathering into a small crowd that is heading toward me.

TJ comes running out his front door, toward my house. I can barely move at all now. Whatever energy I summoned in order to get outside and down the street is gone. I have nothing left. It takes effort just to breathe.

TJ kneels beside me. "Alice, what are you doing? What happened to you?"

I stare at him. He is desperate with worry, I realize. I know exactly how he feels. When I speak, my mouth is dry. It takes all my effort to pronounce my next words. "Sean Morelli took my sister. She's in his basement."

TJ's face crumples. "What?" He turns to our approaching neighbors and screams, "Somebody call the police!"

To me, he says, "Alice, you're shaking." I can barely keep my eyes open. Each breath is so painful that every passing second feels like an eternity. There is a fiery pain spreading through my chest. I can feel my heartbeat slowing.

TJ smacks me lightly on the cheek, trying to rouse me. "Alice. Hey. Alice!"

I manage to speak again. "She's in the sub-basement," I say. "Go."

"Alice." He smacks me again, a little harder. My eyes open and close, open and close, open and close. I try to move my mouth to form words, but I don't have a voice anymore.

All the way down the street, I can see somebody jogging toward us. There is a large dog at his side.

My heart flutters as he gets closer. He pushes past my neighbors. He's coming straight for me.

I am not afraid anymore. I feel calm and sleepy. As the jogging man climbs our porch stairs, he reaches behind his back and pulls something from his waist. His dog sits on the sidewalk, calmly observing the unfolding chaos.

TJ turns to look over his shoulder. "What the hell?" he asks, jumping to his feet, taking a few panicked steps backward. "Oh, Jesus. Oh my God."

The man points a handgun at the space above my head. "Stop," he says. "Everybody calm down."

I can feel myself descending into unconsciousness. The periphery of my vision is starting to blur into nothingness.

With his free hand, he reaches into his pocket. He pulls

out a small silver badge, holding it outward in his palm so everyone can see it.

As my eyes fall shut again, a fuzzy pause surrounds me. After a moment, his voice high and incredulous, TJ says, "Holy shit. You're a *cop*?"

I wish I could see them, but all I can do is listen.

"Yeah," Homeless Harvey says, breathless. "You need to get off the porch." I can hear police sirens approaching from a few blocks away.

"What's happening?" It's TJ.

"Somebody set off the hostage code from this address. I have to get inside." To me, Harvey says, "Miss, are you okay? Miss?"

I remember his straight, white teeth. It seemed so odd that a homeless man would have such good dental hygiene.

I am slipping away. The sounds around me grow fainter, turning into indecipherable murmurs, dissolving into nothing. In my mind, the last thing I see before everything goes blank is the steep hillside beside my parents' car, the big rock in the valley below with its plea scrawled in cursive spray paint: *I loved you more.*

EPILOGUE

Death is a funny thing. It comes for every last one of us eventually, no matter how we might try to avoid it. Despite its inevitability, we are all so afraid of what might happen to us once we've passed on. Why? I remember being young, maybe seven or eight years old, and asking my mother what happens after we die; it must have been obvious to her how much the idea frightened me, because she put her arms around my shoulders, brought her face close to mine, and explained that I already knew the answer—I just couldn't remember it.

"Imagine you're a grain of sand floating in the ocean," she said, "and one day a wave washes you onto the shore. It's a whole different world, like nothing you've ever experienced before. You stay there for a while, but eventually the tide comes in and carries you back to the sea. What's scary about that? You aren't going anywhere you haven't been before."

Her reasoning didn't bring me much comfort. "I'm still scared. I don't want to die."

She smiled at me. "That's not why you're scared, honey. Being dead isn't anything to be afraid of. *Dying* is what's worrying you."

I told her I didn't understand the difference.

"Every person who ever lived is united in death," she said. "The hard part is dying, because each one of us has to do it alone—just like when we're born."

Her words sent a flutter of excitement through my body. "That's not true. I wasn't born alone."

I expected her to explain why I was incorrect, but she didn't. She smiled instead, and pulled me closer to her. "You're right," she whispered. "My girls are special." She kissed me on the forehead. "Neither of you will ever be alone. No matter what, you will always have each other."

This morning was my sister's funeral, which was followed by an informal gathering for friends and family at my grandmother's house. I've managed to slip away from everyone else for the time being, and I am sitting at her kitchen table, thinking about that conversation from so many years ago. I'm surprised by how much comfort it brings me. The grief I've been feeling for the past few days is still present, so consuming and fierce that right now it feels like it will never release its grip on me. And even once it subsides—which seems unimaginable—I know it will stay with me, to some degree, for the rest of my life. There are so many emotions today, and each one feels so distinct and wicked, so powerful, that I can't imagine trying to resist any of them. I am weak and brokenhearted, and I'm more lonely than I've ever been in my life.

Lonely, yes. But not alone. That would be impossible.

When our parents died, my grandmother held a similar gathering in this house after their funerals. I can remember sitting on the living-room love seat, my sister by my side, the two of us silently holding hands as we watched my parents' friends and relatives wandering around the big house, nibbling from Styrofoam plates of finger foods and making awkward conversation with one another. I remember people stealing glances at the two of us, looking on with such pity. We stayed close to our grandma for comfort that day, hiding behind her as she introduced us to the aunt and uncle we'd never met, even though they'd lived only a few miles away our entire lives.

Right now, the kitchen door creaks open, and I turn in my seat to see Kimber stepping into the room. Her long hair is pulled away from her face in a ponytail. She wears a white dress shirt and black pants, along with a somber but nervous expression. Her face is clean and free of makeup. The skin around her eyes is spotted with tiny red dots that are the result of burst capillaries; I'm sure she's been crying just as much as the rest of us in the past few days. I can also see faint, feathery scarring on her jawline, which is usually covered in foundation: marks that map the crawl of fire as it tried to consume her whole so many years earlier.

She sits across from me at the table. There is an empty water glass beside me. I've probably refilled it half a dozen times this afternoon so far. I feel incredibly thirsty, like my whole body is dried out, like I'll never be satisfied no matter how much I drink.

"You don't have to come with me," Kimber says. "I'll understand. You should probably stay here."

"No," I say, "I want to come." The truth is that I don't want to do much of anything, but it will be a relief to get out of here, even if it's just for a few hours.

"Are you sure?"

"Yes." I do my best to smile at her. The gesture sends an achy pain shooting through my cheek. My face is still bruised. My wrists and ankles throb constantly; even the prescription painkillers I got in the hospital don't make much of a dent.

But I'm here. I'm alive.

Two nights ago, Charlie left Sean's house knowing that something was wrong, that he needed help. My cousin programmed the hostage code into the alarm system, and then he hid in the secret stairway, waiting.

The call came in to the police dispatcher, who contacted the closest officer on duty. My neighbors watched as Homeless Harvey pounded on our door, finally kicking it open as his dog barked frantically from the street.

Once he was inside, he found our house empty. Charlie was nowhere in sight. Within a few minutes, the place was swarming with cops, searching the house to look for my cousin. He stayed in the secret stairway for two hours, listening as the searchers called his name, not making a sound. It wasn't until my aunt and uncle came home that he finally surfaced to explain what had happened that night. He was so afraid that he hadn't done enough to help, but that wasn't the case. The hostage code summoned the police to our house. There was nothing else Charlie could have done for us.

After speaking with Sean Morelli for a few minutes, Officer Martin felt satisfied that he was just one of our friendly neighbors with nothing to hide. Before he left, though, he knelt down to pet Sheba. He held out his hand, encouraging her to shake, and Sheba extended one of her front paws, resting it in Officer Martin's palm, just like she'd been taught. When she pulled it away, she left behind a smear of blood.

Before Officer Martin had a chance to react, Sean managed to overpower him and take his gun. He dragged him into the house, beat him unconscious, and tied him up. Then he got in his car and fled. Highway patrol caught up with him a few hours later. He must have understood it was over for him, because he didn't put up a fight. He didn't even ask for a lawyer, not until after he'd already said way too much.

∽

"If you're sure you want to come," Kimber says to me, "we have to leave now."

I nod. "Okay. I'm ready." When I stand up from the table, my legs ache.

We make our way toward the front of the house. We don't say much to the people we pass. They don't seem to mind. They understand. Like everyone else here, they're trying to manage their own grief; I'm sure they can't begin to imagine how I'm feeling right now.

My aunt and uncle are on the porch with Charlie, our grandma, and Homeless Harvey. Except he's not Homeless Harvey anymore; his name is actually David Munroe. He'd been working undercover on the trail for over a year. Apparently there was a lot of drug activity going on near the methadone clinic. He was only a few blocks away when the hostage call summoned him to our house, effectively causing him to blow his cover.

But it was worth it. The events from last week have allowed the police to solve eight murders that took place on outdoor trails in four separate states over a period of fifteen years. They have solved the mysteries of what happened to Rachel Carter and Melissa Bell of Maryland; Shannon Seaver of Virginia; Amy Sloan and Rebecca Dylan and Susan Grimes of Maine; Jennifer Weaver of West Virginia; and, finally, Jamie Slater of Greensburg, Pennsylvania.

David, along with my aunt and uncle, looks through an old sketchbook, astounded by the incredible likeness that was captured in the many portraits of Jamie Slater.

After a minute or so, he notices me standing just behind

him, looking over his shoulder. He glances up at me and smiles to reveal two rows of perfect teeth. His eyes are sad. Nine girls are way too many to lose under any circumstances. But there is wonder in David's gaze as he watches me, observing all my cuts and bruises like he's seeing them for the first time.

My aunt stands up and approaches me. She looks like she hasn't slept in a year. As she gives me a long hug, her body sort of falls against mine, and her arms grip me so tightly that I can tell she doesn't want to let me go, even though she knows I'll be safe. As we stand there together, her breathing is deep and uneven as she tries to keep herself together as best she can. Tonight, I know, she'll go home and fall apart in private.

As she finally pulls away, she asks, "Are you leaving now?"

"Yes," I say. Even though I know she'd rather I stayed, she understands why I feel the need to leave right now. I'm going with Kimber to her father's hearing this afternoon. I don't want her to be alone.

But there is deep concern in her expression. "You're sure you'll be all right?" Her voice is small and hoarse.

"She'll be fine," my grandma interrupts.

"Grandma's right," I say. "Don't worry."

My aunt doesn't seem convinced, but she doesn't have much of a choice. I'm eighteen. I can do what I want.

As we're about to leave the porch and head toward

Kimber's car, I glance down at the sketchbook again. David has turned the page, and it's no longer open to a drawing of Jamie Slater. Instead, it's a portrait of Robin. It's similar to the painting of him that's back at my house, in my room. He is posed the same way, staring outward with a mischievous smile on his lips.

"Who's that?" David asks.

"I've been told that's Robin," my aunt says. She looks up at me, and I nod in agreement.

"It's impossible," she murmurs. But the words sound empty, like she's struggling to believe them herself.

Again, it was Officer Martin who figured it out. When he ran a search on Robin Lang, he was puzzled to learn that a man by the same name had been killed nine years earlier in a car accident. He was the driver. During some routine follow-up with my aunt and uncle a few days ago, Officer Martin showed them the driver's photograph. They were astounded to realize that the deceased Robin Lang appeared identical to all the drawings they'd seen over the past few months—drawings of a man they'd never met, who they'd only known as Robin.

My grandmother—who looks elderly and fragile today, her essence somehow deflated from the events of the past week—leans past my aunt to get a good look at the drawing. She goes still. She stares at it. She reaches toward the paper and brushes her hand across his eyes. "You don't say," she murmurs.

We all look at her. "What do you mean?" my aunt asks.

My grandma's eyes are flat and sad, but for just a moment I see a flicker of light in them, like she's keeping a secret that makes her happy. "Nothing," she says. "I've seen him around, that's all."

Just before Kimber and I walk away from the house, I glance up to see Tom standing in the doorway. His parents are at his side. When our eyes meet, he gives me a tentative, sorry smile.

I'll talk to him soon. Not right now, but soon enough. We know where to find each other.

⌒

As usual, Kimber drives slower than the speed limit. We don't say much on the ride.

She pulls into a visitor's space in the parking lot and turns off the car.

"Are you ready for this?" I ask her. I stare down at my hands, at the tiny yellow flower knotted around my ring finger.

"I don't know. I think so."

"What are you going to say?"

She squints into the sun, thinking. "I'm not sure. I'm hoping I'll know once I see him."

"Do you forgive him?"

"I'm trying. It's hard," she admits. "I always felt like doing that would be the same as setting him free. I was wrong, though."

"You were?"

"Yes. Because it isn't like that at all. It's the other way around. If I let go, then *I'll* be free." She pauses. "I think. I hope."

The silence between us is thick, full of everything we're both thinking, though neither one of us will say it.

I open my purse. Inside is the bag of black licorice Tom gave me to try to cheer me up, but that's not what I'm looking for right now. The tiny monkey, carved from a peach pit, is tucked into the inner pocket. I take it out and hold it in my hand, staring at it. I don't know how much time goes by, but it's long enough that Kimber finally nudges me and says, "Rachel? Are you sure you're up for this right now?"

I nod, still looking at the monkey. "Yes."

"What is that?" Kimber asks.

I smile, closing my hand and slipping the monkey back into my purse. "It's for good luck."

We get out and start across the dusty stone parking lot, toward the massive brick building, its periphery surrounded by high barbed-wire fences. As we're walking, Kimber shades her eyes and stares at the sky. There are only a few clouds, which hang low and puffy, like cotton. There's a name for them, I know, but I have no idea what it is. If Alice were here, she'd be able to tell me.

"Rachel?"

"Yeah?" I glance at Kimber, who is a few paces ahead of me in the parking lot.

"Are you coming?"

Cirrus clouds. That's what they're called. Somehow, I just know.

ACKNOWLEDGMENTS

Hoo boy, where do I even begin? I want to thank Stacy Abrams, who believed in this book from the beginning and worked so hard to help me bring these characters to life. Any thanks and recognition that I can give her seems so inadequate compared to her amazing effort and dedication. Stacy, I adore you.

To Emily Easton, who oversaw a great deal toward the end of this project and offered such wonderful insights—your attention and concern has made this book 100 percent better, and I cannot thank you enough for your persistence and dedication. I know it couldn't have been easy to step in at such a late stage, but I'm so grateful for everything you've done. And everyone else at Walker—you are all wonderful, and I feel so fortunate to be working with you. Beth Eller, Kate Lied, Katy Hershberger, Laura Whitaker, Rachel Stark . . . you're such a fabulous group of people; none of this would work without all of your efforts!

To my agent, Andrea Somberg—surely you know how awesome you are, right? If I had someone like you to handle every aspect of my life, people would really think I had it together! Not only are you great at what you do, you're also one of my favorite people. Please consider me for any outrageous favor you ever find yourself in need of; I will happily oblige.

To my husband, Colin . . . what else is there to say to you? After twelve years, you're still my closest friend and biggest supporter. Thank you for being a witness to my life, for all your love and hard work and devotion to our family. You are stellar in every way. I love you.

This book wouldn't exist had it not been for the inspiration given to me by the coolest redheaded twins I know, Mallory and Amanda Warman. You're both so beautiful, and I'm so proud to call you my (almost) sisters. (Also, I'm crazy about your big brother!) I also want to thank my critique partners, Mary Warwick and Cheryl Alsippi, for keeping me motivated, even when these Pittsburgh winters make us all want to crawl back into bed for the day.

Finally, I have to recognize Michael Merck. Out of every person I know, you are by far the most positive and cheerful, even in the bleakest of situations. Your optimism and enthusiasm for every aspect of life is truly inspirational. I've never met anybody else who can look at the most hopeless situation and find a way to turn it into something good. You're like the Mister Rogers of Regent Square. (Your wife is pretty cool, too! Jennifer Merck, you write a mean haiku!)